THE HOSTAGE IN HIDING

HENRY VOGEL

Published in the United States of America by Rampant Loon Press, an imprint of Rampant Loon Media LLC, P.O. Box 111, Lake Elmo, Minnesota 55042. "Rampant Loon Press" and the Rampant Loon colophon are trademarks of Rampant Loon Media LLC.

www.rampantloonmedia.com

Cover by Miblart.com

ISBN: 978-1-958333-00-6 (ebook)

ISBN: 978-1-958333-01-3 (paperback)

ISBN: 978-1-958333-02-0 (hardcover)

First publication: April, 2022

For Chris Pierce and Dixie Hickman. This book wouldn't be nearly as good as it is without your advice and suggestions.

AN UNTIMELY BREAKTHROUGH

You want to know what's worse than your parents having high expectations for you? Everyone else in the world having even higher expectations than your parents. So here's my advice to the future generations of the galaxy.

Don't be born to heroic parents. Famous, heroic parents are even worse. Rich, famous, heroic parents the absolute worst.

You want to know why?

Rich kids exceed society's expectations if they aren't entitled jerks. It's not exactly a high bar to clear, you know? And if you ask me, any kid who can't even do that is kind of pathetic.

Kids of famous parents can claim, "I love my parents, but I just want a normal life out of the limelight." And everybody nods, says how smart the kid is, and lets them get on with life.

But the first-born daughter of the fantastically rich, galactically famous, historically heroic Matt and Michelle Connaught? I'm supposed to *do* something with my life. People don't expect me to change the galaxy like Mom and Dad did, but they still expect Great Things from me. (You can hear the capital letters every time someone says that about me. Not kidding.) And they expect Great Things even though I'm a complete flop as a psychic.

I'm supposed to be a powerful empath like Dad. Except I'm not. All I can sense are my family and a few close family friends. (Most of them are history-book famous, too, but no one expects me to live up to their standard *and* my parents. Mostly no one, anyway.) Dad swears I have plenty of psychic power. If I do, I sure can't find it. At least Dad has my younger sister Nancy and baby brother Eric to train. *They* have psychic power to spare.

I'm also supposed to be a kick-ass fighter, like Mom. And I'm actually pretty great at it. I ought to be. Mom and Granddaddy have been training me for as long as I can remember. Since I didn't have to spend time learning how to use my virtually non-existent psychic powers, Mom made sure I got *lots* of extra martial arts practice. That's why I can wipe the mat with either of my siblings. I'm a crack shot with a blaster, too.

Yay, me!

But I'm no hero. Nancy and Eric are, though. A couple of years ago, they used their psychic abilities to find a lost kid, and even rescued her from drowning in the river. Me? I've never done anything close to heroic.

That's why I'm so excited about going away to college. I even get to go to Draconis, a world that rivals Earth in importance to the Terran Federation. The planet has nightclubs. An amazing music scene. A fashion industry. *Shopping*. And people. Lots and lots of people. Draconis has cities with more people than all of Ark's Landing. There are so many people that maybe I can blend into the crowd. Be a regular eighteen-year-old girl without all the expectations I face here on Ark's Landing. When I told that to Mom, she gave me a typical "Mom" response.

"You know your father and I are proud of you just the way you are?" When I nodded, she continued, "I hope you can find what you're looking for, honey. But remember that life doesn't always give us what we want."

I resisted the urge to roll my eyes. "I know, Mom."

She smiled and rolled her eyes for me. For someone with no

psychic abilities, she's great at figuring out my moods. Since she started it, I went ahead and rolled my eyes, too.

"But," Mom added, "sometimes life gives us what we *think* we want."

I grinned and gave in to the urge to roll my eyes. But I should have paid more attention to Mom. If I had, I'd never have boarded the starliner to Draconis.

~

Everyone turned up at the spaceport to see me off. Both sets of grandparents, all my adopted and honorary aunts and uncles (I have a *lot* of those. Mom and Dad brought home a bunch of strays during their adventuring days), my sibs, and my parents. And something like half the colony's population. Okay, not really, but a few thousand colonists turned out to cheer me on.

See what I mean about expectations?

When the shuttle from the *Pegasus* (that's the starliner) landed, my family suffocated me with hugs, good wishes, and advice.

"Don't embarrass us," Eric said.

"Leave a few cute guys for me, when I follow you in two years," Nancy added.

"While you're on the *Pegasus*, always wear an atmosphere harness under your clothes," Granddaddy said. "Did you memorize the ship's layout, Nora?"

Grandmama gave him a gentle slap on the arm. "Jonas, dear heart, you're *supposed* to tell your granddaughter that you love her. Give the security advice to her bodyguards."

"Conley and Barber already have their instructions." Granddaddy glanced at my two-man security detail. "Right, men?"

"Yes, sir," they said in unison.

I hugged my grandparents. "It's okay, Grandmama. That's

how Granddaddy shows his love. And, yes, Granddaddy, I memorized the ship's layout, including the maintenance tunnels."

I hugged Dad, and whispered, "I'll make you proud."

"You always do, honey," he said.

Mom joined our hug. "Don't forget to have some fun, too."

Captain Riggs, the *Pegasus's* skipper approached, doffed his cap, and said, "We've loaded Miss Connaught's bags on the shuttle, and will depart as soon as she's ready."

Yeah, the captain really came to personally escort me to the ship. You get pretty amazing service when your family owns the cruise line.

I disentangled myself from my family, wiped my suddenly damp eyes, and followed Captain Riggs onto the shuttle.

After the shuttle docked with the *Pegasus*, Captain Riggs showed me to my suite. It's the largest one on the *Pegasus*, but that's not saying much. It's got two tiny bedrooms, one for me and one my bodyguards will share, and a sitting room barely big enough for its sofa and two armchairs.

Then Captain Riggs presented a pretty, dark-haired, hazel-eyed girl about my age. "This is Sofia Olson. She'll be your personal attendant during the trip."

My *what*? We might be rich, but we don't even have servants at home. Why would I need one on a spaceship? I opened my mouth to say as much, but then Sofia *curtseyed* to me.

Her eyes lit up, and she flashed a dazzling smile. "I'm very pleased to meet you, Miss Connaught."

Faced with Sofia's enthusiasm, I swallowed my planned comment and said, "Just call me Nora." I jerked a thumb towards Barber and Conley. "Those guys are the only people who call me Miss Connaught."

Uncertainty crossed Sofia's face, and her eyes cut to Captain Riggs. He gave a microscopic nod, and she said, "Thank you, Miss—Um, I mean, Nora."

A few minutes later, Sofia crowded into my bedroom with me

and helped me unpack. I saw her eying one dress in particular, and said, "Why don't you try it on?"

"What?"

I pointed to the dress, "Try it on."

"Oh, I couldn't!"

"Why not? We're about the same size."

"It wouldn't be proper."

I adopted a rural Ark's Landing accent, "Yeah, well, I ain't proper much, anyhow."

That drew a giggle from Sofia. "Are you sure?"

"I insist."

I liked the dress well enough, but its light colors provide little contrast to my pale skin, blonde hair, and blue eyes. But it was *perfect* for Sofia's coloration. I was about to say so when Captain Riggs came on the ship's intercom.

"All hands and passengers, prepare for wormhole entry."

I must have tensed up, because Sofia said, "There's nothing to worry about. Because of the inertial dampeners, we won't even notice the transition."

A few seconds later, Captain Riggs announced, "Wormhole entry complete."

Something inside my head shifted, and my brain exploded.

A torrent of emotions flooded my mind and swept away everything before them. My thoughts, my feelings, my... everything vanished, drowning beneath the torrent as every emotion the *Pegasus's* crew and five thousand passengers felt pummeled my brain.

Joy. Bright and bubbling. It warmed my soul and made my heart sing.

Romance. Indulgent and fanciful. My entire body tingled as this longed-for emotion swept over me.

Wonder. Strange and surprising. The tingling faded, washed away by the awe of discovery.

Why had Dad spent so much time warning about the

emotional deluge that came with a breakthrough? It felt fantastic!

Doubt. Hesitant and distrusting. I pulled my knees up to my chest and curled myself around the sudden distress that overwhelmed everything good inside me.

Anxiety. Tense and apprehensive. My breath came in short, sharp gasps. A scream formed in my gut, but it took up residence there and churned my insides.

Depression. Bleak and foreboding. My vision blurred, and I felt tears trickle down my cheeks. Darkness closed around me, and I welcomed it.

Far away, in a foreign world where people only felt their own emotions, hands grabbed my shoulders. Wide hazel eyes caught my gaze. A distant voice said, "Nora? What's wrong?"

Sofia's touch brought a new emotion.

Fear. Raw and primal. Sharp and urgent. A spike that destroyed everything in its path. A blazing call to fight or flee. An old emotional friend, one I've lived with since I first felt the weight of expectations pressing down on me. I mentally grabbed the fear and held on for dear life.

Sofia gave me a little shake as her fear intensified. Yes, Sofia. More. Give me more. Your fear is the only thing keeping me sane.

"What should I do, Nora?" Sofia asked. "Do I call your bodyguards?"

She pulled away, but I grabbed her hands and held on. I fought for the breath to say *no*, couldn't find it, so just shook my head.

Sofia moved closer and caught my shoulders again. "Don't go?"

I nodded my head.

Sofia pulled me into a hug. "Okay, Nora, I'll stay here as long as you need me."

Her warm touch eased the tension in my shoulders. But, spurred by my responses to her questions, Sofia was mastering her fear. My lifeline began fading, and five thousand emotions raged just on the edge of my perception. The minor part of me that was still simple Nora Connaught had an idea. Knowing I'd hate myself later—if there was a later—I threw my body into false convulsions.

Sofia's fear spiked. The emotional tumult baying at the edge of my mind receded. I kept my limbs jerking and twisting while I clawed through my memories for any advice from Dad that might help. There was something, somewhere. I just knew it, but I couldn't remember...

Wait! Not advice. A story. The one about Dad's psychic breakthrough, and how Grandmama Connaught helped him control it. By doing... what? My memory was blank.

Blank.

Blank!

Picture a blank sheet of paper. Or the deep blackness of space. And concentrate on it.

Dad used space, because he'd just spent twenty minutes floating in it. I went with paper, because I've never been out in space.

I stopped twitching and turned all my concentration to picturing a bright white sheet of paper. It's harder than it sounds. Try it sometime, if you don't believe me. But I created a tiny splotch of white inside my mind. Emotions sparked and raged all around it, but I pulled it and stretched it and it grew. It blotted out intruding emotions and grew faster. Then, finally, mental whiteout.

Those horrible emotions circling my mind like hungry sharks vanished. I gasped in relief and drew a deep, shuddering breath. "I'm okay, now, Sofia."

She still radiated fear, but I picked it up from the tension in her body and her rapid breathing rather than from my empathic abilities. Sofia relaxed a little and eased her hold on me.

"What happened, Nora?"

"My empathic abilities just, um... I guess *blossomed* is the word."

"And I grabbed hold of you!" Sofia released me and sprang back. "Oh my gosh, Miss Connaught, I'm *so* sorry! The company gives us a little training in dealing with psychics, and I know that touch makes emotional transfers stronger. I—"

"Saved me." I grabbed her waving arms and held them still. "You saved me, Sofia."

"I did?"

"Yeah. Your fear dammed the flood long enough for me to remember what to do. If you hadn't hugged me..." I shuddered at the thought. "Thank you."

I forced a bright smile onto my face, even as a new emotion poked a hole in my imaginary sheet of paper.

Hatred. Deep. Implacable. And aimed directly at me.

The hatred directed at me shredded my flimsy defense, and the torrent of emotions poured through the tattered remains of my mental whiteout. I stumbled under the renewed onslaught and fell back onto the bed. My knees drew up to my chest. I wrapped my arms around my head, opened my mouth, and, despite my best efforts not to, screamed.

The door to my bedroom flew open. My bodyguards rushed in and leveled their blasters at Sofia.

"Down on the floor!" Conley said. "Now!"

Sofia gaped at the two men and waved her hands in panic. "It's Miss Connaught—"

Barber dove across the bed and tackled poor Sofia to the floor. Her cry of terror cut off as Barber's weight landed atop her and drove the breath from her lungs.

"What did you do?" Barber demanded.

Sofia just coughed and wheezed.

No! I tried shouting to my bodyguards to stop, but the emotions raging through my brain robbed me of the power of speech. But I *had* to speak. I *had* to defend Sofia.

If only I could recreate my mental whiteout. But I'd only

succeeded last time, because Sofia's fear shielded me from the worst of the emotions laying siege to my mind. She'd been touching me then, but she now was on the floor beneath a hundred kilograms of bodyguard in full-on protection mode. Barber would never let Sofia lay hands on me.

If she couldn't reach me, maybe I could reach her. But could I find the willpower to move my arms?

"What is wrong, Miss Connaught?" Conley asked. "Should I call the ship's doctor?"

I ignored him, which was dead easy with all the stuff happening inside my head, and fought to reach a hand for Sofia. Nothing happened. My fear of the rampaging emotions kept my hands clasped around my head.

But I'd underestimated Sofia. Through her own terror, despite the weight pressing her into the floor and her breath-deprived body's resistance to movement, she pulled an arm out from under Barber. Her hand slapped onto the bed and moved back and forth, searching for me.

"Watch out!" Conley yelled, and reached across me for Sofia's hand.

With one last lurch, her fingers brushed my arm and latched onto it. Her terror—far more for me than for herself—blasted through her touch and exploded into my mind. I grabbed her terror like the lifeline it was, and held on as it overwhelmed the other emotions, and shoved them aside. With just Sofia's fear and the unknown person's hatred left to deal with, I could finally concentrate. I imagined the blank sheet of paper again.

The mental whiteout returned. With it came control over my body.

"Stop," I croaked. "It's not Sofia. Let her up."

Conley holstered his blaster and bent over me, concern etched on his face. "What happened, Miss Connaught?"

I drew a deep breath, "It's the family legacy."

His brow drew down in puzzlement, then cleared. "Did your empathic abilities manifest, Miss Connaught?"

I nodded.

"Is that why you screamed?" he asked.

"No... Well, yes, but only because I thought I had everything under control."

Barber helped Sofia to her feet. "I apologize for the rough handling, Miss." He guided Sofia to the side of the bed. "Lie down and stretch your diaphragm. It will help you regain your breath."

After she did as Barber suggested, I clasped her hand in both of mine. "You saved me again, Sofia."

She directed a weak smile at me. "It's just another facet of the exemplary customer service you'll find aboard every ship in the Connaught Starline."

Sofia's comment caught me just right, and I burst out laughing. It had a hysterical edge to it, but it still made me feel much better. And my laughter bolstered the whiteout, which I totally didn't expect. Dad never told me that laughter could do that. I couldn't imagine he just forgot to mention it, so maybe it was something unique to me? I filed that away for future consideration.

I looked from Barber to Conley. "Guys, someone on board the *Pegasus* hates my guts."

Barber's and Conley's faces went blank. Uh oh. I know exactly what those expressions mean. Okay, their *lack* of expressions, but you know what I'm saying.

Super protective mode: engaged.

Their eyes darted around my bedroom, searching for threats. I'm pretty sure they knew there weren't any to find. It's a really tiny room, and the four of us only fit inside it because Sofia and I were on the bed. But the guys can't stop themselves. It's something Granddaddy's training instills in every bodyguard in the family's security detail.

After a few seconds, Barber nodded. Then Conley nodded.

Conley looked at me and asked, "Who hates you, Miss Connaught?"

I shrugged. "How should I know? It's not like I can read minds."

"I know, Miss Connaught, but I'd be remiss in my duties if I didn't ask."

"Can you do the pointing thing your father used to find his parents?" Sofia asked.

Conley, Barber, and I all turned inquiring expressions on Sofia. I also raised my left eyebrow. (I did that to my sister once, and it irritated Nancy so much I kept doing it. Mom says it's an endearing quirk. I just hope the boys on Draconis see it the same way, because I can't break the habit.)

Sofia's eyes darted between the three of us, then she looked down away. "When Captain Riggs told me I was going to be Miss Connaught's—"

"Nora's," I corrected.

"*Nora's* attendant, he had me read up on her family history. I read how Mrs. Connaught helped Mr. Connaught clear his mind and instinctively point toward his parents." Sofia raised her eyes and looked at me. "Since your mother already figured out what to do, can't you just do that?"

"I don't think so," I said. "Unless you know a super cute guy who's secretly in love with me."

Sofia looked puzzled. "I don't get it."

"Mom and Dad had been in love with each other for years, but never told each other. And what Mom did to help Dad was have a hot and heavy make-out session with him. She waited until Dad really got into it, then told him to point towards his parents."

Dad loved telling that story, so we kids heard it *a lot* growing up. I thought it was romantic when I was eight, when Dad just told us they kissed. But now that I'm eighteen and know the whole story? Ew! I mean, yeah, I know my parents love each other and all that. And they... did stuff. Did *it*. But there are some things about parents a kid just doesn't want to think about. If you think I'm being childish, take a minute and imagine *your* parents going at it. Still feel the same way? Yeah, I thought not.

Sofia looked abashed. "Oh. I... didn't know."

"I don't think my parents shared that bit outside the family, so how could you?" I adopted a nonchalant air, "But, if you know any cute guys onboard, I'm willing to make out with them and see what happens." Conley frowned at me, so I added, "Purely for scientific reasons, of course."

Sofia giggled at least.

I dropped the light tone and added, "But I'd have to open my mind to the flood of emotions, again. And I don't think I can take that. I'm barely holding on, as it is."

Barber asked, "If you were touching someone, do you think you could read their emotions while maintaining your defenses?"

"Maybe?" I turned to Sofia. "Are you willing to let me try with you? No pressure, and I'd understand if you—"

Sofia took my hand. "Sometimes you talk too much, Nora."

"Yeah, Nancy and Eric say the same thing." I remembered Sofia hadn't met them, so added, "They're my brother and sister."

"I know. Remember when I said Captain Riggs had me read up on you? Now, try reading my emotions."

My sibs could have read Sofia, no problem. They wouldn't even need to hold her hand. And Dad could probably have read her from, I don't know, another star system or something. But I'm just plain old No-Talent Nora. I think I felt Sofia's emotions gently poking at the other side of my white wall of defense. But so many other emotions were doing the same thing that I'm not sure it was Sofia I felt. Still, I tried to make a tiny pinprick hole in my wall, one just large enough to let only Sofia's emotions through. I tried as hard as I've ever tried to do anything.

And I couldn't do it. I was too afraid. Afraid of another emotional deluge if I opened my defenses even a little. Afraid I'd never rebuild my defenses. Afraid I'd lose myself forever.

My shoulders slumped. "Sorry, I can't."

"It's just as well," Conley said. "I wouldn't want to let someone who hates you get that close."

Barber nodded. "The logistics of testing everyone on board the *Pegasus* would have been a nightmare, anyway."

"Besides, it's not like hating me is against the law," I added.

Conley and Barber gave reluctant nods, and I got the idea they thought there *should* be a law against hating me. Body-guards, right? (That's a joke. I know most people don't have bodyguards. In fairness to me, most people don't need body-guards, either.)

"What will you do now?" Sofia asked.

She was asking me, but Conley answered. "We'll take the safest course available to us. I'll tell Captain Riggs to turn the *Pegasus* around and take Miss Connaught back to Ark's Landing."

My jaw went slack, and I just stared at Conley. He was going to ask the captain to *turn the ship around?* He obviously never paid attention to any of the lessons Aunt Nancy gave us kids. (Mom and Dad named my sister after Aunt Nancy. And no, she's not really my aunt. But she's been an honorary member of the family since before I was born.) She's a retired Federation Navy starfighter pilot, so Mom and Dad got her to teach us all about orbital mechanics, stellar navigation, and a lot of high-level stuff about spaceships.

Yeah, I had an unconventional education.

The thing is, you can't just turn a spaceship around and go the other way. Not like you can with an aircar. And definitely not like they show it in adventure vids. The ship uses up tons of fuel reverse thrusting to bring it to a stop. Then tons more fuel going back the other way. And I mean real tons, too. That's not just teenage girl speak for 'a whole lot.'

But I didn't say anything to Conley or Barber. From the looks on their faces, they needed to hear that from someone other than the girl they'd guarded for the last eight years. So I sat quietly with Sofia while Conley called Captain Riggs. Conley had to talk his way past the comm officer and the first officer before Captain Riggs appeared on the comm screen.

"Captain Riggs," Conley said without preamble, "please turn the *Pegasus* around and return us to Ark's Landing. Miss Connaught's life may be in danger."

"I can't," Captain Riggs said.

"You *will*," Conley growled, "or I'll personally see that Mr. Connaught relieves you of duty."

"I didn't say I *won't* turn the *Pegasus* around," the captain snapped, "I said I *can't*. The *Pegasus* is in the middle of a wormhole transit. It's impossible to turn the ship around until she exits the wormhole."

Conley sighed, "Very well. Turn the ship around once it—"

Without conscious thought, I said, "She."

"What?" Conley asked.

"Ships are female."

"What difference does it make?"

"Ask Aunt Nancy next time we see her. And tell me before you do, because I want to watch."

"Fine," Conley sighed again, "turn the ship around once *she* leaves the wormhole."

The first officer suddenly appeared in the comm screen background. "Captain Riggs? I must speak with you about an urgent matter."

Conley began, "It can wait until—"

"No, *you* can wait," Captain Riggs said, and hit the mute button.

Conley and Barber clenched their jaws in frustration, but they couldn't do anything else. In the comm screen, the first officer spoke urgently for a few seconds. Captain Riggs said something in reply, and the first officer hurried off. When the captain unmuted the comm, he wore a troubled expression.

"Please stay there. I'm on my way to Miss Connaught's suite." Without another word, he ended the call.

I glanced at Sofia and she looked just as surprised as I felt. Ship captains simply do not visit passenger's rooms. Not even passengers like me. Captains run the ship. The concierge and the stewards deal with the passengers. What was so important the captain would take time away from doing his job just to talk to me?

We met Captain Riggs in the suite's sitting room. Sofia and I sat quietly on the sofa while the three men loomed over us.

Conley spoke first. "Have you come to tell me you'll turn the ship around once it— once *she* leaves the wormhole?"

"No, that would be a terrible idea," Captain Riggs said. "Especially in light of the reason I came to Miss Connaught's suite."

That sounded ominous, so I asked, "What's happened, Captain Riggs?"

"One of the *Pegasus's* messenger drones launched shortly before we entered the wormhole. The crew didn't discover the launch until First Officer Blair interrupted your call."

Yep, it was ominous.

"Do you know who launched it?" Conley asked.

"The crew is investigating that right now," Captain Riggs replied. "I wish I could say otherwise, but it's likely someone will be waiting for us when we exit the wormhole."

"Who?" Barber asked.

"I must assume it will be pirates." Captain Riggs continued, "There has been increasing pirate active in this sector over the last two years. The *Pegasus's* sister ship, the *Perseus,* vanished without a trace last year. Her last known position was a star system just two wormhole jumps away from the one we're approaching now."

Conley and Barber exchanged worried glances. I didn't blame them. Space pirates aren't exactly the kinds of threats they're trained for.

"What can you do to insure the ship's safety?" Conley asked.

"The *Pegasus* carries armament on par with a navy destroyer, but speed will be our best defense," Captain Riggs replied. "Pirates can't capture a ship they can't catch."

"What about the Federation Navy?" Barber asked.

"We're dozens of light years beyond the Federation's borders. I have another messenger drone prepped and will launch it the moment we exit the wormhole, but it will take the drone four days to reach the nearest naval base." Captain Riggs spread his hands, "Whatever is waiting for us when we exit the wormhole, the *Pegasus* will face it alone."

The captain and my bodyguards exchanged grim stares for

several seconds. Then Captain Riggs looked at me. And it didn't take empathic abilities to read his dominant emotion. It blazed in his eyes like a beacon.

Hope.

Directed at me.

No-Talent Nora.

I could only think of one reason why he felt that, and it made my already churning stomach start doing flips. And flops. Lots and lots of flops. I prayed I was wrong, but had to know for sure.

I drew a deep breath, steeled myself, and asked, "Why did you tell us this in person, Captain Riggs? I appreciate your consideration, but you could have explained it over the comm."

The captain waved at one of the two empty chairs and raised his eyebrows. I nodded, of course. It's not like I'm royalty or something. He doesn't need my permission to sit in my presence. Especially not on board the ship *he* commands.

Captain Riggs sat, then he removed his hat and stared at it while he turned it over and over in his hands. My heart began pounding, thumping so hard I felt like it might burst out of my chest. My already taut nerves felt as if someone was tap dancing on them, and my left eye began twitching. And, worst of all, my mental wall of white shuddered and cracks formed in it.

The raging, roiling emotions of five thousand people lurked just beyond my meager defense. Watching my wall. Searching for a weakness. Ready to pounce the moment they sighted their prey.

Me.

My mind.

My sanity.

Somehow, Sofia sensed my distress. She clasped my right hand in both of her hands. Warmth flowed into my hand and the tremor I hadn't even realized I had eased.

Captain Riggs heaved a sigh. "There is a traitor among my crew, Miss Connaught. I don't know who it is, and am unwilling to risk the wrong person overhearing what I'm about to say."

From the corner of my eye, Conley and Barber gave simultaneous nods of approval at the captain's caution. Bodyguards *always* assume they're the only ones in the galaxy with any security sense, and that's an attitude Granddaddy encourages.

Captain Riggs continued, "When I return to the bridge, I will make a ship wide announcement confining passengers and non-essential crew to their quarters. I can't do that without a good reason, so will have to tell everyone that we might find pirates waiting for us when we exit the wormhole. From the command crew down to the youngest child, the news will terrify everyone on the *Pegasus*. And with good reason."

I felt certain I knew the answer to the question I was about to ask, but I voiced it anyway. "Why are you telling me this, Captain Riggs?"

He met my gaze. "Because I hope you inherited your father's ability to draw emotions out of people and project them at others. Then you could absorb everyone's terror, hold it until we emerge from the wormhole, and then project it at the pirates. Assuming there *are* pirates."

And now it was out in the open. Captain Riggs felt his best chance of escaping pirates lay with the hoped-for psychic abilities of an eighteen-year-old girl who had heroic parents. I'd thought going off to college would get me *away* from high expectations. But it did just the opposite.

My vision blurred as tears welled. I opened my mouth to crush Captain Riggs' hopes, but nothing came out.

"Nora can't do it, sir," Sofia said.

Captain Riggs blinked and looked at Sofia, almost as if he had forgotten she was here. "What's that, Miss Olson?"

"She can't do what you're asking, sir. Nora's psychic abilities just showed up after we entered the wormhole, and she's had a hard time controlling them."

I found enough of a voice to snort. "What Sofia isn't saying is that I'd be a drooling imbecile right now if she hadn't been here to help me get through my ability's sudden arrival."

"I see. Well, it was a long shot, to begin with." Captain Riggs stood and turned towards the door. "I must return to the bridge."

"Captain Riggs?" Sofia asked. When the captain looked over his shoulder, she continued, "May I stay here with Nora when you confine everyone to their quarters? She may need me if her psychic ability overwhelms her again."

The captain's mouth stretched with the hint of an approving smile. "Of course you may." Then his eyes flicked to Conley and Barber. "Please keep Sofia as safe as possible, gentlemen."

"We will," Conley said.

Captain Riggs left without another word.

I thought my bodyguards would start discussing their chances of keeping Sofia and me safe from pirates. Instead, Conley looked at me and said, "You look tired, Miss Connaught. Why don't you and Sofia get some rest?"

I knew Conley just wanted us out of the way so he and Barber could discuss bodyguard stuff without us overhearing. I was so wound up, I doubted I could fall asleep. But I just nodded and led Sofia back to my bedroom. We lay down on the bed and just stared at each other in wide-eyed fear. Then, to my amazement, I fell asleep.

~

White light blinded me. Whispers surrounded me. I blinked and squinted into the light, searching for the source of the voices. Too low to understand but too loud to ignore, the whispers were an irritating itch I couldn't scratch.

Some whispers sounded urgent, but I couldn't heed their warning.

Others carried ominous tones, but I couldn't comprehend their threat.

But most of them were barely more than background noise. Susurrations just on the edge of hearing. Distractions that kept me from hearing the warnings and threats.

"Stop whispering!" I screamed, punching the air in a vain attempt to silence the voices.

They remained.

Another voice burst through the others.

It seethed.

It burned.

It writhed.

Its whisper cried hatred.

It was one whisper among thousands, but I recognized the voice. Even as it changed tone.

It reveled.

It rejoiced.

It exulted.

Its whisper proclaimed triumph.

I gave the voice my full attention, turned all my anger on it, and screamed, "Shut up!"

It fell silent.

But why?

"Nora?" A hand shook my shoulder. "Wake up, Nora."

I cracked one eye open, drawn by a voice I could understand. "Wha—?"

"You were thrashing in your sleep. I thought it might be a nightmare and woke you up." Sofia sat up. "Was it? A nightmare, I mean?"

"Yeah."

I said that to protect Sofia's feelings. Because it wasn't really true. I mean, I heard whispers while I was asleep. But I *still* heard the whispers now that I was awake. Except for the one that fell quiet. I wonder what caused that? Or was that voice the real nightmare, and the rest was just reality intruding on my dream?

"Lights," Sofia called.

When the little cabin's lights came on, I noticed Sofia had a red spot on her cheek. I pointed at it. "Did I hit you?"

Sofia touched her cheek. "Not on purpose."

"I'm sorry."

She grinned. "You pack a wallop. If we end up fighting pirates, I'm glad you'll be on my side."

"That's Mom's and Granddaddy's training. I'm sorry you ended up feeling it."

Sofia rolled her eyes. "Stop apologizing, Nora."

She suddenly cocked her head, as if listening for something. Did she suddenly hear the whispers, too?

"What are you list—"

"Shush!" Sofia hissed. After a few seconds, she added, "Do you hear it?"

"Hear what?"

"Nothing."

A surge of the irritation I felt in my dream surged through me. With the whispers coming from beyond my mental whiteout, I'd never hear silence again, and snapped, "If you don't hear anything, why did you bother asking me if I heard it, too?"

Sofia was immediately contrite. "I'm sorry, Nora. I wasn't trying to make you mad. It's just that the *Pegasus* is never silent. There's always something making noise, like the engines or life support or something. But there's *nothing* right now, except our voices."

Now that I knew what spooked Sofia, I concentrated on the ever-present background noises she mentioned. And they weren't there.

"Maybe they're doing some repairs?" I suggested.

Sofia shook her head. "Not unless it's something absolutely critical. You heard what Captain Riggs said about speed being our ally. There's no way he'd shut down the engines. Not this close to exiting the wormhole."

"Maybe the *Pegasus* came out of the wormhole while we were sleeping?"

"I don't think so, but let me check." Sofia reached for the suite's data pad. She tapped through two screens, then spun the pad to face me. "According to the ship's schedule, wormhole exit isn't for another ten minutes."

"Sabotage, then?"

Sofia shrugged, "Your guess is as good as mine."

She was right, but I couldn't help feeling like my guess shouldn't even be a guess. Dad and my sibs could just get an emotional reading of the bridge and figure it out from there. Supposedly, I could, too. I just had to focus my ability. And then ignore the emotions from five thousand people long enough to rebuild my mental wall after I got my reading. But even if I couldn't do either of those things, I could always use Sofia as a lifeline.

Right?

Probably.

No.

Definitely.

Confidence is half the battle, just like Mom and Dad taught me.

Something must have shown on my face, because Sofia said, "Don't do it."

"We need to know if this is intentional or not."

"We don't need to know *that* badly, Nora. I'm sure Captain Riggs—"

"Is *really* busy right now, or there's nothing to worry about." I held my hands out to Sofia. "Please?"

She sighed and took my hands. "I still think this is a terrible idea."

"You're probably right, but I've got to try this on my own sometime. Since Conley and Barber need to know if there *is* something to worry about, that time might as well be now."

I remembered my inability to drop my wall earlier and used that failure to feed the anger I still felt after my dream. Without giving myself more time to think about it, I kicked down my mental wall.

THE DARKNESS REMAINED

Thousands of emotions flooded my mind. But this time, I'd invited them in. Because I knew what to expect and was ready for it. Totally. Ready. And if I kept telling myself that, someday I might even convince myself it was true.

Okay, I wasn't ready. As before, the torrent battered me from all sides. As before, I felt a rising panic as it threatened to sweep me away. As before, I knew I risked losing myself in emotions not my own.

I felt as if I'd been caught by a surprise ocean wave. Engulfed in it. Tossed about by its irresistible power. Unable to breathe. Terrified I might never breathe again.

But this time I was somewhat better prepared than before. This time I had a lifeline.

Sofia held my hands, and the physical contact brightened and strengthened my ability to recognize her anxiety and fear. Her emotions dangled before me, a familiar rope amid the torrent. I latched onto it, just as I had before.

I didn't try blocking everything else out. There was simply too much.

I didn't try rebuilding my mental wall. Damming the flood wasn't my goal.

I waited.

I held on.

I breathed.

Rapid, at first. Panting, almost. Then slowing and deepening.

The emotions still swirled around me. They still threatened to suck me under and drown me.

But I *breathed*. And if I could breathe, I could survive the flood. As long as I had Sofia's fear and anxiety as a lifeline.

Now that I wasn't in as much danger of losing myself, I sifted through the emotions filling my mind. I'd opened my mind to find the bridge crew and read their emotional state. But where were they amid everyone else?

I plucked an emotion at random from the thousands around me.

Frenzied, fear-fueled passion filled me. I panted with a desperate desire for life-affirming love and intimacy. Heat coursed through me, and...

Okay, I thought, releasing that emotional strand. *Definitely not someone in the bridge crew.*

I caught an emotion coming from another direction.

Raw terror blazed through the strand. But not terror for self. Terror for others. For... children?

I dropped that emotion as if it had burned me. And maybe it had. Because now I could imagine how a mother felt in the face of a space pirate attack.

As remorse, shame, grief, despair, anger, and a hundred more emotions swarmed around me, I realized it would take forever to find someone in the bridge crew by random sampling. But I also realized the emotions came at me from all around. Did they flow in a straight line between the person feeling the emotion and me? They must, otherwise Dad could never have used his ability to find his parents all those years ago.

Okay, if I looked in the bridge crew's direction maybe I could find one of them. But I had no idea where the bridge was from here. Did Sofia know? Could I even ask her? What would happen if I took my attention off Sofia's emotional lifeline? Would I lose my hold and then lose myself?

I had no idea. Dad and my sibs could talk and do normal stuff while using their abilities. So it was possible. The only question was whether I could do it. But I had to try.

I took a deep breath, steeling myself for the worst, and forced my eyes open. Sofia's fearful gaze met mine.

I took one more breath, turned my attention away from my lifeline, and whispered, "Bridge. Which way?"

Sofia's eyes widened in surprise. "What?"

"Point to bridge," I gasped.

She looked around the room, as if getting her mental bearings. Meanwhile, her posture relaxed. Her rigid shoulders slumped. The creases in her brow vanished. Her death grip on my hands eased. The corners of her mouth turned up in the beginnings of a smile.

Sofia vented an enormous sigh. "Nora, you can control your ability!"

I felt something change in my mind and immediately turned my attention inward. Sofia vanished as I searched for the problem. I found it immediately.

When I'd spoken to Sofia, I'd soothed her fear and eased her anxiety. Those twined emotions were all that anchored me against the raging sea of other emotions. But Sofia's fears were fading quickly, taking my lifeline with them.

I felt Sofia's fears for me unraveling and slipping from my mental grasp. With the collected emotional tsunami from the *Pegasus's* passengers and crew poised to crash down on me and sweep me away, I chased after my fast-receding lifeline. I clawed and scrambled through terror and love and anger and every other imaginable feeling in search of some remnant of the lifeline Sofia's emotions wove for me. But her once-firm fears kept fading and slipping from my grasp.

I felt panic rising within me like the dark hand of doom. It snatched for my own trailing emotions, and I fled farther up the one thing that kept me tethered to the real world. I felt my growing panic closing in. It flowed up and around me, pulling me under its dark depths. And if it ever closed over my head, if it ever cut me off from Sofia's lifeline of fading fears and ebbing anxiety, I was lost.

Totally, irrevocably lost.

Pushed beyond my limits by terrors of my own making, I made one last, desperate lunge for Sofia, and...

Silence.

Blissful.

Dark.

Life-saving.

Silence.

My panicky hand of doom? Vanished.

The constant assault from five thousand emotions? Repelled.

Sofia's lifeline? Gone.

But *I* was still here. Still myself. And at peace for the first time since the *Pegasus* entered the wormhole and my psychic abilities manifested. I was safe.

Except for the possibility of a space pirate ambush when we exited the wormhole in... Hey, how long was it until the *Pegasus* returned to normal space? The wormhole transit had another ten minutes to go when Sofia took my hands and I kicked down my mental wall. And nearly lost myself forever. So, yeah, no more kicking down mental walls. Not until Dad's around to help me, anyway.

But back to the *Pegasus's* wormhole exit. There was a simple way to find out how long we had left. Just open my eyes and look at a clock.

Hey, weren't my eyes already open? I'd looked at Sofia and didn't remember shutting my eyes again. But I must have, since it was totally dark in here. Right? Yeah, no problem. I'll just open my eyes.

Nothing happened.

Nora to eyes! Wakey, wakey. Time to open.

No brilliant burst of light appeared.

Weird.

Was I dreaming? No, it couldn't be that. I've had cusp-of-waking dreams before, and I always wake up the moment I'm aware it's a dream.

Had I built such a perfect mental fortress that I'd cut myself off from the rest of my mind? Was that even possible? It never happened to Dad or my sibs, but it seemed like my abilities worked differently than theirs did. So, maybe?

In that case, all I had to do was replace the super strong mental walls surrounding me with my original whiteout defense. I kind of hated the idea of doing that because all those emotions continuously poked and prodded and pushed on the whiteout's paper thin barrier. But if I ever wanted to open my eyes again, I didn't think I had any other choice.

I drew a deep breath. Or tried to. Maybe I did. I couldn't feel myself breathing any more than I could make myself open my eyes. Okay, *that* was scary. Was my body slowly suffocating while I cowered inside this quiet, dark fortress I'd built inside my head?

No, that couldn't be. Breathing is involuntary. At the worst, I'd pass out from lack of oxygen and then my body would start breathing again. Not the best solution, but...

What would happen to me if my body passed out while I was still stuck in this silent corner of my brain? Would I find myself permanently trapped here? Or would I just be stuck here until someone got Dad so he could come inside my head and find me? *Or*, if space pirates captured the *Pegasus*, would they just take me for dead and toss me out an airlock?

Wonderful as the silence felt, it wasn't worth taking any of those risks. I steeled myself and kicked at the dark wall surrounding me. And I missed.

Talk about lame. How could I miss my own mental barrier?

I kicked again. And again. And again. And I kept missing the barrier.

Okay, Nora, kicking isn't working. Time to try something else. Think it through. What else could protect me from outside emotions this completely?

A room? Had I built a fully sealed room inside my head and then shut myself in? It *seemed* logical. I mean, as logical as anything dealing with psychic abilities ever is. So I just had to find the door to my little room and open it. It would be a lot easier to do that if I had some light inside my mental hideout. So...

Let there be light!

And... the darkness remained.

Okay, time to feel around for the door. Assuming there was a door. Which there had to be, because I somehow got myself into the room, and ought to be able to get myself out the same way. Yep. Logic.

I cast my mind out into the darkness, imagining hands searching for a doorknob hidden by pitch black darkness. And I found something almost immediately. Not a doorknob. Not a wall. It was... squishy... I know what you're thinking. How can I feel something if I can't even tell if I'm breathing? The thing is, I didn't feel it. *It* gave me a squishy feeling.

I turned my attention to the thing. Without further prompting, it opened. But it wasn't a door out of the room. It was an emotion. It was warm, fuzzy, comfortable love for a man and a woman. For parents. Except they weren't *my* parents, and it wasn't *my* emotion.

I cast the emotion aside and discovered another squishy emotion. It gave me the tingling thrill of a first kiss with a first love. But I've never had love's first kiss.

I found another random emotion. Anxiety for a big test in school. But I never attended a regular school.

I sensed another one. The sharp pang of loss when a close friend moves away. But I was the first girl in my small circle of friends who left Ark's Landing.

Had I trapped myself inside my head with emotional memories stolen from the passengers and crew of the *Pegasus*? No, that couldn't be it. Dad could pull emotions out of other people, but they were just feelings. They didn't have associated memories.

And there was something familiar about all the emotional memories I examined. Something they all had in common. As if they all came from the same person. From the way the emotions felt, the person was a girl. And I got the idea she was about my age. And...

It came to me in a rush. Oh, God, I wasn't trapped inside *my* mind. Somehow, someway, I was trapped inside *Sofia's*.

I sensed more of Sofia's feelings and their associated memories all around me, with more... *Approaching* isn't the right word, because I didn't get the idea the emotions were moving around inside Sofia's mind. But I don't have words to describe what was happening. So I'm stuck using words for stuff that happens in the physical world while I'm in the... Metaphysical world? I *think* that's right.

This isn't a vocabulary test, Nora. Get your thoughts back to figuring out how to get out of Sofia's mind.

Another of her emotional memories popped open, and the heartbreak Sofia felt when she lost her first love washed over me. Then came the simple joy of snuggling down in a warm bed. Followed by the soothing feel of a cat's purr.

More and more emotional memories burst around me. They brought pain, relief, envy, sympathy, and the rest of the full range of human emotions with them. And suddenly Sofia's mind wasn't the refuge I originally thought it was.

I mentally curled myself up into a ball and screamed, *Leave me alone! Please, just go away!*

And... they did.

Sofia's emotional memories stopped revealing themselves to me. The squishy feeling I associated with them retreated. I could think again. Which was good, because I had to figure out how to get out of Sofia's head and back into my own. That's assuming I *could* get back.

That was the one idea I had tried my best to keep out of my mind. Because the thought of being stuck in here forever was even more terrifying than the thought of being overwhelmed by the thousands of emotions assaulting my mind back there in the real world.

I felt panic stalking around the edges of my mind. Biding its time. Watching for the right moment to leap fully into my mind and rip control away from me. (Yeah, I know the panic is part of me, not some weird emotional predator. But anyone who's ever panicked can tell you it can still take over your mind and make you do irrational things. And if there's one thing I can't afford right now, it's irrationality.) I turned my attention away from my emotional fringe and considered my situation.

Okay, start at the beginning. Mind, how did you get us into Sofia's head?

I don't know.

Yes, you do, you just haven't given it enough thought, yet.

Fine, I'll think. I was safe inside my own head, clinging to Sofia's lifeline of fear and anxiety. And then it all went wrong.

How did it go wrong?

She stopped being afraid and anxious. So the lifeline started unraveling.

Then what?

I chased after the receding lifeline. And then I was in here.

Oh. My. God. I followed Sofia's emotions right inside her mind! How was that even possible? I never heard of any empath ever doing something like that before. Dad knew more about empathic abilities than anyone in human space, and he taught us kids as much as he could, just in case we inherited his abilities. So he must not have heard of anything like this, either.

Hey, did that mean No-Talent Nora was really New-Talent Nora? That was a pretty zing idea.

And one that isn't helping us return to our own mind.

Right. Sorry.

Okay, if I followed Sofia's emotions into her mind, I should be able to follow more of her emotions out of her mind. I think. But do I need to ride an emotion directed at me to get back to myself? I don't know. But better safe than sorry.

All I had to do was wait for Sofia to get worried about me. I guess that would happen if I was unresponsive long enough. But how long would that take? Did I even experience time the same way in Sofia's mind as I did in mine? Would I go crazy in here, waiting for Sofia to finally get scared?

Too many questions. No answers. And I was already talking to myself. That's never good.

Could I find some way to prompt Sofia's emotions?

That thought came with a recent memory of my own. Afraid of being overwhelmed by Sofia's emotional memories, I told them to back off. And they did. But did that mean I could order up emotions on a whim?

I'd like the Fear For Nora platter, with a side of Anxiety, please.

Stop it, mind. That's not helping.

Yes, it is. Just try it.

If I do, will you shut up?

No. You have to use me to place your order.

Fine.

Sofia, be afraid for Nora. She's in danger. She's losing herself. Feel fear! Feel anxiety!

A bright, pulsing shaft of sheer terror laced with deep anxiety leapt into existence next to me. The panic hovering on the edges of my mind chose that moment to pounce, and it drove me, clawing and climbing up Sofia's emotion.

But, if this was my way out of Sofia's mind, what would happen when I emerged? Would I just hop back into my own body? Would the flood of outside emotions sweep me away before I knew what was happening?

A bright, burning feeling filled my senses. I tightened my

hold on Sofia's shaft of fear and anxiety as the brightness washed over me.

There was nothing easy about returning to my own mind. The outer fringes of Sofia's mind held her own emotional defenses. They formed a barrier protecting her against ridicule and rejection and all the other emotions people inflict on us, or the self pity and doubt and everything else we throw at ourselves. I crashed through Sofia's own version of my mental whiteout and slammed back into my own mind.

It was *not* gentle, and my mind reeled from the impact.

The surge of emotions I hoped for—prayed for, even—hammered me from all sides. For a second, I felt like someone dying of thirst who gets caught in a sudden downpour. The deluge told me I hadn't marooned myself forever inside Sofia's mind and also got myself back into my own head. But it still threatened to sweep me away.

My grip on Sofia's fears and anxieties slipped. I felt a surge of terror well up inside me and turned all my attention on that life-line. Once I had a firmer hold, I tried building my mental wall against the emotional onslaught. My first attempt was too hasty, and it shredded under the pressure. I guess I was still recovering from my sudden return to normal.

God, what was happening to me? When did *this* become normal?

This isn't the time for existential questions, Nora.

Right. Right. Sorry. It's time to concentrate on my mental defenses. But if I'm not stuck in Sofia's head anymore, why am I still talking to myself like this?

Nora!

Ack! The emotions washing over me make it so easy to lose focus. And if I couldn't regain it, I could lose a lot more than that. I could lose myself.

And?

That would be bad.

Look beyond us. Who else is affected if we lose ourself?

Sofia! She might think it's all her fault. It's not, but she won't know that.

Concern for Sofia sprang into existence inside my mind. Bright and strong. I started building a new mental wall, but this time I reinforced it with the concern I felt for my new friend. And it held. It turned the emotions aside. Working with hasty deliberation, I expanded the wall. Bolstered by my concern for Sofia, it went up quickly. And...

Whiteout.

Mental barrier built.

The thousands of emotions still pounded at my head. I still felt them out there. But they were quieter, somehow. Sort of like a ringing in your ears. Irritating if you pay attention to it, but it fades into the background once your attention turns elsewhere.

I drew a deep breath of relief. And I *felt* the air rushing through my nose and filling my lungs. I released the breath with a sigh, blinked my eyes, and looked at Sofia.

I saw a pale face, and wide, terror-filled eyes stared back at me. I felt a surge of guilt at Sofia's appearance and mental state. I'd done that to her. Maybe I didn't have a choice, but that didn't ease my guilt.

I squeezed Sofia's hands. "I'm all right."

"What happened, Nora? I thought everything was fine. I mean, you looked at me and talked to me. But then you just went all still. And your eyes!"

"What about my eyes, Sofia?"

"They... changed. Lost their sparkle and turned dull. They looked really creepy, Nora, and I guess your eyes frightened me. Because I suddenly felt a stab of pure terror."

"How long did my eyes have that dull look?"

"A couple of seconds. Not very long, but..." Sofia shuddered. "I don't think I'll ever forget that look. It was like... I don't know. Like you weren't in there anymore."

"That's because I wasn't. In my own head, I mean."

Sofia's mouth opened in an astonished O, and she covered it with her hand. "What happened? Where did you go?"

I couldn't think of an easy way to tell Sofia where I'd been, so I caught her gaze and said, "I was in *your* head."

Sofia stared at me with incomprehension for a second. A little color had returned to her face, but it drained out of it, again. She dropped my hands like they were too hot to handle, and then crossed her arms over her chest defensively.

I couldn't blame her for that reaction.

"You were in *my* head?" she asked.

I nodded.

"Did you go pawing through my thoughts?"

I winced at her tone. But I *had* seriously invaded her privacy. "No. Not on purpose. Some of your emotional memories revealed themselves to me, but once I figured out where I was, I made them back off." I gazed into Sofia's cold eyes, and my heart broke. "I'm sorry, Sofia. I didn't mean to. I didn't even know I could do that. I didn't even know *anyone* could do that."

Sofia held my gaze. "Did you have anything to do with the terror I felt just now?"

"Yeah."

"How could you do that to me? I thought we were friends."

"We are!" I hung my head, lowered my voice, and said, "I didn't want to frighten you, but I got into your mind on the fear you felt for me. I just hoped I could get out again the same way."

"Couldn't you have tried some other emotion first? Compassion, or something else like that?"

"Maybe. Probably. But I was so scared I'd *never* get out that I just went with the first idea that came to me." I reached for one of Sofia's hands, afraid she'd jerk it away. But she let me take hold of it. "I truly am sorry, Sofia."

Her frozen gaze thawed. "I know, Nora. It's just..." She waved her free hand. "*So* weird."

I offered a tentative smile. "Oh yeah. To quote my mom, it's *totally* weird."

"Do you think you can do it again? On purpose, I mean?"

My eyebrows rose. "You *want* me in your mind, again?"

"Not really, but you need to figure out how this stuff works, and I'm right here."

Sofia had a point. A really good point. And she was willing to do something she found incredibly uncomfortable just to help me learn how to use my new ability. But I wasn't so sure I wanted to dive into her head again. Not yet, anyway.

Before I could reply, Captain Riggs came on the ship's intercom. "Wormhole exit in thirty seconds. Passengers, I am sealing your cabins until further notice. Crew, if pirates are waiting for us, let's give them a fight they'll never forget. Prepare to repel boarders!"

SURRENDER

Sofia and I exchanged frightened glances. Then we both about jumped out of our skin when someone knocked at the door to my bedroom.

"Miss Connaught? Miss Olson?" Conley called. "May I open the door?"

Sofia and I had slept in our clothes, so we didn't have to worry about dressing. I cocked an eyebrow at Sofia in question. She nodded in answer.

"Sure, Conley," I said. "Come on in."

The door slid aside and revealed my two grim-faced bodyguards. They scanned the room for threats, even though they had guarded the only entrance to my room. The only publicly known entrance, anyway. Both held blasters, naturally.

"We must hide you, Miss Connaught, and I suggest you take Miss Olson with you."

Sofia's eyes darted around the small room. "Hide where? The closet is too small for two people, and it's kind of an obvious hiding place. The bathroom isn't much bigger."

"My grandfather had a few special touches added to the owner's suite after the starliners were built," I said. I pointed at a corner of the room. "There's a secret entrance to the maintenance tunnels over there."

Sofia leaned closer to the wall I'd indicated and squinted. "I don't see anything."

"That's the whole idea," I said, then turned my attention back to Conley. "But if pirates do attack, hiding me won't do any good. A simple scan of the passenger manifest will tell them I'm on board. If they really want me, they'll tear the ship apart looking for me. People could get hurt, and the pirates will still get me."

Conley shook his head. "At the first sign of a pirate attack, Captain Riggs will trigger a process to wipe all crew and passenger data from the ship's computer system. That's part of the emergency protocols on all Connaught Starline ships."

"Then Sofia can hide in the tunnels and stay safe, at least," I said. "But I was the last passenger brought on board. The captain escorted me, himself."

Sofia asked, "Did you see any other passengers when Captain Riggs led you here from the shuttle bay?"

Barber immediately replied, "No, Miss Olson, we did not. May I assume the captain made no ship-wide announcement about the stop at Ark's Landing?"

Sofia shook her head and added, "Every member of the crew knows passenger privacy is paramount. They drill that into us during training. A few officers will know Nora is on board, but that's it. The captain only told me about her because she's my special assignment on this trip."

"You're all forgetting one thing," I said. "*Someone* on this ship hates me. Their hatred is so strong it punched through the first mental wall I built. They must know I'm on the *Pegasus*. They're probably the same person who launched the drone before we entered the wormhole. That means they're working with the pirates." I looked at Conley and Barber. "And *that* means the pirates will know I'm onboard."

"We can't simply let you fall into pirate hands, Miss Connaught," Conley said.

"Why not?" I asked. I'd have felt more courageous if my voice hadn't quavered when I asked that question, but I forged on. "They can make a fortune ransoming me back to my family, so they'll take good care of me."

In a tentative voice, Sofia asked, "What if Nora could hide *and* the pirates could still capture her?"

"You've lost me, Sofia."

"What if the pirates *thought* they had you? Then you'd be safe hiding in the maintenance tunnels."

"What do you have in mind, Miss Olson?" Conley asked.

Sofia's hands shook, but her voice was firm when she said, "I'll take Nora's place, and we let the pirates capture me."

I stared at Sofia, incredulity written all over my face. Conley and Barber are as stoic as they come, but their eyes widened in apparent surprise.

When I finally found my voice, I said, "It'll never work. You don't look anything like me."

Sofia shrugged. "We're about the same size—you said it yourself when you told me to try on some of your clothes. The rest won't matter."

"Won't matter? Are you crazy, Sofia? I'm a blue-eyed blonde. You're a hazel-eyed brunette. Those aren't minor details. People *will* notice."

"I know that, Nora. But do *you* know how well your family has kept images of you, your siblings, and your cousins out of circulation?"

I glanced at Conley. "They have?"

He nodded. "Your grandfather is extraordinarily cautious, Miss Connaught. Your parents made more than a few enemies, and he feared those enemies would seek revenge by attacking their children."

Sofia added, "The Connaught Starline files don't even have

your picture. I never knew what you looked like until Captain Riggs brought you on board."

"I knew Granddaddy was paranoid, but not *that* paranoid." A sudden thought occurred to me. "How did he ever agree to me going to Draconis with only two bodyguards?"

Conley looked distinctly uncomfortable. "He didn't. The rest of your security detail left by private transport yesterday."

Wow. And here I thought I was finally going to get away from most of that security stuff. I guess I should have known better. A tiny flame of anger ignited in a corner of my mind at Granddaddy's sneaky move. But it was nothing compared to the anger I felt at the darker side of the expectations I've lived with my entire life. Granddaddy's plans must always revolve around the expectation that some low-life will use my sibs or me to get revenge on my parents.

Sofia brought me back on topic, "If there are pirates, chances are none of them know what you look like."

"You're forgetting the person on the *Pegasus* who hates me."

Sofia shook her head. "No, I'm not. I'm on the *Pegasus*, too. I even read everything we have on you and your family. If I didn't know what you looked like, neither will he."

I sighed. "You're still not thinking it through. What difference will it make if I'm free or not? Sure, I can handle myself in a one-on-one fight, but I can't take on a whole shipload of pirates. And I'm stuck going wherever the *Pegasus* goes, too. So why bother with the switch?"

"Because you're our best hope for rescue," Sofia said.

"Me? That's the craziest thing you've said so far!"

Sofia met my gaze and asked, "What is the first thing your father will do when he finds out you've been captured by pirates?"

"He'll... Ohhhhhh!"

"Right," Sofia nodded. "He'll use his empathic ability to find you, just like he used it to find his parents."

"Yeah, that makes sense. And Dad will probably bring half

the Ark's Landing Navy with him. But he can do that whether I'm hiding in the maintenance tunnels or in the pirates' hands."

"Unless the pirates have some way of neutralizing his connection to you. The pirates have to know how your father tracked his parents, so would they even risk taking a ship you're on if they couldn't block his ability? Is there anything you know of that can block psychic powers?"

I shrugged. "I think psychic nulls can."

"What's a psychic null?" Sofia asked.

"Someone with a natural psychic shield that's so strong most psychics can't even detect a person with one. Surround me with three or four psychic nulls and they'd keep Dad from using his empathic ability to find me." A small part of Mom's and Dad's story surfaced. "Except Dad found a way to detect a null and break his shield."

"Could he do that across dozens of lightyears?"

I wanted to say yes, but couldn't lie. "Probably not."

"All the pirates had to do was recruit a few of those nulls, then."

"You're forgetting one other thing the pirates could do to keep Dad from finding me," I said. "They could just kill me. Or you, if we switch."

Sofia's complexion paled, but she met my gaze. "I'm trying not to think about that, but I didn't forget it."

"And you're *still* willing to take my place?" I asked.

She hesitated for a moment, then nodded slowly. "There are five thousand people on the *Pegasus*, including children and friends I've made in the crew. What happens to them if pirates capture the ship?"

"The pirates will probably take the ship to the outer rim and sell the passengers into slavery. Or," I shuddered, "cut them up for parts."

"Being captured terrifies me more than dying, Nora. Suffering through weeks of dread before being sold. Or waiting to have my organs harvested. Listening to the screams of parents as their children are taken from them. And that's nothing compared to hearing the cries of those children. I... I'd rather be dead than go through that. If risking death by taking your place gives everyone else a chance of escaping those fates, I'll do it."

I caught Sofia's gaze and held it for a few seconds. I didn't need empathic abilities to know she was scared. But I also didn't need them to know she meant every word she'd just said.

My eyes cut to Conley and Barber. "What do you guys think?"

"I don't like the idea of leaving you alone in the tunnels, but Miss Olson makes a compelling case," Conley said. He looked at Sofia. "Are you certain you want to do this?"

Sofia didn't hesitate this time. "Yes."

Conley turned his attention back to me. "Then I suggest you pack a small bag of emergency supplies, Miss Connaught."

"And don't forget your blaster," Barber added.

I wasn't in a joking mood, but rolled my eyes anyway. "I'm my mother's daughter. She'd tan my hide if I didn't pack my blaster."

"I am your grandfather's employee," Barber said. "He'd flay me alive if I didn't remind you."

I went to the little closet, pulled out the backpack I planned on using for college, and stuffed it with two pairs of underwear, two shirts, and a pair of pants. Next, I opened the false bottom of my largest suitcase and pulled out my blaster. It went into the pack, along with two spare battery packs for it. Then I tossed several energy bars into the pack with everything else. If nothing else, I'd have chocolate to keep me company.

I glanced at Conley. "What else do I need?"

"Are you wearing an atmosphere harness under your clothing, as your grandfather instructed?"

I pulled my shirt up enough to show the harness under it.

Conley nodded. "A data pad might come in handy. I also suggest you take a paper notebook and a pen. That way you can leave notes for us, if you need to communicate."

"Or," Sofia said, "Nora can just pop into my head and send emotions directly to me."

Conley's brows drew down, and he cocked his head. "She can do what?"

"Um, yeah," I said, "that's a new development. But this probably isn't the time to go into it."

"Agreed," Conley said.

Barber had gone to my bodyguards' shared room while I packed. He returned and handed me a tiny comm unit. "Put it in your ear, Miss Connaught. Once we install nano transmitters on the rest of us, you'll be able to hear everything that goes on around us."

"What kind of transmitters?" Sofia asked.

"Nano," Barber replied. He held up a small injector tube. "They're microscopic and go in your ear. Anything you hear, they'll transmit to Miss Connaught's comm. They are short range and pose no danger, Miss Olson."

Sofia shrugged, "Even if there was a danger, it can't be worse than what I've already volunteered for."

Barber inserted transmitters in Sofia's ear, then Conley's, and then his own. Meanwhile, Conley showed me how to switch the comm between channels. I left it set for Sofia's channel, since she was going to be pretending to be me.

The ship-wide comm came to life, and Captain Riggs said, "All passengers and crew, my worst fears have been realized. Pirates were waiting for us at the wormhole exit. Worse, since someone has sabotaged our engines and weapons, we can neither outrun nor outfight the pirates. The pirates contacted me and demanded our surrender. When I refused, they threatened to blast the *Pegasus* apart.

"I offered my surrender, believing we could still defeat the pirates after their ship docked with the *Pegasus*. But whoever sabotaged the ship's systems is also in communication with the pirate ship. The pirates knew of our preparations and gave me five minutes to have the crew stand down. If I do not comply, the pirate spy will alert the pirates and they will simply destroy the *Pegasus.*

"I cannot put five thousand lives at risk for no possible gain. As much as it pains me to admit, the pirates have us where they want us. Therefore, I order all crew to stand down, store all weapons, and return to your quarters. I repeat, all crew stand down by order of the captain.

"To all aboard, I suggest you put your faith in almighty God and pray for our salvation."

The comm fell silent. Sofia and I stared at each other in mute despair while my bodyguards checked their weapons. Seeing that, I said, "Conley, you and Barber can't fight the pirates by yourselves."

"Perhaps not, Miss Connaught," Conley said, "but we must try. It comes with the job."

"No, it doesn't," I said. "Your job is protecting me, and you can do that best if you're alive. Sofia is going to need your help to pull off this switch. I need the pirates to accept the switch if I'm going to stay free in the tunnels. That means you have to stay alive if you want to protect me."

Conley and Barber exchanged glances, then Barber ejected his blaster's charge pack. "She's right."

Conley nodded, disarmed his blaster, and looked at me. "Stay safe, Miss Connaught, and stay alive. You are our best hope for salvation."

I gave my bodyguards a weak smile, surprised them by hugging both of them, then gave Sofia a hug and whispered in her ear, "Take care of yourself."

"You do the same," she whispered back.

I found the tiny retina reader for the secret exit to the tunnels. It scanned my eye, and the door popped open. I peered into the dimly lit tunnel, and it looked surprisingly spacious. I'd have to walk hunched over, but it wouldn't give me claustrophobia. Burdened with a new and extraordinarily heavy set of expectations, I entered the maintenance tunnel and shut the door behind me.

AN EYE FOR AN EYE

I spent ten seconds finding the retina scanner on the tunnel side of the hidden door. Just when I found it, the comm in my ear crackled to life.

Conley said, "Miss Connaught? Please knock twice on the door if you can hear my voice."

I dutifully knocked two times.

Conley's voice sounded again. "Good. We have full confidence in you, Miss Connaught, as does your grandfather."

I rapped on the door once more in acknowledgement.

Sofia added, "Come visit me sometime, Nora. If you can find my mind without touching me."

I knocked again to show I'd heard her, but also considered the problem. Could I filter Sofia out of all the other emotions hammering at my mind? Then shook my head at myself.

Now isn't the time for psychic experiments, Nora. This is the time for exploring the tunnels and matching the layout you memorized to reality.

It's not that I was worried the tunnel configuration was different from the diagrams Granddaddy gave to me. It's that the real world always has surprises that maps and schematics never show. Nooks and crannies to serve as quick cover. Small alcoves for hiding in case the pirates decide to sweep the tunnels. And the more familiar I was with this new environment, the more comfort-able I'd be living in it. Or fleeing in it. Or, God forbid, fighting in it.

Without another unnecessary word to myself, I rose from my crouch next to the door, bent *way* over at the waist, turned left, and headed down the tunnel.

In case you're wondering, walking in a crouch gets uncom-fortable fast. Within a few meters, a burning sensation began building in my lower back. It quickly spread down into my thighs and knees and up my spine to my neck. Only one minute in the tunnels, and I already wanted to stand straight. But my backpack brushed the tunnel's ceiling, so that was impossible.

And then I noticed something moving to my left. I didn't actually see the thing move, but I definitely sensed it. I whipped my head around to see what it was. And nothing was there. Well, there was the tunnel wall, but I saw nothing else. I ran my hand over the smooth metal. It was cool to the touch and absolutely couldn't move. I glanced all around me. Nothing.

It's your imagination playing tricks on you, Nora. Creepy tricks, but just tricks. Ignore them and keep moving.

The comm in my ear came to life as Sofia said, "Please tell me everything you can about Nora's family. If anyone asks me about them, I want to be as truthful as possible."

There was a pause for a minute, then Conley said, "Miss Connaught's family loves her very much, and her parents have tried to give her as normal a life as is possible for the daughter of billionaires."

As much as I wanted to listen to Conley and Barber dish on my family and me, I couldn't risk having my concentration divided between their stories and my exploration of the tunnels. I raised a finger to my ear and turned down the comm's volume. I could still hear Conley's and Barber's voices, but could only make out their exact words by concentrating on them.

Two steps later, the same something moved to my left. My eyes cut to the left, and there was nothing there. Again.

I gave a shake of my head. *Get a grip, Nora. This isn't the time to start acting like you're the fog-bound blonde girl in a horror vid. The one who's only there to bounce, act like a moron, and become the psychopathic murderer's first victim.*

I started walking again, but kept up my internal discussion. *And why is it that the smart and capable girl is always a brunette? I mean, talk about stereotyping blondes! I'm blonde, and I could kick those psycho killers' butts into next week.*

And I sensed the thing a third time. Still to my left, but now I realized it was more behind me than next to me. That was weird. It's like whatever was pinging my senses wasn't moving with me.

I kept my head turned to look backwards, put a hand on the tunnel wall for guidance, and walked on. I felt it again. The sense that something was behind me and I was walking away from it. I had to figure out what was going on. If this was a threat, I needed to deal with it. If it was just a distraction, I needed to know I could ignore it.

Turning around, I retraced my steps and concentrated on the thing I sensed. If it was just my imagination playing tricks on me, concentrating on the sensation would make it go away. But it stayed with me. And it felt nearer as I walked.

An idea popped into my head. But I didn't let myself believe it until I walked past the hidden door into my cabin. The sensation came from there. From my cabin. From Sofia.

But why could I suddenly sense her better than the thousands of others hammering on my empathic senses? And the answer was obvious once I gave it a moment's thought. I hadn't just sensed Sofia's emotions. I'd been inside her mind. Could my ability have forged a stronger connection with Sofia during that time?

That had to be it, right? I mean, nothing else explained what was happening to me.

A different range of emotions interrupted my thoughts. Malicious glee. Greed. Hunger of the most appalling kind. And I knew where those emotions came from.

The pirates had boarded the *Pegasus*.

I*felt* the pirates spread out through the ship like a disease. It wasn't because I'd suddenly figured out how to locate people from the emotions they broadcast—I could only do that with Sofia—but because the pirates' foul emotions infected and tainted the feelings of everyone they came in contact with.

Courage became fear, then fear curdled into abject terror. Hope gave way to despair. Impotent anger surged and faded.

The children's emotions were the worst. Theirs were so close to the surface that they shone sharp and bright and lashed my mental wall like hot, jagged metal.

None of the emotions got through to me. My wall held against the onslaught. It kept them all at bay. I wasn't afraid I would lose myself and drown in an unending tidal wave of emotions. They couldn't hurt me.

But they did *affect* me.

I stood in the eye of a vast and terrible emotional storm as it raged all around me, bringing destruction to everyone except me. I witnessed the devastation, but was helpless to do anything about it.

My entire world became unrelenting terror and desperation, driven by sick and twisted glee. There was no way to look away because it was all around me. There was no way to ignore it because I couldn't turn off my brain.

Somewhere inside the ship—somewhere inside my head—panic burst forth. Fury rose alongside it. Horrible feelings suddenly exploded and briefly washed away every other emotion. Pain. Incomprehension. Loss. Sorrow.

A tiny emotional spark winked out.

Death.

The next thing I knew, I was on the tunnel floor, curled up in a ball. My arms wrapped around my head as if protecting it from physical blows. Tears ran down my cheeks, and my breath came in ragged gasps.

Oh God. I'd *felt* someone die.

How can you live with this, Dad? How can you be so happy and upbeat all the time if this is what it feels like inside your head? Is this the reason you and Mom stayed on Ark's Landing even after it was safe for you to return to the Federation? Because the entire colony had fewer people than a small city on Draconis? So you could surround yourself with a loving family and get away from the rest of humanity?

I tried to imagine Dad's response to my questions, but it was beyond me. The thousands of sharp emotions jabbing at my wall made thinking almost impossible. But I had to do it. If I couldn't think and act while my mind withstood the passengers' unintentional psychic assault, I wouldn't be any good to anyone.

No-Talent Nora chose that moment to surface in my mind. As usual, she brought gobs of derision with her. *You don't seriously think you can do anything except hide? You're not a hero, Nora. Everyone else in your family is, but not you.*

I snarled and sat up. *I'm not useless, and maybe I can do something besides hide. Go away, No-Talent Nora. I have a talent, and I don't need you.*

I don't know if my self doubts would have had a response to my declaration, but sound suddenly erupted from the comm in my ear. I'd turned the volume down earlier so I could figure out what was pinging my senses—it turned out to be Sofia—but now I needed to hear what was happening in my tiny shipboard suite. A few taps on the comm brought the volume level up.

"Stay behind us, Miss Connaught," Conley said.

I had a brief flash of confusion before I realized Conley was speaking to Sofia, who was pretending to be me.

A fist hammered on the suite's door and a muffled voice shouted, "If you got weapons, you better put them down. We'll blast anyone even holding a weapon. Got it?"

"Please do as they say," Sofia said.

"If you say so, Miss Connaught," Barber said.

I heard two blasters clatter to the deck, then Sofia called, "My bodyguards have disarmed themselves."

With a hiss, the suite's door slid aside. I heard many feet. Then the previously muffled voice asked, "Are you Nora Connaught?"

Somehow, Sofia's voice didn't quaver as she replied, "I am."

The voice vented an unpleasant laugh. "Let's go, girl. The captain is anxious to meet you."

My awareness of Sofia's psychic presence rose as fear flashed through it and slammed into my mental wall like a battering ram. Had we not switched places, I knew I'd be terrified and feeling horribly alone. Oh, God, how could I have put her in this position?

Because it was the only way to ensure Dad could use his psychic ability to find me. He could sense me across light years, but not if the pirates used psychic nulls to block him. Sofia and I had understood the rationale intellectually. But, despite everything that happened during this short space voyage, neither of us truly understood the emotional toll Sofia would pay when she came face-to-face with the pirates.

I heard the shuffling of feet, and Sofia's psychic presence began moving. She must be walking out of the suite with the pirates. I trailed after her, relieved the maintenance tunnel I was hiding in ran parallel to the ship's corridor. Sofia only took a few steps before a voice from the suite made her stop.

"Not you two," a man said.

"We must accompany Miss Connaught," Conley said.

"Uh uh. You're staying right here."

"You have our weapons," Conley countered. "What difference will it make if we go with her?"

"The captain asked for *her*, not you. That means she goes and you stay. Got it?"

Sofia said, "Do as they say, Conley. I'll be—"

The first pirate's voice interrupted, "Keep walking."

Sofia's presence lurched into motion again, and I imagined the pirate had grabbed her arm and pulled her after him. Anger replaced some of the fear pulsing through my connection with Sofia. Fabric rustled, and the pirate gave a grunt of surprise. Had Sofia brushed the pirate's hand from her arm?

In a tart tone, Sofia said, "I can walk on my own, thank you very much."

You tell him, Sofia!

"Looks like we've got us a feisty one, boys," the pirate said.

Harsh laughter sounded around Sofia. Her anger wilted, but at least it didn't vanish completely.

"Why is the captain so anxious to meet me?" Sofia asked.

"That's the captain's tale to tell," the pirate replied.

How could the captain have a tale about me? I'd never been off Ark's Landing before this trip, and the only people I knew who'd gone off planet were members of my family and friends so close to us they might as well be members of my family. This pirate captain simply couldn't have any stories about me.

It says a lot about my mental state that I didn't figure out what was coming. In general, if not in specific. In my defense, the last ten hours of my life had been really busy and more than a little emotionally draining. And that's without even taking the pirate attack into account. So, I think my lapse in memory can be excused.

Sofia and pirates walked on in silence, and I followed them from the maintenance tunnel. Soon, I heard indistinct shouting through the comm. Random screams and wails followed the shouts. And, finally, the low murmuring of a lot of people talking quietly. The voices all had an echoing quality to them that made me think they came from a large room. Probably *Pegasus's* passenger dining room.

The voices grew louder, and Sofia and her escort approached the source. Then the pirate who'd done all the speaking called, "Hey, Boone, clear the doorway."

A different pirate—Boone, I guess—yelled, "Everybody stop and clear the door!"

"But my son just went through!" a woman said. "He'll be scared without me!"

As if on cue, a very young boy's voice called, "Mama? Mama!"

"See?" the woman said. "Please, just—"

A loud slap sounded, and the woman cried out in pain. "That was a warning, woman. Clear the door or I'll burn you where you stand."

"Mama!" the child called.

The woman sobbed quietly, but must have followed Boone's orders because his next words were directed to the man leading Sofia. "That's her, huh?"

"Yep."

"She's pretty. That'll please the captain."

The echoing increased as Sofia and the pirates entered the dining room. The nearest voices fell silent, I assume because they turned to stare at the girl being escorted by a gang of pirates. Silence spread quickly, and I imagined more and more heads turning to watch Sofia's progress through the room.

"Ah," a voice called, "I see our guest of honor has finally arrived!"

A triumphant voice.

A cruel voice.

A *woman's* voice.

"Bring her to me, boys," the woman purred. "I want to get a closer look at Matt Connaught's first child."

Venom dripped in the pirate captain's voice when she spoke Dad's name. Its timbre suggested a deep and abiding and long-standing hatred. It sounded as if the pirate captain nursed and stoked and cherished her enmity year after year, holding it in check until just the right time to unleash its pent up fury. And that moment had finally arrived.

"Well, well, well, look at you." Something in the way the

captain's voice changed made me think she was pacing around Sofia. "You're a pretty little thing, aren't you, Nor*a*?"

The captain's voice rose, and she almost sang the 'a' in my name. Her mocking tone would have been comical under less dire circumstances.

The captain raised her voice. "Isn't that right, boys?"

A ragged chorus of men called, "Aye!"

"But," false disappointment filled the captain's voice, "you obviously didn't inherit your looks from your dear mother. Feisty little Michelle was quite the beauty back before she married your father. In truth, little Nor*a*," the captain did the mocking sing-song thing again, "you're plain compared to your mother."

While the pirate captain needled the girl she thought was Nora Connaught, I wracked my brain trying to figure out who the captain was. She obviously hated my parents—especially Dad—but I couldn't imagine why. Mom and Dad made plenty of enemies during their adventures, but the pirate thing had me convinced this woman was connected to the pirates who held Dad's parents hostage for seven years.

It was a safe assumption some of those pirates were women. But all the pirates my parents fought during the rescue were men. So, I was at a complete loss who this woman pirate captain was and why she hated my parents so much.

Through my new link with Sofia, I felt tension building on top of her fear. A similar tension grew inside of me. Right next to my new feelings of self-loathing for agreeing to let Sofia pretend to be me.

Sofia interrupted my thoughts by speaking. Her voice only trembled slightly as she asked, "What are you going to do with me?"

"That *is* the question, Nor*a*. What, indeed?"

"If you're smart, you'll hold me for ransom."

"Oh ho, listen to little Nor*a*. Are *you* lecturing *me* on how to do my job?"

"I'm just pointing out that my family will pay a lot to get me back safely. Enough to make every member of your crew millionaires."

Excited babbled rose around Sofia as the rank-and-file pirates voiced their approval of that idea.

"*Silence*!" the pirate captain snapped. "We're going to make plenty from this haul, as it is, boys. Don't let this girl's pretty words distract you from that. Besides, you all know I've been looking forward to getting my hands on a Connaught for years. And it wasn't just so I could pick the Connaught's pockets for a few million credits."

"A few *hundred* million credits, you mean," Sofia countered.

A slap sounded. "That's enough from you, little Nor*a*."

The fear and tension flowing through my connection to Sofia kept rising. And I didn't blame her one bit for it. The unnamed pirate captain obviously had a vendetta against my parents and, by extension, me. And whatever drove her went beyond getting a lot of money from the Connaught family. But I couldn't figure out what it was.

The captain must have leaned close to Sofia, because she whispered the next words so quietly that only Sofia could hear them. And me. I heard them. And they sent a shiver down my spine.

"You might think your family's money will save you, little girl, but I wouldn't get your hopes up." The captain's voice dropped even lower. "Have you ever heard this ancient saying? An eye for an eye. A tooth for a tooth?"

I heard Sofia's breathing grow ragged and rapid. "I... Yes."

"Well," the captain murmured, "I've come up with a new addition to it. Would you like to hear it?"

"No."

"Too bad. You're going to hear it, anyway." The captain paused for several seconds, then hissed, "My new addition is, a daughter for a son."

DIAMOND-HARD TRUTH

What was going on? What did this woman, whoever she was, have against me? My mind raced, searching for the reason behind the pirate captain's hatred. But nothing came to me.

I'm just No-Talent Nora! I've never done anything special. Definitely nothing that would cause the loathing I heard in the pirate captain's voice.

Over the comm, I heard Sofia gasp. Over my mental link to her, I felt panic bubbling just beneath her emotional surface. Not that I blamed her. I'd be panicking, too, if Sofia hadn't made the colossal mistake of switching places with me. Of assuming the pirates would value me for the ransom I'd bring.

"Why—?" Sofia choked on the question. She took a steadying breath and tried again. "Why do you hate me so much? What did I ever do to you?"

The captain stopped whispering and spoke so all could hear her. "You were born, child."

Sofia sobbed softly, "I don't understand."

"Are you crying, girl? Can it be that the great and wonderful Matt Connaught's daughter is a coward? Can it be that the coldly beautiful Michelle Connaught's daughter cannot face her death with dignity?" The captain sniffed. "I shouldn't be surprised, what with your soft, privileged life on Ark's Landing. You never struggled for survival, did you, girl? Death didn't lurk down every corridor and beyond every airlock like on Rockville Station."

I'd thought the captain's tone was as cold as possible, but it dropped to the absolute zero of deep space. "But Death never caught my son in those places. No, Death came for my Paco through your father's hands. With two blaster bolts to the chest."

Oh, no. No no no no no no no!

I knew all about the shooting of Paco Rivera. I knew because Dad told me about it before he let Granddaddy teach me about guns. I knew because Paco's death still haunts Dad to this day. I looked into his eyes when he told me how he felt after he shot Paco. I saw the grim pain taking a life inflicted on him. And that, as much as Dad regretted killing Paco, Dad didn't doubt he'd done the right thing. That he'd do it again if he had to.

And that meant I knew the details this pirate captain wouldn't admit. Maybe she couldn't admit them. But it didn't change the facts. Dad shot Paco because Paco was trying to kill Mom. And if Paco had gotten her, he'd have turned his blaster rifle on Dad. It was self defense all the way. The security vids confirmed the story, and Rockville Station officials never even pressed charges.

I don't know if Sofia was familiar with the Rockville Station Shootout—that's what the writers named it—but that wouldn't help her. She was openly crying now, terrified out of her wits, and all alone. So horribly alone.

But she didn't have to be. I could be with her. I could provide comfort. And whatever came next, I could make sure she didn't face it alone.

Just because you got inside her head once doesn't mean you can do it again, Nora.

Get out of my way, No-Talent Nora. I don't need you anymore.

You'll always need me, because you'll never measure up to the Connaught name.

Over the comm, Sofia whispered, "Please…"

Just that one word. And Sofia wasn't even talking to me. But it burned through my mind like a laser.

Don't even think—

I cut No-Talent Nora off mid-derision. My friend needed me. She needed me *now*.

And, without another doubt, without conscious thought, I went to her.

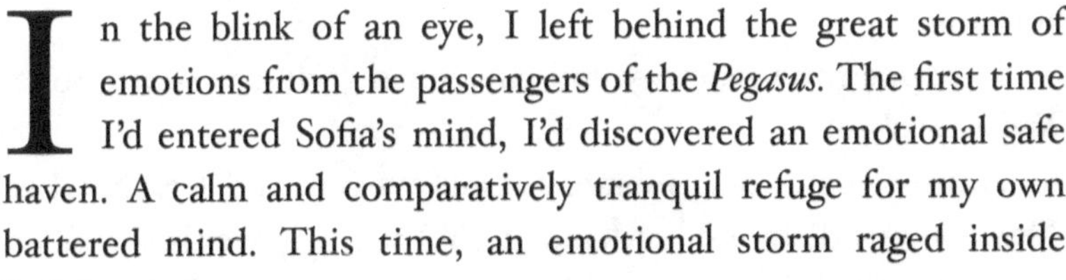

In the blink of an eye, I left behind the great storm of emotions from the passengers of the *Pegasus*. The first time I'd entered Sofia's mind, I'd discovered an emotional safe haven. A calm and comparatively tranquil refuge for my own battered mind. This time, an emotional storm raged inside Sofia's mind.

It picked me up and flung me around like a leaf caught in a tornado. Terror buffeted me in ever-growing waves. Despair sucked me into its depths and threatened to drown me. It was all I could do to hold on to my own sense of self under the assault from Sofia's emotional turmoil.

I felt something vast and terrible lurking in the darkness that engulfed me. Its looming presence drove Sofia's emotions before it like a wolf pack stampeding a flock of sheep. The thing must be Sofia's emotional impression of the pirate captain, and it was horrible in ways I had never imagined. Sofia's panic burst into my mind and crashed against everything that makes me who I am.

I felt reason slip.

I felt sanity crumble.

In desperation, I cried, *It's me, Sofia! Stop panicking! I'm here! I'm with you!*

Sofia's emotional assault on me eased. *Yes, that's it! Breathe, girl. Let me be the calm in your storm.*

The terror that battered me didn't disappear, but it lessened and swirled around me instead of over me. Sofia's panic responded in the same way, and I finally got a chance to find my bearings inside her mind.

Emotional memories tumbled inside the river of terror and panic that flowed around me. Without conscious thought, I caught one. Last time I was inside Sofia's mind, the memories were small, squishy, and warm. The fresh memory was nothing but deep shadows briefly illuminated by flashes of painfully bright light that gave me the briefest glimpse of something I couldn't quite make out. But it was dreadful beyond comprehension.

I dropped the memory and continued trying to sooth Sofia. *You're not alone!*

Another emotional memory came my way, and I grabbed it. This one was diamond hard and as cold as the grave. It was filled with deep shadows and mocking laughter. The appallingly frigid memory burned my mind, and I threw it from me in disgust.

All the while, I sent soothing emotions into Sofia's mind. *We'll get through this together, Sofia. You and me. Don't worry.*

But suddenly Sofia's emotional storm strengthened. Her panic surged over me and sent me reeling. Fresh emotional memories smashed into me and I caught brief impressions of what she was feeling now.

The hideous effect of the pirate captain's casual hatred.

The warmth-draining feel of gun metal against her skin.

The inexorable pressure of the blaster pushing against her forehead.

Those feelings smashed through my pathetic attempts to sooth Sofia. Smashed through the idea that I could help Sofia if I was with her. And in a moment of absolute clarity, I realized my mistake.

Whether calm or panicked, there was nothing Sofia could do

to stop the pirate captain from killing her. Sofia could die crying and begging for her life, or she could die looking the pirate captain in the eye. But she would die either way. Because the pirate captain held all the power. All the rage. All the pent-up emotions tied to her son's death twenty years ago.

I'd let my own emotions affect my judgment. I'd let myself get swept up in what I heard and felt from Sofia. I'd entered her mind in a vain attempt to help. And I was certain I *could* help. Just not from where I was.

Entering another's mind had been the right thing to do. I'd just entered the wrong one.

With a strength of mind fueled by desperation, I pushed aside the stinging lash of Sofia's inner terror and searched for her outward projecting fear. It blazed inside her mind like a column of fire. And just like I'd done the first time I exited Sofia's mind, I grabbed onto her fear of the pirate captain and willed myself to go with it. Her white-hot fear seared my mind, but I didn't let go.

Sofia's fear carried me towards a seething black pool that I prayed was the pirate captain's mind. I smashed into the pool and darkness engulfed me.

Jagged, rasping emotions roiled and boiled all around me. Tongues of dark flame flicked over my...sense of self? Emotional awareness? Whatever held me together inside this new mind, the murky fire scorched what it touched. Searing pain lanced through me and new emotional memories tap danced on the fresh burns.

Joy, when a nurse placed an infant in her arms. Resentment as a man —her husband?—took the baby from her. A wail rose from the child at the man's rough handling. Relief mingled with fear when the man shoved the baby back into her arms.

Was the baby Paco? Was the man Paco's father? Um... Hector? Yeah. Mom and Dad told us about Hector, along with Paco. They said Hector was part of the space pirate gang that kidnapped Dad's parents.

Hot flames washed over me again, bringing more pain and more emotional memories tied to Paco.

Agony warred with impotent anger as Hector towered over her. Paco, now a child no older than four or five, stepped between her and his glowering father. The boy's posture screamed defiance. Hector's proclaimed fury. Terror surged in her when an enormous fist fell and Paco crumpled.

I would have cried at the memory if tears were an option. God above, it appeared Paco's father was an even worse man than Mom and Dad thought. And that says a lot, since they already thought Hector was lower than slug slime.

The pirate captain's fiery emotions engulfed me a third time. As before, they brought emotional torment.

Joy warred with despondency as she held another baby. A preteen Paco stood before her, insolence and sullen hatred smoldered in his eyes when she showed the infant to him. Paco's eyes darted to the baby, softened for a second, then flicked back to her. Without a word, he turned and walked away. And Hector watched it all with a tight smile.

More emotional memories scalded me. I saw Paco scorn her affections. Hector ignoring his wife and new daughter. Paco giving his sister the love his mother longed for. Her daughter doting on Paco's every word. And Paco's mother basking in her son's devotion to his sister and vicariously claiming a sliver of Paco's love through her children's bond.

The darkest flame yet swept over me. I writhed under its blistering heat and would have screamed if I had a mouth.

A girl on the cusp of womanhood stood before her. Tears streamed from eyes filled with loss and anguish. The pirate captain extended her arms towards the girl. Anger flashed in her daughter's eyes. She shouted and evaded the proffered hug.

That emotional memory—I guessed it was when the pirate captain and her daughter learned of Paco's death—triggered a cascade of other emotions.

Relief when the Federation imprisoned Hector for piracy. Despair as her daughter grew distant. Determination to win love from her daughter.

Hatred for the chosen source of all her despair—the fugitive heir, Matt Connaught. Resolve to even the score with him.

I almost felt sympathy for Paco's mother.

Almost.

Yeah, she had a tough life. My brief glimpses into her marriage to Hector horrified me. Stuck on Rockville Station, escape from that life was probably impossible. I could even sort of understand the twisted logic that fueled her hatred of Dad and, by extension, me. But the woman's solution to her vendetta against my family utterly turned me against her.

I mean, piracy? Come on, what kind of person decides it's okay to ruin thousands of lives just to take revenge for an innocent man's imagined crimes against her? One with a tenuous hold on sanity, I guessed. And any doubts I had that Paco's mother could kill Sofia vanished.

The first time I entered Sofia's mind, I learned I experienced time differently inside another head than I did inside my own mind. But that didn't mean I had a lot of time to spare. I felt certain Paco's mother had a gun pressed against my friend's forehead.

Would the pirate captain draw out the scene? Would she search for satisfaction from Sofia's suffering? Or would she decide that would only come from pulling the trigger?

Whatever she decided, I had mere seconds to stop her.

Earlier, Sofia's emotions responded to my mental commands, so I tried the direct approach first. I reminded myself that the pirate captain thought Sofia was me and sent a command at the captain.

You don't want to shoot Nora Connaught. She's innocent, and killing her will only make you feel worse. You'll feel guilt that will consume you from the inside out.

The pirate captain's mind roared, drowning out my mental voice. The emotional conflagration raging around and over me doubled in ferocity, fanned and fed by the force of her rejection of my command. Barbed shards of memories tied to Paco and her daughter lashed my senses, ripped open my soul, and poured bitter, stinging memories into the fresh emotional wounds.

I felt the captain's mind crumble. Watched her rebuild her identity around a core of burning hatred for my father. Reveled in that hatred as it consumed her every waking thought. Heard the captain infect her daughter with it and shape the girl's will.

Malice for everyone and everything associated with the Connaught name smashed into me and tore away my meager emotional protection. Loathing for my family oozed into me through the tattered remains of my emotional self. My grip on reality—already slipping away under the emotional assault I'd been under since my empathic ability burst forth—loosened further as the captain's insanity insinuated itself into the very core of my being.

I flailed for a lifeline to pull myself out of the captain's mind. But I couldn't find the shaft of terror I'd ridden from Sofia's mind into the captain's. I was sure the pirate still terrified Sofia, but neither of them were empaths. Their emotions wouldn't extend into another person's mind. At least, not without help from me.

The captain's rage seethed all around me, and it led straight to the girl she thought was me. But the insane anger frightened me more than anything else I sensed inside the pirate captain's mind. If I took hold of the enmity the captain felt for my family, I felt certain my touch would be the last spark that tipped the captain over the mental edge. She'd pull the trigger of her blaster, and Sofia would pay for my mistakes with her life.

Something soft and fuzzy crashed into me. It felt so different from the ragged-edged emotions pummeling me that I thought Sofia had somehow thrown me an emotional lifeline. I scrambled after it as the out-of-place bundle of emotions and memories bounced off me. It almost eluded my grasp, but I flicked a tendril of desperation at the fluffy ball. My mind sank into the thing and...

Four-year-old Paco faced her. Terror and confusion filled his innocent face. He held his arms out, seeking solace and safety in her warm embrace. One hand held a toy gun someone had given him for his birthday. A gigantic shadow fell over Paco, plunging the boy into darkness. A monstrous capering caricature of Matt Connaught appeared behind the boy. Twisted glee danced in Matt's glowing red eyes. A long tongue flicked over blood-red lips as Matt lifted a huge blaster and pointed it at little Paco. Matt met her gaze. His mouth split in an impossibly wide grin. A bolt flashed from the blaster and right through Paco. The little boy stumbled. One tiny hand reached for her. Then he fell. Above her, demonic Matt Connaught laughed maniacally.

In the moment that I experienced the pirate captain's false memory, I hated Matt Connaught, knew him for the monster he was, and despised him with every fiber of my being.

Then my senses hit something hard and sharp beneath the fluff of the captain's insane reconstruction of her son's death. That touch washed away the myth she'd built out of my mind and showed me the emotions and memories she couldn't face.

She watched a vid replay of the Rockville Station Shootout. A dozen members of Paco's gang hid behind packing crates and shot at a young man and a young woman—Matt Connaught and his future wife, Michelle—as they ran through a warehouse. The gang's intended victims returned fire as they ran. Michelle shoved Matt aside, and a bigger, brighter blaster bolt seared the air where Matt had just been. Paco snarled and turned his blaster rifle on Michelle. She dove to the side and rolled as Paco poured shot after shot at her. Unnoticed by Paco, Matt rose up on one knee, took careful aim at Paco, and put two shots into her murderous son's chest.

The truth of the incident was self-evident in the security recording. Something about the sharpness of this memory told me she'd watched the vid over and over, desperately searching for some reason to cast Paco as the victim. When she couldn't find one, the pirate captain must have created the entire soft and fluffy scene to protect herself from recognizing Paco's guilt. And that true memory might be the one thing that could save Sofia's life.

Ignoring the rage swirling inside the pirate captain's mind, I ripped the soft and fuzzy cover off her memory of the vid and shoved the diamond-hard truth into her emotional maelstrom.

The pirate captain's emotional vortex recoiled from the truth she'd hidden from herself for twenty years. The maelstrom whirled around that truth but couldn't affect it. Then the captain's protective core of rage and lies converged on the tiny kernel of truth, and I felt certain the kernel would be crushed.

If I had eyes to close or a face to turn away, I'd have done so. But I couldn't turn off my empathic abilities like that. I... "watched" isn't the right word, but it's the closest one I've got. I watched the rage that fueled the pirate captain's desire for revenge smash into that one true memory I'd found in her mind. The self-deluded insanity that put Sofia's life in danger piled on. And the small, bright light of truth vanished beneath the onslaught.

Virtually every emotion inside the captain's mind flowed towards Sofia. I made mental preparations to jump back to Sofia's mind so I could influence her empathically. Persuade her to admit she wasn't me. The captain could send the pirates into the maintenance tunnels to find me, drag me before their captain, and let her vent her wrath on a real Connaught.

But just before I latched onto the captain's emotional flow, the real memory of Paco's death burst through shards of anguish and shone forth again. The captain's mind sprang to defend its precious delusion, pummeling the kernel of memory again and again. And every emotion, every manufactured memory shattered against the impervious truth the captain had hidden from herself for so long.

Something truly dark and sinister rose around me and engulfed the terrible truth the captain could not—would not—face. And that tiny spark of light absorbed the darkness, growing larger and larger as it... fed on the darkness? I really don't know how to describe what I felt happening all around me. I'm pretty sure I'm the first person in humanity's history to witness an insane mind's destruction in the face of a reality it denied. Watching it. *Feeling it*. From the inside, I mean.

It was awe-inspiring and terrible at the same time. But a whole lot more terrible than awesome. I suddenly wanted nothing more than to get out of the pirate captain's mind.

Even as I tried wrenching my attention away from the pirate captain's collapsing mind, something primal howled inside her head. It picked me up and flung me away.

I felt a rushing sensation, then crashed hard into something familiar. Something warm and comfortable.

My mind.

In *my* body.

I drew a ragged breath, opened my eyes, blinked against the light in the maintenance tunnel, and realized I was curled up into a ball on the deck.

"Please..." a voice sobbed in my ear. "Don't..."

Sofia! In my relief to be back in my body, her situation almost slipped my mind.

I immediately reached for the comm in my ear so I could transmit my surrender, then remembered it wasn't tuned to the *Pegasus's* shipboard comm. But the maintenance tunnels have permanent comms every ten meters, so repair crews can easily report to their superiors. If I could just get to one in time, I could turn myself in and save Sofia!

I spotted a comm just out of reach. A quick roll brought me closer. I pressed the button and—

A voice sounded in my ear. But it wasn't Sofia. The captain screamed in agony, horror, despair, and loss. Her voice turned raw with the depth and power of the scream. And it just went on and on, becoming less human and more bestial with each passing second. The scream's pitch rose until it hurt my ear through the comm. I couldn't even imagine what Sofia must have felt listening to that wail.

Abruptly, the captain fell silent. Through the comm, I heard her draw one deep breath, then she murmured, "No. No. *No. No!*"

I heard Sofia draw a sharp breath. "Oh my God!"

In a soft, almost loving voice, the pirate captain said, "You don't have to be alone anymore, Paco. Mama's coming."

A blaster shot sounded.

Sofia cried out in horror.

Passengers screamed.

A terrible, wet thump sounded nearby. Somehow, I knew it was the pirate captain's body dropping to the deck.

Right on cue, No-Talent Nora cried, *You killed that woman!*

No, I kept her from killing Sofia.

Sofia wouldn't even have been in danger if you hadn't switched places with her.

It was her idea.

Which you accepted with cowardly quickness.

Which I accepted because Sofia wanted to make sure I stayed free so Dad could find me with his empathic ability. Just like he did with Grandmama and Granddaddy Connaught before I was born.

Yeah, keep telling yourself that. Because—

Hush!

What did you say?

I said hush. But I meant shut up.

How dare you—

Shut. Up. Something different happened when the pirate captain threw me from her mind. I need to figure out what it was.

I waited for an argument from No-Talent Nora, but she stayed quiet. I tuned out the emotions battering against my mental wall of white and tried listening with my ears. And something *was* different, but it was so subtle I couldn't figure out what it was.

Were pirates sneaking through the maintenance tunnels, looking for passengers or crew hiding in the tunnels with me? Or had someone realized the truth about Sofia's switch with me? Were the pirates scouring the *Pegasus* for me, their super-valuable hostage?

I put my hands on the deck so I could push myself to my feet. The deck was cool to the touch, and the vibrations of a spaceship underway felt reassuring.

Wait, that was it! The constant hum from the *Pegasus's* engines and life support systems—the ones Sofia noticed were gone just before we exited the wormhole—were back. I guessed that meant the pirates had complete control of the ship and were taking it... wherever the pirates take their captives before selling them into slavery on the frontier. Or ransoming the rich ones back to their families. Or whatever other sick things the pirates did to their captives.

I imagined the soul-shredding emotions from those things and shuddered at the thought. Not because of what those emotions would do to me, but because I'd experience the victims' suffering and have no way to help them. I just prayed my mental wall would hold against it, because I...

A new thought popped into my head. When I got back inside my own head a few minutes ago, I was hit with a flood of terror and hysteria from the *Pegasus's* five thousand passengers and crew. My mental defenses went up the second I got back. That's why I'd been free to consider Sofia's situation and plan to surrender. It was why I was free to reach for the comm. I'd been so worried about Sofia, I hadn't even thought about rebuilding my mental defenses. I'd just done it without thinking.

Just a few hours ago, I'd have leapt up and done a little dance of joy. Don't get me wrong, I was still thrilled with this development. But now I was excited because having better control over my new psychic abilities meant I had a better chance of using those abilities to help the passengers and crew of the *Pegasus*. Especially Sofia.

Voices from the comm in my ear interrupted my thoughts.

"Stop your caterwauling!" a harsh voice yelled over the continuing crying and screaming from the passengers. "Shut it, all of you!"

Someone, probably Mr. Harsh Voice, fired a blaster four times.

"I *said* to shut it!" Harsh Voice shouted.

Silence fell over the crowd. People still talked in the background, but I guess that was quiet enough for Harsh Voice.

"What do we do now that the captain done shot herself?" a second voice whispered.

I assumed that was one of the pirates who brought Sofia to the pirate captain. Anyone else would have been too far from Sofia for her nano transmitters to pick up.

Harsh Voice whispered back, "Somebody's got to tell the first officer."

"Sounds like something another officer should do." Despite everything that had happened, Second Voice laughed as he added, "*Sir*."

"Don't you sir me, boy," Harsh Voice retorted. "My parents were married."

Second Voice asked, "Was that before or after they kicked you out on the street?"

Harsh Voice said, "Before, I think. Don't matter much, now."

Geez, those two guys were literally standing over their captain's corpse making jokes? I knew normal people didn't become pirates, but I'd never understood just how psychopathic these pirates were until that moment.

Second Voice interrupted my thought. "What do you want me to do with our special hostage while you go tell the first officer about the captain?"

Harsh Voice considered this for a moment, then said, "Take

her back to her cabin, I guess. Might help keep her bodyguards in line if they see she's okay."

After everything Sofia had been through, how could that idiot think she was even remotely okay?

"Up you go, girl," Second Voice said.

Sofia must not have moved fast enough for the pirate's satisfaction. A slap sounded, and Sofia cried out in pain.

Second Voice snarled, "I said, *get up*."

I made a mental note to find out what that pirate looked like. If I ever got the chance, I would pay him back for the way he treated my friend. Pay him back extra, I mean. Because, if it was the last thing I did with my life, I was going to make sure all of the pirates paid big time for their cruelty.

I used the link I'd formed with Sofia to keep track of her while the pirates escorted her back to my suite. The one I'd dubbed Second Voice was chattier than he'd been when he took Sofia to meet the pirate captain.

In a casual, almost friendly tone he said, "Girl, I don't know what you did to the captain to make her shoot herself like that. But I sure wouldn't want to be in your shoes when the first officer hears about it."

"I didn't do anything," Sofia muttered. "You were holding me the whole time."

"Yeah, but your daddy is a hotshot super psychic. For all I know, you killed the captain with your mind."

It's crazy how many people think all psychics can just think people to death. There's only ever been one psychic who could do that, and she was dead.

A hint of disdain entered Sofia's voice. "If I could do that, you'd already be dead."

The smack of a hand against a cheek sounded. "Don't get uppity with me, girl. You're in enough trouble as it is. Don't go looking for more."

I wondered if I could jump inside Second Voice's mind and

maybe make him treat Sofia a little better? It was worth a try, at least.

I centered on my connection to Sofia. Once I had that, I groped around for any emotions coming from near her. It... didn't work. I didn't have enough control to sift through the thousands of emotions swirling around just beyond my mental wall to separate a specific person. Maybe if the pirate had stronger feelings directed just at Sofia—who he still thought was me—I could have found something. But I don't think he saw her as anything more than a product to sell or ransom. That would explain the casual greed that mingled with the passengers' apprehension and terror.

Maybe I could hop into Sofia and ride from her to the pirate? It worked on their captain. And if Second Voice was holding Sofia's arm, the physical contact might make it even easier. I think.

I was just about to try it when I heard a door hiss as it slid open. Second Voice said, "In you go, girl."

The door hissed shut, and Conley asked, "You have blood on your dress, Miss Connaught? Did those scum hurt you?"

"No..." she began. "I mean... Not really. They— She—"

Sofia burst into tears again. And who could blame her? She put up a brave front after the captain killed herself and during the walk back to her suite. But I didn't have to imagine what the pirate captain put her through. I'd been inside her head. I felt it all. And I desperately wanted to go comfort my friend.

Something suddenly muffled Sofia's crying. I felt a stab of alarm, but it eased when I heard Conley murmur, "There, there. Let it all out."

My mind reeled when I realized Conley must be hugging Sofia. Proper, respectful, unemotional Conley? *Hugging* someone? He'd never hugged me once during the eight years he'd been on my security detail. Of course, I'd never gone through anything close to what Sofia just went through.

Wow. So he *was* human, after all.

Then Conley ruined my new image of him by whispering in Sofia's ear. "Miss Connaught, I believe Sofia would benefit from a friendly female face. Come back to the bedroom entrance. As long as you don't hear any pirate voices over the comm, knock once to alert us of your presence."

Conley had hugged Sofia only for an excuse to whisper directly into her ear. It explained his behavior. But... it wasn't totally inhuman of him. I mean, he recognized Sofia needed comfort and found a way to tell me it was safe to pay a quick visit to her.

I reached the hidden door a few seconds later. The only sounds over the comm were Sofia's crying and Conley's and Barber's stilted words of comfort. I rapped on the door once.

Conley breathed into Sofia's ear, "Come in, Miss Connaught."

I looked into the retina scanner, and the secret door slid aside. Conley stood inside the tiny bedroom, his posture stiff, but with his arms wrapped protectively around Sofia. Over her head, he mouthed, *Leave the door open.*

A good idea, in case I had to scoot back into the tunnels on short notice. I entered the room and opened my arms for Sofia. Conley gently turned her around and guided her into my embrace. Then I held Sofia while she cried out her fear and horror.

～

After a while, Sofia's sobs turned to whimpers. Those faded into gasps, and then to sniffles. Finally, she took a deep, shuddering breath, gave me one last squeeze, and released me.

She wiped her eyes, and whispered, "Thank you."

I shook my head. "Why are you thanking me? You almost got killed pretending to be me. You should be royally pissed off at me for abandoning you."

Sofia straightened in apparent surprise. "What? You didn't abandon me!"

"You're kidding, right? You had to face the insane pirate captain while I hid in the tunnels. If that's not abandoning, I—"

"Stop it, Nora! I know you were inside my head the whole time. I felt your encouragement. And I felt it when you left me." Sofia caught my gaze and asked, "Did you go inside that woman's head?"

I shrugged. "I thought she was going to kill you. Getting inside her mind was the only way I could think of to stop her."

Concern flooded Sofia's eyes. "Did you make her shoot herself?"

"If you mean did I control her mind or something like that, no." I felt tears of my own well up in my eyes. "But, yeah, I killed her."

Conley and Barber stood stolidly by the bed while I comforted Sofia. At my words, they stirred.

"How did you do that, Miss Connaught?" Conley asked.

"Does it really matter how?" I asked.

"If this is a new facet of your ability," Conley said, "it matters very much."

I sighed. "I... made the captain face something she hid from herself twenty years ago. The truth destroyed her insane delusions. You know the rest."

I felt a tear roll down my cheek, and it was Sofia's turn to wrap her arms around me and pull me into a tight hug. "You didn't kill her, Nora."

"I didn't pull the trigger, but she wouldn't have shot herself if I hadn't forced that memory into her conscious mind."

"No, she wouldn't have shot herself," Sofia agreed. "She'd have shot *me*."

More tears followed the first. "I know. And that would have been my fault, too!"

"That is irrational, Miss Connaught," Barber said.

"Barber is correct," Conley added.

"Guys, you're not helping," Sofia said. She rocked me gently, just as I did with her minutes before, and whispered, "Let it out, Nora."

And it was my turn to sob and whimper and gasp. All the while, Sofia held me close and let me purge the horror from the captain's insane mind.

After a minute, I forced back my tears and sniffed. "Can you believe me? I grew up hearing Dad's stories about his psychic adventures, and this is how I react to my first one? It's too bad one of the family heroes isn't here in my place, huh?"

Sofia gave me a gentle shake. "Take that back right now!"

"Take what back?"

"The part where you say you're not a hero."

"But... I'm not."

Sofia made a frustrated sound. "How can you say that? Did you *like* being inside that woman's mind?"

"What? God, no!"

"So why didn't you leave as soon as you saw what it was like in there?"

"She was going to shoot you! I couldn't let her do that."

"You know, most people can't handle insanity when they see it from the *outside*. But you were *inside* it. You faced it, and you beat it. And you did it all for someone else. If that's not the definition of a hero, I don't know what is."

I offered a tentative smile. "If so, I'm not the *only* hero in this room. I mean, *you* took my place and almost got killed."

Conley caught my attention. "Miss Connaught, I deployed nano transmitters on the wall outside your door when we boarded the *Pegasus*."

I glanced at Sofia and rolled my eyes at the things my body-guards do to keep me safe.

He continued, "They are picking up multiple footsteps coming this way. As a precaution, you should return to the tunnels."

Sofia nodded her agreement and gave me a gentle shove

towards the open door into the tunnels. I ducked through and closed the hidden door. Ten seconds later, I heard the hiss as the door to my suite slid open.

"We got a visitor for the girl," a pirate said.

Someone walked into the suite, and with them came the sudden stab of a familiar emotion. Hatred, deep and implacable, for Matt and Michelle Connaught's oldest daughter. I wanted to warn Sofia, tell her to be on her guard, and there was only one way to do that. But before I could settle myself enough to enter Sofia's mind, I heard that someone enter my bedroom.

A woman's voice asked, "Hello, Miss... Olson, isn't it? Where is Nora Connaught?"

The unknown woman stood no more than two meters from me, in my bedroom. Worse, she knew Sofia. Worst, she was the person on the *Pegasus* who hated me. And she had asked Sofia where I was.

The woman's question hung in the air for a second. Just long enough for me to imagine bursting through the hidden doorway and gunning her down in a blazing hail of blaster fire. Not that I'd have ever actually done that. As they say in the rural areas on Ark's Landing, my momma didn't raise no fools.

"Um, what are you doing here, Lieutenant?" Sofia asked.

The woman was a member of the crew, then. No surprise, since she recognized Sofia. And also no surprise that the Lieutenant became my leading—and only—suspect for sabotaging the *Pegasus's* engines and weapons.

The Lieutenant sighed, "I'm looking for Miss Connaught. That should have been obvious from my initial question."

In a wounded tone, Sofia said, "I'm sorry, Lieutenant. This hasn't exactly been the best day of my life, you know."

The Lieutenant's voice took on a hard edge. "You're hardly the only person on board who feels that way. You selfish girl, have you even considered what Miss Connaught went through just a few minutes ago?"

"I know *exactly* what Miss Connaught went through," Sofia snapped.

"How could you possibly know?" The Lieutenant's tone dripped with more disdain than No-Talent Nora ever dumped on me.

"Because *I'm* the one they dragged in front of the pirate captain," Sofia shouted. "*I'm* the one she threatened. She put her blaster against *my* head. *That* is how I know."

"You?" The Lieutenant sounded confused. And that confusion tinged the sharp spike of hatred she felt for me. "But I was told they dragged Nora Connaught in front of the pirate captain."

"That's because I told them I was Nora."

Apprehension joined the Lieutenant's emotional spike. "No, that can't be right."

"Well, it is," Sofia said. "You can ask the pirates guarding the door, if you don't believe me."

"But I had assumed Nora made the captain shoot herself," the Lieutenant muttered.

"How? Did you think the other pirates just let Nora grab that woman's arm and make her turn the gun on herself?"

"Of course not," the Lieutenant snapped. "But everyone in the Federation knows her father is a powerful psychic. Surely, his daughter inherited his powers."

Incredulity filled Sofia's voice. "You believe Nora *thought* the pirate captain to death? Did you even pay attention to the company's psychic training? Psychic abilities don't work that way."

"Then why did the captain shoot herself?"

"How should I know?"

I heard the Lieutenant drew a shuddering breath. She took another, stronger breath. "I'm sorry, Miss Olson. We have gotten away from the subject of my visit. I came here to comfort Miss Connaught after her ordeal, only to discover *she* wasn't the one who faced the pirate captain."

I felt disgust join the Lieutenant's other mingled emotions and her voice grew reproving. "I assume the real Nora was too afraid to admit who she was? Did she just hide in the bathroom or something?"

Even though I hid at Sofia's insistence, the officer's guess was closer to the truth than I wanted to admit.

The Lieutenant's voice rose, "Stop cowering and come out, Miss Connaught!"

Sofia snapped, "Nora isn't the cowering type, Lieutenant Riva."

Riva? That was way too close to Rivera, the late and unlamented Paco's family name. Unlamented except by his mother, dead by her own hand. And by his sister. Who would undoubtedly hate Nora Connaught. Just like this woman did.

"If Miss Connaught isn't a coward," Lieutenant Riva snapped back, "where is she?"

As much as I trusted Sofia, my heart began pounding when I heard that question. Sofia thought she was talking to a trusted member of the crew, not the daughter of the pirate captain, who almost shot her. Would Sofia tell the woman where I was, thinking the Lieutenant could help me more than she and my bodyguards could? I tried clearing my mind of turmoil long enough to dive inside Sofia's mind and send warning emotions to her, but I remained stubbornly stuck inside my head.

I also shouldn't have worried.

Sofia sighed, "I don't know."

"How can you not know?" Riva asked.

"Nora slipped out of the suite when everyone else was busy unpacking."

I held my breath, wondering if Riva would accept Sofia's lie.

"Well, where did she go?"

Sofia was silent for just long enough that I could imagine her looking at Lieutenant Riva as if she was an idiot. "If I knew that, I'd know where she was. Wouldn't I?"

"Watch your tone! I'm still your superior onboard this ship."

I was afraid Sofia might mouth off again, not realizing who she was talking to. But her voice sounded contrite when she replied, "I'm sorry, Lieutenant Riva. Like I said, it hasn't been a good day for me."

I heard Riva draw a deep breath. "Let me rephrase my question, Miss Olson. Do you have a guess where Nora went after she slipped out?"

"You've seen how some of those rich girls act after they board the *Pegasus*."

"Yes," Riva said. "It's like they think they own the ship."

"Yeah, only Nora really *does* own it," Sofia said. "If you ask me, now that Nora is out from under her parents' thumb, she's off looking for a boy to get into trouble with."

"In that case, she's probably with the rest of the passengers in the dining hall."

Riva sounded relieved at her conclusion. Too bad she was in for disappointment.

But if she was the late pirate captain's daughter, what would she do when she couldn't find me hiding among the other passengers? The answer was as chilling as it was obvious. She would order the pirates to search the entire ship from bow to stern. With the entire crew to call upon, I had no chance of escaping their search. Despite everything Sofia went through to keep me free, the pirates *would* find me.

While I wracked my brain for a way to evade the coming ship-wide search, I heard a faint rustling of cloth. That was probably Riva standing, now that she had the information she thought she needed.

"Please come with me, Miss Olson," Riva said.

"Captain Riggs assigned me to Miss Connaught. Shouldn't I wait for her?"

"Miss Connaught isn't here, nor do I think she will return. Meanwhile, the *Pegasus* has thousands of other passengers who could use your services." The door to the bedroom slid open.

"I'm sure Miss Connaught would approve of you assisting passengers who need you more than she does."

Riva's voice had an edge to it I didn't like. Sofia didn't care for it, either.

"I don't know if—"

"I am not *asking* you, Miss Olson. Follow me. Now."

My bodyguards must have overheard the last bit through the open door, because Conley said, "Is there a problem here?"

"Nothing that concerns a passenger," Riva snapped.

Instead of accepting Riva at her word, Conley asked, "Are you all right, Miss Olson?"

"She's fine," Riva said.

"Lieutenant Riva is right, sir," Sofia said. "She's just reassigning me to serve the other passengers. They need me more right now."

"I'm glad you finally recognize that," Riva said. "Come along."

A few seconds later, I heard the suite's door whoosh open and then hiss shut.

In the corridor outside my suite, Riva said, "Take this girl to the dining hall with the other passengers. I have plans for her."

A man's voice I didn't recognize but assumed belonged to a pirate said, "Yes, ma'am."

Sofia gasped, "You're with the pirates?"

"With us?" the pirate cackled. "She be our new cap'n."

A second man asked, "Do you have a message for the new first officer, ma'am?"

"Yes," Riva said. "Tell Boone to keep a guard on this girl. I don't want anything happening to my bait."

"Bait?" Dread crept into Sofia's voice as she said, "You're going to threaten me to make Nora surrender!"

"Aren't you a smart girl?" Riva purred. Her tone turned neutral. "I have a few last details to attend to for mother's send off. Make sure Boone understands he's to do nothing until I arrive."

"You got it, ma'am."

Through my link with Sofia, I felt her move down the corridor. I thought my mind was whirling as fast as it could go when I needed a way to avoid pirate search parties. But now Sofia's life was back on the line, all because she'd been assigned as my personal attendant. I pushed aside every other concern racing through my mind and concentrated on just one thing.

I had to get Sofia away from the pirates!

Without giving it another thought, I hurried through the maintenance tunnel as fast as my hunched over posture allowed. I guess the pirates were in no hurry. From the first time the pirates led Sofia to the dining hall, I knew the route they'd take and hurried to get well ahead of them.

The tunnels had several doors out into the corridor, but I had a particular one in mind. It opened into a section that ran along the ship's hull. The designers put a row of observation windows there so passengers could gaze out into the depths of space, with sharp bends in the corridor at each end of the windows.

I guess they did that to make the spot feel more isolated or something. It must have worked, because the stuff Granddaddy had me study said it was a popular place for onboard marriage proposals. When I read that, I thought it was super romantic. But I needed the isolation for something else. I needed to take out the two pirates with Sofia quickly and silently *and* get away before more pirates showed up. That stretch of corridor gave me the best chance of pulling it off.

I reached my chosen tunnel door well ahead of the pirates. My link told me they were approaching the bend that would bring them into the observation area. I unslung my backpack, pulled out my blaster, and set it to stun. I didn't do that out of compassion for the pirates, but in case Sofia stumbled into my line of fire.

I had time to take one deep breath, and then I felt Sofia pass by my position. As quietly as possible, I opened the door into the corridor. It was time to put my years of martial arts training to good use.

SOFIA'S PLAN

I slipped into the corridor and softly closed the door back into the tunnels. Mom always taught me to keep the fighting ground clear of obstacles, and that included open doors.

I glanced to my right. Clear corridor. The pirates were three meters to my left, walking just behind Sofia. They were both men, which was good and bad. Good, because they had a great vulnerable point between their legs. Bad, because they were each at least ten centimeters taller than me, a whole lot heavier than me, and stronger than me.

I wasn't surprised. There's probably a good reason you don't hear many stories about tiny pirates. Stealth and speed were already my greatest allies. I'd just need more of it with these guys.

Standing, I padded down the corridor after the pirates and Sofia. For this part of my rescue, I loved the thick carpet under my feet. But I'd hate it the first time I slammed a pirate down onto it. Assuming I managed to do that.

Think positively, Nora!

I know what you're thinking. Why didn't I just go ahead and stun the two pirates with my blaster? Because unmuffled blasters are *loud*. I had no idea how many pirates were nearby, but anyone who heard the shots would come running. Sound carries a long way down metal walled corridors, too. The last thing I needed was a running gun battle with pirates. Because that's something I would totally lose.

The one on the left looked a little bigger and stronger, so I chose him as my first target. From the angles of the pirates' heads, I felt certain they were watching Sofia's butt. Typical guys. That also meant they weren't expecting any trouble.

I came up behind the guy on the left. Snaked my left hand up under his chin. I clamped the hand over his mouth, kicked him hard in the back of his right knee, and yanked him backwards. The pirate lost his balance and fell. I spun around him and used my weight to drive him into the carpet. We landed with a muffled thump, and I immediately drove an elbow into his solar plexus. The pirate's eyes bugged out as the pain hit him and his breath blew out around the hand I still had over his mouth. For good measure, I cracked the butt of my blaster against his temple. The pirate wasn't out yet, but at least he was out of the fight for the moment.

As I sprang off the downed pirate, his buddy and Sofia turned to see what caused those strange sounds.

"Nora?" Sofia gasped.

A grin spread over the second pirate's face as he snapped off a kick at my head. "Cap'n's gonna gimme—"

From years of training with better fighters than this pirate, I saw his kick coming and spun around it. I caught his leg with my left hand and yanked him towards me. At the same time, I rammed the barrel of my blaster into his now unprotected groin. His eyes filled with tears and he automatically closed his legs around my hand.

Perfect.

I pulled the blaster's trigger. The man's legs muffled the shot beautifully. His eyes rolled up into his head and he collapsed.

Before the second pirate hit the carpet, I dove back at the first pirate. He had curled up around his stomach. It's the body's natural reaction to my attack. And another ready-made muffler for my blaster. The pirate clawed at my hand as I shoved the blaster into his stomach. But he was still too busy fighting for breath for that to have much effect. I pulled the trigger again. As I'd planned, the pirate's body muffled the sound, and this pirate went as limp as his buddy.

I jumped up and ran to Sofia. She reached out to hug me, but I hissed, "No time for that."

Grabbing her hand, I dragged Sofia down the corridor and into the maintenance tunnels.

As I shut the tunnel door, Sofia whispered, "Where are we going?"

Keeping my voice as low as Sofia's, I replied, "Somewhere far away from here."

Without another word, I grabbed my backpack. Then Sofia and I ran as fast as the low ceiling allowed.

Running hunched over isn't easy. Try it sometime and you'll see what I mean. The burn started in my lower back. It didn't take long before it spread down to my thighs and up to my neck. Sweat beaded on my brow and ran into my eyes. It stung, but I felt sure getting shot by pirates would sting a whole lot worse, so I kept on going.

Sofia stayed right behind me as I led her through the maze of maintenance tunnels winding through the *Pegasus*. She gasped and panted, fighting for breath, but fear kept her going. Or maybe it was the same determination that made her volunteer to swap places with me when the pirates first invaded the ship. Whatever drove her, it kept her from begging me to stop or even asking me to slow down. And my already sky-high admiration for her grew with each meter we ran.

Finally, after we'd been running for nearly ten minutes, I

ducked into a tool storage alcove and stopped. Sofia collapsed next to me, red-faced, sweating, and chest heaving. I sat next to her, wiped a sleeve over my own sweaty face, hung my head, and just concentrated on breathing.

After a minute, Sofia said, "Remind me... never... travel... with you... again."

I gave a short laugh. "I'll do my best. How do you feel?"

"Terrible." Sofia took a moment to control her breathing, then looked into my eyes. "Thank you."

"There was no way I could let that bitch use you as bait to lure me out. And, you're welcome."

"I can't believe Lieutenant Riva is the traitor. She was always stern, but to betray us like this?" Sofia shook her head.

"Oh, you'd believe it if you knew her real name. It's Rivera, not Riva. She's Paco's little sister and the dead pirate captain's daughter."

"Everyone keeps talking about some guy named Paco, like it should mean something," Sofia said. "Who is he?"

"More like who *was* he," I said, and then gave her a short version of the Rockville Station Shootout.

When I finished, I fished two water bottles and two chocolate energy bars out of my pack and handed one of each to Sofia. "Drink slowly and take little bites."

"Yes, mother," Sofia said with a grin and a roll of her eyes. The grin faded quickly, and she asked, "What do we do now?"

"I'm trying to figure that out."

"Have you got any ideas?"

"No," I admitted.

Sofia looked out of our alcove at the passageway. "Do you even know where we are?"

"Yeah."

She turned wide eyes back to me. "How? I don't even know how many turns we took!"

"Thirteen." With a shrug, I added, "My grandfather made me

memorize the ship's layout, especially the maintenance tunnels. I kept the map in my head while we ran."

"Wow. I can't imagine keeping all of that straight while running for my life at the same time."

"You could if you had the training Granddaddy and Mom put me through."

"I'd say they sounded paranoid, only someone really *did* spend twenty years plotting revenge against your family."

I offered a slight smile, "I was ten before I realized no one else on Ark's Landing grew up preparing for... Well, for something like this."

"So, where are we?"

"Um..." I consulted my mental map again. "Just outside the long, port side corridor connecting crew quarters with passenger quarters."

"How long do you think we have before the pirates start searching the ship for us?"

"Five minutes? Maybe ten?" I leaned back against the alcove wall. "But that's not even my biggest worry."

"It's not?"

I shook my head. "How long it will take Rivera to figure out she can force me to give up by threatening anyone on board the ship. I'm terrified the next thing we're going to hear is her on a ship-wide broadcast where she threatens a crying child. Or, if Rivera is really sadistic, she'll make the child's mother beg me to turn myself in."

"I hadn't thought of that."

"The thing is, I can't think of anything I can do to stop her."

A contemplative look crossed Sofia's face. "What if we can convince Rivera you aren't on the *Pegasus* anymore?"

Sofia flashed a quick smile after she dropped her bombshell question on me. I tried hiding my incredulity, but must have failed miserably. My reply didn't make things any better.

"Um, you know we're in space, right Sofia?"

"I've been working on the *Pegasus* for nearly a year," she said. "Of course I know that. I'm not stupid."

"I know you're not. It's just..." I shrugged, "We can't just walk away from the ship."

"No, but the *Pegasus* has a lot of lifepods," Sofia said. "Most of them are back in passenger territory, but a few are kept just outside crew quarters. Those are just down the corridor from us."

"But if a lifepod launches, the first thing Rivera will do is blast it into a million pieces."

"No, Nora, the first thing she'll do is make sure we're in the pod. *Then* she'll blast it into a million pieces."

"Well, in that case, what are we waiting for? Let's hop in a lifepod and fly to our deaths."

Sofia shook her head. "We won't die because we won't actually be in the pod. We just need to make Rivera think we are."

"How are we going to do that?" I asked.

"Have you still got the comm that Conley gave you when you first hid in the maintenance tunnels?"

I pulled the comm out of my ear and showed it to Sofia. "Yes."

Sofia eyed the comm. "Please tell me you can change the channels it sends and receives on?"

"Yeah. Being able to change frequencies is just basic security stuff. Along with code words for compromised channels and—"

Sofia interrupted, "That means you can set your comm to the same emergency channel lifepod comms are set to?"

"Sure."

"There you go, then. Set your comm to the right channel, launch the lifepod, we hide in the tunnels again, and then gloat or act terrified or whatever if Rivera sends a message on that channel."

I considered Sofia's plan from all angles. "No one who knows anything about me would believe I was stupid enough to get in that lifepod."

"Rivera doesn't know you. Were you listening in when she talked to me in your bedroom?"

"You mean before she had you dragged off to use as bait to draw me out? Of course I was."

"She didn't even bat an eye when I suggested you were just like most of the other rich girls who board the *Pegasus*—spoiled, demanding twits who expect to have everything handed to them on a silver platter." Sofia looked away. "To be fair, that's what I was afraid you'd be like, too."

"Good. That's one worry down."

Sofia looked back at me. "You have more?"

"Lots, but Rivera's reaction was my biggest one."

"What else is there to worry about?" Sofia asked.

"Rivera will probably make her crew search the ship anyway. Not so much to find us, especially if she thinks we're dead, but to make sure no one else is hiding from her. And if Rivera is as paranoid as her mother, she might have her communications officer trace my comm broadcasts before she destroys the lifepod."

"She doesn't know anything about you. Not even what you look like." Sofia's brows drew down in puzzlement. "Why would she think you have a comm?"

"She might not," I admitted. "But how many of those other spoiled, demanding rich girls you compared me to had comms?"

"Um, all of them."

"So it's a safe bet Rivera will assume I have one, too."

Sofia's shoulders sagged. "I hadn't considered that."

"That's just because you haven't had the benefit of my grandfather's training."

"I'm sorry, Nora," Sofia sighed. "I guess my idea isn't all that good after all."

"Wrong, Sofia. It's a great idea that just needs a few tweaks." I smiled at her. "We can find ways to work around my worries."

"You're sure?" When I nodded, she continued, "Even if Rivera traces the comm broadcast?"

"That one is trickier, but I think I have a way around both that and getting away from a determined search by the pirates."

Sofia's eyebrows rose. "How?"

I took a deep breath, then said, "We're going to hide outside the ship, on the hull."

Sofia's eyes widened in surprise at my announcement. "You want to hide? Outside? On the hull?"

"Yep."

"But..." Sofia gave a quick shake of her head. "How? We're in *space*, Nora!"

"I know. We just discussed that a minute ago, remember? And you're reacting to *my* suggestion the same way *I* reacted to yours."

Sofia stared at me for a few seconds and nodded slightly. "Okay, Nora. I know you're not stupid, so tell me how we're going to survive outside the ship."

I pulled my shirt up and revealed the atmosphere harness I had on beneath it. "Remember my wonderfully paranoid grandfather I told you about? The one in charge of family security? The last thing he told me before I left was to wear one of these under my clothes."

"That explains how you can breathe outside the *Pegasus*, but most of us don't have grandfathers like yours. How am I going to breathe out there?"

"As long as we stay in contact with each other, the harness will automatically expand its atmosphere shield over both of us."

"It will?"

"That's a safety feature, in case there are more people than harnesses. We'll use up the oxygen twice as fast and will have to come back inside sooner than I'd like."

Sofia cocked her head. "How long do you want to stay on the hull?"

"Preferably until we reach the pirate base."

Sofia's eyes widened again. "Won't we die the first time the *Pegasus* enters a wormhole? I don't know the technical stuff, but before I started working on the ship, I had to sign a waiver releasing the company from liability if the inertial dampeners failed. Wouldn't this be the same thing?"

"No. The dampening field extends beyond the ship far enough to protect sensor arrays and stuff like that. I think we'll be safe out there."

"You *think?* You don't *know?*"

"I can't guarantee it, Sofia. Look, I won't blame you if you want to back out now and give yourself up to the pirates. Just tell them you weren't willing to get in the lifepod. Even if they don't believe you, the pirates won't find me onboard the *Pegasus*, so—"

"I'm not going to abandon you now, Nora," Sofia said. "I just thought I was done with crazy stuff for a while. Let's go find a lifepod while I wrap my mind around this latest idea."

Sofia's lips quirked up in a quick smile, so I nodded, rose to a crouch, and said, "Follow me."

The pain in my neck and back returned immediately. The burn in my thighs took slightly longer. From the soft groan Sofia gave when she stood, her aches and pains must have returned, too.

I concentrated more on moving quietly rather than quickly, and that taxed a new set of leg muscles. So we were both ready to stop when I reached the tunnel entrance nearest to the crew quarters' lifepods.

I crouched next to the door, slowed my breathing, and listened for sounds from the corridor on the other side. No sounds came to me, but that didn't mean the coast was clear.

I glanced at Sofia. "I'm going to drop my mental wall for a bit and see if I can pick out any nearby emotions."

She knew I had virtually no control over my empathic abilities, but if Sofia had any doubts, she kept them to herself and off her face. "Good idea. I'll keep watch while you're busy."

I took a moment to prepare for what might hit me when I dropped my mental wall. The thought that maybe it wouldn't be so bad popped into my head just before I knocked down the wall. Hopeful thinking at its best, but...

The emotional maelstrom *was* less intense. It didn't knock my mind this way and that, buffeted by sharp and wildly unpredictable feelings. The emotions were... muted. Dulled. Maybe people just can't maintain that level of sharp fear and panic forever? Whatever the reason, I wasn't afraid of drowning or getting swept away by the flood of emotions. That meant I could take a minute, look around, and see what was happening.

Strangely, my brain built something like a mental map, organizing everything and color-coding it all. I couldn't identify individual people, but the areas with the most emotional activity appeared bright red to me. I guessed the biggest, brightest red blob was the dining hall, where the pirates took most of the passengers and crew. Blobs of maroon slowly moved around the ship. Pirates, probably.

Something about the maroon movements caught my attention. I watched them for a second and realized those splotches of color moved with purpose and deliberation. As if they were coordinating their movements.

Like a search pattern.

And the nearest maroon blobs didn't feel very far away.

I threw my mental wall up again, and the relative calm made it seem easy compared to previous times. Maybe my mind remembered what it did when it threw up the wall automatically just before the pirate captain shot herself?

Not important right now, Nora!

Right.

"Time to go," I hissed.

Then I opened the door out into the corridor.

I poked my head out the door just far enough to glance up and down the corridor. Not a soul in sight. I listened and heard distant voices. But sound traveled well along metal walls, so I couldn't guess how far away the owners of those voices were.

The closest lifepod was to our right, about a dozen meters away. Without giving myself time to think, I waved Sofia forward and stepped into the corridor. As soon as Sofia cleared the tunnel door, I quickly and quietly pushed it shut. I stood—oh my God, did it feel good to stand straight again—grabbed Sofia by the hand, and set off for the lifepod at a brisk walk. I *wanted* to run, but apparently crew quarters didn't rate the noise-dampening carpets found in passenger territory. Our footfalls were loud enough as it was.

I kept my eyes on the lifepod hatch while my ears searched through the sounds echoing down the corridor for signs of danger. Were the voices behind us coming closer? They seemed a little louder. I think. But was that because of my heightened awareness of every sound around me, or were the speakers heading our way?

Sofia and I about jumped out of our skins as a woman in the

nearby crew quarters shrieked. Something—I prayed it was just a hand—muffled her cry.

We heard rough laughter, and an equally rough voice said, "All right, boys, who goes first?"

Half-a-dozen voices each claimed they should be first, and arguments broke out. Before they decided, an unfamiliar voice shouted, "Hey! No sampling the merchandise. Captain's orders."

The rough voice drawled, "Ain't you heard, chief? The captain's dead."

"Yeah, I heard," the second voice said. "But the new captain hasn't rescinded her mother's orders."

The rough voice was silent for a second, during which we heard the woman's quiet sobs. Finally, he said, "Looks like we don't get to have fun yet. Put her back with the others, boys."

If the pirates in crew quarters headed our way, Sofia and I would have to beat a hasty retreat to the maintenance tunnels. Without conscious thought, I glanced behind us, and noticed the door latch hadn't caught, leaving the door just the tiniest bit ajar. I hated leaving it like that, but I doubted we had time for me to go shut it properly.

As we reached the lifepod hatch, the rough voiced pirate added, "If you see the new captain, tell her she better rescind that order if she wants my boys to vote for her after this raid is over."

Sofia's hand shook with horror at what we heard. I gave it a quick squeeze before releasing it so I could work the hatch controls. They're dead simple to operate. You just push a big green button and the hatch opens. A red button closes it. And a covered yellow button lets someone outside the lifepod launch it. But my hand trembled, too, so pressing the button took more concentration than it should have. The hatch slid quietly aside, and Sofia and I clambered into the lifepod.

The same series of buttons repeated themselves just inside the pod. I tapped the red button, the hatch closed behind us, and I got my first look at one of the *Pegasus's* lifepods. The knot in my gut eased a little bit when I realized it matched the standard lifepod layout I learned from Aunt Nancy's spaceship training. This one was a lot bigger than any I'd seen before, with six *rows* of seats instead of a mere six seats, but the important things were where they should be. A tiny bathroom—home to the pod's maintenance hatch—was to our left, food storage was to our right, and one unexpected addition.

"Sofia," I whispered and pointed to a small control area at the other end of the lifepod, "are those messenger drone launch controls?"

She nodded. "All the lifepods have them. If no one from the crew is onboard, the drone activates automatically one minute after the lifepod launches."

I handed her my backpack. "Fill this with food and water. I'm going to record a message for Dad."

The drone's controls were just as simple as the ones for the hatch. There was a button labeled Record, a second labeled Destination, a third labeled Launch, and a small touch screen. I was fine with the automated launch, so punched the Destination button. The screen lit up.

Nearest destinations:

Ark's Landing - 14 hours

Pelnira Naval Base - 91 hours

Captain Riggs told us he would launch a drone for the naval base as soon as the *Pegasus* exited the wormhole. But even if he hadn't been able to do that, I'd have selected Ark's Landing. Because the sooner Dad heard about the pirates, the sooner he would start looking for me. I tapped the screen.

Destination set - Ark's Landing

I pressed the Record button, and the screen's display changed.

Recording. Press button again to end recording.

I drew a quick breath and said, "This is Nora Connaught onboard the starliner *Pegasus*. We have been captured by pirates.

Get this message to my father, Matt Connaught." I paused for a second, then continued, "Dad, come and get us. I love you!"

I wanted to say more, but Sofia hissed, "I hear voices in the corridor!"

I tapped the Record button a second time.

The screen displayed, *Recording complete.*

I hurried back to Sofia and whispered, "Can you make out what they're saying?"

She nodded her head.

From the corridor, a voice called, "Hey, chief? This door into the maintenance shafts isn't fully closed. You think they went in there?"

"Good eye, Barker," the chief replied. "That would be a great place for them to hide. Peck, check out the lifepods. Everyone else, into the tunnels."

"Why me?" whined a voice I recognized. Peck had the rough voice we heard from the crew quarters.

"Because I said so," the chief snapped. "And Peck? You better search these pods. If you go back and start playing with the crew, I'll space you. Got it?"

"Yeah, yeah, chief, I got it."

With banging and mumbling, the pirate search party filed into the maintenance tunnels. Except for Peck, who, from the sound of his footsteps, was coming our way.

"Get against the back wall," I whispered to Sofia.

She flattened herself against the wall on the right side of the hatch. I did the same on the left. I drew my blaster and carefully engaged the safety. Even the sound of a muffled shot would carry, and the other pirates were too close to risk that. Shooting Peck was out of the question. But I could still club him with the gun butt.

With a soft whoosh, the lifepod's hatch opened.

But the pirate just stood outside the lifepod and muttered in a falsetto voice, "Check out the lifepods, Peck." His tone dropped to a growl. "Yes, sir, chief. Whatever you say, chief. I'll get right on that, chief."

Peck's left foot stepped into the lifepod. "Chief, if I do find those girls, I'm going to have some fun with the fancy rich one. Her daddy will pay just as much ransom for her used as brand new."

His head poked through the hatch. "Maybe I'll make that little crew girl watch. That—"

I raised the butt of my blaster pistol, ready to smack Peck on the head as many times as it took to shut him up. But his head swiveled left, his eyes met mine, and they widened in surprise. Surprise I felt through my newly active empathic ability. Surprise that blazed a path between his mind and mine. Before I quite realized what I was doing, my mind latched onto Peck's sudden surprise and rode it inside his head.

I sensed weird, vaguely humanoid shapes capering in front of me. They formed a circle around something I couldn't see. I felt their shrieks and wails as their circle whirled. The scene inside Peck's head would have terrified me before my trip inside the pirate captain's mind. But that experience showed me insanity from the inside, and I didn't get the same sick sensation from Peck's emotions.

I knew the looming shapes dancing before me were supposed to terrify, but the circle still hid their target from me. Still, something was... off about them. With sudden inspiration, I figured out what felt wrong about the figures.

They flickered.

They weren't solid.

And they only had two dimensions.

They were projections from whatever was inside the circle.

Unlike the pirate captain, who buried the true memories of her son's death, I got the idea that Peck knew exactly what these projections hid and that it was something he didn't want to see.

I charged one of the flickering projections and... I don't

know how to say what I did. Smashed it with my fists? Kicked its ass? However you say it, the figure shattered. That set off a chain reaction as the other figures cracked and collapsed, too.

And I found myself face-to-face with Peck's emotional self image.

It was... pathetic.

A caricature of a man was curled up in front of me. Thin arms wrapped around spindly legs and pulled them close to a shrunken chest. A pencil-thin neck bent under the weight of a too-large head from which wide eyes darted this way and that, as if constantly on the alert for threats.

Like most kids, I heard all about how bullies picked on other kids to hide their own fear and insecurities. I thought it was a load of crap, then. But this glimpse into Peck's emotional core at least showed there was some truth to it. It didn't change my mind about *every* bully, but it was obviously true for some of them. Maybe even most of them.

But I overheard Peck terrorizing a poor woman who had the misfortune to end up in his power. I overheard his plans for me if he caught Sofia and me. So pathetic as Peck was, I felt no pity for him.

I guess I projected the disgust I felt for Peck, because the figure's eyes turned my way and it hunched even tighter into its ball. I felt the urge to kick him while he was cowering, but wouldn't let myself sink to Peck's level.

Too bad I can't think him into unconsciousness. It would save me a lot of time banging on his head when I return to my body.

There was a sudden burst of light, and something threw me from Peck's mind and back to my own. I rebuilt my mental wall, blinked twice, and took in my surroundings. Peck lay on the deck. Sofia bent over Peck and whacked him on the head with a big wrench. From the matted blood on Peck's head, it wasn't the first time she'd hit him.

Sofia lifted the wrench for another go. Now that I had my

bearings, I caught Sofia's hand. She glanced at me with wide, wild eyes.

"I think he's out, Sofia."

She tried pulling her arm from my grip. "Let me hit him a few more times to make sure."

I pried the wrench from her hand. "No."

"But you heard him. He—"

"Won't get a chance to carry out any of those threats." I held up the wrench. "Where did you get this?"

She pointed to a tool locker built into the lifepod's bulkhead. "When the two of you went real still right after he poked his head into the pod, I figured I wouldn't get a better chance to knock him out without him yelling for help." Sofia's hand covered her mouth. "Did I hurt you? I didn't mean to, I was just—"

"I'm fine. You just knocked me back into my own mind." I glanced into the tool locker and spotted just what I needed to immobilize Peck. "Help me drag this guy all the way into the lifepod. Then hand me the duct tape."

A moment later, we had Peck's hands taped behind his back, his legs taped together at the ankles and knees, and tape covering his mouth.

"Now what?" Sofia asked.

"Now we go through the lifepod's maintenance hatch," I said. "It's time to find out if my plan for fooling the new pirate captain will work."

Sofia looked around. "What are you talking about, Nora? I don't see a maintenance hatch anywhere."

"That's because it's in here." I said as I opened the bathroom door.

I crouched, reached under the little sink, and felt around until my fingers discovered a small handle against the bulkhead. I caught hold of it and pulled. The entire bathroom floor, which wasn't much more than a meter square, slid smoothly aside. The hatch was beneath it.

"Why is it hidden away like that?" Sofia asked.

I turned and raised one eyebrow. "You work with passengers every day. Do you *really* need to ask that question?"

"Yeah," she nodded as a ghost of a smile appeared, "we see stupid passenger tricks all the time."

I flashed a grin, "And they're all stupid, am I right?"

"Every last one of them." Sofia's eyes suddenly widened and her hand flew to her mouth. "Except for you, Nora! I didn't mean to suggest—"

"Hey, *I* said it. You just agreed with me." I turned a mock glare on Sofia. "Besides, you ought to know me better than that by now."

"I do, it's just..." Sofia waved a hand helplessly. "The officers get really upset if a crew member says something like that around a passenger."

I turned back to the hatch controls, but added, "Then it's a good thing I'm not a passenger."

"Right," Sofia drawled, "because saying that in front of an owner is *so* much better."

I unlocked the hatch and pressed the open button. The hatch slid smoothly aside. Lights came on outside the lifepod, I assume, triggered by the opening hatch.

"Come on," I said, and slithered through the hatch.

A moment later, Sofia and I stood in the maintenance area that surrounded the pod. My shoulders brushed the lifepod's hull on one side, and the launch bay's bulkhead on the other. I'm about average size for a girl and couldn't imagine a burly engineer having any room to maneuver in the narrow space. Maybe lifepod maintenance fell to women or small men?

Focus, Nora.

Right.

I walked towards the nose of the lifepod. It was a lot longer than I expected, probably thirty meters, but the *Pegasus's* outer hull finally came into view.

I released breath I hadn't realized I was holding. There, at the end of the passageway, was another lifepod launch control. If you're anything like me, you're wondering why one lifepod needed *three* launch controls—the ones outside the lifepod's hatch, the ones inside the lifepod, and now this set. I asked Aunt Nancy about it, and she made me look it up for myself.

The short answer is *redundancy*. Every safety system on a starship has at least two backup systems. Life support has *ten*. Just having three sets of controls was considered the bare minimum for safety.

I gave the control area a quick once over. "Okay, I've seen what I needed to see. Let's go back and get our stuff."

Sofia peered past me. "We're going to use those controls?"

"Yep."

"Won't we get roasted when the lifepod's engines start?"

I shook my head. "The engines don't start until after the launch. The lifepod uses a linear accelerator for launching."

"Okay, but what about—"

"Stop." I looked into Sofia's eyes. "I wouldn't suggest this if it wasn't safe. Please trust me."

She held my gaze for a second, then nodded. "Okay."

As we walked back to the lifepod's maintenance hatch, I felt conflicting emotions coming through my link with Sofia. But the link wasn't strong enough for me to sort through them and figure out what was bothering her. Sofia turned to face me when she reached the hatch, but she didn't meet my eyes.

"So, what are we going to do with the pirate in the lifepod?" Sofia's tone said she didn't care what we did with him. Her stiff posture and her roiling emotions said otherwise.

I shrugged, "We'll get our stuff, shove him out into the corridor, and then follow through with the rest of the plan."

Sofia's body sagged, and I felt her relief through our shared link.

"Good," she said. "That's good."

"Did you think I was going to leave him in the lifepod and let him die if Rivera blows it up? I'm not *that* bloodthirsty, Sofia."

"I know you're not, Nora. It's just... won't we need someone in the lifepod so the *Pegasus's* sensors will detect life forms inside the pod?"

I smiled. "You watch too many adventure vids, Sofia. Sensors like that are really expensive and take a lot of training to use right. I doubt the *Pegasus* is equipped with them. Even if it is, I'd be shocked if any of the pirates knew how to work them."

Sofia gave a quick nod and then squirmed through the hatch. By the time I came through, Sofia had crouched next to Peck.

"He's still out. I think." Doubt clouded her eyes, and she added, "I could hit him with the wrench again to make sure."

Just in case Peck was faking, I said, "Sure, whack a few more times if you want."

Sofia's eyes widened, and I felt more emotions battling each other through the link. Meanwhile, I watched Peck. He never stirred, so either he was a fantastic actor or he really was out cold.

Sofia hefted the wrench. "If you're sure?"

"No, don't hit him again. There's no way Peck would just lie there if he was awake."

Without another word, Sofia and I stuffed supplies into my backpack. I checked the tool locker for anything useful, found an extra safety line, and also grabbed the roll of duct tape and a folding knife. I lowered my pack through the maintenance hatch, then went back to Peck. As Sofia reached for the main hatch controls, we heard a raised voice from just outside the pod.

"Peck?" It was the chief. "Where are you?"

Another man said, "Maybe he got that crew woman and dragged her into one of the pods?"

"Sounds like something Peck would do," a third man said.

Sofia and I glanced at each other, and I was sure my eyes were just as wide and panic-stricken as hers.

What now? she mouthed.

"Peck?" The chief sounded farther away, and I assumed he

was walking down the line of lifepods towards crew quarters. "Come on, Peck! Don't make me open every pod!"

There was no way Sofia and I could afford a face off against three pirates. And that's assuming it was only three. I pointed to the hatch in the bathroom and waved Sofia ahead of me. After she slipped through the hatch, I followed her. Peck's bound, huddled form was the last thing I saw before I closed the maintenance hatch and headed for the launch controls.

I made sure the hatch was shut and then hurried after Sofia. She sidled down the narrow passageway, moving way too slowly. I gave her a gentle push. "Go as fast as you can."

She turned and walked faster, but asked, "What's the big rush?"

"The lifepod can't launch if its entry hatch is open."

Sofia started running. "So, we have to launch it before those pirates get to our lifepod?"

"Yep."

"What if we're too late?"

"Then the pirates will catch us."

Sofia glanced quickly over her shoulder. "Why would they even look out here?"

"Because the bathroom floor is still pushed aside. They'll see the hatch and know exactly where we are."

"And we'll be trapped at the end of this short passage."

Sofia ran faster, and I kept pace with her. Our shoulders bounced off the bulkhead on our left and smashed against things sticking out of the lifepod's hull on our right. I ignored the pain by reminding myself Sofia and I would get hurt a lot worse if the pirates ever got their hands on us.

The gentle curve of the lifepod's hull hid the controls from us until we were five meters from them. The second Sofia spotted them, she put on a burst of speed and stuck her right hand out in front of her. With a sudden jolt of horror, I realized she was going to push the launch button as soon as she reached it.

My mind conjured visions of the launch bay's air rushing out into space after the lifepod launched. And that sudden decompression swept Sofia and me out into space, too. Sofia would suffer a horrible but quick death. Sure, I could activate my atmosphere harness, but that would just keep me from suffocating. After that, I'd be as good as dead, only my body wouldn't know it yet. But my mind would, and I shivered just thinking about it.

"Don't push the button!" I called. "Not yet."

The urgency in my tone cut through Sofia's panic. She lowered her hand and slowed down. I caught up with her just as she reached the controls.

"Put your arms around me," I said.

Sofia did what I asked, and said, "I almost killed us, didn't I?"

"We're still alive. That's all that matters."

I grabbed the safety line I spotted the first time we came down here, wrapped it three times around us, and then clipped it to a safety ring. Finally, I reached under my shirt and activated my atmosphere harness. The soft, blue glow of the oxygen shield enveloped us. Then, I pressed the launch button.

Nothing happened.

Fear-driven adrenaline flooded my body, and my mind screamed, *No! Not after everything we've been through!*

Then the *Pegasus's* hull began vibrating. I heard the soft scrape of metal sliding against metal. A meter to my right, a gap appeared in previously solid hull as the launch bay's hatch trundled open. A high-pitched whistle began as the air in the bay rushed through the opening and out into space.

At first, the escaping air felt like nothing more than a summer breeze ruffling our clothes. Its intensity grew rapidly, as did the sound it made passing through the widening hatch. The whistle became a howl. The breeze became a gale that grabbed our bodies and tried to drag us into space with it.

The safety line snapped taught. The loops I'd wrapped

around us tightened painfully. Sofia and I fought for breath against the constricting safety line.

Then, the last of the air rushed from the launch bay. The vibrations from the hull ended as the hatch finished opening. In a soundless blur of motion, the lifepod shot into space.

INTO THE VOID

Our breathing was louder than I expected. But the vacuum surrounding us cut off every sound except the vague, distant ship sounds that came through the deck.

I gave Sofia a quick squeeze. "Are you okay?"

"I think so," she said. "But what's the blue haze I see in front of me?"

"That's the shield created by the atmosphere harness. It keeps the air in so we can breathe, but still lets us touch stuff."

"How does it do that?"

"I don't know. Dad and Granddaddy Connaught tried explaining it to me one time, but it just confused me more. Anyway, let's get your harness on and activated."

"Do we have time for that, Nora? Won't the hatch close now that the lifepod has launched?"

"No, it can only be closed at a space dock."

"Why is that?"

"It's another safety protocol. Say the *Pegasus* broke down and sent out distress drones. When rescue ships arrive, open lifepod ports tell them people abandoned the ship and they should search for pod beacons." I grabbed the atmosphere harness stored at the launch controls. "Put your hands on my shoulders, Sofia. That will keep my shield around both of us and leave my hands free to put this one on you."

She did as I asked. A moment later, her harness was in place, and I activated it.

"Okay," I said, "you can let go of me."

"Are you sure, Nora? Nothing changed when you turned on the shield. What if it doesn't work? How will I breathe if—"

"Then we'll keep sharing my atmosphere harness. Don't worry. If yours isn't working, just grab hold of me again, okay?"

Sofia gave a nervous nod, took a deep breath, and let go of me. The blue haze from my shield made it impossible for me to see if Sofia's shield was there, but I saw her chest rise and fall as she breathed and she didn't grab for my hand. A little tension flowed out of her posture. Her mouth moved, but with a few centimeters of vacuum between her shield and mine, I didn't hear what she said.

I gently took her hand and said, "We can only talk to each other if our shields overlap."

"Oh, right. That makes sense. Anyway, all I said was my harness is working."

"Good." I looked her in the eyes. "Are you ready to go out onto the hull?"

"No, but do we have any other choice?"

"Not that I can think of."

I took the spare safety line out of my backpack and clipped one end to Sofia's harness and the other to mine. "This line means you don't have to worry if you lose your grip, okay? I can just pull you back to the hull." I flashed a confident smile. "Or you can pull me back if I lose my grip."

"Got it."

I took the loose end of the launch bay's safety line and attached it to my atmosphere harness. "You stay here for a minute while I go outside and fasten this end of the safety line on the outer hull. When I pull on it three times, unclip the line from the ship, then I'll pull you out to join me."

Sofia nodded, but said, "We've got two safety lines, Nora. Won't it get confusing if we use the same words to describe them both?"

"You're right. Why don't you come up with a name for this line?" I held up the line that connected Sofia and me. "And we'll keep calling the other one the safety line."

"Okay." Sofia thought for a second, then flashed a quick grin. "We'll call it Dad."

I raised one eyebrow. "Dad?"

"When you were a little girl, did anyone in the galaxy make you feel safer than your father?"

Memories of me crawling into Dad's lap when I was a little girl appeared in my mind. I always felt so safe sitting there with his arms wrapped around me. "Yeah, that's a good name. Now, I'm heading outside."

I waited a heartbeat in case Sofia wanted to say anything. When she didn't, I released her hand, turned around, and pulled myself along handholds specifically installed for just this purpose. A second later, I reached the launch bay's open hatch. With a deep breath, I pulled myself through it and stared into the dark void of space.

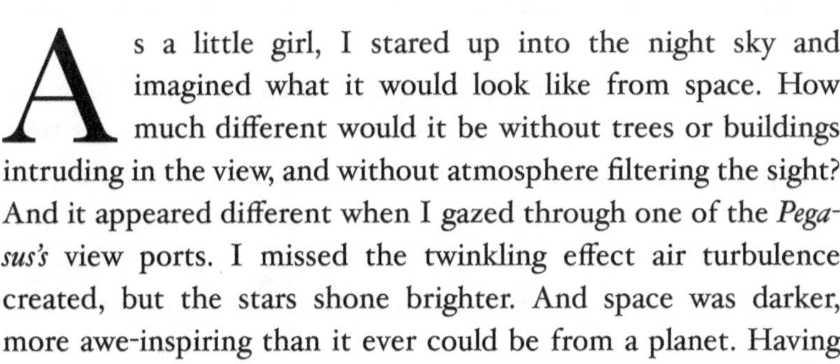

As a little girl, I stared up into the night sky and imagined what it would look like from space. How much different would it be without trees or buildings intruding in the view, and without atmosphere filtering the sight? And it appeared different when I gazed through one of the *Pegasus's* view ports. I missed the twinkling effect air turbulence created, but the stars shone brighter. And space was darker, more awe-inspiring than it ever could be from a planet. Having seen the stars from inside a spaceship, I thought I'd truly seen space.

I didn't realize how wrong I was until I was outside the ship and hanging onto an outer hull safety ring. Pulling myself through the hatch took all my concentration, and I kept my eyes riveted on the handholds. I didn't look up from the ship until I had an arm looped through a safety ring ten meters from the hatch. With a deep breath, I grabbed the clip for the safety line (instead of the clip for the line Sofia named Dad) and detached it from my harness. I snapped it into place on the safety ring, and only then glanced away from the hull.

The enormity of space stilled my breathing. It captured my attention so thoroughly I found I couldn't look away. Not because I didn't want to. Because I *couldn't*. Paralysis spread out from my terrified mind and froze my body in place. I felt as if I dangled over a bottomless pit and the only thing keeping me from plunging to my doom was the arm I'd stuck through the safety ring.

Don't forget Dad.

Right. I'd clipped one end of Dad to Sofia's harness, and the other to mine. So, if I lost my grip, Sofia could just pull me back to the launch bay.

Yeah.

Unless *she* lost her grip, too. Then we'd both fall until we suffocated or died of thirst.

Space seen from space didn't inspire awe. It terrified me like nothing else ever has.

I don't know how long I hung from the hull, staring into the abyss. Long enough that I remembered Mom's story of the time she spent twenty minutes lost in space. She only shared the story after I begged for days, and then with the barest of details. But her eyes told the story more eloquently than terse words could. I watched Mom's blue eyes turn dark and lose focus as she spoke. Life only returned to them when she got to the part where Dad found her with his psychic powers and guided a shuttle to rescue her.

Now I had the vaguest of ideas about how she must have felt while drifting all alone like that. A shiver ran up my spine, and it gave just enough distraction from the horrible, hypnotic lure of the abyss for me to turn away from it. I started breathing again and turned my attention back to the safety line. I gave it a sharp tug to make sure the clip was firmly attached to the safety ring. It was, so I coiled the slack in the line until the bit between me and Sofia drew taut. I made sure I still had my left arm looped through the safety ring, then I gave three sharp tugs on the line.

A moment later, Sofia's head poked out of the hatch. She looked my way, waved, and I realized she held the loose end of the safety line in her left hand. I gave myself a mental smack for not telling her to fasten it to her harness and waved to get her attention. When Sofia looked at me, I mimed attaching the line to her harness. She nodded, and being right-handed, instinctively pulled that hand back to handle the clip. That would have worked fine in a gravity well. In space, she kept drifting forward.

Sofia realized her mistake a second later and lunged for the nearest handhold with both hands. The end of the safety line slipped from her grasp. Since I had my end of it attached to the same safety ring I had my arm looped through, Sofia should have just ignored the safety line. But alarm crossed her face and Sofia grabbed for the line as it drifted away from her. She misjudged the distance and knocked the clasp farther from her. But far worse, dividing her attention between the safety line and handhold meant she drifted far enough that the handhold was out of reach.

A look of sheer terror froze her face as she drifted away from the *Pegasus*. Sofia flailed with both hands, desperate to find something to hang onto. That set her spinning, which only fed her fear.

In her panic, Sofia must have forgotten that Dad still connected us. All I had to do was reel her in and everything would be fine. And surely her terror would ease once she felt me pulling her back to the ship.

In my haste to help Sofia, I almost made the same mistake she had made. I grabbed Dad with my free hand and unlooped my arm from the safety ring so I could use both hands to retrieve Sofia. Somewhere in the back of my mind, alarm bells rang just before I pulled my hand completely free from the ring. Adrenaline flooded my body and jolted me to action. I grabbed the ring with fanatical strength and then carefully looped my arm back through the ring.

With my heart hammering so hard I could hear it, I turned my attention from Sofia for a moment and used my free hand to pull the drifting safety line to me. Then I snapped its free end to my safety harness. Now that we were attached to the ship again, I used my free hand to pull Dad taut. Then I reeled Sofia back to the ship.

I held Sofia while she mastered her panic, and she held me while I mastered my own terror.

With one second of inattention, I nearly doomed us. Unlike my mother, nobody would have come for us. Nobody would have found our bodies. Nobody—

I forced my mind away from those morbid thoughts and silently swore I'd keep my eyes locked on the hull rather than staring into the terrible and irresistible abyss. Then I asked, "Are you okay, Sofia?"

She didn't answer immediately, but finally said, "I think so, but I hate being out here!"

"Me, too. I promise we'll go back inside the ship as soon as we think it's safe."

Sofia drew a deep breath and asked, "What now?"

I considered how close we'd come to disaster just moving ten meters from the launch bay hatch. "I'd planned on working our way to the back of the *Pegasus* before I had that comm conversation with Rivera. But that's *way* too dangerous for a couple of newbs like us. I think we'll just stay here."

"Oh, thank God," Sofia said.

I triple checked the safety line's and Dad's connections to the hull and our harnesses. Satisfied, I raised a hand to my ear, activated the comm, and switched it to the emergency channel.

The comm crackled, and Rivera said, "I know you can hear me, Nora, so you might as well answer."

I gave Sofia a weak smile and mouthed *Showtime.*

I waited two seconds after Rivera finished speaking, vented an irritated sigh, assumed my leave-me-alone tone of voice, and said, "Fine, I can hear you. Are you satisfied?"

"Very much so," Rivera purred.

"Good." I grinned at a wide-eyed Sofia. "Now shut up and leave me alone."

Rivera's tone turned conversational. "I'm afraid I underestimated you, Nora."

I couldn't help rolling my eyes. "There's a shocker."

Rivera ignored my comment. "Here I was expecting a foolish little rich girl with no skills beyond wielding a credit stick. You can imagine my surprise when I discovered you weren't as stupid as I'd imagined. Hiding in the maintenance tunnels was even mildly clever."

"Clever enough to avoid your idiot pirates," I said.

"Child, I *always* order a sweep of the tunnels once we've secured a ship. Even if you hadn't staged your little ambush, we'd have captured you eventually, Nora."

With false concern in my voice, I said, "Gee, I hope I didn't hurt your men *too* badly."

"Cook and Wells will recover in time, though it was rather low of you to shoot poor Wells in the groin."

I drew on my martial arts training and said, "He should be happy I only had a blaster with me."

"Oh?" Rivera sounded curious. "And why is that?"

"If I'd been a typical rich girl wielding a credit stick, he'd be dead."

"I must admit you've lost me, Nora."

"If you know where to stab, a credit stick makes a passable stiletto." In a conspiratorial whisper, I added, "And I know *exactly* where to stab."

Sofia's eyebrows rose in shock or surprise at my response. But Rivera's response was more satisfying. From the forward end of the *Pegasus*, I felt a sharp spike of hatred laced with anger. I guessed I was finally getting on her nerves.

"You know, it's too bad mother died before you met her," Rivera snarled. "She'd have beaten the smugness out of you."

I adopted a sickly sweet tone of voice, and said, "Oh, Rivera, you haven't figured it out yet, have you?"

Genuine confusion filled Rivera's voice as she asked, "Figured what out?"

"I met your mother."

In a scornful tone, she said, "I don't believe you. Passengers weren't allowed near mother during the roundup. Besides, you were cowering in the tunnels while poor Miss Olson faced mother's wrath in your place. No, if mother had met you—"

"I didn't say she met me."

"Ah, you think spying on her through some vent is the same as meeting her? Really, Nora—"

Time to twist the knife.

"Do you remember when you two heard that Paco got himself killed?"

Rivera hissed, "Murdered, you mean."

It was my turn for scorn. "Oh, please. You're not stupid, Rivera, and you're not insane like your mother was. You know as well as I do, Dad shot Paco in self defense. Paco might still be alive today if he'd just let Mom and Dad leave peacefully."

"You dare to—"

"But, I was talking about what happened when you got the news." I switched to a nonchalant tone and said, "Your mother reached out to hug you. But you dodged around her and ran off."

Rivera stayed silent, so I continued, "Do you have any idea how badly you hurt her when you did that? She was grieving, too, though I can't imagine why anyone would care that much about a lowlife like Paco."

"Shut up!" Rivera snarled.

I ignored her, of course. "I'll bet your reaction to her is what started her down the road to insanity. It's kind of sad, really."

"Shut. Up!"

"Can't handle the truth, can you, Rivera? I guess that's no surprise. I mean, look at what your mother did to avoid facing it."

In a whisper so low I had trouble hearing it, Rivera asked, "What do you mean by that?"

"Oh, didn't you realize? She knew that Paco got what he deserved. But she hid it from herself. She even dressed it up to make it look like Dad was the murdering psycho instead of her precious Paco."

"How can you know any of that?"

"Are you serious, Rivera? I mean, I know Rockville Station is out in the galactic boonies, but I'll bet the news about Dad's psychic powers got there a long time ago. And, well, I *am* my father's daughter."

Rivera growled, "You were inside my mother's head?"

"Yep. And let me tell you, she was *really* messed up."

"You controlled mother and made her kill herself!"

"Don't be stupid. No psychic can do that. I just found the memory your mother hid from herself, dusted it off, and shoved it into her conscious mind." In a derisive tone, I said, "She couldn't face that memory, so she took the coward's way out."

Through my new psychic abilities, I felt rage replace the anger Rivera radiated earlier. It pushed her hatred for me far beyond anything I'd felt before.

Rivera was silent for a long time. Loathing filled her voice as she said, "I wish I could kill you with my bare hands."

"Well, you can't."

"No, but I *can* kill you."

I looked out at the abyss of space and let myself imagine

falling forever. I didn't have to fake the panic that filled my voice. "What? No! How?"

Rivera gave a dark laugh and said, "The *Pegasus* is well armed, girl."

"But the weapons were sabotaged!"

"By *me*, you idiot! I used a virus to override the controlling software. Needless to say, I had the passcode necessary to disable the virus." Her voice lowered slightly, as if she'd turned away from the comm. "Have you targeted the lifepod?"

"Yes, ma'am," a distant voice replied.

"Fire."

A missile burst from one of the *Pegasus's* launch tubes and streaked away.

"No!" I cried. "Please, don't!"

I saw a flash far behind us, and it briefly washed out several stars in the area. I immediately muted my comm so I couldn't accidentally broadcast anything.

Satisfaction filled Rivera's voice as she said, "Goodbye, Nora Connaught."

Rivera gave a delighted chuckle. "My, that *was* fun. But it's time to get back to business. Ortiz, return the comm to the ship-wide channel."

I assumed Ortiz was the pirate's communication officer. He obviously obeyed Rivera's order, because my little comm immediately stopped receiving. But I couldn't get Rivera's exultant tone out of mind.

My stomach suddenly fluttered, and the feeling spread from there through my body. I drew legs up to my chest, wrapped trembling arms around them, and fought to still my suddenly shaking body.

Sofia laid a hand on my cheek and firmly turned my gaze away from the darkness of space. "Are you okay, Nora?"

My vision blurred with sudden tears, and I tried blinking them away. But without gravity pulling on the tears, all I did was smear them around.

"Close your eyes," Sofia said. When I did, she gently wiped the tears from my eyes. "Do you want to talk about it?"

"Talk about what?"

"Whatever Rivera said that upset you so much."

I tried brushing her concern aside. "It was nothing. Probably just the after effect of all the adrenaline that's been running through my body."

"Right," Sofia scoffed. "Your voice is quavering, Nora. That's not from adrenaline."

I stared into Sofia's eyes and saw exactly what I knew would be there—compassion and concern for me. She offered an encouraging smile. "Unlike *some* people hanging around on this hull, I'm not psychic. I can't dive inside your head and figure out what's bothering you. But I am your friend, Nora, and friends help each other."

I gave a shaky nod, then said, "It wasn't so much what Rivera said... It was her tone of voice. She was just so... happy that she'd killed me."

"*Thought* she killed you," Sofia said. "But you already knew she wanted you dead."

"Yeah, but... There's a difference between knowing someone wants to kill you and hearing them get all excited when they think they succeeded. But I don't know how to explain it."

Sofia considered my words for a moment. "I think you just did, Nora. You told me about your paranoid grandfather and all the training he and your mom gave you. So, you grew up *knowing* people might want to hurt you. But you never really *understood* what that meant until now."

"I think you're right, Sofia."

"Of course I'm right." She tilted her nose up in an expression of superiority. "As your elder, I possess wisdom beyond your understanding."

I couldn't help giggling. "My elder? Seriously?"

Sofia kept her imperious tone. "I am nineteen, while you are but a child."

"I'm eighteen!"

"Which is less than nineteen."

"I can't argue with math. Thank you for sharing your wisdom, O revered elder." I uncurled from my ball. "When this is all over, remind me to thank Captain Riggs for bringing you into my life."

Sofia lost her lofty expression and shook her head. "I wish I had your confidence."

"The lifepod's messenger drone launched like twenty minutes ago. It'll reach Ark's Landing in just under fourteen hours."

"Then your dad will come find us?"

"Along with the Ark's Landing Navy, yeah."

"So we just have to sit tight and wait for a rescue?"

I *wanted* to say, *Yes, we've done our part.* But I didn't.

My expression must have told Sofia what I was thinking. She sighed, "That looks like a no."

"I'm sorry, Sofia. Really, I am. But I don't know how long it will take Dad to find me. It took him weeks to find his parents. And I know he and Mom had a lot more space to search, but we don't know where the pirate base is, how long their trip will take, or what they'll do with the passengers and crew when we get there."

"Meaning... what?"

"We'll have to play everything by ear. I mean, I hope Dad swoops in and rescues us just as much as you."

"But?"

I shrugged. "If he doesn't, we're going to have to rescue ourselves."

"And five thousand other people."

"We can't exactly leave them in pirate hands, can we?"

Sofia's gaze unfocused for a moment. I think she was remembering what that slime ball Peck wanted to do to one of her fellow crew women. "No, we can't."

I suddenly remembered Peck has been on board the lifepod. *I guess he's the* late *slime ball Peck now.*

My thoughts turned inward, too, as a sudden surge of guilt accompanied that recollection. Absently, I asked, "Sofia, do you feel guilty about Peck?"

"For hitting him on the head so many times?" She gave a firm shake of her head. "Absolutely not."

"No, for leaving him to die when the lifepod blew up."

Sofia took a moment to consider my question, then she said, "A little. But what choice did we have? If we opened the lifepod hatch to push him out, the pirates in the corridor would have caught us. We didn't have time to drag him out the maintenance hatch, either. And it's not like *we* blew up the lifepod."

"You're right... At least I have a better idea how Dad felt after he shot Paco."

We shared a few seconds of silence before Sofia said, "We can't do anything about Peck, and we don't know what we'll have to do when we reach the pirate base. Do we know what we're going to do right now?"

I considered her question, then replied, "Let's have some chocolate."

"You're a genius, Nora!"

I carefully fished two of the energy bars from my pack. As I handed one to Sofia, I couldn't stifle a yawn. "And after the chocolate, I think I'll take a nap."

Perhaps inspired by me, Sofia yawned, too. "Another good idea. This has been the hardest day of my life."

"Mine, too."

Minutes later, I used quick release knots on our safety lines, lashing us close to the safety ring. Neither of us wanted to wake up drifting fifteen meters from the ship. Exhaustion drove everything from my mind—even my guilty feelings and the emotions radiating from everyone inside the *Pegasus*. I closed my eyes and slept.

MONSTER

A terrified Peck struggled with his bonds as Rivera pronounced his death sentence. He made desperate mewling sounds through the tape over his mouth as he wormed his way towards the lifepod's comm. He went rigid when the new pirate captain said, "Fire!" The back end of the lifepod vanished, and a wall of flame swept towards him. The tape binding him vanished. Peck raised his hands as if they could shield him from death. Then he screamed and screamed and screamed as the fire engulfed him.

I awoke with a start, and a sense of disorientation flooded through me. Why was I tied to my bed and floating a meter above it? Why did that bed look so hard and unyielding? My eyes wandered to something floating nearby. Sofia floated next to me, her face peaceful in sleep. And beyond her...

The abyss of space.

My stomach roiled at the sight, and my eyes darted back to the comparatively safe view of the *Pegasus's* hull. As I shook off the last vestiges of sleep, my disorientation fled. The memories of my dream faded, leaving only the knowledge that it hadn't been a pleasant one.

Time to take stock of your situation, Nora.

How long had I slept? I checked the time and learned it was

nearly 7:00 AM ship's time. Then I remembered I hadn't checked a clock once since I came on board the *Pegasus*, so knowing the time didn't tell me anything useful. I tried guessing when we fell asleep by working through everything that happened to me since I left Ark's Landing, from my suddenly blooming psychic talent to the pirate takeover to the original pirate captain's suicide to...

I shook my head in frustration at the immensity of it all. How could one girl's life change *so* much so quickly?

As if in answer, I felt a sharp spike of terror through my empathic ability. The fear spread for a moment before it faded. Was it a child having a nightmare? A parent waking to discover reality was far more terrifying than anything their sleeping mind concocted? Whatever caused that spike, it reminded me I was only one of thousands whose lives were turned upside down in the last twenty-four hours.

Sure, I had to deal with the unexpected and deeply unsettling arrival of my psychic ability on top of the pirate attack. But I spent my entire life wishing it would finally show up. I couldn't exactly call it a burden now that I'd gotten my wish. Besides, after the first few terrible hours, when it took all my concentration to keep the flood of emotions at bay, my mind had adjusted. I wouldn't say I had firm control of the ability—especially since it manifested in ways I'd never heard of before—but I no longer feared losing myself in the sea of emotions surrounding me. That was good, because I'd had no time to think about controlling my talent since the pirates arrived.

Or maybe I developed what control I had *because* I'd been forced to think about other things. I mean, people can adapt to just about anything, right? And I only stopped feeling overwhelmed by my ability after the pirates invaded the ship. Because I had other, more important things to worry about. It's like—I don't know—like I got out of my mind's way, stopped interfering with its attempts to adapt to the ability, and let my mind do its thing.

God, from this train of thought, it almost sounds like I'm saying the pirate attack was a *good* thing! No way, brain. I'd rather have gone insane and gotten lost in that sea of emotions than have pirates capture the *Pegasus*. But maybe, just maybe, the control I'd developed would make a difference in my battle with the pirates.

But how could I turn empathy—something I bet pirates don't have a lot of—against them? Memories of the brief time I spent inside the original captain's mind rose, and with them came the first stirrings of an idea.

Next to me, Sofia stirred. Her eyes fluttered open, and I saw the same disorientation reflected there that I felt on waking. I said, "We're hiding from the pirates on the hull of the ship."

Her eyes flashed with comprehension, and she nodded. "I remember, now. How long have you been awake?"

"Not long." A smile stretched my lips. "But long enough to come up with an idea for battling the pirates."

"Are you out of your mind, Nora? They outnumber us a hundred to one! We'll get slaughtered."

"Cut me some slack, Sofia. I'm not stupid enough to go rampaging through the *Pegasus* with guns blazing."

"Sorry. I know you're not stupid, but you said you wanted to battle the pirates. How else can you do that?"

I grinned. "Have you ever heard of psychological warfare?"

Sofia actually rolled her eyes in response to my question. Her reaction was so normal, so totally out of place from our situation —I mean, we had tied ourselves to the *Pegasus's* outer hull while hiding from space pirates, for God's sake—that I couldn't help laughing.

"Sorry, Sofia," I said. "That was a stupid question."

"You think?" Her sarcastic tone made me laugh again. Sofia waited until I stopped giggling, then asked, "You're planning on going into the pirates' minds, aren't you?"

I was my turn for sarcasm. "We could always try sneaking up

on them and whispering in their ears. But I think it'll be a lot safer if we use my new ability."

Sofia ignored my tone and asked, "Safer for who?"

I pasted a confident grin on my face. "Both of us."

I didn't fool Sofia. "Are you sure?"

"Why wouldn't I be?"

"You didn't answer my question."

"Of course we'll both be safe, because we'll stay out here on the hull. We won't even come close to any pirates. Are you satis-fied now?"

I tried glaring Sofia into accepting my answer, but she wasn't having any of it. After a few seconds, she said, "You *know* that's not what I meant."

My eyes darted away from hers, and I said, "Fine. You'll be completely safe. I probably will be, too."

Sofia and I were already holding hands so we could talk to each other, but she added her free hand to it. "It's not like I can stop you, Nora. But you've been inside two pirates' minds. Whatever you saw in their heads had an effect on you—and it wasn't a good one."

She fell silent for a couple of seconds, then said, "Just promise me one thing? Promise me you'll stop if I ask you to. Because everyone on the *Pegasus*—passengers and crew—needs you. Maybe they don't know it, but I sure do."

This is when the doubting voice inside my head usually popped up with some cutting comment about how nobody ever needed No-Talent Nora. But the voice stayed silent. Maybe that's because I knew Sofia was right. And *that* responsibility was a lot scarier than anything the voice inside my head ever said to me.

"Okay, I'll stop using my ability whenever you say to. I prom-ise." I gave a little shrug. "That's assuming I can even make this work. I only got into those minds by following strong emotions back to their source."

Sofia waved my comment off. "You'll do it."

"What makes you so sure?"

"Because you're Nora Connaught. Too many people are counting on you for you to let yourself fail."

I raised one eyebrow. "You've only known me for one day. What makes you so sure I won't screw this up?"

"You haven't yet, and you know more about your power now." Sofia bit her lip briefly, then said, "I'm not saying your psychological warfare plan is definitely going to work, though I *think* it will. What I'm saying is that I believe you will find a way to get inside these pirates' minds. Because you won't let yourself rest until you figure it out."

"So, no pressure, right?"

Sofia shook her head. "Lots of pressure, but that's part of being a hero. And isn't that who you always wanted to be?"

"It's who I *thought* I wanted to be."

I suddenly remembered what Mom said to me back on Ark's Landing, before we left for the spaceport. *Sometimes life gives us what we think we want.* Yeah, it had definitely done that, and I absolutely hated life for pulling such a dirty trick on me.

I rolled stiff shoulders and realized the weight of responsibility wasn't any lighter in zero gravity. I drew a deep breath, and said, "Okay, let's say I figure out how to get inside someone's head from out here. Where should I start?"

"Isn't it obvious?"

"I wouldn't be asking if it was."

"Start with Rivera." Sofia grinned, "It's time for the ghost of Nora Connaught to haunt her dreams."

In response to Sofia's suggestion, I felt my mouth stretch into a grin that matched hers. "Oh, yeah, haunting Rivera's dreams will be totally zing!"

Sofia's head bobbed in enthusiastic agreement. "I just wish I could be in her nightmares and watch her running from big, bad Nora the ghost. You *are* going to give yourself fangs and claws and red eyes and scary stuff like that, right?"

"Obviously. But I don't want to get too weird, since I want to make sure Rivera recognizes me."

"She's never seen you before, Nora. You're going to have to tell her who you are." Sofia raised one hand and waved her fingers in the universal signal for eerie happenings. She pitched her voice to match, and said, "*I am the ghost of Nora Connaught! You murdered me, and now I'm here for your soul!*"

"Nice spooky voice, Sofia! I think that's just..." My voice trailed off as a sudden thought popped into my head, something from Granddaddy's training. I sighed, "I think that's just what I *shouldn't* do."

Confusion filled Sofia's eyes. "Why not?"

"It's something my grandfather said to me."

"You mean the paranoid one?"

I almost nodded in agreement, but another thought occurred to me. "I'm hiding from space pirates on the hull of a spaceliner, and the only reason the pirates haven't caught us is because of everything he and Mom taught me. Since people really were out to get me, I don't think I should keep calling him paranoid."

As if she'd forgotten where we were, Sofia glanced around us. Like me, she avoided looking out into deep space. After a second, she nodded. "Yeah, I see what you mean. So, what did your... um... really well-prepared grandfather say that made you change your mind about haunting Rivera?"

"Never interrupt your enemy when she's making a mistake. Granddaddy and Mom said it was some old Earth book. *Really* old, like from the time before space travel."

"Wow, that's ancient! But Rivera and her pirates took over the *Pegasus* without any trouble, and now she's taking the ship to her pirate base so she can sell five thousand people into slavery. What mistake is she making?"

"She thinks we're dead." I considered how to explain my realization, then said, "Rivera isn't stupid. If I pop into her head and haunt her thoughts and dreams, it might scare her a little bit. But she's bound to remember that I told her I went inside her mother's mind. Sooner or later, Rivera's going to put two and two together and figure out I'm not dead. Once she does that..."

"She'll order another search of the *Pegasus*," Sofia said, "and when they don't find us, she'll threaten to space passengers unless we give up."

I nodded. "She'll know I have a comm, and just broadcast over the ship-wide channel. Which reminds me, I ought to change to that channel and see if she has anything to say."

With a few taps, I changed my comm's channel. The ship-wide comm was silent. I offered a brief prayer of thanks for that, and said, "There's nothing on the comms right now, but one of us should listen to this all the time."

"Can you show me how it works?"

"Sure." I carefully removed the comm from my ear, showed Sofia how to change the volume, the channel, and the mute button. Then I brushed Sofia's hair away from her left ear and inserted the comm. "How does it feel?"

"A little weird, but I can get used to it if you ever want me to monitor the ship's comm."

"Good, because I want you to do that now."

"Okay. Is it because you need some more sleep?"

I shook my head. "I can't hear anything when I'm inside someone else's mind."

Sofia's eyebrows rose in surprise. "But I thought we agreed you shouldn't do that!"

"We agreed I shouldn't haunt Rivera's dreams. But I bet I can still learn something useful from inside her mind. Besides, there are a lot of other pirates in the *Pegasus*. I can scout their emotions, figure out how to upset them, and use that in my psychological attacks. It's probably better to undermine Rivera's authority with her followers than it is to haunt her, anyway."

"I guess so... You'll be careful, right?"

"Caution is my middle name."

"Your middle name is Erin."

"Wow, that file you read on me was thorough! Okay, how

about, I'm my mother's daughter and my grandfather's granddaughter? Better?"

"Much. But I have one question for you."

"Shoot."

"What should I do if I hear something important over the comm while you're off inside some pirate's head?" Sofia's gaze filled with uncertainty. "Do I shake you? Shout in your ear? Or just wait for you to come back to yourself?"

"I don't really know," I replied. "I can't feel my body when I'm inside someone's head, so... I guess you should just wait for me to come back?"

Sofia didn't like my answer—I didn't either—but she nodded, and said, "Good luck."

Without another word, I closed my eyes and looked for sharp emotions. I found a bunch of them—mostly from terrified passengers, but also pirate's greed or twisted lust. I hated the idea of diving into those minds, and almost involuntarily turned my attention to one other source of strong emotions.

Hatred bolstered by smug satisfaction shone like a beacon, sharp and strong. Rivera. Her emotions pulled strongly, and without conscious thought, I rode them to her. With a jarring mental crash, I entered Rivera's mind.

I had no idea what I would find inside Rivera's mind. Something like the horrible turmoil inside her mother's diseased head, I guessed. Or maybe even something pathetic, like the self-image I found in Peck's mind. But Rivera's mind was nothing like those. It reminded me of the first time I entered Sofia's mind. Rivera's mind was... tranquil.

A bright meadow surrounded me, stretching as far as the eye could see in all directions. The colors weren't quite right, but I couldn't put my figure on what was wrong. Then I remembered Rivera grew up on a space station, where wide open views didn't exist except through a view port. She probably never saw a meadow in her life, and what surrounded me was a child's imagined vision of one.

With that realization, I knew what was off about the view. The colors didn't come from nature. They came from a box of crayons. And now that I knew what to look for, I spotted places where green spiked into the too-blue sky. As if an enthusiastic child had colored outside the lines.

Suddenly, a looming caricature of Rivera's mother appeared before me. She moved jerkily back and forth in front of me, her legs and arms waving wildly. A blaster appeared in her hand, and she lifted it to her head. A crayon-yellow flash shot from the gun's barrel, then a round, black hole appeared in her head, and she fell over.

Fingers reached up from inside the hole, gripped the edge, and a person pulled herself out of Rivera's mother's head. The person looked at me and I realized it was a demonic version of my mom. Demon Mom held a bunch of strings in one hand, and those stretched back inside the hole in the dead woman's head. Mom grinned, pulled on a strand, and River's mother's hand moved.

Oh. That wasn't Mom. It was me. Only Rivera didn't know what I looked like, so I guess she assumed I looked like my mother. (I sort of do, except I'm not gorgeous like Mom. She and Dad say I am, but that's what loving parents *would* say. You know?)

Weird dream me reached out one hand. Sofia appeared and took it. Then the two of us skipped away across the meadow in the same jerking way the caricature Rivera's mother moved. The ground suddenly shook, and the skipping girls stumbled and fell. A towering version of Rivera came into view, a gleeful grin on her face. As dream me and Sofia raised their arms in terror, she raised a foot and stomped on them.

Rivera ground her foot on top of the squashed dream versions of Sofia and me. At the same time, a boy in his late teens or early twenties appeared. I'd seen him before in Rivera's mother's memories, so I knew it was her brother, Paco. He smiled up at giant Rivera and clapped for a moment. A bright circle of light suddenly appeared next to Paco. With a wave, he walked into the circle and disappeared.

The scene vanished, and the darkness I'd seen inside other minds replaced it. But with the darkness came one overwhelming emotion—deep contentment, the kind that comes from a job well done. I always heard about people who finally got what their heart desires the most, only to realize they were happier before they got everything they wanted. Rivera wasn't one of those people. On the heels of her feelings of satisfaction came bubbling joy.

I searched everywhere inside Rivera's head for some semblance of guilt, and I couldn't find the tiniest shred of any. Nor did I find anything like grief over her mother's death, not even in the darkest corners of Rivera's mind. All I found was happiness. All because she thought she'd killed an eighteen-year-old girl who never did anything to her or her family. Whose only crime was being born to parents Rivera learned to hate while growing up. It was like the idea that she might have made a mistake never even occurred to Rivera.

No remorse.

No regret.

And if Rivera didn't feel any of that over the girl she thought she killed, she wouldn't feel any guilt over selling her captives into slavery, ripping children from their parents, letting her crew have their way with a few selected captives, or cutting healthy people apart so she could sell their organs.

Unwilling to spend more time inside Rivera's mind, I found the spike of hatred she still held for my family and rode it back to my head. When I opened my eyes, I saw a concerned Sofia watching me intently.

"Nora, are you okay?" When I shook my head, Sofia enveloped me in a hug, and said, "Tell me what happened."

I hesitated for a moment, then the words came tumbling out. I described Rivera's dream as briefly as possible, then said, "Nothing that's happened bothers her. Not her mother's suicide. Not thinking she killed us. Her mother was insane, but Rivera is a monster pretending she's human."

Sofia tightened her hug, adopted a light tone of voice, and said, "Then it's a good thing we're on the case, right?"

I was still reeling from what I saw in Rivera's mind, so was I slow on the uptake. "What case? What are you talking about?"

"How do people deal with monsters in fairy tales?" she asked.

I furrowed my brow in confusion. "They run away and hide, like we did?"

"Yes, but then they track the monster to its lair and beat it." Sofia cocked her head to one side. "And who better to do it than Connaught and Olson, Interstellar Monster Hunters?"

I felt my gloom lift, and snorted a quick laugh. "How come you always know just the right thing to say to make me feel better?"

Sofia grinned. "Superior customer service training, courtesy of the Connaught Starline."

"When this is all over, remind me to ask Dad to give the trainers a raise."

"Hey, don't I get a raise, too?"

It took all my concentration, but I gave a nonchalant shrug. "If you want to stay on the *Pegasus*, sure. Or you could come be my roommate in college."

"I'd love that, Nora, but there's no *way* I can afford college right now."

"You saved my life, Sofia. Twice, even."

"And you saved mine, Nora."

"Okay, but I could never have done that if you hadn't saved me first. That means my family owes you big time, and Connaughts *always* pay their debts."

"Meaning?"

"My family will pay your tuition, room, and board."

Sofia studied me for a minute. "Are you serious?"

"Yes, but there *is* a downside to accepting."

"Like what?"

"You'll have to get used to Conley and Barber hovering protectively over you."

Sofia smiled. "I think I can live with that... roomie."

I pushed thoughts of Rivera, the pirates, and the fates of thousands of crew and passengers from my mind, and spent a moment concentrating on the idea of sharing an apartment and college classes with Sofia. I felt a smile stretch my lips, and said,

"Just don't hog all the cute college boys, okay? Leave one of them for me."

Sofia's eyes widened and her mouth moved, but no words came out.

"What?" I asked.

"You're kidding, right?"

"About what?"

"About *me* hogging all the boys. Are you crazy, Nora?"

"You're so pretty and friendly. The guys are going to follow you everywhere, Sofia."

"I know they will," she muttered, "but that's because I'll be walking next to *you*."

"Don't remind me." I grimaced, "Before I left, Mom and Dad talked to me about boys who would try to get close to me just because my family is super rich."

"Yeah, there will probably be a few vurgs, but—"

"What is a *vurg*?" I asked.

Sofia frowned. "You don't use that word on Ark's Landing?"

"I wouldn't ask if we did. The planet isn't exactly galactic central, you know. It takes a while for the latest slang to reach us."

"How about..." Sofia's eyes lost focus for a second. "What was the word Mom told me they used when she was a girl? Slo something?"

"Do you mean sloid?"

"Yes, that's it! A *vurg* is the same as a sloid." Having given an answer of sorts, Sofia continued, "But don't worry about vurgs— we'll spot them easily enough. The rest of the guys will follow us because you're friendly, famous, and—most of all—drop-dead gorgeous."

"You're confusing me with my mother."

"Uh, no, I'm not. Those files I read about your family had pictures from when your parents were just married. Your mom was beautiful, your dad was really cute, and—"

"They still are. Though I think Dad's too old to be called 'really cute,' anymore."

"*And*," Sofia continued, "you inherited your looks from both of them. God, Nora, didn't at least one boyfriend tell you how beautiful you are?"

I glanced away, "I've never had a boyfriend."

When I looked back at Sofia, she gave me an incredulous stare, and said, "You have *got* to be kidding? How is that even possible?"

I shrugged. "Ark's Landing isn't like the Federation. Most of the colonists still do things the old-fashioned way, and that includes courting."

"Courting? Are you serious?"

"Yes."

"Nora, are you telling me you've never been on a date?"

I shook my head.

"Then it's a good thing I'm so much older and wiser than you. Just trust me when I say a fully charged blaster won't keep the boys away from you."

I considered her words for a moment, but then said, "We can worry about my love life later. Right now, I need to get started on the psychological warfare."

The change in topic caught Sofia by surprise. "Um, okay... Are you sure you're up to it?"

"I have to be. I mean, it's not like we've got another empath to take my place."

Without giving myself time to reconsider, I closed my eyes and searched for emotions I thought a pirate would feel. Fear remained the dominant emotion on board the *Pegasus*, but it was also concentrated in one place—in the dining hall where the pirates had the crew and passengers. That made it easier to find the minds filled with greed, lust, and cruelty. I didn't want a repeat of the stuff I saw inside Rivera's head, so searched for the least slimy-feeling bundle of emotions. That search proved futile, so I just picked a mind at random and followed the greed it broadcast.

I still felt as if I smashed through a barrier when I entered the pirate's mind, but it wasn't as jarring as with Rivera or Rivera's mother. Was that because I was getting more used to being in another person's head? Or maybe this pirate had a weaker mind than the mother and daughter? Whatever the reason, I wasn't going to complain.

Remembering the lurking emotional horrors I'd found inside the two Riveras' minds, I steeled myself against whatever sick stuff I might discover in this pirate's mind and went to war.

Figuring I was as ready as I'd ever be, I probed the pirate's mind with my empathic ability. I found something that felt unreal, like Rivera's dream had, but this dream looked like something from the Teenage Boy Fantasy Handbook.

Pegasus crew uniforms were strewn about the floor while their owners—half-a-dozen naked girls, all about my age—flitted around a naked guy stretched out on a couch. The guy was *way* older than the girls. I mean, he had to be at least thirty! One girl dropped grapes into the pirate's mouth. Another stood ready with a beer. Three others caressed the guy's chest, while the sixth...

Ew!

I ignored the scene as best I could and went on the emotional offensive. When I'd been inside other heads, I'd ordered their minds to feel particular emotions. I tried taking it a step farther with this pirate. Conjuring the giant image of Rivera I'd seen in her dream—the one who squashed dream Sofia and me—I focused on projecting the vision into the pirate's dream.

For good measure, I imagined her shouting, *I ordered you to leave the crew alone! Do you* want *me to throw you into space?*

The pirate's fantasy burst like a bubble. The girls vanished, leaving the pirate naked before his giant captain.

No messing with the crew, got it? Not even in your dreams.

As the pirate nodded and covered himself, I let Rivera's image fade away. After she vanished, I sent one order to his mind.

You're angry at the new captain. She's got no right giving orders against having fun with the captives. No one like that should be a pirate captain!

I prayed my suggestions didn't make this pirate ignore the standing orders against messing with the crew, but that was the only emotional lever I found. Satisfied I'd done what I could, I abandoned his mind and looked for another.

I flitted from pirate mind to pirate mind, dug into their most sharply felt emotions, and did my best to twist those against Rivera. The things I saw in their heads made me want to puke. Two of them were so twisted, I took one look and got out of their minds as fast as I could. Yeah, they were even worse than what I'd seen inside Rivera's and her mother's heads.

I almost gave up on my plan after I found the first of those two psychos. But one glance at the bright red blob of fear coming from the passengers was enough to make me dive back in again. I lost count of the minds I visited, and none of them were what I'd call normal. Maybe that made what I was doing easier. Because emotions drove every pirate mind I visited.

They wanted riches, so stole the lives of those who had what they desired.

They wanted to forget their own miserable lives, so used their stolen treasure to buy drugs and cheap lovers.

When the money ran out, the pirates did it all over again. With no thought to the future, and no care or compassion for the lives they ruined along the way.

After I finally returned to my own mind, I spent a few minutes recovering from the greed and lust and misery I'd found in the pirates' minds. I gave a mental shudder, thinking about how I loved pirate adventure vids growing up. My run through pirate minds put those stories in a totally different light, and I knew I'd never be able to watch anything like that again.

I wasn't quite ready to open my eyes yet, but I heard Sofia gasp. My eyes flew open, and I asked, "What's wrong?"

Wide-eyed, she said, "Nothing was happening on the ship-wide comm, so I checked in on Conley and Barber. We can't talk to them, but I thought I'd see how they were doing, what with Rivera saying you're dead."

I felt a pang of guilt that the same idea hadn't occurred to me. "How are they doing? Do they believe Rivera?"

"They..." Sofia waved her hands helplessly.

"They *what*, Sofia?"

"They think they failed your grandfather. Worse, they think they failed *you*. And it's tearing them up."

Incredulity filled my voice. "Emotions? From Conley and Barber?"

"They may hide it, but those men love you like a sister." She drew a deep breath. "And they're planning on avenging your death—even if it means sacrificing their own lives."

TRAPPED

"**Y**ou're kidding, right?" Surprise and fear mingled in my voice. "Conley and Barber are willing to sacrifice their lives to avenge me?"

"Why does that surprise you?" Sofia asked. "You said they've been with you since you were ten."

"Yeah, but they've always been distant. The cool professionals, you know? Why didn't they ever say anything?"

Sofia shrugged. "Maybe they kept quiet to protect you?"

My eyebrows rose. "From what?"

"Getting too attached to them? I mean, how would you feel if they treated you like their kid sister and then one of them died saving your life?"

"Horrible. But I'd have felt just as horrible if one of them died regardless of how they treated me."

"Of course, but don't you think it would feel worse if you loved them like they love you?"

I opened my mouth to deny it, then made myself stop and really examine my feelings. You'd think an empath would be really good at figuring out feelings, but my ability is still new to me. Maybe all that understanding stuff came later? All I know is

I didn't have any better insight into my own feelings now than I had back on Ark's Landing.

"You're probably right." I closed my eyes, sighed, and said, "It figures those two would worry more about my feelings than about one of them dying."

Sofia pulled the comm from her ear and handed it to me. "So, give them a quick call and—"

As I slid the comm into my ear, I said, "The pirates will have taken all of Conley's and Barber's stuff long ago. That's why they put those nano transmitters in their ears and yours. We can hear what they hear, but we can't talk to them."

"What about using your psychic powers?"

"Oh my God! Why didn't I think of that?"

"Probably because you're too busy worrying about your bodyguards." Sofia smiled, "So it's a good thing you have me around to think of that stuff for you."

I closed my eyes and concentrated on finding Conley and Barber. But the red blob of the passengers' emotions overwhelmed everything in passenger territory. Earlier, I only found the pirates' minds because they weren't near that blob of concentrated terror. My bodyguards were too close to the other passengers for me to have any hope of finding them.

I opened my eyes and shook my head. "I can't find them. Maybe I could if I had more experience with my ability."

"Then what are we going to do?"

"*You* should wait here."

Sofia gave a firm head shake. "That's not going to happen."

"But you'll be safer—"

"Nora, how do you think I'll feel if I stay here and you get captured or killed?"

I saw determination in Sofia's eyes. "Okay. We'll both go."

"What are we going to do when we get there?"

"Once I'm sure no one is in the suite, I'll open the hidden door and—"

Sofia smacked her forehead with her free hand. "I'm such an

idiot. I should have told you that Conley and Barber are in the dining hall with all the other passengers."

That brought all my brilliant planning to a halt. "When did the pirates move them?"

"I don't know. They'd already been moved when I switched to their channel. But I heard lots of other voices talking around them and assumed those came from other passengers."

I gave a slow nod. "Yeah, that makes sense. There's no good reason for Rivera to keep Conley and Barber separate from the other passengers."

"How are we going to warn them now?"

"I don't know. We'll just have to look at the situation and see what we figure out."

Sofia's eyes darted around our little section of the *Pegasus's* hull. "Um, I don't see an airlock anywhere. How are we going to get back inside the ship?"

"We'll go in through the lifepod launch bay."

"It doesn't have any air, Nora. Won't that keep the hatch from opening?"

"Yeah, but there has to be a way to pressurize the bay. I mean, imagine if a crewman launched a lifepod using the same controls we did. There would have to be some way for him to get back inside the ship, right?"

Sofia gave a cautious nod. "I guess so..."

"And the controls have to be easy to reach for the same reason. We just have to find them. Then, after we pressurize the launch bay, we sneak back into the maintenance tunnels, head for the dining hall, and then let Conley and Barber know we're not dead."

"You make it sound so easy, Nora."

I put all the false confidence I could muster into my voice. "That's because it will be easy. You'll see."

Sofia drew a deep breath, then released it. "When do we start?"

"It's still early morning, ship's time. With luck, the pirates who aren't on duty guarding the passengers or flying the ship will still be sleeping. We might as well go now."

"Okay. Let's do it."

Returning to the launch bay wasn't quite as terrifying as I thought it would be. But that's probably because I kept all my attention on the safety lines and Sofia and didn't look into deep space even one time. Once I was safely inside the bay, I reeled Sofia to me.

It was a huge relief having gravity again, but I was still tethered to the safety ring inside the launch bay. Then we began searching for the controls I prayed would be there. God—and the design engineers—answered my prayer before I even sent it, and Sofia found the controls on the other side of the bay. Once again, the controls were so simple, even a passenger could figure them out. I activated the control and, after an interminable ten-second wait, the pressure was high enough for us to hear the hiss of air pouring into the bay.

"Nora, the launch hatch didn't close. What's keeping the air inside?" Sofia asked.

"Probably a bigger version of the shields our atmosphere harnesses use."

Five minutes later, the pressure gauge on the control turned green. My stomach fluttered when I turned off my harness, but I had no trouble breathing. I even spotted the light blue haze of an atmosphere shield stretched across the opening to space.

When Sofia saw me breathing normally, she turned her harness off, too. I coiled a safety line and stored it in my backpack. Then we made our way back to the hatch that led into the *Pegasus*, pressed our ears against it, and listened intently. Neither of us heard anything.

I closed my eyes and checked my psychic mental map for nearby people. The closest ones weren't moving around, at least.

I glanced at Sofia and nodded. And she nodded back.

I opened the hatch and stuck my head just far enough through the hatch to glance up and down the long corridor outside the launch bay. It was empty, but I heard low voices coming from the crew quarters. The voices didn't grow louder, which probably meant their owners weren't moving our way.

Granddaddy always told me to make a decision and go with it, because indecision kills more people than mistaken decisions. I took a deep breath and stepped through the hatch. Sofia followed me out and pressed the button to close the launch bay hatch. Then we walked purposefully towards the maintenance tunnel entrance.

My heart hammered in my chest and I thought our footsteps sounded like a pair of giants stomping through the corridor. The half-height maintenance tunnel door was only a dozen meters away, but being out in the open made it feel more like a dozen kilometers. I kept my blaster drawn and ready while praying I wouldn't have to use it.

As we approached the tunnel entrance, Sofia sped up just enough to get there first. As she opened the door, the voices from the crew quarters grew louder and more distinct.

"Hurry!" I hissed. "They're coming this way!"

As Sofia ducked through the door, the voices got close enough for me to make out the last few words the pirates said.

"Don't see why we gotta waste time in the tunnels."

A chill ran down my spine as I crouched and followed Sofia.

"The captain says we guard 'em. I don't need no other reason."

The tunnel door clicked shut, cutting off the voices. But I had to assume the pirates were on their way to the door we just went through. We had to get far from the door quickly and quietly.

Sofia turned a pale face my way and whispered, "What now?"

"Stay quiet and follow me."

The closest side tunnel was five meters away, but it was aft of us. That was the opposite direction from where we wanted to go. Without hesitation, I headed towards it. I stopped at the corner where the side tunnel intersected ours and cautiously glanced around the corner.

No pirates lurked in it. It went about five meters and turned, heading aft towards crew quarters again. Still not the way I wanted to go, but it wasn't like we had any other choices.

I led Sofia into the new corridor, and we scurried down to the corner where it turned. Behind us, the tunnel door we'd just gone through clicked open.

"Wilkins, you patrol aft," a woman ordered. "The rest of you —you're for'ard with me."

"Got it, chief," another woman—Wilkins, I guess—replied.

I heard someone enter the main tunnel and head our way. We had to get out of sight of the main corridor *now*.

A man whined, "*I* wanted aft."

It went against my training to round the corner without looking, but we had to get out of sight before the pirate reached our side tunnel. I led Sofia around the corner. The tunnel went another three meters and dead-ended in a door. I had Sofia go around me while I crouched at the corner. If Wilkins came our way, we'd be trapped between the door into the unknown and the pirate. Could I take her out without alerting the other four pirates, or were we better off going through the door?

As the remaining four pirates entered the tunnels, the woman in charge said, "No way. After that stunt Peck and you tried with the crew woman yesterday, the captain don't want you anywhere near the crew."

Wilkins barked a laugh, and it was so close I almost jumped out of my skin. Her footsteps paused when she reached our side tunnel.

"Hey, chief?" Wilkins called.

"Yeah?" the woman in charge of the tunnel guards replied.

"Got any idea what's down this tunnel?"

"Hang on, let me check the map." A few seconds passed, then the chief said, "It's just a back way into the engine room.

You can check it now and then go on into the engine room, or do it at the end of your rounds."

I turned off the blaster's safety and changed the setting from stun to kill. If the pirate came this way, maybe I could make her keep quiet by threatening to kill her.

But Wilkins still hadn't decided. "You got any idea who's on duty in the engine room?"

Behind me, the door softly clicked open. I whipped my head around in time to see Sofia peek through the door.

The chief replied to Wilkins, "York and his boys."

"Thanks!" Wilkins called. Under her breath, she added, "If I know York, he's got coffee going. Could use me some of that."

I heard Wilkins start down the tunnel towards us. Sofia crawled through the door and waved me after her. With a mental prayer for divine protection, I followed Sofia into the *Pegasus's* engine room.

Sofia glanced right and left and apparently decided. She stayed crouched and hurried to her left. I took a few precious seconds closing the tunnel door, then followed her without hesitation. With the pirate Wilkins mere meters behind us, it's not like I had any other choice.

I heard voices behind me. They rose above the soft sound of machinery, but didn't sound alarmed, so I ignored them. Five meters ahead of me, Sofia ducked behind some kind of console. She glanced back and waved frantically, exhorting me to move faster. I quickened my pace while Sofia kept her gaze locked on the tunnel door.

As soon as I was within her reach, she grabbed my arm and dragged me behind the console with her. The move caught me by surprise, and I sprawled across Sofia. I'm sure it hurt, but Sofia never made a sound. Instead, she released my hand, grabbed my legs, and pulled them up to my chest.

The tunnel door slammed open just after Sofia dragged me out of sight. She all but cradled me in her lap as we both held our breath.

"What the—?" a man called as all the other voices fell silent.

"Ha!" Wilkins crowed. "Gotcha, York!"

"Don't go doing that, woman," York said. "I thought you were the captain doing one of her surprise inspections."

Wilkins' voice faded a bit, as if she turned away from us. "You worried about her finding something wrong?"

"She always does," York growled.

Footsteps sounded as Wilkins walked towards the pirate engineer. "Yeah, she can be a real pain in the ass."

"Why are you up so early?" York asked. "And what are you doing in the maintenance tunnels?"

"Gimme some coffee, and I'll tell you."

Wilkins and York fell silent, I assume, while York got coffee. With the pirates distracted, Sofia and I untangled, and I got my first good look at the surroundings.

Our hiding place was a typical starship's console. It was a little over a meter high, three meters wide, and gave good cover only as long as the pirates stayed away from it. We'd be in big trouble if one of them came our way to check readings on the console.

"We can't stay here," I whispered. Pointing at the other end of the console, I continued, "Can you crawl down there and look around it? Look for more maintenance tunnel doors. And pirates, of course."

Sofia nodded and turned away. Meanwhile, I cautiously peeked around my corner.

Fifteen meters away, one woman—Wilkins, obviously—and five men gathered around a small table. In one hand, the woman held a mug with the Connaught Starlines logo embossed on it. She gestured with her other hand while she talked.

"We ain't had much luck with captains on this trip," Wilkins said. "The first went crazy—"

"Crazier, you mean," a man said.

Wilkins barked a sour laugh. "You got that right. Anyhow,

the first went and shot herself. You mark my words, that'll bring us bad luck."

"Already did," a second man said. "Look who be captain now."

"That's my point," Wilkins said. "And what did our new captain do? She went and killed that rich girl! We coulda sold her back to her folks for more money than we'll get for everyone else on the ship."

A third man spoke, and I recognized York's voice. It had an edge to it as he said, "Are you suggesting we mutiny?"

Wilkins waved her free hand in negation. "Nah. But we're gonna have to elect a new captain when we get back to the base. I don't care if she's a worse psycho than her mother, I just don't want anyone who lost us hundreds of millions of credits running our gang."

York shook his head. "Blasting that lifepod wasn't stupid. We couldn't leave that girl alive to tell tales."

"We coulda come about and picked 'em up," Wilkins said.

"Would have wasted too much time, especially after the lifepod launched a drone back towards Ark's Landing. I don't know about you, but I don't want to still be in this system when the girl's daddy comes hunting for her with a battle cruiser."

"We coulda sent *our* ship to get 'em, if the dead captain hadn't sent it on ahead."

In case you're wondering, it's pretty weird sitting around listening to people debate whether your supposed death was a good idea or not. But compared to some of the unsettling stuff I'd experienced in the last twenty-four hours, this conversation wasn't even in the top five.

Sofia tapped my knee and whispered, "There's another maintenance tunnel door on the other wall. It's about five meters away, and there's nothing to hide behind."

"Could you see any pirates?"

She shook her head. "I think they're all getting coffee."

"Then let's get out of here while the getting is good."

Sofia and I crawled to the other end of the console, rose to a crouch, then she peered around the corner. She waved us forward, and we came out into the open. The tunnel door was right where Sofia said it would be, and we hurried towards it.

Just as we reached the door, I heard Wilkins say, "Thanks for the coffee, York, but I better get back to my rounds. Wouldn't want the new captain thinking I wasn't doing my job."

"Have fun," York said.

"Riiiight," Wilkins drawled. "Which way to the nearest tunnel entrance?"

"Over this way."

Footsteps sounded, and they were coming our way!

NO-TALENT NORA RETURNS

The pirates' footsteps sounded ominously loud on the engine room's metal deck. Worse, the pirates would have a clear view of us over the control consoles in less time than we needed to run back to our original hiding place. That left only one choice for us.

I reached past a fear-frozen Sofia, opened the tunnel door, and shoved Sofia in the back. "Go, go, *go!*"

My push broke Sofia's paralysis, and she scooted into the tunnel. I stayed right on her heels. The door made an audible click when I pulled it shut. I just prayed the engine room's background noise drowned out the sound of the door closing.

A maze of maintenance tunnels surrounded the engine room, so we had our pick of directions. Sofia turned towards the closest side tunnel, but I caught her attention and shook my head.

"Take the third tunnel on the right," I whispered.

She nodded and headed for it, but asked, "Why that one?"

"According to the tunnel map Granddaddy had me memorize, it goes inside the engine and has dozens of side tunnels."

Sofia nodded her understanding. Five seconds later, she ducked down that side tunnel. Before I could follow her, I heard the tunnel door open behind me. I immediately dove into the side tunnel, tucked, rolled up into a crouch, and waited for Wilkins' cry that she spotted me.

Instead, I heard York say, "You can ignore all the side tunnels around the engine room. Me and my team are always going in and out of them. I got three in there right now. They know the captain's latest code words, so give the guys a chance to speak before you go raising an alarm."

"Gotcha," Wilkins said. "Catch you on my next circuit. And keep the coffee hot for me."

I listened to that exchange as Sofia and I moved away from the main tunnel as quietly as possible. We ducked into the first side tunnel we came to, pressed up against the wall, and listened as the tunnel door slammed shut behind Wilkins.

"Ow, my back," Wilkins groaned, "I'm getting too old for crawling around like this."

Her footsteps echoed down the tunnel as she approached the first turn we'd taken. She passed it without pausing, and I sighed with relief. That feeling lasted all of three seconds.

"Hey!" Wilkins called. "Who's down there?"

Sofia and I exchanged worried glances. Without a word, we set off down our latest tunnel and away from Wilkins.

"I can hear you moving around down there," Wilkins called. "Give me the code phrase or else."

Ahead of us, a man's voice yelled, "I'm busy."

We stopped, stuck between Wilkins behind us and the unknown pirate ahead of us.

"What?" Wilkins called. "You got to speak clearer."

I pointed back to an alcove we had just passed and led Sofia back to it.

"I *said*, I'm busy!"

"Still can't understand you over all the engine noise," Wilkins shouted. "You gotta come out here so I can see you."

The alcove was less than two meters long, with access to all sorts of conduits and other stuff I didn't understand.

"Yeah, yeah," the man yelled. "Gimme a minute."

I pushed Sofia into the back corner and crouched protectively in between her and the alcove's entrance.

"What are we going to do?" she hissed.

"I don't know. Pray the guy is mad enough that he doesn't see us?"

"There's got to be *something* we can do!"

Wilkins yelled, "Get out here! *Now!*"

"Okay," the man called. "I'm coming. I'm coming."

We heard the pirate moving our way down the tunnel.

Something niggled at the back of my mind. A story Dad told me about how he used his empathic ability to hide in plain sight. But what was it he did? My attention must have been on something else when he told the story, because I—

Wait! Inattention. That was it! Dad broadcast indifference, and the man searching for them overlooked them. Could I do that with the approaching pirate?

I glanced at Sofia and whispered, "Hide behind me as best you can. I have an idea."

I turned away from my friend, closed my eyes, called up my mental map of the surrounding emotions, and found a blob of irritation coming our way. The pirate's emotion was far weaker than Sofia's fear or Rivera's hatred, but it was all I had to work with. I reached out with my empathic powers and groped for his thread of irritation.

As the pirate neared the alcove where Sofia and I hid, his wispy strand of irritation flitted around me like a leaf caught in a whirlwind. I had three or four seconds to get inside the man's mind, but his emotion didn't have a single focus. Sofia's fear anchored on me or Rivera, and Rivera's hatred fixed firmly on me. But it seemed as if the approaching pirate was just in a bad mood.

I got the idea the pirate was irritated at Wilkins for demanding he show himself to her and give the code phrase. Then something else drew Bad Mood Boy's attention and became the new source of his ire. His lack of focus meant his strand of irritation kept moving. I'd reach for it with my ability, but it would flick away just before I grabbed it. The whole situation would have been comical if Sofia's life and mine didn't hang in the balance.

Since I hadn't entered the pirate's mind, my normal senses still had access to the real world. Out there, I heard Wilkins shout, "Hurry up! I ain't got all day."

I assumed that her demand would draw Bad Mood Boy's attention, made an educated guess where his emotion would point, and lunged for it. The strand whipped my way, and I grabbed it with my empathic ability. The line into the Bad Mood Boy's mind felt fragile, like I'd break it if I didn't handle it with care. But I didn't have time for that kind of caution, and pulled myself along the thread of irritation as quickly as possible.

And...

I slid seamlessly into Bad Mood Boy's mind without a jarring crash. One instant I was inside my mind, and the next I was inside his. I don't know if I was getting better at this stuff or if I was just invading weaker minds, but I didn't waste any time considering the issue, either. As the darkness of his mind enveloped me, I began issuing commands.

Boring. Everything is so boring. Nothing ever happens. Because it's boring. So boring you don't care about anything anymore. There's nothing to see. No one to notice. No reason to even look around. Because it's so boring.

You couldn't care less about anything but getting to the irritating woman who keeps shouting at you, and giving her the code phrase. That's the only *thing that matters now. Nothing else is worth noticing.*

You don't care about the job.

You don't care about anything around you.

You don't care about anything at all, except for giving her the code phrase.

Once my commands for indifference and boredom got into a basic rhythm, I turned part of my attention towards figuring out how long I'd been inside Bad Mood Boy's head. Was he approaching the alcove that served as our entirely inadequate hiding place? Was he right there at the alcove's entrance? Or had he already passed by it?

I had no guess. Because when I was in another person's head, I didn't experience time the same way as when I was in my own head. But there had to be *some* way I could figure it out. Or at least make an educated guess. But how?

On the edge of my perception, I felt Bad Mood Boy's irritation whip off in another direction. Man, the guy really had the attention span of a gnat. He couldn't even keep his irritation focused on one thing for more than... one... second... at a time.

That was it! By the time I entered Bad Mood Boy's mind, he was almost at the alcove. Assuming he didn't stop or change his pace, he'd be past the alcove in two or three seconds. I'd give him four just to be safe. All I had to do was count the number of times he directed his ire at something new and pop out of his head after the fourth time.

I was so pleased with my idea, I almost forgot to keep the stream of boredom and disinterest orders going. But even as I did a little mental happy dance for my idea, I kept the orders flowing into Bad Mood Boy's mind.

Meanwhile, his irritation flickered again. And then a third time. Then, finally, a fourth time. Hoping I'd guessed right, I followed Bad Mood Boy's irritation out of his head and snapped back into my own mind.

I opened my eyes, afraid I'd find a pirate glaring at us in the alcove's entrance. No one was there. Better, I heard footsteps receding.

I turned to a white-faced Sofia and whispered, "How did it go?"

She gave a little shake, and replied, "He looked down here, and I thought we were dead. But his eyes just slid over us and he kept going."

"I can't wait to tell Dad how his old stories saved us. Let's give him another few seconds, then get out of here."

"Aren't he and that Wilkins woman blocking the way?"

I shook my head. "There are lots of ways in and out of the tunnels around the engine. But there are also two more pirates in the area, so we'll have to be really careful."

Sofia offered a weak grin. "I thought you said caution was your middle name?"

"I did, but *you* said it was Erin."

"I changed my mind. Caution can be your middle name. Especially now."

In the distance, Bad Mood Boy's footsteps became noticeably quieter, as if he'd turned a corner. I thought about listening for the code phrase, but decided against it. We wanted to be as far from this alcove as possible by the time Bad Mood Boy returned.

I rose to a crouch. "Let's get going, Sofia."

I led Sofia away from Bad Mood Boy's receding footsteps, which also took us away from his impending meeting with Wilkins. The maintenance tunnels twisted and turned through the *Pegasus's* enormous engines. We passed access panels and control boards and a lot of other stuff I didn't recognize. All the while, I watched my mental map of emotions and compared it to the tunnel layout Granddaddy had me memorize.

I took a longer route than necessary to avoid the two other pirates working the tunnels. Fortunately, they weren't moving around, so avoiding them was time-consuming but not dangerous.

The small part of mind that remembered my life before pirates captured the *Pegasus* boggled at the idea that sneaking through maintenance tunnels to avoid blood-thirsty pirates wasn't dangerous. Has my concept of safety truly changed that radically?

You spent the last eight hours tied to the outer hull of the Pegasus,

Nora. And you did it because it was safer than staying inside the ship. So, yeah, your idea of safety is totally out of whack.

To think my parents did this sort of thing not once, not twice, but *three* times. I mean, how were they still even sane? Sure, I told friends on Ark's Landing that my parents were crazy all the time. And they all nodded and said their parents were the same. That's what kids are supposed to do, right? And I'm the dutiful oldest child, so I'm always trying to live up to their expectations.

Is that why you're pretending you're the hero, Nora? Because you know it's what your mother and father would do? Only they wouldn't have to pretend.

Wow, I really had *not* missed No-Talent Nora and her downer comments. I even hoped she was gone for good.

You can't get rid of me that easily. You got lucky a couple of times, Nora. That doesn't make you a hero.

Shut up! I'm sick and—

"Nora?" Sofia asked. "What's wrong?"

"Huh? What makes you ask that?"

"Your posture just got all stiff, like you were angry at something."

With my attention divided between the mental maps, my internal discussion, and Sofia's question, I accidentally told her the truth. "I'm just arguing with No-Talent Nora."

Sofia's eyebrows rose. "Who?"

"It's nothing."

Sofia obviously didn't believe me, but she didn't press. Not until we reached a section of tunnels far from any patrolling pirates and took a few minutes to rest.

As I sipped from my water bottle, Sofia asked, "Who is No-Talent Nora?"

I thought about waving off the question, but Sofia nearly died protecting me. If anyone deserved honesty, it was her.

"She's me," I said. "A little part of me, anyway. She first showed up when my sister's empathic ability manifested. Nancy was six, but suddenly she had abilities like Dad and I still didn't. No-Talent Nora started whispering that I didn't deserve powers. She got louder and more insistent when Eric got his powers a couple of years later." I shrugged. "No-Talent Nora has been with me ever since."

Sofia was silent for a moment, then asked, "Even now?"

"Yeah."

"What was she whispering to you just now?"

"That my parents are heroes, and I'm just a little kid pretending I can be like them."

"Humph! You tell No-Talent Nora that *I* say you're the bravest, most heroic person I know."

I couldn't stop a wry smile from forming. "She'll tell you to get out more." I wiped the smile from my face and looked at Sofia. "Or just look in a mirror."

Sofia shook her head. "I'm terrified, Nora."

"But you haven't given up, Sofia. And that's what makes you so brave."

"You haven't given up, either, Nora."

I looked down at the deck. "I've just had more training than you."

"That makes you better prepared." Sofia put a hand under my chin and lifted my head so she could look into my eyes. "But no matter how well-trained you are, it still takes courage to keep going."

"I... guess?"

Sofia blew out an exasperated breath. "Would your parents have done anything different if they were here?"

"Yeah. Dad would have sucked up all the passengers' fear and then blasted the pirates' minds with it. Then Mom would have kicked the crap out of any pirates still standing, disarmed them, and captured them all."

"But what would their eighteen-year-old selves have done?"

I opened my mouth to say they'd have done the same thing,

then remembered that was before Dad's ability broke through. I closed my mouth.

Sofia said, "Right, they'd have done the same things you did. Except your father couldn't have gone inside minds, like you can. So stop comparing yourself to your parents. When they were your age, they hadn't done anything close to what you've done so far."

"That's only because—"

Sofia covered my mouth. "Stop inventing excuses for why you don't think you measure up to them. *I* say you do, and we've already agreed that I'm older and wiser. So tell No-Talent Nora I said to shut up and go away."

Did you hear what Sofia said, No-Talent Nora?

She didn't respond.

"Good," Sofia said. "Now, don't we have a couple of your bodyguards to save?"

I put away my water and rose to a crouch. "Yep."

I summoned my emotional map, checked it against the tunnel layout, and saw that none of the pirates were nearby. Without another word, Sofia and I started forward to find and warn Conley and Barber.

Sofia and I communicated with simple hand signals as we crept through the maintenance tunnels. I couldn't tell her much beyond *stop, go,* or *turn here,* and a part of me wished I'd taken the time to work out a more detailed set of gestures. The rest of me remembered how long it took me to learn the complex set of signals Granddaddy devised for my bodyguards and knew a more complex series of gestures would have confused Sofia. We had enough problems with the patrolling pirates without adding miscommunication to the mix.

I tracked the pirates with my empathic ability and overlaid their movements on my memorized tunnel layout. And it was mentally exhausting. Sure, I'd used my ability to check on the pirates' locations before Sofia and I slipped through the ship's corridors. But that was just a quick scan I did and I dropped it almost immediately. Keeping constant track of five pirates and their locations in the tunnels took almost all my concentration. I had enough brain power left to see my surroundings, move quietly, and make those simple hand signals to Sofia, but not much more. But that wasn't the worst thing I discovered.

As we drew closer to the huge red blob of the passengers' emotions, I realized the pirates would vanish into the blob when they patrolled close to the dining hall. It wasn't a problem at the moment, but it would be huge when we neared the dining hall. I'd lose the ability to track the movement of the pirates most likely to discover us. Maybe the passengers' emotions would be so overwhelming, I'd lose track of *all* the pirates. Either way, it would leave Sofia and me way more vulnerable than I was comfortable with.

I'd always known we'd be vulnerable during the few seconds it would take me to dive inside Conley's or Barber's mind. (And that was assuming I could pick them out from the mass of frightened and angry passengers.) But the new vanishing pirate bit meant we'd be trusting to luck and our normal senses to avoid detection. For *minutes* rather than seconds.

I doubted that much luck existed in the galaxy, much less around Sofia and me. Besides, Granddaddy taught me, "Lady Luck exists, Nora, but you must never count on her favors to keep you alive. Graveyards are full of men and women who relied too much on luck and too little on their abilities." Then he surprised me by pulling me into a hug and whispering in my ear, "For God's sake, remember this. It would tear me apart if anything ever happened to you."

Granddaddy hardly ever showed his emotions like that. (Where do you think Conley and Barber got the whole stoic bodyguard thing? Yeah, they picked it up from Granddaddy.) I mean, I always knew he loved me and all, but I had to learn how to see it. It helped that Mom and Grandmama were around to translate Granddaddy's gruff manner, but I knew his ways well by the time he gave me the Luck Hug. Yeah, I named it, because it made a *huge* impression on me. Knowing Granddaddy, he probably planned it exactly that way.

But it worked. I'll never forget his point. That's why I never once stopped tracking the pirates. And avoiding them was dead easy while we crossed from crew territory to passenger territory. But the closer we came to the dining hall, the harder it was to dodge patrolling pirates. We ended up backtracking almost as often as we went forward, all to avoid the pirates' patrol pattern. The worst part of the whole thing was the pirates obviously knew what they were doing. Someone must have planned their routes using the same tunnel diagrams I memorized.

Without my empathic abilities as a guide, I know the pirates would have caught us. But the constant concentration really took a toll on me. I didn't even realize how bad it was until Sofia caught my hand and pulled me to a stop.

"You've got to rest, Nora," she whispered. "You're worn out."

I panted, "I'm... fine."

I hadn't even realized I was gasping for breath until that moment. Without speaking, I raised a hand in surrender to Sofia. But where could we go where I could drop my mental tracking and truly rest? The pirates were all over the tunnels around us, so hiding in them was out.

Sofia had obviously been thinking about just that. "Go to your suite. With Conley and Barber gone, the pirates don't have any reason to check on it."

I nodded, recognizing her idea was better than anything I'd come up with. We set off for the hidden door into my suite. What should have been a one-minute trip took fifteen since we still had to dodge pirates. But we finally reached the door. I concentrated my ability on the suite on the other side of the bulkhead and found nothing. The retina reader scanned my eye, and the door softly popped open.

Sofia and I crowded into my tiny bedroom. She closed the door behind us while I quietly searched the rest of the suite. Satisfied we were the only occupants, I returned to my bedroom and shut the door. If anyone entered the suite, they wouldn't immediately spot us.

I showed Sofia how the blaster worked, handed her the comm unit, and said, "Listen in on Conley and Barber. Wake me up in an hour, or if it sounds like my bodyguards are getting ready to take their revenge."

I stretched out on the bed, dropped my mental tracking of

the pirates and felt immediate relief to have the now-normal mental whiteout replace it. Seconds later, I fell asleep.

~

My mental alarm clock woke me after one hour. That's something Mom and Granddaddy taught me, and another in an ever-growing list of skills I never thought I'd need. I mean, who needs a mental alarm when you can set your comm to do the same thing? And, being a smartass kid, I said as much to them.

He gave me a typical Granddaddy non-explanation. "If you ever find yourself on the run, you'll be glad you've got it."

"What your grandfather means," Mom said, "is that exhausted people sleep through alarms all the time. But if you train yourself to wake up on a schedule you set, you won't have to worry about that."

And they were right. Not that it really mattered this time, since I saw Sofia leaning over me when I opened my eyes.

"You're already awake?" At my nod, she asked, "Do you feel better?"

My eyes felt gritty. My thighs and lower back were still sore from being hunched over in the maintenance tunnels. And my brain still felt foggy. So I said, "Yeah, I'm fine. What about you? How are you doing?"

She flashed a half smile, half grimace. "I spent half the time you were sleeping massaging my legs, and the other half stretching my back."

I sat up and stretched, and it felt so amazingly good. I stood and stretched some more.

"I'm sorry I'm putting you through all this, Sofia."

"Well, I'm not."

I paused mid-stretch. "You're not?"

"It's got to be better than being in pirate hands. That crew woman we heard screaming and crying in the crew quarters could have been me. Or they could have forced me to watch, helpless to do anything but pray they didn't pick me next. Compared to what could happen to me, sore muscles are nothing." Sofia flashed an honest smile. "Besides, I'm one of only two people on the *Pegasus* who knows there's hope for a rescue."

"So, no pressure, huh?"

I meant it as a joke, but the fear that I would fail everyone on board the ship leaked into my voice.

"That's No-Talent Nora talking." Sofia crossed her arms and glared at me. "And I've already told you my opinion of *her*."

Sofia looked so fiercely protective, I couldn't help giving a short laugh. "Yes, mother."

Sofia gave an imperious sniff. "That's better. Now, young lady, don't you have a pair of bodyguards to contact?" When I nodded, she said, "We're a lot closer to the dining hall now. Is there any chance you can pick them out from here?"

I shrugged. "It's worth a try."

Closing my eyes, I brought up the mental map of shipboard emotions. As before, the dining room was one big, red blob of fear. Lots of little maroon blobs moved around the rest of the ship, and I realized a few of them were brighter and easier to track. I guessed those were the pirate minds I entered when I started waging psychological warfare on them. One of the brighter blobs approached the passengers, accompanied by two duller blobs. The dull ones vanished into the roiling sea of emotions created by the passengers, but the mind I'd entered stood out from everyone else.

Could I enter that mind and ride with him while he wandered among the passengers? I couldn't see why not. I mean, I'd entered his mind before, and I already knew the second time was easier than the first. But would it do me any good? Even if I could ride inside the pirate's mind, it wouldn't make finding Conley and Barber easier. I could read the pirate's emotions, but wouldn't have any way of telling if the pirate went near my bodyguards. And even if he did, he'd have to direct an emotion towards them. If he did that, I could probably ride that emotion from the pirate into one of my bodyguards' minds.

But what were the odds the pirate would even consider finding Conley and Barber?

The odds are really good if you enter his mind and order him to feel something associated with them.

Of course! That was how I could find my bodyguards! Fighting to keep my expectations low, I dove into the pirate's mind.

~

I pushed through the mental barrier that surrounded every mind I'd ever entered, and found myself back inside the pirate's head. Just like normal. Or new normal, since popping in and out of people's heads was something I'd only been doing for a day.

Or was it two?

I realized I had no idea how much time had passed since the *Pegasus* entered the wormhole that changed my life. Before that, a psychic ability was something I dreamed of having, and pirates were just rogues—lovable ones, most of the time—in adventure stories. And here I was, just a short time later, using my strange version of Dad's empathic ability to enter the mind of a real pirate, one who had nothing in common with the ones in stories. All so I could keep my bodyguards from getting themselves killed to avenge my death. Well, supposed death, since that was just a ruse to get the new pirate captain off my back long enough for Dad to get my message, mobilize the Ark's Landing Navy, track me down with his empathic ability, and save the day.

No wonder I've been so tired lately.

Anyway, back to the pirate's mind. His was filled with the filth I expected from this bunch of psychopaths who captured the *Pegasus*. Sparks of lust flashed through his mind nonstop. It's like the guy couldn't look at a woman without imagining having his way with her.

Were all guys like this pirate? Surely not, right? I mean, after twenty years of marriage, Dad still only had eyes for Mom. My brother Eric didn't make a drooling fool of himself whenever my friends came over for a visit. And I already knew the pirates were a bunch of sickos. So most guys were probably fine. For the sake of my future dating life, I sure hoped I was right.

I'd let my mind wander, so yanked my attention back to the pirate's emotional landscape. It was just as barren of warm, human emotions as all the other pirate minds had been. I dodged the sparks of lust as best I could and shuddered at the visions carried by the ones I couldn't avoid. Flashes of greed hit me now and then, too, but there weren't as many of those as I'd expected. Maybe that was because the pirate had women all around him and the money he expected to get for the passengers wasn't in his hand yet?

Whatever. I wasn't inside the guy's head to figure out what drove his depraved desires. I was here to get him to go to Conley and Barber.

If I was a telepath, I could probably just give him a direct order to go to my bodyguards. But I'm an empath. How could I do that just by using the guy's emotions?

I had to try something, so I ordered, *It sure would be fun to taunt the dead rich girl's bodyguards. Laugh at them for completely failing at their job. Yeah, that would be the funniest thing ever. I bet it will scare the rest of the passengers, too, and that will make them easier to handle.*

I stopped sending orders and watched the emotions flying around me. Since I wasn't dodging the sparks, a lot more of them hit me. At first, the sparks were the usual mix of lust and greed. If I'd had a stomach, those visions would have turned it. So, I guess it's just as well I couldn't feel my body while I was inside another mind.

Then a spark filled with malicious glee hit me. Another

followed. Then another. They all conveyed visions of a mighty pirate looming over two cringing men and laughing.

Bingo!

Yes, I ordered, *go lord it over those two bodyguards! They deserve it. Living the easy life with those rich people, when you have to risk your life as a pirate just to get money and women! Oh yeah, you should definitely make those guys regret the day they ever saw you!*

Maybe I was pouring it on a bit thick, but none of the emotions flying around me held any suspicion. They just held more and more sadistic joy.

And then the sparks of emotion coalesced into a bright beam streaming out of the pirate's mind. Praying that meant Conley or Barber were at the other end of the beam, I caught hold and rode the pirate's cruelty out of his head and into the unknown.

STRAWBERRIES MEAN LIFE

I crashed into the strongest mental barrier I'd run into yet. Unlike all the other barriers I'd run into, I didn't simply smash through this one. I got stuck, instead. I felt like I'd tried wriggling through an opening that was too small for me and my hips got stuck.

In the real world, I'd try going backwards. Okay, in the real world, I'd never have tried pulling myself through such a small opening. Not unless whatever was behind me was worse than the thought of getting stuck. But that was the situation I faced now. *Not* entering this mind meant giving up on my bodyguards. Or letting them throw their lives away for no reason.

I couldn't do that. For eight years, Conley and Barber had been there for me. Ready to trade their lives for mine. There was no way I could let myself fail the first time they needed me to be there for them.

So I pushed and pulled and squirmed and wriggled and cursed and clawed and suddenly popped through the barrier and into the mind beyond. But was it Conley's or Barber's mind, or some random passenger the pirate felt like taunting?

I was pretty sure the mind belonged to one of my body-guards. I mean, they're about as strong-willed and hard-headed as two men can be. That's why Granddaddy put them in charge of my security team. The guys in charge of my sibs' teams were so similar that the three of us used to swap you-won't-guess-what-my-bodyguard-did stories. We'd whisper and laugh and cast surreptitious glances at our bodyguards to see who watched us with the most expressionless stares. Conley and Barber almost always won that competition. They *never* let emotion show. Never let it show to us kids, at least. And the surrounding mind was exactly like those faces.

Emotionless.

Dark.

I expected that. What I didn't expect was the oppressive weight I felt. The mind around me felt... thick? No, not that. Restricting. Controlled. Hard to move through. And that gave me more hope that I'd entered one of the two minds I wanted.

I... *swam* is the best word I can come up with. I swam through the darkness, looking for some sign of emotional life. This was only the second non-pirate mind I'd entered—Sofia's was the first, obviously—and I hadn't considered the difference between the normal and pirate minds until now. Every pirate mind I'd seen was filled with flitting, flashing emotions. So many emotions I couldn't dodge them all, no matter how hard I tried. But I had to go looking for emotions in the other minds. Except for when Sofia faced Paco's mother, but then her emotional over-load made sense. But the pirate minds were all emotion, all the time. It was like the pirates never grew up. Like they never learned to think beyond their latest whim or desire.

I spotted a light in the distance, abandoned all thoughts about pirates and their minds, and swam towards the bright spot. The light came from a bunch of fuzzy balls. I recognized those from the first time I was inside Sofia's head. They were memories that evoked powerful emotions. As I neared the scene, I realized the balls floated around the dark, vague shape of a man.

The man caught a bundle of light and cradled it. After a

moment, he released the ball and reached for another. Then another, and another. Each time the man released a memory, his form was darker than it was when he caught it.

Why was that? I'd seen nothing like it in the other minds. Then it came to me.

It was grief. And every memory drove his mind deeper into it.

That meant this *had* to be Conley's or Barber's mind, right?

There was one way to be certain. I reached out and caught a passing memory.

Bright afternoon sunlight shone through the leaves of a tall tree. One I recognized from our backyard on Ark's Landing. I watched through someone else's eyes as a preteen girl scampered through the tree's lower limbs. Those limbs were three or four meters off the ground, and the girl zipped around on them without a care in the world.

I watched her grab a small branch and put too much trust in its strength. The girl's weight shifted. The branch broke. She lost her balance and—

Fear shot through the watcher as the girl fell from the branch. He threw himself beneath her, just in time to break her fall with his body.

Another man—Barber—rushed into view, and asked, "Are you all right, Miss Connaught?"

She waved the question off with a laugh. "Yeah. I got lucky and landed on Conley."

I had my own memory of that fall. But mine was comical, and all about how my highly trained bodyguard couldn't get out from under a falling girl. Why had I never realized why I landed on Conley instead of the hard ground? Because it made a better bodyguard story to share with my sibs? Whatever the reason, I felt ashamed at the memory now.

But I also felt relief that I was inside Conley's mind. Now all I had to do was figure out how to tell him I wasn't dead. Maybe the answer lay inside one of Conley's memories of me?

Praying that was the case, I tossed aside the memory of my fall and reached for another ball of light. I had a lot of memories to sort through and was short on time. I had to find just the right memory before the pirate who brought me to Conley taunted my bodyguards into killing him.

I grabbed another of Conley's memories.

He stood in a wide-open meadow, his eyes roaming the countryside. On the edge of his perception, a group of teenage girls sat in a circle, whispering and giggling and listening to music. The oldest of the bunch—the older sister of Sandra, my best friend at the time—held court, telling us about the boys vying for her hand.

I didn't know exactly what kind of memory I was looking for, but that one wasn't it. I tossed it aside and reached for a third memory.

He entered our house's security room. Barber sat at a desk watching a bank of monitors.

"How is she?" Barber asked.

"Probably crying her eyes out, now that she's alone." The view wavered as Conley shook his head. "She was barely holding it in when we got to her room. I didn't want to embarrass her, so I did my security sweep as quickly as possible, then cleared out."

"She's a tough kid," Barber said. "But there's no excuse for that boy to be so rude to her."

Even though I never knew about this conversation, I felt sure I knew who they were talking about. When I was thirteen, I'd gathered all my courage and told a seventeen-year-old boy that I loved him. He laughed at me. But that memory wasn't what I needed, either.

I grabbed a fourth.

Conley and Barber standing watch outside a friend's house while I attended a sleepover.

A fifth.

Watching me ride my bike.

A sixth.

Watching me sit alone in our backyard, making a daisy chain.

I pawed through memory after memory looking for something, *anything*, that might help me get through to Conley. At first, I held the memories in both hands and dove into them. But that took too long, so I began scooping them up in one hand, taking a quick peek, and then tossing them aside.

Watching me sit alone at a local dance.

Helping me with homework.

Discussing me with my parents.

Security reports to Granddaddy.

Watching my sibs and me pick wild strawberries.

Making the nighttime security rounds at the house.

Wait!

Strawberries!

That was an old code word. One that told Conley and Barber I was okay. Maybe I could use that memory to send my message to Conley. I lunged after it, grabbed the wrong one, and then found the strawberry memory. Holding it tightly, I waded through the memories piled up around the shadowy figure of Conley.

Thick, oppressive grief made for slow going, but I pushed my way through it and the memories surrounding Conley's mental image of himself. He held one in his hands, and I felt waves of anger and sorrow radiating from him.

I only discovered what he was holding when I tried taking it from him. It was him watching me disappear into the maintenance tunnels after Sofia returned from watching the first pirate captain kill herself, and I'd come back to the suite to console her. That was the last time Conley saw me. Worse, he thought he'd never see me again.

It was time to show him he was wrong. I kicked that memory away and shoved the strawberry picking one into his hands. Conley dropped the strawberries and reached for the one I'd just knocked from his hands. I caught the strawberries and shoved it back in his hands. He dropped it. I put it back.

Drop.

Put back.

Drop.

Put back.

Drop.

Desperate to get through to Conley, I issued emotional orders. *You must feel hope! You must not grieve! Be happy! Be hopeful! Because I'm alive!*

Then I shoved the strawberry picking memory into his hands again. Conley didn't immediately drop it, so that was progress. He sat there, examining it. I got the idea he was trying to figure out why that one kept coming to mind.

Come on, Conley, you can figure it out! Be hopeful! Don't grieve! Strawberries, Conley. My old code word. God, please help him remember! Strawberries mean safety! Strawberries mean life!

With a suddenness that left me disoriented, the oppressive darkness vanished, washed away by the bright light of hope. Conley's mental image of himself stood and... Oh. My. God. He *danced*. Hugging the strawberry picking memory, Conley spun and leapt and pranced. Joy radiated from him.

Part of me wanted to stay and watch Conley's mental dance, but that would be foolish. I quietly withdrew from his mind and returned to mine.

Blinking, I sat up. Sofia turned a questioning expression my way.

I nodded. "I got through to Conley. I think."

Sofia smiled and then held a hand to the ear with the comm. "He just told Barber that you were alive. So you definitely got through."

"Did I miss anything while I was away?"

Sofia's smile faded. "Rivera made a ship-wide announce-ment telling her crew the *Pegasus* was about to enter a wormhole."

I shrugged. "We knew they were going to make a wormhole jump sometime."

"I know, but that's not all, Nora. Rivera said it was their *third* wormhole transition. And—"

"Third? When were the other two?"

"It's just a guess, but they probably happened while we were sleeping outside on the hull. But that's not all, Nora."

I felt my gut tighten at Sofia's tone of voice. "What else did Rivera say?"

"She told the crew to prepare for arrival at their base."

Sofia's words stunned me so much, I asked, "Arrival at the pirate base? Isn't it too soon for that?"

Sofia shrugged. "I don't know. It depends on which wormholes Rivera took the *Pegasus* through. Maybe Rivera knows some that aren't on the regular charts. Or the base might be in a star system so dead it's the perfect hiding place for a pirate base. It wouldn't be the first time pirates set up shop so close to major shipping lanes."

I raised an eyebrow. "Wow, it looks like Connaught Starlines' training is more thorough than I thought."

Sofia's cheeks reddened for a second. "I didn't learn all that in training."

"Do tell?"

"A boy joined the crew the same time I did, only he was a temp working for his passage to the Scout Academy on Draconis. We hit it off, and he told me all sorts of stories about space exploration, famous Scouts, and the Scout Corps battles with pirates. Then we reached Draconis, and he left to attend the Academy."

"Do you still miss him?"

"A little, at first. He left six months ago." Sofia paused, then asked, "I wonder if he still thinks of me?"

"He definitely will when he finds out you took down a pirate gang while he was still at the Academy!" I rolled off the bed and changed the subject. "And on that note, we need to get moving."

Sofia stood. "Moving where?"

"Back to the lifepod launch bay. I think it's the safest hiding place available to us."

"Is it worth the risk of going back through the maintenance tunnels?"

"I'm hoping Rivera pulled her people out of the tunnels to help prepare for arrival. Hang on while I check."

I closed my eyes, lowered my mental shield, and let the emotional map of the *Pegasus* form. The bright red that represented all the passengers pounded against my mind. No doubt, their panic flared up at Rivera's announcement. Frightening as their captivity aboard the *Pegasus* was, the pirate base was a terrifying unknown to them. Just two days ago, their vortex of fear would have battered my mind, sucked me beneath its roiling surface, and destroyed my sanity. Even now, it took almost all my concentration to keep it at bay. That meant I only had time for a quick look around the rest of the ship.

Maroon blobs representing pirates moved in the tunnels. But were they still following a search pattern, or were they retreating from the tunnels? I forced myself to stand against the emotional pounding from the passengers, did my best to ignore the headache it induced, and watched the pirates. It felt as if it took ages for me to figure out that the pirates *were* retreating from the tunnels. Then I reformed my mental shield and breathed a sigh of relief as my wall held against the passengers' emotional assault.

I opened my eyes and found Sofia before me. She offered a cup of water and two pills. "Take these. They'll help with the pain."

I accepted both, but asked, "What makes you think I'm in pain?"

"Your face went pale right after you closed your eyes. I got these from the suite's bathroom just in case you needed them."

The pills went down easily, and the water felt cool when it hit my stomach. "Thank you, Sofia."

"Don't mention it." She glanced at the corner that had the hidden door into the tunnels. "Is the way clear?"

I nodded. "At least until we reach the long corridor that connects crew quarters and passenger territory. I'll need to do another emotional scan when we get there."

I went to the hidden door, glanced back at Sofia, and asked, "Are you ready?"

She stretched her back, something she wouldn't be free to do in the tunnels, and said, "Let's go."

I put my eye to the disguised retina reader, and the door popped open with a soft click. We entered. I carefully closed the door behind us, then we started our crouching walk to the other end of the *Pegasus*.

We stopped four times so I could do an emotional scan of the ship. By the fourth scan, the only pirates left in the tunnels were the ones working in the engine room, and they weren't moving much. We made it back to the same tunnel exit we'd used before. Only a dozen meters of corridor and the hatch stood between us and the relative safety of the empty launch bay.

"Let me scan the corridor," I said. "Be ready to move the second I give the signal."

"I'm ready, Nora."

I closed my eyes and lowered my shield. The storm of passenger emotions still raged and pounded on my mind. But the headache it created was nothing compared to the pit that formed in my stomach when I checked the corridor. Dozens of maroon blobs moved purposefully through it, blocking our path to the empty launch bay.

MASSIVE DECOMPRESSION

I wanted to drop my mental map and put my whiteout wall between me and the dark storm of fear raging inside the dining hall. But I couldn't do that. Not with dozens of pirates just beyond the maintenance tunnel door in front of us. I opened my eyes and looked at Sofia.

She leaned forward and reached for the door handle. "Is it clear?"

I caught her hand and pulled it back. "Not even close. There are at least thirty pirates in that long corridor."

Sofia's face paled. "What do we do now?"

"Get away from this door." I rose into the now-familiar crouch and headed back the way we'd come. "I don't think the pirates need anything in the tunnels, but staying here is too risky."

We backtracked through three side tunnels until we reached another alcove, one we used the last time we stopped, so I could scan the tunnels for pirates. It wasn't a great hiding place, but it was at least two hundred meters and several turns from that corridor full of pirates.

I gave the maintenance tunnel system another quick scan. The only pirates in here with us were two near the engine room.

Neither one had moved, which meant they were probably doing engine crew stuff. Monitoring the plasma flow or reversing polarity or whatever technobabble engineers always use in adventure vids.

Aunt Nancy's reaction to what she called 'stupid starship scripting' popped into my mind, and I wished desperately I could ask her what to do next. But she was back on Ark's Landing, blissfully ignorant of my situation.

No, I realized. *It's been way more than fourteen hours since we launched the lifepod. Its messenger drone should have reached my homeworld at least ten hours ago. If I knew Aunt Nancy, she was in the cockpit of a starfighter right now, leading her squadron to the rescue. And Dad would be right alongside, guiding the pursuit.*

Next to me, I felt a shiver run through Sofia's body. I pulled her into a hug and asked, "Are you cold?"

"No. I just..." Her voice trailed off, and she rested her head on my shoulder. "Nora, I'm scared. Not that I wasn't before this —I mean, the first pirate captain completely terrified me—but... I don't know. Everything we've done and everything that's ahead of us—it just hit me all at once."

As if triggered by Sofia's words, the full weight of our situation crashed down on my shoulders. I couldn't stop a shiver of my own. Tears welled up in my eyes and, in a quavering voice, I said, "Yeah."

Sofia returned my hug and also blinked back tears. We held the hug for a minute, both of us giving and receiving the comfort you can only get from a close friend. We squeezed each other tighter for a few seconds, then we broke our embrace.

I wiped away my tears and smiled weakly at Sofia. "Hey, something dawned on me just before our crying jag. The messenger drone I sent to Ark's Landing must have arrived hours ago. By now, my dad and Aunt Nancy are on their way to rescue us."

Sofia offered a brighter smile than I managed. "Please tell me they're bringing a few friends with them."

"Knowing Dad and Aunt Nancy, they probably had more volunteers than they could bring."

We sat in silence for a minute, then Sofia asked, "With all that help on the way, do we just sit tight and wait?"

"I don't know. I guess it depends on what the pirates do. They're bound to have some kind of procedure for this, but I'll bet their procedure doesn't take *us* into account."

Sofia's eyes widened. "Nora Erin Connaught, what are you planning?"

"Nothing!" Sofia gave me a dubious look, so I shrugged. "I can't make any plans until I see what the pirates do. But if I see an opportunity to raise our chances of being rescued, I'm going to take it."

The doubt in Sofia's eyes gave way to resolve. "No, Nora. *We're* going to take it."

I looked at the determination burning in Sofia's eyes, and my first inclination was to shake my head. Tell her she'd done enough. *More* than enough. That it was time for her to keep her head down, stay safe, and keep as far away as possible from a trouble magnet like me.

But what safety could there be for her on the *Pegasus* or at a base filled with pirates? Especially pirates who thought we were dead? I could only imagine the cruel tortures Rivera would come up for us if we ever fell into her hands. As much as I wanted to keep Sofia safe, we only had two paths to safety.

We could sit tight and wait for rescue. Or we could stay alert, learn the pirates' routines, and plan an escape.

I knew which approach *I* preferred. Sofia obviously felt the same way. And who was I to turn down her help? I mean, without Sofia, I'd already be dead or captured.

So I buried my fears, smiled at Sofia, and said, "The pirates will never know what hit them!"

Any reply Sofia had in mind cut off when Rivera's voice rang out from the ship-wide comm. "All crew to wormhole exit stations. We transition to normal space in ten minutes."

Sofia said, "This might be our last chance to sneak into the empty launch bay. Can you tell what the pirates in the corridor are doing?"

I closed my eyes and summoned my mental map. As always, the bright red from the passengers dominated the emotional landscape. It even affected my reading of the corridor we had to take when we slipped from the tunnels to the lifepod launch bay, blurring my reading of the corridor into a long, maroon splotch.

I shook my head. "All I can say is there are still pirates between us and the launch bay's hatch. I can do better if we're closer, but I don't know how safe we'll be."

"We can stay here if you think it's best," Sofia said. "But I really think we should do our best to get back to the launch bay."

"Why?"

"Maybe I'm being foolish, Nora, but won't the pirates notice the atmosphere shield covering the open hatch? I mean, glowing blue might stand out, right?"

I felt like smacking myself. "Oh my God, Sofia! You're right. Why didn't I think of that?"

"You've had a lot on your mind. Literally, since you're still learning how to use your psychic ability."

"But—"

"That's No-Talent Nora's talking again, and I already told her to shut up." Sofia caught my head with her hands and forced me to look into her eyes. "No one thinks of everything. Not you. Not me. Not your mother or father. And not even that super-prepared grandfather of yours. So stop putting all the pressure on you. Got it?"

I reached up and took Sofia's hands, squeezed them gently to show my appreciation, and nodded. "Thanks."

"Anytime." Sofia rose to a crouch. "Let's get going."

We took extra time returning to the tunnel door, stopping twice so I could check my mental map for pirates wandering the tunnels. As before, the only ones in here with us were the two in engineering. They had changed stations since my last check, and ended up farther away from us. We reached the tunnel exit with two minutes remaining before the *Pegasus* exited the wormhole. I took a last scan, noting two pirates moving around in crew quarters but none in the corridor.

"Go!" I said.

Sofia opened the door, glanced both ways, then went through the door. I followed close on her heels, and once again took care, shutting the tunnel door behind me. The walk to the launch bay hatch was anticlimactic until suddenly it wasn't.

From crew territory, a pirate's voice echoed down the hallway. "All aft crew are at their stations, Captain."

The voice sounded far too close for comfort, so Sofia and I picked up our pace. As we reached the door, the same pirate said, "Roger, Captain. Ortega and I are returning to the bridge now."

Purposeful footsteps echoed off the metal deck as the pirates headed our way!

I hit the green button that opened the launch bay hatch. It slid open with a hiss that sounded far too loud to my ears. Sofia squeezed through the opening as soon as it was wide enough.

"Hey," a new pirate voice said, "did you hear something from up ahead?"

The sound of the pirates' purposeful walk changed to pounding footfalls as they ran our way.

I crowded after Sofia and whispered, "Close it!"

Sofia pressed the red button inside the launch bay. The hatch paused for an agonizing fraction of a second, then began closing.

I pulled the safety line from my backpack and clipped it to Sofia's oxygen harness. "Stay here and listen at the door. And turn on your oxygen harness."

Holding the other end of the line, I sprinted for the panel that controlled the atmosphere shield. Even my soft-soled shoes sounded loud against the metal deck as I ran.

Behind me, Sofia called softly, "The pirates are in the corridor now!"

Afraid to slow down as I approached the bulkhead, I stuck my arms ahead of me to cushion myself from the collision. Even then, I hit the bulkhead with a hard thump.

"They heard that!" Sofia gasped in a voice laced with fear.

It took all my willpower to resist the urge to drop the atmosphere shield immediately. The first time the launch bay decompressed, the force of it would have blown Sofia and me out into space without the safety lines holding us in place. That time would be like a summer breeze compared to a hurricane when the shield fell. With such a large opening into space, thousands of cubic meters of atmosphere would blow out into vacuum in one or two seconds. Unless I tethered Sofia and me to the ship, such a massive decompression would blast us into the void with the venting atmosphere.

Sofia called, "I can hear them coming closer!"

Terror and stress and the awful weight of responsibility sent adrenaline coursing through my body. I thanked God the life support controls had a big, wide safety ring right next to them. My shaking right hand couldn't have threaded the line through anything smaller. I caught the end with a shaking left hand and yanked it towards the ring on my oxygen harness.

Sofia hissed, "Hurry!"

It took both hands to hold the clasp steady. But it finally snapped onto my harness. Relief flooded through me as I slapped the button controlling the launch bay's atmosphere shield. A message began flashing below the button.

Decompression warning! Press button again to deactivate atmosphere shield.

Sofia backed away from the hatch. "Nora, they're here!"

I punched the button again.

The shield vanished.

An invisible hand grabbed hold of me and hurled me towards the void of space.

The safety line connecting Sofia and me pulled taut. It yanked Sofia off her feet. I absently noted the blue haze surrounding her. At least she'd turned her oxygen harness on. But I shouldn't be able to see Sofia's shield. Unless...

I'd never turned my harness on!

My right hand darted for the harness's switch. But before I could turn it on, I slammed into a bulkhead next to the opening into space. My head rang. Vision blurred as tears flooded my eyes. The force of the blow knocked out the breath I had left.

The rushing wind swirled around me and pulled my limp body around the lip of the hatch. Then it sucked me out into space. I hurtled away from the *Pegasus* until Sofia crashed into the bulkhead next to the life support controls. The safety line went taut and stopped me with a horrific jerk.

I tried turning on my oxygen harness, but my hands were slow and uncoordinated. My body fought for oxygen that wasn't there as darkness clouded my mind. Just before it overwhelmed me, I got one last look inside the launch bay.

Sofia, my only hope for survival, hung limp from the other end of the safety line.

~

Comfortable darkness wrapped around me like a blanket. The pain from my empty lungs faded. My frantic fight to move my hands eased.

Let go, Nora. It's okay to give up. You did your best. It just wasn't enough.

I recognized that voice. I knew its message. And I hated it.

Why don't you just crawl off somewhere and die, No-Talent Nora?

Oh, I will, Nora. I'll die when you die, a victim of your continuing inability to live up to the Connaught name.

At least one positive thing will come from my death.

That's because you're not thinking of all the people you're letting down when you die. Your parents and grandparents. Your brother and sister. Poor Sofia, who will blame herself for not saving you. Malicious glee entered No-Talent Nora's voice. *And then there are Conley and Barber. Think how deeply they'll grieve when you turn up dead just minutes after you convinced them you were alive. It will destroy them.*

Shut! Up!

Die, Nora, and I'll be silent forever.

No.

Not now.

Not ever.

I will not give up. I will live, and I will do it just to spite you, No-Talent Nora.

I expected some snide reply from her, but something weird twisted inside my head and she fell silent. As did all the danger signals from my body. Had I jumped into another mind? That would explain the strange sensation, but the darkness surrounding me didn't feel right.

Fear churned it.

Desperation writhed through it.

The darkness fought.

But against what?

Something moved nearby, swirling in the roiling blackness. I went to it. It brushed against my senses, and a vision flooded through me.

Fear of capture by the pirates held me rigid. Through the blue haze of my oxygen harness, I watched my best friend in the galaxy hit the control that dropped the atmosphere shield. Then an invisible hand swept her away from the control panel. The safety line connecting us pulled me after her. But the line ran through the ring next to the controls. As I careened towards the bulkhead, my friend smashed into the lip of the launch bay's hatch. The unseen hand swept her rag doll body into space. Then I hit the bulkhead and stars exploded in my head.

My first guess was right. I had jumped from my dying mind and sought my one hope for survival—Sofia's mind! But the last time I saw her, she wasn't moving. Could I do anything to help her help me?

Yes. I would try. I would fight on. I would do exactly what No-Talent Nora told me I couldn't do. I would *not* give up.

Sofia, I yelled into the surrounding darkness, *help me! I'm dying! You must feel urgency! You must feel desperation! You must overcome your own darkness and help me! I know you can do it, Sofia! And you must believe you can save me, too! Because you* can *do it!*

A shock wave ran through the darkness. Its force knocked Sofia's most recent memory from my hands and ended the roiling motion surrounding me. A second, stronger wave followed the first. I no longer had the strength to stand against it. The wave picked me up and carried me away.

I hung limp in calm darkness. Far away, a light winked into existence. It grew brighter, bigger, and it flowed towards me. Was it the tunnel of light everyone claims you see when you've died? Did it mean I was dead?

The light washed over me. And the light brought sensations with it.

Odor, as the stench of fear assaulted my nose.

Pain, as something pushed my head back.

Touch, as lips pressed against mine.

Taste, as moist air blew across my tongue.

Sound, as a quavering voice demanded, "Come on, Nora, breathe!"

Pressure, as a hand pushed against my chest and my back pushed against the deck.

Touch. Taste. Pressure.

Touch. Taste. Pressure.

My lungs cried for air. Begged for it. Demanded it.

A cough exploded from me. And I breathed.

My eyes fluttered open. Sofia hovered over me, her face pale and eyes wide in terror.

"Oh, thank God!" she cried. As I drew another shuddering breath, Sofia hugged me and whispered, "I thought you were dead."

"Don't be silly," I gasped. "I can never die while you're around to save me."

Sofia shook her head. "I could only help you because you came into my head and got me going."

"Water?" I asked.

Sofia pulled a bottle from my backpack and trickled water into my mouth. It felt cool and wonderful going down. After another sip, I took the bottle from Sofia and emptied the bottle.

"Tell me what happened," I said.

Sofia shrugged. "I felt your cry for help, and that sent a jolt of adrenaline through my body. It brought me to my senses, and that's when I saw you drifting outside the ship. I grabbed the safety line, pulled you inside the ship, and turned on your oxygen harness. But you weren't breathing, Nora." Sofia lowered her head, and a tear trickled down her cheek. "I was afraid you were dead."

"But you gave me mouth-to-mouth resuscitation, anyway."

"Everyone in the crew gets emergency training. I just did what the trainers taught me."

I blew out an exasperated breath. "What's your middle name?"

Sofia gave me a confused glance. "Huh?"

"Your middle name. What is it?" When Sofia still didn't answer, I said, "I nearly died. Humor me."

"It's Nadia."

"Thank you." I drew a deep breath, adopted a forceful tone of voice, and said, "Sofia Nadia Olson, when are you going to stop deflecting credit for all the amazing things you've done for me?"

Her eyes went wide. "Um... Are you feeling okay, Nora?"

"I feel fine. *Because of you*. I'm alive. *Because of you*. But *you* keep passing the credit to some corporate trainers who probably never dealt with an actual emergency in their lives." I shook my head. "When this is all over, I'm going to make you sit down and talk with Mom and Granddaddy. They have tons of stories about people who froze up in emergencies despite having a lot better training than you."

A faint smile creased Sofia's face. "After everything you've told me about them, I'd be honored to meet them."

"Yeah, about that honor bit. You remember me telling you about all the honorary aunts and uncles I have?" Sofia nodded, and I continued, "My parents are going to be thrilled to add an honorary daughter to the family."

Sofia's eyes flew wide and her hand flew to her mouth. "What?"

I hugged her, and whispered, "And I'm thrilled to have an honorary sister."

I leaned against the bulkhead after giving Sofia her welcome-to-the-family hug, closed my eyes, and—

With a gasp, my eyes opened wide. The pirates outside the hatch!

I grabbed Sofia's wrist so hard she cried, "Ouch!"

Loosening my grip, I asked, "What happened to the pirates out in the corridor?"

Sofia's gaze darted to the hatch. "I... I don't know! I was so worried about you I forgot all about them!"

I rose and hurried to the door, dragging Sofia behind me. I put my ear against the hatch. Sofia did the same, and we both held our breath. Distant ship sounds came through the hatch. But I didn't hear any voices. After half a minute, I released my held breath, took another, held it, and kept listening.

The two of us stood there for at least five minutes, breathing little, and listening for pirate voices. Neither of us heard anything, so I finally let myself slump to the deck.

Sofia slid down next to me, took my hand, and asked, "Do you think they gave up and went away?"

"The hatch won't open when there's a vacuum in here. So we can hope that convinced them whatever they heard couldn't have come from in here. Or at least wasn't made by people hiding in here."

"The *Pegasus* makes lots of noise at the best of times," Sofia said. "Walking her corridors, I've been startled by strange sounds lots of times. So space pirates ought to be used to hearing spaceships make odd noises."

I shrugged. "There's nothing we can do about it, either way."

With obvious reluctance, Sofia said, "We could go out on the hull, again."

"No. I think I'd rather get caught by the pirates than do that again."

Relief lit Sofia's face. "Good. Um, what do we do now?"

"I'm just going to sit here and see if my heart will stop pounding."

"Sounds like a plan, Nora."

I released Sofia's hand and concentrated on breathing. Dull pain pulsed through my gut with each breath I took. I think I strained my diaphragm when I fought for breath in the vacuum of space. Here's a handy tip for future plucky girl pirate hunters —space wins that fight every time. That's why smart girls always have a pluckier girl rescuer at their side. Because someone has to bring the smart girl back from the dead when she's too smart for her own good.

Okay, I'm making light of nearly dying. Being one of those smart girls, I even know why. Because such a close brush with death is absolutely terrifying. Worse than staring into the void of space. Far worse than living out my life in my sibs' shadow ever could have been. But that's the problem with life. You don't know how good your life was until it's snatched away from you. You don't know how foolish your dreams of heroism were until you think you've taken your last breath.

Sofia's arms wrapped around me, held me tight, and she whispered, "It's okay, Nora."

That's when I realized I was shivering. Not because I was cold, but because my body had its own reaction to its near-death experience, followed by panic over the pirates. Where my mind made lame attempts at humor to ward off the horror I felt drifting in the void, my body only had one way to tell itself it was still alive. It shivered. Violently.

I don't know how long I shook while Sofia held me. But I know it would have lasted longer without her warmth and the soothing words she whispered while I vibrated in her arms. When my body finally stilled, I gave Sofia a tight squeeze and released her.

"Thank you, Sofia. Again."

"I'll always be here when you need me, Nora. Just like you'll always be there for me. And have *already* been there for me."

"Yeah, same here."

Sofia looked out the launch bay's open hatch. Her brows furrowed, so I followed her gaze. It took me a few seconds to see what caught her attention. Without thinking, I raised an eyebrow in the way that irritates my sister Nancy so much.

"Sofia? Is it my imagination, or does it look like we're approaching a planet?"

"If it is a planet, it's the smallest one I've seen during my year on board the *Pegasus*. Maybe it's a moon?"

"Do you think the pirate base is there?" I asked. "I mean, I can't think of any other reason they'd come this close to it."

"It's kind of cliché, but I guess clichés have to be based on something." Sofia turned back to me. "What do we do next, Nora?"

"Do you have any idea how long we have before the *Pegasus* lands?"

Sofia shrugged. "I can only guess. But a pilot told me the final approach was always tricky and took way longer than most people think it should. I think we still have a few hours."

"In that case, we should take turns napping. God only knows how long it will be before we have another chance to catch some sleep. I had the last nap so—"

"That was hours ago, Nora! You've done a lot since then."

"So have you. So shut up and go to sleep. I'll wake you up in a couple of hours."

Sofia opened her mouth to protest, but I let go of her hand. Since our oxygen harnesses didn't overlap anymore, I wouldn't hear anything she said. Sofia caught on immediately, folded her arms over her chest, and stuck her tongue out at me. I gave her my oldest-child glare, which my sibs hate dearly, and waited for her to do as I instructed. She resisted for ten seconds, then gave in and stretched out on the deck. She fell asleep less than a minute after closing her eyes.

I spent the time watching the moon grow larger and larger. An hour and a half after we first spotted it, the *Pegasus* entered her approach to orbit. And that's when I got my first look at the pirate base.

A massive complex of buildings and landing fields spread over at least one square kilometer of the moon's surface. I'd expected something sparse, four or five buildings with a dirt landing area. Not something as huge and sophisticated as this place.

Seeing the base below, I suddenly felt very small, extremely insignificant, and *way* out of my depth.

～

I studied the pirate base until the *Pegasus's* orbit took us beyond its horizon. The ship was way too high above the surface for me to make out minor details, but I still learned a lot from that first pass above it.

First, the moon didn't have an atmosphere distorting my view of the surface. The large, visible details of the base were too clear, and the sunlight was too harsh. No clouds floated above the surface, and I didn't see evidence of a single storm raging across the plain surrounding the base.

Since Sofia and I had oxygen harnesses, we wouldn't have trouble breathing. But to get inside the base's buildings, we'd have to go through airlocks. Not a problem if the pirates didn't post guards, and why would they on a barren rock like this? But airlocks took time to cycle. Time during which we'd be sitting ducks for a passing bunch of pirates. Since there wasn't anything we could do about that, I turned my attention to other things I saw.

The base supported *four* landing fields. Two of them were in use and had ships sitting on them. But I was positive one of those ships was the *Pegasus's* sister ship, *Perseus*. According to Sofia, the *Perseus* vanished without a trace a year ago. She had to be the ship I spotted in one of the landing fields, the huge one that dwarfed the other ships parked around her. What I didn't know was whether the smaller ones were other pirate ships or other pirate prizes.

Part of me hoped those ships were prizes. Because if even a few of them were pirate ships, we were facing a *much* bigger gang. Or maybe it was gangs? There are stories of pirate gangs cooperating well enough to share the costs of a large base. But would the gangs mix with each other when they weren't out ravaging and pillaging? And if they did, would that make infiltrating the base easier, or harder?

Yeah, I *hoped* Sofia and I could just stay on the *Pegasus* and wait for Dad and Aunt Nancy. But if we couldn't, I *think* we'd have an easier time moving around the base if everyone was used to seeing people they didn't recognize. But if there were several pirate gangs based here, that would also make a rescue much more difficult to pull off.

I mean, how many rescuers would die storming a pirate stronghold? And how many passengers would get caught in the crossfire? I'd been so busy staying out of pirate hands and waiting for those rescuers that I hadn't considered how many good people might die in the attempt. They'd die ridding the galaxy of a bunch of bloodthirsty pirates, and that would be a good thing in the long run. But people live in the short run. How much comfort would the families of the dead take from that?

It suddenly dawned on me *I* might be a member of one of

those grieving families. Because Dad or Aunt Nancy or both of them could end up among the dead.

Because of me.

Not that I thought the pirates picked the *Pegasus* just because I was on it. But I saw what was inside the insane captain's mind before she killed herself. I saw the dream her psycho daughter had when she thought she'd killed me. I might not be the *only* reason the pirates targeted the *Pegasus*, but I was *a* reason.

Fair or not, I bore some responsibility for the attack. If I'd been content to go to a college on Ark's Landing, it's possible the *Pegasus* wouldn't have been a target. So, fair or not, I'd bear some responsibility for the deaths among the rescuers.

If Sofia was awake, she'd tell me I was crazy. She'd even point out that I deserved credit for being the one person who made the rescue possible. And she'd be right. That still didn't make my realization any easier to take.

But there was nothing I could do about it, right? I mean, it's not like I could storm the base by myself. Even if I could, it would take *forever* to get five thousand people back to the *Pegasus*. But—

Wait! It would also take forever to move five thousand people *off* the *Pegasus*. But from what I'd seen of the pirates' emotional state, they wouldn't have the patience for that. Not right after landing, anyway. Sure, they'd probably take some people away. The crew, definitely, and maybe some hostages to make sure the rest of the passengers behave. But they might leave most of the passengers onboard until after the pirate crew blew off a little steam. And if that was the case, I just had to figure out how to spring the *Pegasus's* crew and the others the pirates took from the ship.

Then we could return to *Pegasus* and escape with everyone!

I let Sofia nap for an hour before I woke her.

She yawned and rubbed sleep from her eyes. "I miss getting a full night's sleep. After your father rescues us, I'm going to sleep for a whole day."

"You and me, both," I said.

Sofia peered at me. "But?"

"What makes you think there's a but?"

"Because I know you, Nora. Your expression changed when I talked about your father rescuing us. Did you hear anything over the comm? Something that makes you think he's not coming?"

With absolute conviction, I said, "*Nothing* will stop my father from coming for us. Even if no one else was willing to help, he and Mom would come by themselves. You can count on it."

"I believe you." She paused for a second, then asked, "But?"

Unwilling to meet Sofia's eyes, I looked at the deck. "But I don't know how long it will take them to get here. What if the pirates start sending passengers off to rim world slave markets before then? Or... I've seen the emotions that drive those animals." I shuddered. "What if they pick some crew members and passengers for... entertainment? I don't know if I can block that kind of emotional suffering. I *do* know I can't just sit by and do nothing."

"You aren't willing to wait for a rescue that might not happen for days?" At my nod, Sofia's face cleared. "That's the *but* you left unsaid?"

"Yes."

"Is that all?"

Sofia's offhand tone surprised me. I met her gaze and asked, "*Is that all?* I'm talking about the two of us sneaking *five thousand people* out from under the pirates' noses!"

"I know." I guess my face still registered surprise, because Sofia added, "We discussed this back in the tunnels, Nora. I distinctly remember saying that if *we* saw a chance to rescue everyone, *we* were going to go for it. And the way you're acting, I think you have a plan for doing just that."

I shook my head. "*Plan* is much too grand a word for what I've got."

"Fine. You've got a *scheme* you think might work. Am I right?"

I considered that for a moment. "Yeah, scheme is a good word for it."

Sofia rolled her eyes. "Now that we've agreed on terminology, it's time to share. Spill your scheme, Nora."

"Let me ask you one question, first." Sofia nodded, so I asked, "How long would take to move everyone off the *Pegasus*?"

"Through the ship's air locks?" Sofia's eyes unfocused for a moment, then she said, "The *Pegasus* hasn't been totally empty since I came aboard, so this is just a guess. But I think it would take at least four hours. And that's if everything went smoothly."

"That's less time than I hoped, but I'll bet it's still longer than this bunch of pirates will want to spend after the ship lands."

"Plus, it'll take about twice that long to get everyone settled inside the base. That's if the pirates just cram people into the nearest rooms and bring them the minimum food and water necessary to survive."

"I hadn't thought about that. I *know* these scummy pirates won't wait twelve hours before they start drinking and, um, doing other stuff."

"Okay, Nora, I answered your question. Are you going to tell me your plan—excuse me, scheme—now?"

So I did. To my relief, Sofia nodded as I described it. I felt confident in my reasoning, but it felt good having her agree with it.

When I finished, she asked, "You know Rivera will leave some of her gang on board as guards, right?"

"Yeah, but I'll bet the guards are going to be more worried about the drinking they're missing out on than guarding a bunch of scared passengers. Besides, the guards are the one thing I *do* have a plan for." I grinned. "Once we free the crew and any passengers the pirates take from the *Pegasus*, I'm going to send Conley and Barber in to take out the guards."

"What makes you think your bodyguards will be among the ones the pirates take off the ship?"

"Rivera is a psycho, but she's not stupid. She'll want to keep guys with their training under closer guard. At least, that's what I'd do in her place."

"I suppose that makes sense... My next question is a lot tougher."

"Let me guess; this is an airless moon. How is everyone going to breathe between the base and the ship?"

"Good guess. Do you have a good answer?"

"Not really. I *hope* we can find more oxygen harnesses for everyone. Or at least enough so small groups can share one harness. But that's something we're just going to have to play by ear."

"I have one more question, Nora."

I gave a faint smile. "Only one?"

Sofia didn't return my smile. "You remember how Rivera sabotaged the *Pegasus's* engines so we couldn't run from the pirates? What if she does the same thing after we land? We can't escape if the engines are offline."

"I thought of that, too. But right before Rivera launched that missile at the lifepod she thought we were on, she told me she had a code that unlocked the weapons. Since the *Pegasus's* engines are running now, she must have one that unlocked them, too."

"I guess that's right. But she'll never tell us the code willingly."

"Then I'll just have to go into her mind and trick her into revealing it."

I thought Sofia might gasp in horror at the thought of me diving into Rivera's head a second time. (My imagination can be a little melodramatic. It came up with No-Talent Nora, after all.) My friend just nodded as if I'd said exactly what she thought I would.

"Well, you won't be able to do anything useful with your psychic ability unless you get some rest," Sofia said. She pointed at the deck. "Take a nap."

"I want to, but—"

Sofia pulled the same trick on me as I did to her. She released my hand, so she couldn't hear anything I said. Then she crossed her arms, gave me her own version of the oldest-child glare, and pointed at the deck.

I reached for her hand so I could finish what I wanted to say. When Sofia swayed back out of reach, I grabbed her ankle. "As I was saying, I want a nap, but I need to study the base's layout when we fly over it next time."

Sofia sighed and pointed at my backpack. "Have you still got the pad of paper and pen Conley suggested you put in your backpack?"

"Yes."

"Give them to me. *I'll* sketch the layout while *you* get some sleep. Then you can study my drawing after you wake up."

A protest formed on my lips before I remembered something Granddaddy told me long ago.

"Sleep is your best weapon, Nora. Fatigue-clouded minds make mistakes. And mistakes...?"

"Mistakes get you killed, Granddaddy."

"Right. All the training your mother and I are giving you won't make a bit of difference if you're too tired to use it properly. So...?"

"If I ever find myself in so much trouble, I have to rely on your training to stay alive. I'll sleep whenever I get the chance."

Granddaddy nodded. "Never forget that, Nora."

I almost *had* forgotten it. But Sofia's behavior reminded me. I released her ankle, pulled the pad and pen from my backpack, and handed them to Sofia. "Make sure I'm awake before the ship lands."

I stretched out on the deck, closed my eyes, and immediately fell asleep.

A hand shook my shoulder. "Wake up, Nora."

I opened my eyes and yawned as I propped myself up on an elbow. "What's happening?"

"I think we're on the final approach for landing."

I sat up, brushed hair away from my face, and asked, "Did you have time to make the sketches?"

Sofia bit her lip, nodded, and shyly handed me the pad. Instead of the primitive blocks, circles, and lines I'd have drawn, an amazing, three-dimensional drawing of the base covered the page. She'd labeled the airlocks, included estimated distances between buildings, between spaceships and the nearest airlock, and even showed where she thought the pirates would land the *Pegasus*.

I looked up. "Sofia, this is *amazing*! You must have drawn it really fast, since the base is only in sight for a few minutes each pass."

"Oh no, I'm nowhere near fast enough to do that. I, um... I

studied the base while it was visible, then I drew from memory while I waited for it to come back into sight."

My eyes went wide with surprise and appreciation. "Wow. I mean, seriously, *wow*. I had no idea you had so much artistic talent. Why didn't you tell me?"

"You've been busy. And it's not like art is real important right now. Not like your empathic ability is."

I held up Sofia's map of the base. "This says different. Can you make copies? If we have to free people from the pirate base, it would really help if we could give them maps leading back to the *Pegasus*."

"Yeah, sure."

I handed the pad back to Sofia. "I'm curious about the landing spot you picked out for the *Pegasus*. What made you pick that spot?"

"I figured they'd land us near the *Perseus*, since they'd need the same facilities to unload the *Pegasus*. And that's the only spot in the same landing field with enough room for a ship as big as the *Pegasus*."

"That's a good observation."

"Thanks," Sofia said.

She turned her attention towards copying the map. I watched in fascination as another copy of the base layout emerged from her swift and sure pen strokes.

After a moment, I turned my attention back to the original map and tried figuring out what the pirates would do when we landed. There was a large building next to the landing field—probably a warehouse—that looked large enough to hold as many as a thousand people. More, if the pirates packed people in there as tightly as possible. But I thought doing that would probably overwhelm the life support systems. After the pirates went to all the trouble of capturing the *Pegasus*, I couldn't imagine them just letting people die for no reason. I mean, there's no profit in dead people, right? Even if the pirates had an organ harvesting operation, they'd want their intended victims healthy until they opened them up.

The horrific image of a surgical disassembly line remained stubbornly in my mind until the pirate base came into view again. This time, the *Pegasus* went through a series of more complex maneuvers before settling gently to the ground. Right where Sofia predicted they'd land.

There was only one problem. Our open hatch didn't face the nearby buildings, where I thought the pirates would take the crew. The *Perseus* sat about a hundred meters away, blocking our view of the moonscape. As much as I wanted to stay hidden in this launch bay, I wanted to see where the pirates took everyone even more.

Sofia eyed the *Pegasus's* sister ship and asked, "What now?"

"We can't free the people they take off the ship if we don't know where they are. So I guess we go back out onto the hull, peek over the top, and see where the pirates take them."

Sofia glanced out of the launch bay at the desolate landscape between us and the *Perseus*. She sighed, and said, "At least the ship isn't moving anymore."

"No, but nothing else on this moon is moving, either. That means we have to be really careful when we move around. Nothing attracts attention like movement where there shouldn't be any."

"That'll be a good idea outside the *Pegasus*, anyway." At my blank expression, Sofia added, "Because of the moon's gravity."

"Oh yeah. I, um, forgot about that."

Sofia grinned. "You'd have remembered it as soon as you stepped outside the ship's artificial gravity, Nora."

Images of me unintentionally launching myself into low-moon orbit ran through my mind, complete with pirates far below, pointing and laughing and taking potshots at me as I waited for the moon's weak gravity to bring me down. No, it wasn't a realistic, imaginary vision. I'd probably just end up tumbling down somewhere between the *Pegasus* and the *Perseus*.

That would be almost as bad, since a pirate would just have to look out one of the view ports on this side of the *Pegasus* to see me flailing around on the ground.

"Maybe we should keep ourselves tethered with the safety line," I said. "Just until we adjust to the moon's gravity."

"That sounds like a good idea." Sofia walked over to the safety ring I'd threaded the line through just before getting blown out into space. She unclipped the line from her harness, pulled it through the ring, and then clipped it back to her harness. "Are you ready to learn about really low gravity?"

"Sure. Got any suggestions for me?"

"I spent a week on the moon—Earth's moon, I mean—before I shipped out on the *Pegasus*. The trick is to make slow, controlled movements."

"That sounds easy enough," I said.

"It's not, because you have to think about every move you make. Seriously, Nora, moving around in very low gravity is exhausting. It's hard on your muscles, but all that concentration will exhaust your brain."

Thinking about how much my recently awakened psychic ability taxed my mind, I muttered, "Gee, I can't wait."

"But you probably won't have to do a lot in this low grav. I'll bet the pirate base has an artificial gravity generator."

I cocked my head and asked, "Why?"

"Because the pirates haven't had any trouble moving around in the *Pegasus's* gravity. And they never changed the ship's gravity setting from Earth normal, which is the first thing they'd do if they weren't used to it."

"Wow, Sofia, you've really thought this through. I'm impressed." After a brief pause, I added, "Again."

Her cheeks colored briefly. "I've worked with a few passengers from low gravity worlds, that's all. One man was so miserable he offered to pay Captain Riggs a million credits a day to set the ship's gravity to his world's norm. The captain turned him down, of course."

"Yeah, Captain Riggs doesn't seem like the bribable type."

I walked to the launch bay hatch and peered outside. Nothing moved out there. And that's more than a little creepy. My senses are used to being on a living world, one with wind rustling leaves and tugging at clothing, with birds chirping and animals moving. This moon had none of the smells and sounds and sights of life. The primitive, caveman part of my brain distrusted this dead world and wondered where the monsters were hiding.

But on this moon, the monsters didn't hide from view. They didn't need to, not here at their lair. Hiding was for the hunt, and there wasn't anything worth hunting on this airless rock.

With those monsters firmly in my mind, I looked at Sofia. "You have the most experience moving around in low gravity. Do you mind taking the lead and showing me how it's done?"

"Nope. Are you ready?"

I nodded, and Sofia reached for a handhold on the *Pegasus's* hull. She carefully pulled herself out of the ship's artificial gravity and began her slow climb. I watched everything she did, took a deep, calming breath, and followed her onto the hull.

I thought low gravity would feel a lot like no gravity, just less frightening because I wouldn't suffer from the ever-present horror of the void. But just having some gravity fooled my brain into thinking everything was normal, and I didn't concentrate hard enough to keep my muscles from reacting as if that was true.

I caught the handhold on the outer hull and swung myself out of the *Pegasus's* gravity field. But every part of my body except my arm was still in Earth-normal gravity, so I took an Earth-normal step out of the hatch. Wide-eyed, I swung past the line of ascending hand holds. Only my suddenly white-knuckled grip on the one outside the launch bay hatch kept me from taking a slow tumble towards the ground thirty meters below. My body pivoted around my anchored hand and smacked into the hull. I didn't hurt anything but my pride, but that was plenty bruised.

What gravity there was outside the ship took hold of me, and my feet slowly dropped towards the moon's surface. I still had my death grip on the handhold, so didn't worry about falling. But part of my mind wondered how badly I'd get hurt by such a fall. Sofia and I had the safety line connecting us, but even in this gravity, its full length would be a long way to fall.

I took a moment to get my bearings. Then, moving with the exaggerated deliberation required by the low gravity, I got my hands and feet positioned for climbing to the top of the *Pegasus's* hold.

From above, Sofia gently touched her foot to my hand. After our oxygen shields merged into one, she asked, "Are you okay, Nora?"

I nodded, then said, "If you want to say *I told you so*, go ahead. I deserve it."

"There's no need. I can't say anything that's worse than what you're already saying to yourself. But I will tell you not to be so hard on yourself. Everyone I know messed up the first time they dealt with low gravity."

"Even you?"

"Oh yeah. When I took my first step into low gravity, I went somersaulting for five meters down the docking tube. And I was wearing a dress." She reddened slightly at the memory, then asked, "Ready to climb?"

"Yes."

Without another word, Sofia pulled her foot away from my hand and began climbing. She moved slowly, concentrating on her hands. She only moved her feet after both hands had a firm grip on the next handhold. I copied her moves exactly and quickly saw just how mentally and physically exhausting this kind of movement could be. But I didn't go tumbling again, so I must have been doing something right.

We made slow but steady progress toward the crest of the

Pegasus's curving hull. Moving in such a carefully controlled manner never got less tiring, but I fell into a solid routine before we were halfway to our destination. I soon realized I could turn my attention elsewhere during the few seconds I spent waiting while Sofia finished climbing up one step.

In case you're wondering, staring at a hull forty centimeters in front of your face gets boring really fast. When the *Pegasus* was in space, looking away from the hull meant looking into the terrifying void of space. Now I looked aft along the *Pegasus's* hull at the moonscape visible beyond the ship's engines. It appeared even more exotic because I'd never been on another world before this. The view was incredibly clear without the softening effect of an atmosphere. There was grandeur in the distant, jagged hills, and beauty in the stark wasteland.

It was the very starkness of the view that made the splotch of colors stand out. I noticed it from the corner of my eye, and without conscious thought I turned my attention to it. It took a moment before my brain figured out what I was looking at.

A garbage pile.

My disgust with the pirates rose another notch at their casual disregard for the pristine landscape. With no atmosphere to support insects or bacteria, their little garbage dump would stain the moon until the end of time.

Just as I turned away, something moved next to the garbage pile. I gave it my full attention and saw more movement along the dump's edge.

The figure of a man tossed more trash on the heap.

He turned and looked at the moon's newest sight—the *Pegasus*. Despite the distance, I saw his posture stiffen. I felt certain unexpected spots of color and movement attracted his eyes, just as they'd attracted mine. And the only colorful things moving on the *Pegasus* were Sofia and me!

WHAT IS GREEN?

I reached up and grabbed Sofia's ankle. "Don't move!"

She froze in place, and asked, "What's wrong?"

"Someone is looking our way."

"From where?"

"Aft of the *Pegasus*. A man dumping trash looked this way, and he got all stiff, like he was concentrating on something."

"You think he saw us?"

"Our clothes are too brightly colored. They have to stand out big time against the gray hull." I sighed, "So, yeah, I think he sees us."

"Can you get inside his head and make him unsee us, Nora? Like you did with that pirate in the tunnels around the engines?"

"I got to the guy in the tunnels before he spotted us and made him so disinterested that he didn't notice us. I'll try it on the trash pirate, but I don't think it will work on someone who's already seen us."

I called up my mental map of the emotions surrounding us. As before, the passengers and crew held in the dining hall shone bright red. I spotted Conley's bright spark in the middle of all that red. Scattered around the ship were the sparks for pirates whose minds I had entered. Strangely, the rest of the pirates showed up as dull purple now.

What did *that* mean? Maybe anticipation for the drinking and... other stuff to come? I'd thought maroon was just the pirates' normal emotional color. Now, I wondered if the color represented a different fear than the passengers felt? Or maybe tension from staying alert on the job?

Now isn't the time to answer that question, Nora!

Right. Ignoring the shifting pirate emotions, I turned my attention aft. The man at the dump shined as brightly as the passengers' sea of red. I felt certain the brighter the colors on my mental map, the more vivid the emotion. That's why the passengers' fear showed up as bright red. I knew whatever that man felt, he felt it strongly. But his emotion shined bright green.

"What does *green* mean?" I muttered.

"Green?" Sofia said. "I don't understand."

"Sorry, I'll explain later." I drew a deep breath, released it, and said, "I'm going into the trash man's mind. Don't let me fall."

I felt a gentle tug where the safety line hooked to my oxygen harness and knew it came from Sofia taking up the slack in the line. Confident she had me, I closed my eyes and aimed my mind at the bright green spot. Since trash man wasn't on the *Pegasus*, I felt as if he was farther away than any mind I'd entered. But I don't think he was any farther away than Rivera was when I entered her dreams. I held onto that thought as I flew across the two hundred meters separating me and the strange, green emotion.

I hit the man's mind and slipped inside without the usual jarring crash. Either I'm getting better at it, the man had an open and accommodating mind, or maybe it had something to do with green emotion. Whatever the reason, I was thankful for the easy entry once I got a look at the inside of the man's head.

Gray surrounded me and weighed heavy on my mind. Its oppressive nature reminded me of the grief in Conley's mind before I convinced him I was alive. But this gray felt dull where Conley's anguish felt sharp, and numb where Conley's despair hurt. The mind around me almost felt dead.

But *something* moved around me. Hidden by the drab gray, but there all the same.

Tendrils of gray swirled as the something zipped by. I reached for it, but it vanished before I touched it. A dark ball rolled out of the gray mists. I caught it, thinking it was a memory, but it didn't feel like any memory I'd found before.

A hard shell surrounded the ball. Did it shield the mind from the memory? Or was it protecting the memory from the awful gray? There was only one way to find out.

I concentrated on the shell and hit it with everything I had. The shell cracked, so I hit it again. And...

Alarms blared as I cowered behind a chair. A man and a woman— my parents—stood between me and a door. With a metallic squeal, something pushed between the door's edge and the frame. As it pried the door open, my father leapt forward and thrust a knife through the small opening. Someone outside the door snarled in pain.

A light flashed. My father stumbled backwards, then collapsed on the deck. Horrible, sightless eyes looked at me, and I screamed.

A man squeezed through the widening opening. Blood oozed from a deep gash on his arm. My mother punched him right on the wound. He roared and backhanded her. She fell, stunned, and the man kicked her in the stomach.

A woman slid through the door and surveyed the scene.

The snarling man pointed at the gash on his arm and then at my mother. "She's mine, Captain. Paid for her in blood."

The woman, the captain, waved permission at the man. "Do what you want with her, Hyde."

The captain kicked my father's body aside and approached the chair. Cold eyes stared at me, and she said, "Come out, boy. You're mine, now."

I dropped the memory as if it burned me, and the shell repaired itself before it rolled away.

I recognized the captain in the memory. I'd been inside her mind. I'd witnessed her insanity. I'd forced her to face the past she denied. It was Rivera's late, unlamented mother in this man's memory.

Was he a slave of the pirates, or was he just the pirate who got stuck with the worst jobs?

I sensed something coming and recognized it as the thing that passed near me earlier. This time, I touched it as it swept by. Green sparks flew where my hand touched it, and the unseen thing changed course. It brushed around me before speeding off into the gray distance.

But while it touched me, I felt an emotion. One under tight control. Precious and fragile. And I got the idea the man never thought he'd feel that emotion again.

Hope. Hope is green.

The thin green thread of hope flowing through the trash man's mind flitted away. But it zipped back immediately and entwined itself around me.

"Yes," I said, "feel hope!"

The green brightened, and the thread thickened.

"Rescue isn't far away."

The strand of hope didn't change. Why not? Then it dawned on me. Rescue is a concept, not an emotion. And I'm an empath, not a telepath. Getting rescued is very emotional. You just have to look at how Sofia and I have bonded over the last two days to recognize that. Compassion, love, trust, reliance, joy—they're just some of the emotions I had experienced because of stuff Sofia did for me. But none of them conveyed the idea of rescue. What else could I try?

Salvation? Maybe, but the word is so closely linked to religion that I was afraid it might confuse him.

Deliverance? Still not an emotion.

Release? Freedom? Escape? They were great words but crappy emotions.

Man, I never imagined I'd need a huge vocabulary just to be a successful empath. Then again, most empaths just receive emotions. Broadcasting empaths are super rare, and I've never heard of any empath whose ability worked quite the way mine did. It'll be such a relief when Dad shows up and—

Relief? It's not a perfect match for rescue, but it's not a bad one. Most importantly, it's an emotion.

"Relief is coming!" I said. "Relief from the pirates. Relief from this life. Feel relief, because it's not far away."

The green grew brighter, and the thread got fatter. Not bad, even if I say so myself.

I never know how much real-world time passes when I'm inside someone's head. However long it had been, I didn't want to stay in the man's mind longer than necessary. I needed to send one more message, then wrap things up.

But what should I send to him? Having someone help us from inside the pirate base would be huge, especially if he knew his way around the base. But how could I ask him for help? (And why is it that all the things I *really* want to communicate are concepts rather than emotions?)

I wanted to avoid the pirates, so how did they make me feel? Duh, threatened.

"We feel threatened!" I said, as the green strand of hope spun and danced around me. "But we want to feel... safe!"

The thread didn't change, but I felt confusion rise somewhere inside the man's mind. I guess I didn't do a good job asking for help. But I didn't want to leave him confused, either, so sent a follow-up message.

"Feel hope! Above all else, feel hope!"

The confusion lessened as my latest message caught the man's attention. Figuring I'd done all I could do, I pulled out and returned to my own mind. I was immediately aware of something pulling at my harness. I opened my eyes and saw Sofia had hold of the safety line clipped to my oxygen harness. Then I realized the line was the only thing keeping me from falling off the hull, and quickly grabbed the closest hand hold.

Once I had my feet beneath me, Sofia asked, "Did you keep him from noticing us?"

"I didn't need to. He's a pirate slave, and he hopes we're part of a rescue attempt or something like that."

"Why wouldn't he just think we're a couple of pirates?"

I shrugged. "I'm guessing, but maybe it's because we're not dressed like pirates? Or maybe pirates never climb around the hull of a captured ship right after it lands. For all I know, he's got great vision and figured out we're girls."

"Why would that matter? I mean, their captain is a woman."

"I said I was guessing." I pointed towards the crest of the hull. "Let's get going, again."

With deliberation, Sofia resumed her climb. I cast one last look at the trash pile, saw the man walking away, and began climbing.

When we reached the top, we spent two minutes maneuvering ourselves on the hand holds so we could both peek over the top easily, but duck out of sight just as easily. I looked for the trash man and spotted him approaching an airlock.

I pointed to him and said, "Remember that building. We can go there if we need help."

A dozen bare metal frame vehicles emerged from what looked like a warehouse or parking hanger for small ships. The telltale blue haze of an atmosphere shield surrounded each driver. When they stopped, the vehicles formed a line between the warehouse and the *Pegasus*.

"Any idea what that's for?" I asked.

Sofia shook her head. But we learned the answer almost immediately. Each driver did something with their vehicle's controls, and a translucent blue corridor sprang up between the *Pegasus* and an airlock into the warehouse. Moments later, armed pirates emerged and lined up along the temporary corridor joining the ship and the warehouse. They all held clubs, probably for prodding their prisoners to move faster.

The crew came next, with Captain Riggs leading the way. He

walked with the same commanding bearing he had on board his ship and ignored the pirates lining his route. The ship's officers followed the captain, then came the crew.

But the crew weren't alone. They all carried or led *children* from the ship.

Sofia gripped my arm. "Why did the pirates take the children? They'll be harder to control."

"Yeah, harder for the *crew* to control."

I pointed at a woman who was midway between the *Pegasus* and the warehouse. She pulled a little boy by the hand as the boy cried and waved his free hand towards the ship. I couldn't hear his wails, but knew the terrified child wanted his mama. The crew woman stopped and tried gathering the boy in her arms, but the child pulled free and dashed back to his mother.

The nearest pirate casually lifted a foot and kicked the little boy through the blue haze of the atmosphere shield. He sprawled on the ground, gasping for breath he could never draw. The crew woman hesitated for a second, drew a deep breath, and plunged through the shield after the child. She scooped up the boy and staggered back inside the pressurized tunnel between the *Pegasus* and the warehouse. As the woman checked the child's breathing, the same pirate who kicked the boy through the shield hit her on the back with his club. She stumbled forward, fighting for balance as the pirate yelled at her.

"That's barbaric," Sofia gasped.

I couldn't respond because the scene reminded me of my far-too-recent battle for breath in a vacuum. I felt the same empty ache in my lungs and the same dull pain from my diaphragm as it fought for air that wasn't there. My breath came in short, panicked gasps and—

Sofia squeezed my arm. "You're okay, Nora. Close your eyes and take a deep breath, okay?"

I did as she said and it surprised me how much concentration it took to breathe deeply. But once I managed the first one, a second was easier. By the third, I opened my eyes and glanced at Sofia.

"Thanks. I guess I, um, identified too much with that little boy."

"That's no surprise. Empathy *is* your birthright, isn't it?" Sofia offered a weak smile. "It probably helps that you're not a psycho pirate, either."

"Thanks, I think."

We watched the rest of the parade of crew and children in silence. As I predicted, Conley and Barber were also among those sent to the warehouse. They brought up the rear, and the pirates took no chances that either of them would cause trouble. My bodyguards carried two squirming, crying young children apiece. With all their attention directed at the kids in their arms, neither man could cause problems for the pirates. Not that they would do anything right now.

I mean, what's the point of starting something when you have no hope of accomplishing anything? Don't get me wrong, Conley and Barber *wanted* to smash as many pirate faces as possible, but they knew timing was everything. And this was definitely not the time to kick asses. They would willingly sacrifice their lives fighting the pirates, but only if the gain was worth their loss.

I felt exactly the same.

Although I grew up with men like Conley and Barber all around me, this moment was the first time I think I truly understood them. That those two men spent years putting my life ahead of theirs humbled me. And it shamed me to think how I had taken them for granted. I watched those two amazing men march past the pirates, who took sadistic glee in smacking them with their clubs. Conley and Barber turned and twisted so the blows hit them rather than the children clutched in their arms.

Without conscious thought, I whispered, "I will get you out of this. I will make these pirates pay for what they've done. And this scum will rue the day they dared cross the Connaughts."

"And the Olsons," Sofia said. "So help me, God. Amen."

The moment Conley and Barber entered the warehouse, the pirates split into two groups. A dozen returned to the *Pegasus* while the rest followed my bodyguards into their temporary prison. The men in the twelve metal frame vehicles shut down the atmosphere shields connecting the ship and the warehouse. Personal oxygen harnesses glowed blue around each man as they parked the vehicles next to the building and followed their pirate buddies inside.

As the enormous warehouse's outer airlock door trundled shut, Sofia asked, "Why didn't they park inside the building like before?"

"Maybe it's just one big room in there and they don't want the crew getting any ideas about escape?" I said.

"I suppose that makes some kind of sense. At least we won't have to look for them when the time comes to make a break for it."

I grinned at Sofia. "Listen to you sounding all optimistic! I'll make a Connaught out of you, yet."

Sofia sniffed, "I thought I already *was* an honorary member of the family."

"Forgive me, sis. It slipped my mind for a moment."

"Don't let it happen again, young lady." Sofia turned serious again. "What do we do next?"

"I think I should check the emotions of the parents of the kids the pirates took, and then get an emotional read on the pirate base."

Sofia gazed out across the huge base. "Will your ability work across all that distance?"

"Dad wouldn't even break a sweat doing it. Me? I don't know. I could read everyone on the *Pegasus*, and she's a big ship." I shrugged. "There's only one way to find out."

"Let's tie you to a handhold first, Nora. I don't want you falling because my attention wandered for a few seconds."

We spent a minute securing ourselves to the hull. Then I

closed my eyes, took a deep breath, and lowered my mental shields.

Emotional waves crashed into me, crushing the confidence I'd developed in my ability under their weight. The ever-present fear the passengers felt had ratcheted up to terror for their children. The bright red I'd associated with them now pulsed and seethed, and it was laced with strands of bright blue.

Great, another new color-coded emotion.

A few blue strands split into multiple strands. Some of those split again. And that's when I figured it out. Desperation. Blue was desperation. Some of the parents must be psyching themselves up for a revolt. And their desperation infected others among the prisoners. It was only a matter of time before they took matters into their own hands. And then a lot of people would die.

No. Not on *my* watch, they wouldn't!

If I could just get inside the minds of some of the passengers, maybe I could persuade them to be patient and wait for rescue. I found my way to Conley's mind by riding a pirate's mind in among the passengers. Maybe I could do the same thing to reach one of the passengers? I scanned the ship for pirate minds I'd entered, but none of them remained on board.

What now? From the way the blue strands multiplied, I feared the situation would boil over in less than thirty minutes. There was no way Sofia and I could rescue the crew and children in that time.

I briefly considered going back inside the *Pegasus* and ambushing the pirates myself, but that had to be an absolute last resort. As well trained as I am in that stuff, I'm *nothing* compared to Conley and Barber. And I couldn't drag Sofia into something like that. She had no training at all.

As those thoughts flashed through my mind, another half-a-dozen blue strands split. There had to be *something* I could use to lock onto a single mind. Some difference that—

The blue strands! Those must come from individuals. And they split when one of those people convinced someone else that the situation called for desperate measures. It made sense. I think.

Don't think, Nora, do!

Right. I found the biggest, thickest blue strand among the passengers. With a mental prayer for divine guidance, I caught hold of the strand and rode it into the darkness of a new mind.

DESPERATE HOPE

I expected turmoil inside the passenger's mind, and boy, did I get it.

A dense, red fog of dread shrouded everything around me. It weighed heavily on my mind, and it wasn't even my fear creating the mist.

A gale force wind of desperation howled through the mind, buffeting me from all sides. It drove the fog before it without ever clearing it away.

Bright blue bolts of desperation crackled and flashed in the fog. They lit the mind around me but revealed nothing but black desolation and bright red terror. One bolt arced through me, and its touch burned me with a sharp lance of pain. It seared with the agony I imagine a parent must feel when danger looms over their child.

I spun about, looking for something, anything positive. Nothing. I didn't see the barest glimmer of hopeful green.

Another blue bolt sizzled through the mists before me, followed immediately by another that scorched me again. In the time I spent getting my bearings, the blue flashes appeared more frequently. That wasn't good. Not good at all.

Time to see what I can do.

"Feel hope!" I said. "Feel hope that your children are safe!"

The wind blew my words into the fog, where my command vanished so quickly I wasn't even sure I'd said anything.

This time, I shouted. "There *is* hope! Feel it! Believe it! You must have patience!"

I don't know how much effect the words had, but the fog didn't swallow them. Not completely, anyway.

"Your children will be safe! Rescue is coming!"

Nothing changed.

"You must believe! You must feel hope! You must have patience! All will be well if you do that!"

I think the wind's mournful wail subsided. Just a bit. And so little that I wasn't sure if I'd imagined it.

But then something caught my attention—a tiny spot of green. It spun and twirled and danced in the wind. But it was there. *Hope* existed in the passenger's mind!

"Yes," I cried, "hope! Feel it! Embrace it! There *is* hope!"

As I watched, the green grew into a small blob.

"Yes! That's it! Hope!"

A blue bolt slashed through the fragile fragment of hope, and I feared desperation would destroy hope. It didn't. Green merged with blue, and suddenly the fog filled with blue-green flashes. More bolts than I'd yet seen inside this mind.

What did *that* mean? The horrible truth dawned on me as soon as I asked the question.

Hope and desperation became one in this mind. The passenger heard my call, but he—I felt certain the passenger was male—didn't interpret it in the way I meant. He must believe his act of desperation was the only hope for his children!

Oh God, what have I done?

I entered his mind, hoping to calm him down, to allay his fears. Instead, I'd fanned them. I'd driven his mind to greater desperation.

Terrified of doing further damage, I fled to the safety of my own mind.

I drew a ragged breath and opened my eyes. Tears immediately filled them, blurring my vision. I slapped a hand across my eyes to clear my eyes and failed. I slapped again to punish myself for believing my few minor psychic successes meant I had mastered emotional manipulation, and it hurt. Good. I deserved it.

Sofia caught my hand before I could smack myself again. "Stop it, Nora! What do you think you're doing?"

More tears flooded my eyes. "I ruined everything, Sofia. I made it worse, not better."

Sofia wrapped an arm around me and gave my hand a reassuring squeeze. "It can't be *that* bad! Tell me everything."

I blurted it out in one nonstop sentence. The flowing tears kept me from seeing Sofia's reaction, but I felt her growing tension through her embrace. I finished by muttering, "I screwed up royally, and others will pay for my mistake."

"It's not good, that's for sure," Sofia said.

I sniffled and said, "With all my training, you'd think I'd have some idea what to do next. But I don't have a clue."

"That's okay." Sofia released my hand and gently wiped tears from my eyes. "You'll figure it out."

"I will?"

She nodded. "I have absolute confidence in you."

"So, no pressure, right?"

"Break it down, Nora," Sofia said. "We have to stop the passenger revolt *and* free the crew and children before the pirates finish celebrating. Just set your priorities and get going."

Something in Sofia's expression made me ask, "You've already figured out *your* priorities, haven't you?"

She nodded. "I'm the last member of the crew on the *Pegasus*. My first duty is to the passengers still on board. Splitting up seems like a horrible idea, but the clock is ticking."

"Time is tight, but it isn't *that* tight. I agree we have two things to do, but we *need* each other." I met Sofia's determined gaze with one of my own. "Sure, splitting up sounds like the thing to do, but my gut tells me to stick together. Maybe it's an unconscious warning from my psychic ability, something from my training, or, I don't know, a woman's intuition. But I will fail if you're not at my side, Sofia."

"No you won't," Sofia said. "You're Nora freaking Connaught, the Badass Babe of the Cosmos! I'll just slow you down."

"Oh yeah? Do you know what I'd be if you hadn't been at my side? I'd be Nora freaking Connaught, the Deadass Dummy of the Cosmos." Sofia opened her mouth to protest, but I cut her off. "You know it's true."

"Okay, but you're not the only one who owes a debt of gratitude. I'd be dead or captured if it wasn't for you."

"All the more reason for us to stay together, don't you think?"

Sofia paused for a moment, then nodded.

"Now that we've settled that, you were right about one thing. The clock *is* ticking. Let's get back inside the *Pegasus* and find a way to stop the passenger revolt."

Without another word, we untied ourselves from the hand-holds and began our descent.

～

I resisted the urge to kiss the *Pegasus's* lifepod launch bay deck when we re-entered her Earth-normal gravity field. But not having to concentrate on every move felt so good it was a close thing. I activated the bay's atmosphere shield and slumped against the wall while the bay pressurized.

Sofia touched my arm. "Are you okay?"

"Yeah, just mentally worn out. I didn't realize how much concentration my mental shield took until I had to concentrate on moving, too."

"I had no idea." Sofia began kneading my shoulders. "Wow, Nora, I've felt softer bulkheads."

"Where did you learn to do that?" I groaned in pleasure. "Wait, let me guess—Connaught Starlines corporate training?"

"No, I used to do this for Dad when he had a rough day at work." She sighed, "I miss him."

"I talk about my family all the time, but that's the first time you've mentioned yours."

The motion of Sofia's hands changed just enough to make me think she had shrugged. "Your family is connected to just about everything you've done since your psychic ability first showed up. It's natural that you'd talk about them. This is just the first time I did something with a family story behind it."

"I hope you'll introduce me to them when this is all over."

"Of course I will. They're going to love you just as much as you say your family will love me. And that's without the whole saved-their-daughter's-life thing."

The pressure monitor on the launch bay's controls turned green. I turned off my atmosphere harness and pulled away from Sofia's magic hands.

"As much as I'd love to hear your family history, we have to get to the dining hall and stop the passenger revolt."

We went to the launch bay's hatch. I closed my eyes and summoned my emotional map of the *Pegasus*. There weren't any pirates in the entire aft half of the *Pegasus*.

"We're clear," I said, and opened the hatch.

We entered the long corridor connecting passenger territory and crew territory. Sofia closed the hatch behind us and followed me forward. I hesitated when we came to the door into the maintenance tunnels. It was definitely the safest route for us, but the tunnel's twists and turns would slow us down. I made a quick decision and passed by the tunnel entrance.

"Nora?" Sofia called softly. "Shouldn't we go into the tunnels?"

"Yes, eventually, but we'll make better time out here right now. Don't worry, the pirates are all up near the passengers."

We moved as quietly as possible on the metal deck and stopped at the hatch marking the end of crew territory and the beginning of passenger territory. I checked my mental map again. As before, the passengers' massed emotions—still bright red laced with an increasing number of blue strands—washed out everything else nearby. I didn't see any maroon dots, which meant the pirates were too close to the passengers to stand out. Even so, being out in the open like this was making me antsy.

"We'll go through this hatch," I whispered, "and then enter the tunnels. There's a maintenance door about twenty meters from here."

"Good," Sofia said, "being in this corridor is making me nervous."

I held a finger over the door control. "Ready?"

Sofia nodded.

I opened the door.

And breathed a sigh of relief at the empty corridor stretching out before us.

We fast-walked to the tunnel door, opened it, and crawled in. A little tension flowed out of me when the door clicked shut behind us. I called up the tunnel map Granddaddy had me memorize and set off for the dining hall.

"Do you have a plan for warning the passengers?" Sofia asked. "Because I do, if you don't."

"Since we can't count on my psychic ability to send a message, I'm going to have to go into the dining hall and talk to them in person."

"That's half right, Nora. *I'm* the one who will deliver the message while you wait in the tunnels."

"I appreciate what you're trying to do, Sofia, but you haven't thought it through. Since I've been inside the ringleader's mind, he shows up on my mental map as a spark of light in the sea of red. You can't find him as quickly as me."

"I can if you guide me."

"How? I can't send directions, just emotions."

"I know that, Nora. But if we set up emotional signals in advance, you can do it. We just need something for hot, cold, left, and right. Oh, and one for when I reach the right guy."

"That won't work. I can't see my mental map when I'm inside your head, and I can't send emotions to you when I'm outside your head."

"It will work if you just pop into my mind long enough to send directions, and then pop back out. Or will that tire you out too much?"

"No, I think I can do that," I said, "but why go to all that trouble when I can just do it myself?"

"Because the passengers are more likely to believe me."

I stopped in surprise and looked back at Sofia. "Huh? How does that make any sense? After all, I'm Nora freaking Connaught!"

"The passengers don't know that. They've never met you, *and* they've been told that you're dead."

"They were told you're dead, too."

"True, but they know *me* because I've served a bunch of them on this voyage. All I need is one passenger who'll vouch for me, and that shouldn't be hard to find."

I considered suggesting we both go. But the plan was risky enough already. Someone needed to stay out of sight and free to roam, and I was the best person for that job.

"Okay," I sighed, "you go and I stay."

We spent the next minute setting up emotional signals. Like *love* means *hot*, and *anger* meant *cold*. When we reached the tunnel exit into the dining hall, I gave Sofia a quick hug.

"Good luck, and for God's sake, be careful!"

"I'll do my best." She turned towards the door, then looked back at me. "Turn your comm to my frequency. That way you can hear what I hear."

I pulled the comm from my ear. "Good idea. Don't forget that I can hear what you say, too."

"Gotcha."

I finished changing the comm's frequency, and then cast a quick emotional scan of the area around the door. The closest passengers appeared as individuals. I didn't see any pirates, so I gave Sofia a nod and opened the door. She flashed a quick smile and slipped into the dining room.

The murmur of a thousand voices sounded from my comm, sent by the nano transmitters Conley and Barber installed in Sofia's ear. I listened for gasps of surprise at Sofia's sudden appearance in the room and heard nothing of the sort. At a guess, most of the passengers had either fallen into depression over their fate or were stoking themselves up for the coming passenger revolt. With their attention turned inward, they simply didn't notice Sofia slip into the dining hall.

In a low voice, Sofia said, "This is horrible, Nora. I've never seen so many terrified people before." She drew a shuddering breath, released it, then added, "Okay, I have my back to the tunnel door. Point me in the right direction."

I checked my mental map. Two sparks stood out from the red flood—Sofia and the man whose mind I'd entered fifteen minutes ago. A sea of bright red separated them, and I prayed it didn't hide any pirates. But I felt certain they'd be outside the dining hall, guarding the doors. Mostly certain, anyway.

I released the map and dove into Sofia's mind. Soothing, emotionally quiet darkness wrapped around me. A soft breeze of anxiety brushed by me, but her mind was remarkably calm considering the stakes.

Feel anger, I sent, using our code to let her know she wasn't close to her quarry.

Feel righteous, I added, telling her to head to her right.

I returned to my own mind, called up the mental map, and watched Sofia's spark move through the red blob. She'd wandered too far to the right, so I entered her mind again.

Feel sinister, I sent, telling her to swing left.

I admit I was kind of proud of that hint. I don't know how many people know that sinister is an archaic word for left-handedness. Heck, I don't even know how *I* know it. But for once, my vocabulary was extensive enough to give me just the right emotion for guiding Sofia.

I bounced back and forth between my mental map and Sofia's mind as my friend gradually closed the gap between her and the man who was whipping up revolution among the other passengers. When I wasn't sending signals to Sofia, I heard snippets of conversation through the comm.

"Little Ruth must be so scared," a woman moaned.

"I can't wait to get my hands around a pirate's throat," a man muttered.

"Please, Carl," a young-sounding woman whispered, "I don't want my first time to be when a pirate forces himself on me."

Nothing I heard surprised me. I already knew the emotions behind the words. But there was something about hearing the desperation and fear in the voices that hit me harder than I expected. As difficult as the last two days were for Sofia and me, at least we were doing something. These poor passengers had nothing to do but dwell on their situation and fear their future.

Sofia's voice suddenly interrupted that train of thought. "Mrs. Stanley?"

I heard an indrawn breath that sounded suspiciously like the prelude to a cry of surprise or alarm.

"Shhh!" Sofia hissed. "Please keep your voice down, ma'am."

Mrs. Stanley slowly released her breath, then whispered, "My God, Sofia? They told us you were dead, killed along with that poor Connaught girl."

"Nora and I tricked the pirates into believing that."

"Nora Connaught? Do you mean to say she's alive, too?"

"Yes, and we have a plan to rescue everyone from the pirates. But it will all fall apart if the passengers stage a revolt against the pirates."

"Revolt? What are you talking about, dear?"

"Some of the others are working themselves up to attack the pirate guards."

"I have heard nothing about it. Are you sure?"

"Yes. I need someone who can vouch for my identity so I can talk them out of it."

"Say no more, dear," Mrs. Stanley proclaimed. "Where are these foolhardy men?"

From the rising and fading voices in the background, Sofia and Mrs. Stanley began walking.

"I don't know for sure that it's just men, ma'am," Sofia said.

Mrs. Stanley sniffed. "I'm sure they have a few women in their group. Men don't have a monopoly on foolhardiness, after all. Though men do have the vast majority of it."

I checked my mental map and saw the two sparks converging. I popped into Sofia's mind.

Feel love, I sent.

Return to my mind.

Check the map.

Back to Sofia.

Feel love!

Return.

Check.

Bingo!

I dove into Sofia's mind one more time and sent the signal for success.

Feel desperation!

Sofia and I had agreed it was the obvious emotion to use here, since the man organizing the revolt was as desperate as they come.

I returned to my mind just as a man's authoritative voice came over the comm. "All right, gentlemen, let's teach that pirate scum just who they're dealing with!"

Over the comm, I heard a chorus of male voices rise in agreement with the unknown man's declaration. Another voice cut through the chatter like a whip.

"Just one moment, young man!" Mrs. Stanley said.

"Sorry, lady," the ringleader said, "I don't have time for gossip right now."

"Or manners, apparently," Mrs. Stanley snapped.

"Look, we're a little busy here, so if you don't mind—"

"I *do* mind," Mrs. Stanley countered. "Throwing your life away on this futile gesture is bad enough. But convincing these other young fools to follow you is downright criminal!"

"Nobody asked your opinion, you old bat!" the ringleader snarled.

"*Stop it!*" Sofia hissed. "Do you want to attract the pirates' attention?"

I nodded at Sofia's sensible question. But Mrs. Stanley had other ideas.

"If it will stop this idiot from making a colossal mistake, I most certainly do."

Sofia kept her voice low. "I sympathize, Mrs. Stanley, but what do you think will happen to me if the pirates discover I'm here?"

Exactly, I thought.

But Mrs. Stanley wasn't so easily deterred. "You're out of uniform, dear. How will the pirates recognize you?"

"Uniform?" the ringleader asked, his voice filled with confusion.

"They paraded me in front of their late captain, Mrs. Stanley." Sofia's tone remained polite—probably more of that Connaught Starlines training—but it acquired a hard edge. "You may be willing to bet my life that the pirates won't recognize me. *I am not.*"

"I had not considered it in that light," Mrs. Stanley said. "Please forgive me, dear."

The ringleader said, "You've completely lost me, ladies. But I have things to do and—"

Sofia interrupted, "Sir, if you go through with this plan, you will accomplish nothing, and doom every passenger and crew member to a life of slavery."

"You can't know that," the ringleader countered.

"She can, and she does," Mrs. Stanley said.

"How?" he asked.

"I'll explain," Sofia said, "but privately. Just the three of us."

Good idea, Sofia! She'd already been forced to reveal more than I felt comfortable about. If she spilled the news that I was still alive in public, I felt certain the news would race through the terrified and bored passengers so fast it would make my head spin.

The ringleader must have hesitated, because Sofia added, "Give me two minutes, sir. That's all I ask. The pirates aren't going anywhere."

"Fine, two minutes," he sighed. He raised his voice, "Guys? Give us some space."

Murmurs broke out among those surrounding the trio, but the voices grew fainter as their owners retreated from Sofia and the two passengers.

"All right, spill it," the ringleader said. "And it had better be good."

"I am Sofia Olson, and the last member of the *Pegasus's* crew still onboard."

"Are you with shipboard security?" he asked.

"No, I'm in passenger services."

"Well," he scoffed, "you'll be the first one I call if we decide to serve tea to those pirates!"

Sofia ignored the comment and said, "Captain Riggs assigned me as the personal aide to Nora Connaught."

"Oh." In a contrite tone, he said, "I'm sorry about my last comment. Losing Miss Connaught must be devastating to you, but—"

"Nora isn't dead. Neither am I, obviously."

"Wait a minute," the man said. "Are you telling me you're the crew member the pirates told us died with her?"

"That is exactly what she's telling you," Mrs. Stanley said. "I can vouch for Sofia. She is just who she says she is."

"Do *you* believe the Connaught girl is still alive?" the ringleader asked.

"Sofia has been nothing but truthful with me," Mrs. Stanley replied.

I know the woman's compliment was for Sofia, but I loved the absolute certainty in Mrs. Stanley's voice. And, hey, *I* can vouch for Sofia's honesty, too.

"Thank you, ma'am," Sofia said. "Sir, please hold this in the strictest confidence. Nora and I have a plan to free the crew, rescue the children, and get everyone off this God forsaken moon."

"We're on a moon?" the ringleader asked. "We don't have any view ports in here. How do you know that?"

"Because I've been outside the ship, sir. Nora and I saw where the pirates took the crew and children. We—"

"That changes everything!" the man said. "With your knowledge and our numbers, our revolt has a much better chance of succeeding!"

Crap! That was an unexpected turn.

"It changes *nothing*, sir," Sofia countered. "Even if you overwhelm the pirates guarding the *Pegasus*, you still have a hundred meters of vacuum separating you from where the pirates are holding the others. All your revolt will do is put the pirates on alert and ruin any chance Nora and I can pull off this rescue."

"Then take me with you," the man said.

"That's a bad idea, sir," Sofia said.

"Nonsense," Mrs. Stanley said. "A strapping man like him will come in quite handy, Sofia."

What? And to think I'd developed warm feelings for Mrs. Stanley's practical nature.

"I'm glad that's settled," the man said.

"You'd best go tell your followers that the revolt is off, young man," Mrs. Stanley said. "They look as if they're getting impatient."

"Of course. I'll be right back, ladies."

Two seconds later, Mrs. Stanley whispered, "This is your chance to slip away, dear. I'll cover for you."

"Thank you, Mrs. Stanley."

"Just be careful, Sofia."

"I'll do my best, ma'am."

A minute later, Sofia tapped on the tunnel door. I opened it and she slipped inside.

As we made our way back through the tunnels, Sofia said, "Remind me to give Mrs. Stanley a great big hug when this is all over."

"You and me, both, Sofia. You and me, both."

I scanned for nearby emotions. The vast blob of passenger emotions still washed out everything else in the area. None of the pirates had wandered far enough from the dining hall to stand out, which meant Sofia and I had little chance of being caught. But we still moved through the tunnels in silence until we left the mass of emotions far behind us.

"Let's stop and rest for a minute," I said, and slumped into a tunnel alcove.

Sofia peered at me and asked, "You look pale, Nora. Are you okay?"

I summoned a weak grin. "I'm a blue-eyed blonde, Sofia. Pale is my natural color."

"But?" she prompted.

"Popping back and forth between your mind and my mental map took more out of me than I expected." I gave a nonchalant wave to dismiss the concern in Sofia's expression. "I'll be fine once my brain rests for a bit."

Unprompted, Sofia scooted behind me and began kneading my shoulders. She worked her way to my neck, and then up to my scalp. I almost melted under her touch.

While she helped me relax, I asked, "Do you think the ringleader caused trouble once he realized you were gone?"

Sofia barked a soft laugh. "Nothing Mrs. Stanley can't deal with. She might look like someone's sweet grandmother—and she really can be quite sweet—but she is... *Formidable* is what Captain Riggs calls her. Once she sets her mind on something, she just plows through objections like they weren't even there."

"And you're sure she handled the revolting guy?"

Sofia snorted a laugh at my unintentional pun. "I'd bet my life on it."

"You *are* betting your life on it," I said, "and the lives of everyone else from the *Pegasus*."

Sofia's tone sobered. "I know. But so does Mrs. Stanley. She won't let us down."

"Maybe I should check my mental map one more time and see if the blue strands of desperation are growing or shrinking."

"Only do that if you're up to it, Nora. But I think we'd already know if she failed."

"How?"

"We'd have heard shouts and screams and blaster fire."

"I should have thought of that."

"Don't be too hard on yourself, Nora. It's really hard to think clearly when someone is massaging your shoulders."

"Then you'd better stop, Sofia, because we're going to need all our wits for what comes next."

"Do you have a plan?"

"Sort of," I replied. "We can't risk using the big airlock into the warehouse the pirates put the crew and children into. Not while there might be pirates in there guarding them."

"So?" Sofia prompted

"Do you remember the guy from the garbage pile? I think we need to find him. He's been slaving for the pirates long enough that I bet he knows his way around this base—including ways to reach the crew and children without being caught."

"Are you sure we can trust him?"

"After what I found inside his mind?" I said. "Absolutely positive."

"Then let's get going."

For our return trip to the lifepod launch bay, we stayed in the tunnels until we reached the exit just a few meters from our destination. It took a little longer, but time wasn't as tight as it had been when we went to stop the passenger revolt. Besides, I wanted to keep my emotional scans to a minimum for a while so my brain could rest. That didn't stop me from taking a quick scan before we exited the maintenance tunnels, but it was the only one I did.

"We're all clear," I said, and led Sofia out into the corridor.

We hurried down to the hatch and slipped through while it was still opening. Sofia closed the hatch while I headed for the bay's launch controls. I opened my backpack and pulled out the two safety lines we used both times we went out on the *Pegasus's* hull. I clipped one of them to the ring next to the controls. Then I clipped the other one to the other end of the first.

Closing my eyes, I took a wider emotional scan, looking for anyone who might be on the moon's surface and near the *Pegasus*. The scan came up empty, so I tossed the safety lines out of the launch bay. They fell in seeming slow motion in the moon's low gravity, but finally the end of the second line hit the surface far below.

I turned on my atmosphere harness, and Sofia did the same. Taking hold of the line, I asked, "Are you ready?"

Sofia nodded. "As much as I'll ever be. Let's do this."

I stepped through the blue haze of the atmosphere shield that protected the launch bay and began my descent.

This time, I knew what to expect from the moon's low gravity. I took a gentle step out of the *Pegasus's* artificial gravity and didn't end up swinging wildly like I did the last time. Then I went hand-over-hand down the safety line.

Sofia watched until my head dropped below the lip of the launch bay hatch, then joined me on the safety line. She mimicked my form while keeping a meter separation between her feet and my head. I just hoped Sofia didn't suffer from a fear of heights, since she had to look down throughout the descent, so she didn't accidentally drop on top of me.

The thirty-meter trip down the safety line wouldn't have been difficult in earth-normal gravity. In the moon's one-quarter gravity, it was dead simple. I only stopped once, and that was close to the ground.

The *Pegasus* had five meters of ground clearance. Once we slid below that, we'd be visible to anyone outside the base. I already knew how easily movement caught the eye on this dead world, so I stopped six meters from the ground. Moving with the exaggerated caution the low gravity required, I flipped around so I hung head down from the safety line. I squeezed the line tightly between my legs and gradually pulled myself down far enough to look under the *Pegasus* at the nearby buildings.

Nothing moved. No colorful clothing stood out from the drab, gray landscape or the darker gray building walls. I hung that way for a slow count to sixty while my gaze swept the landscape three times. Finally satisfied we had the landing field to ourselves, I righted myself and climbed down the last few meters to the ground. My feet sank a couple of centimeters into the deep dust that covered the moon's surface.

From a habit ingrained by Mom's and Granddaddy's training, I went to one knee to present as small a profile as possible. Sofia did the same when she reached the ground.

I put a hand on her shoulder and, with my free hand, pointed to a small building fifty meters to the left of the warehouse turned crew-holding facility. "The guy from the garbage pile went into that building."

"That's not too far," Sofia said, "even walking extra-carefully in this gravity."

She rose, but I pulled her down again. "Not yet. We're not going to take the straight path to that building."

"I know you must have a good reason for that, Nora, but I can't think of it."

"Don't feel bad, I didn't think of it until I saw that." I pointed at the trail of footprints left by the crew, children, and pirates as they walked from the *Pegasus* to the warehouse. "If we just walk straight there, we'll leave a trail even the stupidest pirates can follow."

Sofia nodded, then asked, "Should we walk in a crouch, like we had to do in the maintenance tunnels?"

"I think so. At least, until we reach that pile of garbage and are out of the direct line of sight between the warehouse and the *Pegasus*."

"Maybe the low gravity will make it easier on my back."

I resisted the urge to rub my aching lower back. "God, I hope so."

It didn't, of course. Any easing we got was more than offset by the extra concentration and muscular control required for moving around in such low gravity. Before we'd gone fifty meters, my calves and thighs hated me. After another twenty meters, my lower back began complaining, too. After the first hundred meters, my whole body felt stiff and sore.

Halfway to the garbage pile, I realized I'd discovered the one thing Granddaddy's exercise regimen didn't prepare me for. I spent the rest of the hunched-over trip imagining his looks of shock when I finally had a chance to tell him of the gaping hole in his training. And I grinned at the thought that my sibs would be the ones who paid the price for my brilliant observation. They'd be Granddaddy's guinea pigs as he developed hunched-walking training, while *I* would be safely out of reach at college on Draconis.

It's amazing how little things like dreams of inflicting it's-for-your-own-good levels of torture on your sibs can lift the spirits. Well, they lifted *mine*, anyway.

After long minutes scuttling alongside the *Pegasus*, we finally reached the garbage pile. I half expected it to stink like, well, an enormous pile of garbage does. Of course, it didn't. No life meant no bacteria breaking down the garbage. Besides, no atmosphere meant there wasn't anything capable of carrying the odor, anyway. The pile marked one end of a trail of footprints that stretched to the airlock I'd seen the garbage guy enter earlier.

Sofia and I took a moment to sit down and rest. This time, I rubbed my lower back. And my calves and thighs.

I touched Sofia's foot. Our atmosphere shields merged, and I asked, "How are you doing?"

"I'll live. How about you?"

"The same." Then I told her about the exercise revelation I had during our walk, wrapping up with, "Pretty smart of me, huh?"

"Pretty cruel of you."

I grinned. "Yeah, that too. Are you ready to get going again?"

Instead of answering, Sofia rose to her feet. I joined her and —standing up straight this time—we followed the line of footprints towards the airlock. We reached it two minutes later.

I peeked through the airlock's viewport and saw it was empty. I took Sofia's hand so we could talk. "Let me do an emotional scan before we go in."

She nodded and rested her back by leaning against the airlock. Before I could summon my ability, Sofia gave a start and grabbed my hand.

"I felt vibrations through the airlock!"

Through the viewport, I saw why. The inner airlock hatch was opening!

I ducked below the airlock's viewport. "Someone's coming through the airlock!"

I considered my options. The nearest corner of the building was to my right. It was about twenty meters away, while it was thirty meters to the farther corner. But the nearer one was in plain sight from the warehouse where the pirates held the crew and children. If just one pirate came outside for any reason, we were as good as dead. With only one reasonable option, I headed to my left and dragged Sofia with me.

"We're leaving footprints, Nora," she said.

"I know."

"Won't whoever is coming through the airlock see them?"

"Maybe. But they'll definitely see us if we don't hide."

People think they depend on their sight as a sort of early warning system. But they don't realize just how much they depend on their hearing until they can't hear. I found myself straining to hear the sounds of the inner airlock hatch closing again. Of air cycling out of the airlock. Of the outer hatch opening. But there's nothing in a vacuum to carry sounds. So there's nothing to hear.

I tried trailing my free hand along the building's wall, hoping I could feel the vibrations caused by the airlock's mechanisms. But if the wall transmitted those vibrations, they were too soft for me to feel.

I cast a quick glance over my shoulder. Between the recessed hatch and my angle of vision, I couldn't even see the hatch anymore. It wouldn't matter, anyway, if we didn't reach the corner before someone exited the airlock.

When we finally reached the corner, I pulled Sofia around behind me. Crouching, I cautiously peered around the corner towards the airlock. The front of a float pallet emerged. I ducked back out of sight.

I almost jumped out of my skin when Sofia asked, "What did you see?"

She didn't whisper, which is what really startled me. People *always* whisper in situations like ours. Even though I had *just* finished mentally complaining about sound and vacuums, I had to consciously remind myself that Sofia had no reason to whisper. No one besides me could possibly hear her.

In a level tone, I replied, "Whoever is in the airlock is pushing a float pallet."

"More trash, do you think?"

"That's my best guess." I sidled closer to the corner. "Let me take another look."

I didn't poke my head around the corner this time. Instead, I got the best vision angle possible while staying out of sight. I wouldn't see the person pushing the float pallet until it got at least ten meters from the airlock. But I wouldn't show up in that person's peripheral vision, either. Five long seconds passed before the float pallet entered my field of vision. And, yep, it held a container overflowing with trash bags. A second later, the person pushing it came into view, too.

The blue haze of an atmosphere shield surrounded a man wearing a dark blue jumpsuit. Despite the baggy outfit, I got the idea the man had wiry strength. Beyond that, the only other thing I could tell was he had light colored hair. He glanced at the *Pegasus* a few times—I guess unfamiliar sights aren't common on a moon like this—but otherwise looked straight ahead.

"Is he the same guy whose emotions you read earlier?" Sofia asked.

"I'll check."

I closed my eyes and scanned the area for emotions. The man pushing the pallet didn't have the telltale spark of a mind I'd entered. His emotions were a mixture of bright red and soothing green. Fear and hope. I broadened my scan, looking for the garbage guy's spark, and found it less than fifty meters away. His emotions radiated the same colors as the new trash guy, as did a dozen other spots moving around inside the building. But I also counted four maroon dots, and that meant there were pirates in the building, too.

"It's not the same guy," I said, "but he feels hope. So I'm pretty sure he's talked to my guy."

I quickly relayed what else I learned when I scanned the building. "If they're not too scared of the pirates, I think the dozen hopefuls will help us."

"But how do we deal with the pirates?"

"I don't know yet. But chance has given us a good way to get through the airlock without raising suspicions. I think we have to take it."

"How?"

"Let me see if I can get inside the mind of the guy dumping the trash. Then I'll know more."

I dropped my mental shield and was surprised when a maelstrom of emotions didn't hit me. I saw a storm, but it didn't reach me. Maybe I was far enough away from the *Pegasus* dining hall to be outside its range?

That's a question for another time, Nora!

Right. I concentrated on the lone red-green dot, found a green tendril, and followed it inside the guy's mind. I found my answer and returned to my head.

"That guy's story is like the first guy's. Pirates captured him as a kid, and he's slaved for them ever since."

"So can we trust him?"

"Probably. I think that's going to have to be good enough."

The man reached the garbage pile, worked a control, one end of the container rose, and trash bags tumbled around the end of the pile. A moment later, the container settled back onto the pallet. The man turned it around and began pushing the pallet back to the airlock. He never even glanced at the line of footprints from the *Pegasus* to the garbage pile.

Had he just not noticed them or had he carefully ignored them? Time to find out.

"Come on," I said, "let's show ourselves."

Clutching each other's hand tightly, Sofia and I stepped around the corner and into view.

HIT & RUN

The man returning from the garbage pile widened his eyes when Sofia and I came into view. His step faltered and his jaw went slack. I prayed no one inside the building watched him, because I felt certain his reaction wasn't typical. He regained his composure after two long seconds and resumed trudging towards the airlock.

"Come on," I said. "Let's meet him at the airlock."

"At least he's not shouting a warning or anything," Sofia said.

"It wouldn't do any good in this vacuum. But, yeah, I'll take that as a good sign."

Sofia and I reached the airlock before the man. The outer hatch stood open. I assumed the man left it open to save time when he returned. I stopped next to the hatch, closed my eyes, and ran a quick emotional scan of the area. The red-green hopefuls clustered about ten meters from the airlock. I spotted the four maroon pirates a short way beyond the hopefuls.

As I opened my eyes, Sofia said, "The guy just pointed a finger at the airlock. I think he wants us to go inside."

Without another word, we went through the open outer hatch. Blessed Earth-normal gravity returned the second we crossed the threshold. I led Sofia to the wall next to the inner hatch, and we flattened ourselves against it. Even if a pirate came to the airlock and looked through the viewport, we were hidden from sight.

A moment later, the man pushed the float pallet into the airlock. He tapped a button on the airlock's control panel. As the outer hatch ground shut, he walked around the pallet and glanced through the inner hatch's viewport. Apparently satisfied with what he saw, the man held his hand out to me.

A few weeks before I boarded the *Pegasus*, Granddaddy told me, "People lie easily through big gestures, Nora. They can smile broadly when they'd rather punch you. Offer a firm, vigorous handshake even though they hate you. That's why you must pay attention to their small gestures, the things they do without thinking. Those actions can tell you a lot about someone's true self."

I liked the fact that this man invited me to take his hand rather than just grabbing mine. It bolstered the trust already established after my brief dive inside his mind. With a quick smile, I clasped hands with him. His atmosphere shield merged with mine and Sofia's, letting the three of us speak to each other.

"I'm Shawn."

Like the pirates, he spoke in galactic basic. I guess it's the logical language of choice when your band of outlaws comes from all over human space.

I'd been speaking gal base ever since boarding the *Pegasus*, so said, "I'm Nora. And this is Sofia."

The outer hatch closed and air blew against us as the airlock began pressurizing.

"Mike told us there were two *guys* climbing the hull of that new ship. He's sure you're a couple of Scouts here to rescue us." A sad smile played across Shawn's face. "You're not, are you?"

"Scouts? No," I said. "Here to rescue you? Yes."

His eyebrows arched. "But you're girls!"

"And?" I asked.

Shawn looked flustered, and said, "Um…"

Sofia affected a haughty tone. "For your information, we're the Badass Babes of the Cosmos. We avoided capture by the pirates and then convinced them we were dead. We stopped a foolish passenger revolt, and Nora has a plan to rescue everyone from the *Pegasus*."

"I'm sorry," Shawn said. "The only girls I ever see are the ones the pirates bring here after they take a prize. Those girls usually just cry and cower." Shawn gave a reflective pause, then added, "Now that I think about it, a lot of the guys do the same thing."

"Mentioning the pirates," I said, "do you usually have four of them hanging out with you?"

Shawn's eyes bugged out. "How did you know about the four pirates?"

"I'll explain later. Are those four guarding you or something?"

"Why bother?" Shawn asked. "There's nowhere for us to go. They want us to gather food and water to take to the people they put in the warehouse next door."

Air stopped blowing into the room. Shawn released my hand and turned off his atmosphere shield. Sofia and I did the same.

I pointed at the container on the float pallet. "If we hide in that, can you get us close to those four pirates?"

"I can get you down the corridor and into the same room."

"Okay. Are there tunnels or something like that connecting the buildings?"

"Yes."

"Do the tunnels carry loud noises to other buildings?"

"Not unless it's really loud. There's an airtight hatch between every building and the tunnels."

"Perfect."

Sofia and I climbed into the container. The odor I couldn't smell outside assaulted my nose. I ignored it as best I could, and crouched down out of sight. I pulled my blaster out of my backpack and checked the charge in its energy pack. Satisfied, I made sure the blaster was set for stun and then glanced at our new ally.

"Okay, Shawn, it's time to go pirate hunting."

Shawn hit another button on the airlock controls, and the inner hatch began grinding open. He resumed his position behind the float pallet, but he couldn't tear his eyes away from Sofia and me.

"Stop looking at us," I hissed.

"But you're both so pretty!" Shawn blurted. His face turned bright red, and I got the idea he hadn't meant to say that out loud. "I mean, uh—"

"If you keep staring into this container, you're going to make the pirates suspicious," Sofia said.

"Suspicious pirates will be harder to shoot," I added.

"And they'll probably get a chance to shoot back," Sofia continued.

"Then we might end up as corpses."

"Pretty corpses, but still corpses."

"Unless you want that, Shawn," I wrapped up, "*stop staring at us.*"

Shawn fixed his gaze firmly ahead, and whispered, "Sorry."

The inner hatch finished opening, and Shawn pushed the pallet and us out of the airlock. I could only see above me from my position inside the container. Walls rose on both sides of the pallet, forming the corridor Shawn had mentioned when we were inside the airlock.

Shawn left the inner airlock hatch open and pushed us down the corridor. Shawn's lax attention to basic safety protocols surprised me. Maybe the pirates didn't care about things like massive decompression if the airtight seal on the outer hatch failed? Or was it the pirates' slaves who didn't care?

That's a question for another time, Nora!

In the barest whisper possible, I said, "Stay down until the shooting stops, Sofia."

"I already figured that one out, Nora," she replied in an equally low voice. "Just be careful, okay?"

"As always."

"And don't miss."

As I nodded to Sofia, I heard a door ahead of us whir softly as it opened. I hoped it was an auto-opening door, because anyone manning door controls would have a perfect view of the two girls hiding inside the container. Shawn knew we were here, and he had trouble keeping his eyes off us. I could only imagine how another of the hopefuls would react if they saw us. And I could only shudder at what would happen if a pirate was at the door controls.

"Thanks, Jim," Shawn called.

"No problem," Jim said. "You need any help with that thing?"

"Nah, I got it."

"Okay."

To my relief, Jim's last response sounded as if he was moving away from the door. A second later, Shawn guided the float pallet through the door. The sound of half-a-dozen voices speaking at the same time grew louder.

An unfamiliar voice called, "Get over there and help 'em out."

That told the direction to one pirate. But were the other three gathered around the one who spoke?

"I'm just making sure this is out of the way, sir," Shawn said.

"I said, go help them. Don't make me say it again."

Shawn gave the pallet a shove. "Right away, sir."

Our hiding place coasted over the floor for a couple of meters, then came to a stop. I closed my eyes and gave the room a quick emotional scan. Shawn's red-green dot moved towards the rest of the hopefuls. Off to one side were four maroon dots. By the grace of God and Shawn's final push, none of the hopefuls were between the pirates and me.

With the pirates' positions fixed in my mind, I dropped my scan and prepared for my surprise attack. My heart hammered in my chest as I put a finger on the blaster's trigger. Mom and Granddaddy had me practice snapshots like this all the time, but this was the first time I had living targets. I had time for one shot per pirate, no more. Even then, I was cutting it close.

In a single motion, I rose to my knees and aimed my blaster towards the pirates. I adjusted my aim slightly and squeezed the trigger. The blaster's flat crack echoed off the metal walls as a bright bolt of energy flashed across the room. I had already changed my aim to the next pirate. I squeezed the trigger again just as the first pirate dropped. The second pirate fell as I switched aim. The third pirate's eyes had just begun widening in surprise when I fired.

I saw motion to the third pirate's right and swung my aim towards it. But no one was there. The echoes from my shots faded as the third pirate collapsed. That's when I heard a sound I never wanted to hear. Hasty footsteps descending stairs.

The fourth pirate was awake, alerted, and on the run!

The three pirates I'd stunned sprawled before an open doorway. In my rush to shoot the pirates as quickly as possible, I hadn't noticed it until the fourth pirate vanished through the doorway. The echoing sound of feet pounding down stairs suggested they led to the underground tunnel system that connected the base's buildings. If the pirate got through the airtight hatch at the bottom of the stairs, he could go anywhere in the base. I could still shoot him once he got past the hatch, but the sound of blaster fire would carry a long way through the tunnels and attract the attention of any other pirates using them to move between buildings.

Those thoughts flashed through my mind in the fraction of a second it took me to vault from the float pallet container and sprint through the industrial kitchen after the running pirate. A dozen young men gaped at me as I dashed past them. Even

Shawn, who was in on my ambush plan, stood rooted in place. It didn't surprise me. They spent years in the pirates' clutches, and I felt certain the pirates crushed their rebellious spirit long before the *Pegasus* arrived at the base.

But I had another ally in the room. Behind me, I heard Sofia's feet hit the floor.

"I'm right behind you, Nora!" she called.

"Grab a pirate's gun," I replied. "Just make sure you set it to stun."

"Will do."

I leapt over the three unconscious pirates, then dove and rolled through the doorway. I found myself on a three-meter long landing. Beyond it, the stairs descended five meters to another landing. The stairs switched back from it and descended out of sight below the top landing.

The running pirate stood on the first step of the second flight of stairs with his blaster ready. He fired three shots as soon as he saw me. All three shots scorched the air over my head. I heard the hiss of melting metal as the shots slagged the wall behind me. That told me the pirate had his blaster set to kill.

The pirate snarled a wordless curse as I came up on one knee. He jumped down the stairs just as I fired. My hasty shot flashed over his head. The pirate's leap carried him under the top landing and out of sight. I heard him land heavily and snarl a second curse.

I jumped to my feet and surged towards the stairs, planning to charge after the pirate. But he fired another shot up the stairwell. Neither of us could see the other, and I doubt he thought he'd hit me. It was a warning shot to tell me he *could* shoot me if I dared follow him down the stairs.

It worked. I grabbed the railing and stopped myself. Another shot scorched the air near my hand. I jerked it back from the railing.

The pirate couldn't see me.

I couldn't see the pirate.

Stalemate.

Except it wasn't.

He just had to open the airtight hatch and make shooting him a risky proposition.

I had to stop the pirate before he opened the hatch.

I backed up two steps, took a deep breath, and regretted giving up on gymnastics training when I was fifteen. I just hoped I could pull off a full gainer to the landing below without breaking an ankle and have time to shoot the pirate before he shot me. Sofia caught my arm just before I flung myself forward.

"Wait," she whispered. "Use this while I cover you."

Sofia handed me a huge baking sheet she must have grabbed while chasing after me through the kitchen. She inclined her head towards the stairs. I nodded my understanding.

Sofia leaned over the landing's railing and began firing at the landing below. I jumped onto the baking sheet, sitting feet first on it. Momentum carried the sheet over the lip of the stairway. I leaned back, making as small a target as possible, and tobogganed down the stairs.

The baking sheet hurtled down the stairs. I'm not kidding about the speed. It went so fast that I had no time to react during the slide and even less time to think what to do next.

My makeshift toboggan drifted towards the inner edge of the stairway, and its right front corner struck a railing post. It caromed left and started spinning.

It careened head first towards the stairwell's outer wall. I had just begun tucking my head and wrapping an arm around it when the sheet smacked into the wall with a dull, metallic *clunk*. My left wrist cracked painfully against the wall as the sheet and I ricocheted back to the right. The flat pan spun onto the switchback landing. A railing post blurred way too close to my face, but it slid from sight before my brain registered it was there.

In an adventure vid, the baking sheet would have stopped moving and left me perfectly lined up for a shot at the pirate below. It didn't. The metal pan barely slowed as it crossed the landing and struck the back wall at an angle. The latest ricochet slowed the baking sheet and sent me towards the far wall. I came at it head-first and I ducked and wrapped my left arm and aching wrist tighter around my head. The front corner of the sheet hit the wall and rebounded towards the other flight of stairs.

All the wall-banging and sliding across the landing bled the pan's speed. It slid partially over the landing's edge and teetered on the brink of another plunge down the second set of stairs. The sheet slowly spun in place as I uncovered my head. I had just enough time to realize I'd made a huge mess of things before the baking sheet's spin brought the pirate into view.

He stood next to an airtight hatch that almost certainly opened on the underground tunnels connecting the pirate base's buildings. His left hand hovered frozen near the button that opened the hatch. His right hand hung at his side, a blaster clutched in a white-knuckled grasp. And his face was the picture of stunned amazement, complete with a slack jawed, wide-eyed stare.

The pirate appeared young, probably in his early twenties, and was kind of cute. He looked every bit the lovable rogue that the heroine falls for in adventure vids. Then we locked gazes. His cold, hard eyes shattered the romantic notion he was just a scoundrel whose life took a wrong turn.

The pirate's lips curled in a sardonic smile as he lifted his blaster to shoot me. I swung my blaster around, praying I could stun him before he killed me.

God had other ideas.

We shot at the same time. But extending my blaster changed the baking sheet's balance. We fired just *after* it tipped over the edge of the stairs. It rocketed down the stairs straight at the pirate. I felt the heat as the pirate's killing shot seared the air just over my head. My blaster bolt flashed between the pirate's legs and splashed harmlessly against the hatch.

The pirate snapped off another shot that missed, and the blaster bolt fried the stairs behind me. I didn't even try shooting a second time. I curled into a ball and wrapped my arms around my head again.

The pirate realized his peril and shouted in alarm. He tried jumping over me but it was too late. I crashed into his shins and sent him tumbling through the air. Then I hit the hatch head on and everything went black.

WE'RE THE ONLY ONES WHO CAN

Darkness shrouded my mind for a second, then sparks burst forth from it. A riot of colors filled the darkness around the sparks. Familiar colors.

A cluster of blue-green dots and three sparks from minds I'd entered moved nearby. A maroon dot bounced and jiggled next to me. One spark was Sofia—I can recognize her mind at a glance—so the other two must be Shawn and the garbage guy whose mind I entered an hour ago. Shawn said garbage guy's name was Mike. The dancing maroon dot was obviously the pirate, but I had no idea what he was doing.

I thought I heard shouts from far away and Sofia's spark raced away from me and then back in my direction. Maybe she was running down the stairs? The blue-green dots followed more slowly. As Sofia approached me, I saw the pirate's maroon dot fade to black. What the heck did *that* mean?

Sofia stopped next to me, and the blue-green dots crowded around. I guess they weren't worried about the pirate—who I couldn't even see anymore—so I decided I wouldn't worry about him, either. I wanted to tell Sofia I was okay, but my eyes wouldn't open and my voice remained quiet. Maybe I just needed to rest longer? Hoping that was the case, I turned my attention back to my mental map and the other three concentrations of color.

In one corner of my map, bright red laced with fading wisps of blue pulsed near a single spark. That must be the passengers onboard the *Pegasus*, and the single spark must be the revolt ringleader. I don't know why he wasn't in the middle of everything, but I'd bet Mrs. Stanley had something to do with that.

In the opposite corner of my mind, maroon tinging towards crimson surrounded two dozen sparks of the pirate minds I'd entered last night. I knew the pirates' emotions showed up as maroon in my mind, but what did the crimson mean? Here at their base, it couldn't be fear. But crimson was so close to the passenger's bright red that I felt certain it represented something similar to fear.

A second blob of bright red lay in between the other two. And a thin band of crimson wrapped around the red. The crew and children, but the second appearance of crimson confused me. A single spark—I recognized Conley almost as easily as I did Sofia—shined from the crimson ring. What emotion could Conley and some of the crew possibly share with the pirates?

I was so busy wondering about crimson that I almost missed the lone spark moving away from the pirates' maroon blob. But that spark captured all my attention once I noticed it. Rather, noticed *her*. Because the spark was Rivera. She had left the party the pirates threw for themselves and was going... where?

To her quarters?

To the warehouse holding the crew and children?

I might figure out her destination if I dove into her mind and examined her feelings. Did I dare dive into her mind while Rivera was awake? Right before Rivera launched a missile at the lifepod she thought I was on, I bragged that I'd entered her mother's mind. What if I gave my presence away? Would that drive Rivera to conclude that I still lived?

Something from outside intruded on my wonderings. It wasn't much. Just a gentle shake. But it caught my attention.

With the shake came a faint call, as if from a great distance. I turned my attention from the map of emotions and listened hard.

"Nora?" Faint as it was, the voice sounded like Sofia.

I felt the gentle touch of a hand probe the top of my head. It felt nice until—

"Ouch!" I said.

The hand lifted from my scalp. "Nora?"

I pried my suddenly cooperative eyes open and blinked at the bright light. Sofia's head moved into view, blocking some of the light. Far above her, others peered down at me. I recognized Shawn among the faces.

Sofia glanced up. "Nora's awake."

"Is she okay?" Shawn asked.

"Let's find out." Sofia looked back at me. "Do you know who you are?"

"You just called me Nora, so..." I saw Sofia's brow crease in concern and realized just how worried she was. I forced myself to smile through the pain, and said, "So I must be Nora freaking Connaught, Badass Babe of the Cosmos."

Sofia's worried expression eased, but she still asked, "How does your head feel?"

"It hurts."

She held a finger up in front of me. "Look at my finger. Is it blurry?"

I did as instructed and saw a perfectly normal finger. "No."

"Follow my finger without moving your head."

She moved her finger back and forth in front of my face. I dutifully tracked it without moving my head, then asked, "Isn't that for figuring out if someone is drunk, not if they have a concussion?"

"Maybe, but it was worth checking." Sofia leaned back. "Do you feel up to standing?"

"Sure."

Sofia rose smoothly to her feet and offered me a hand up.

Shawn extended a hand, too. I took their hands and let them help me to my feet.

"How's your balance?" Sofia asked. "Any dizziness?"

I released their hands and stood on my own. "None."

"Walk around a bit."

The landing at the bottom of the stairs wasn't large and all twelve hopefuls, Sofia, and I were packed on it. "Where? There's no room."

Shawn waved his fellow hopefuls towards the stairs. "Give her some space, guys."

They retreated onto the stairs. That's when I caught sight of the pirate I'd crashed through just before smashing my head on the airtight hatch. His head was twisted at an impossible angle and dull, sightless eyes stared at the hatch.

Sofia followed my gaze, and said, "He came down on his neck."

I'd never killed anyone before and wanted to look away. But I forced myself to look at what I'd done to the pirate. I felt bile rise in my throat and swallowed hard to send it back down. I took a deep, shuddering breath. Then I walked to the pirate's body, went to one knee next to him, and closed his eyes.

I offered a silent prayer for his soul. Then I stood and walked back to Sofia.

"Satisfied?" I asked.

She nodded.

From the stairs, Shawn said, "He'd have killed you without giving it a second thought, Nora."

"I know, Shawn. I just..." I shook my head. Which still hurt. "Have you guys got anything for a headache?"

"No," he said. "We're just supposed to tough it out when we get hurt."

"Then I'll have to do the same." I looked at Sofia. "We need to act fast. Rivera left the pirates' celebration."

"Maybe she's tired and just decided to go to bed early?"

"I didn't go into her mind, so you could be right. But my gut says she's up to something."

Sofia didn't waste time questioning my instinct. "What do you think we should do?"

I met her gaze and said, "We take out the pirates guarding the crew and children, return to the *Pegasus*, and get out of here."

The dozen hopefuls erupted in a barrage of questions. The close walls in the stairwell amplified the cacophony to a point where I couldn't understand a word. And it made my aching head hurt so badly that I covered my ears with my hands.

Noticing that, Sofia raised her hands over her head and waved for silence. To my surprise, the guys stopped talking. In the sudden quiet, Sofia said, "One at a time. You start, Shawn."

I lowered my hands as he asked, "What about us?"

"I hope you're willing to help Sofia and me," I said. "It'll be dangerous, but—"

"That's not what I meant, ma'am." Shawn caught my gaze. "Will you take us with you?"

My eyebrows rose in surprise. "Of course."

Relieved smiles broke out among the hopefuls as Shawn said, "That will make us very happy. How do you plan on defeating the pirates?"

I shook my head. "I don't know enough about the situation to have a plan yet. But I hope you guys can help me come up with one."

"Us?" a hopeful asked, his voice filled with doubt.

"Sure. I bet you know the base's layout even better than the pirates do." A dozen pairs of eyes stared at me with incomprehension, so I flashed my best smile at the group of young men. "Am I right?"

The hopefuls fidgeted and refused to meet my eyes. Even Shawn looked at the floor rather than at me or Sofia.

Sofia leaned close and whispered, "Do you have any idea what's going on, Nora?"

"They're obviously reluctant to help. But I don't know why. I mean, did they think we could beat the pirates all by ourselves?"

"Let's ask." Sofia turned back to the hopefuls. "I thought you said beating the pirates and leaving this rock would make you happy."

"It will," one said.

"Then why aren't you willing to help Nora and me?"

"Because the pirates will punish us if we help you."

"Only if we fail," I said. "But you'll be free if we succeed."

The hopefuls shuffled their feet and exchanged glances among themselves, but remained silent.

I looked at Shawn. "Do you honestly think two girls can beat an entire pirate gang without any help?"

He glanced my way, his expression filled with trepidation. "Can't you?"

"No, Shawn, we probably can't. We'll still try."

"And probably die," Sofia added.

"What we *won't* do is sit around and wait for someone else to do it," I said.

The only response was more fidgeting and shuffling from the hopefuls.

I took a different tack, folded my arms across my chest, hardened my gaze, and channeled my mother. "Do you like being slaves to the pirates? Is this all you ever want for your lives? Because this is as good as your life is ever going to get as long as you sit around and wait for someone else to rescue you. But, hey, at least it's *safe*. Right?"

Indecision filled the dozen faces arrayed before me. As much as Sofia and I needed their help, we couldn't force them to move beyond mere hope and into action.

Suddenly, a voice crackled from the floor next to me. I jumped, afraid the dead pirate had spoken. Then I spotted a hand radio dangling from the pirate's belt.

The voice issuing from the radio was female, and I recognized it.

Rivera asked, "Are you there, Marsh?"

I had just enough time to worry that Marsh was dead at my feet before a male voice said, "I'm here, Captain."

I realized Marsh must be one of the pirates guarding the warehouse and sighed with relief.

"The mood at the celebration took a nasty turn after the gang got a few drinks in them," Rivera said.

"They still angry that you offed that rich girl?" Marsh asked.

Rivera vented an exasperated sigh. "Yes, and they don't care that I didn't have any other choice. Logic is completely lost on them."

"It looks like those suggestions you planted in all those pirates' minds are working," Sofia said.

From the radio, Rivera continued, "I have to get their minds off the money they think they lost when I blew up the lifepod."

"You want the usual?" Marsh asked.

"I hate wasting pristine merchandise, but I don't see any other options." Rivera replied.

"How many?"

"Forty and ten should do."

"I'll get on it right away, Captain."

"Good. I'll be there in fifteen minutes to collect them." Rivera paused, then added, "Pull ten very young children out of the crowd and tie them to the catwalk railing. Start shooting them if the merchandise doesn't cooperate."

"Got it," Marsh replied. "See you soon, Captain."

Sofia and I stared at each other in horror, then I looked at the hopefuls. They all looked as disturbed as I felt.

"Shawn," I asked, "did that conversation mean what I think it means?"

"Probably," he replied. "Marsh is going to pick out the forty best-looking girls and the ten best looking boys so the Captain can give them to her crew."

"What about the ten children?" Sofia asked.

Shawn looked at the floor again. "The pirates usually don't have to shoot any of them."

"But they will?"

He nodded.

My mind recoiled at what could happen to those children and what would happen to the fifty people Marsh chose. From Sofia's expression, she felt the same way.

I bent down and took the dead pirate's blaster and hand radio. "Come on, Sofia. Let's get the other pirates' guns."

"What are we going to do?" Sofia asked.

I shrugged. "Whatever we can. I won't hide while the pirates ruin sixty lives."

Shawn asked, "Can you succeed?"

I gave him a brutally honest answer. "Probably not."

Another asked, "Then why do you insist on trying?"

I walked over to him and lifted his head so he had no choice but to look me in the eye. "Sofia and I will try because we're the only ones who can."

I shoved past him and started up the stairs. Sofia followed without hesitation. When I reached the switchback landing, I heard the sudden slap of footsteps on the stairs.

"I will try, too," Shawn said.

"Thank you," I said.

"Welcome to the Badass Babes," Sofia said, "even if guys can't be babes."

"Sure they can," I said. "Mom has called Dad 'babe' for as long as I can remember."

"Zing," Sofia said. "I guess you get to be a babe, too, Shawn."

Three more hopefuls pounded up the stairs and joined us.

"We are babes, too," one announced.

That broke the others' resistance, and they rushed to join us as we left the stairwell.

I looked at Shawn. "The pirates wanted you to bring food and water to the warehouse, right?"

"Yes."

"Do you use float pallets for that?"

"We do."

"Okay, listen up, guys. You're going to smuggle Sofia and me into the warehouse in a float pallet. We'll hide under food packages. Once we're inside, I'll guide you to a couple of men on the inside who can help us."

"What will they do?" a hopeful asked.

"God willing, they'll shoot the pirate guards before anyone gets killed."

"And then?" another asked.

"Then we'll make a break for the *Pegasus*."

We returned to the industrial-sized pantry where I'd sprung my ambush on the pirates. The three I'd successfully stunned were still sprawled on the floor. I dug into my backpack for the roll of duct tape and the folding knife I grabbed from the lifepod supplies before we launched it into space.

God, could that really have been only two days ago? It felt like two years. I shook myself out of the brief reverie and handed the tape and knife to a hopeful.

"Secure these pirates with the tape. Arms behind their backs. Wrap tape around their wrists, elbows, ankles, knees, and over their mouths. Okay?"

"Yes, ma'am."

"Just call me Nora."

"Okay, ma'am."

I didn't roll my eyes at his formality, but it was a close thing. "After you do that, can you get someone to help you bring the corpse up here? I'm sure it'll be unsettling but—"

"It won't be the first dead body I've moved, ma'am." The guy's face went rigid and his eyes lost focus for a second. "At least the pirate deserved what he got."

I couldn't imagine the horrors he had witnessed since the pirates captured him, so smiled, gave him an awkward pat on the shoulder, and said, "Thank you."

Sofia held up the three blasters and radios she'd taken from stunned pirates. "What should I do with these?"

"First, set the guns to stun and turn off the radios. All it would take is one radio message at the wrong time and this plan is toast."

While Sofia got busy with that, I looked around for Shawn. He stood nearby, organizing the food gathering effort with the rest of the hopefuls. I walked over to him and asked, "Do you know what we'll find inside the warehouse? How the pirates array themselves, what weapons they'll have, and stuff like that?"

"Yes," he said. "If they do things like they did when they captured that other big starliner last year, the pirates have a couple of guards at the tunnel entrance and ten to fifteen more watching the prisoners from the catwalk that goes all the way around the walls of the warehouse."

That was both good and bad. The good was, anyone on the warehouse floor would have a clear shot at the guards on the catwalk. The bad was that the catwalk gave the pirates a good view of what happened on the floor below them.

"And the ten children will be on the catwalk, too?"

He nodded, caught my gaze, and asked, "Can you save them? Because the pirates watching the kids will either hide behind them or start killing them as soon as they realize they're under attack."

"We'll do our best, Shawn. Those two pirates will be our first targets."

He remained silent, apparently satisfied with my answer. But I still had questions.

I pointed at the stunned pirates, and asked, "Do you think they were among the ten to fifteen guards you mentioned?"

"They have been in the past."

"Good. That leaves six to eleven for us."

"Plus the two guards at the hatch into the tunnels."

"Yeah," I said, "they're a weak link in my plan. We can't shoot them going in because the pirates in the warehouse will hear the shots. But the two at the hatch will hear the shooting when we spring our ambush."

"What are you going to do about them?" Shawn asked.

"Leave them alone when we go in and hope we can send someone to shoot them before they vanish into the tunnels." I sighed, "I'd feel better about that if I knew the code Rivera used to unlock the *Pegasus's* engines and weapons."

Shawn looked at me in alarm. "Your ship cannot take off or fight?"

I shook my head. "Not yet. But the lovely Captain Rivera will provide the code."

He barked a derisive laugh. "If you believe that, you are a fool. Nothing you do will make Rivera say anything to you."

"I just need her to remember setting it, Shawn."

"I do not understand."

"I'm psychic. If we can get her to remember the emotions she felt when she entered the codes, I should be able to watch her memory."

"How will you make her remember?"

"*I* won't. Rivera needs to keep believing Sofia and I are dead for this to work. So keep her as far from us as possible after we capture her."

Shawn's eyes bulged, and he shouted, "You want to capture the Captain? Are you out of your mind?"

Everyone around us stopped what they were doing and stared at me. Though I felt anything but calm, I forced a calm expression onto my face. My gaze swept the gathered hopefuls. "Yes, I want to capture Captain Rivera. No, I am not out of my mind. If we're going to escape, we will need her."

A nearby hopeful said, "If you plan on using her as a hostage against the other pirates, it won't work."

Sofia said, "We've seen the way the pirates work. Nora knows they won't care about hostages." She looked at me. "Do you have a plan for capturing her?"

"She told Marsh she would see him in fifteen minutes." I

checked my chrono. "That was eight minutes ago. We just have to time our arrival at the warehouse, so we get there just after she does. Then we stun her right along with the other guards."

Shawn gave me a doubtful look. "How will you make her remember if she is unconscious?"

"The ship's doctor can give her an injection to counteract the effects of the stun," I said.

"Are you sure the medbay has that?" Sofia asked.

"According to Granddaddy, it's part of the medbay's standard supplies. But my bodyguards also carry doses of it as part of their standard equipment." I smiled at Sofia. "If we can get Rivera onboard the *Pegasus*, we can wake her up. And if we can wake her up, I believe I have a way Conley and Barber can make her remember entering the code."

"Then make sure you don't get yourself killed, Nora," Sofia said, "because this plan falls apart without you."

I raised one hand and solemnly intoned, "I swear I will make sure I don't get killed."

Sofia's gaze hardened. "I'm serious, Nora."

I looked her in the eyes. "So am I, Sofia."

She gave a slight nod. "Good."

I turned to the hopefuls. "Make sure you're all wearing atmosphere harnesses, or this all falls apart."

Without another word, Sofia and I climbed into the container atop a float pallet and stacked the extra blasters between us. The hopefuls buried us under food packages. Then we set off for the warehouse.

Shawn and the hopefuls crowded a dozen float pallets onto the lift down to the tunnels connecting their pantry with the rest of the base. All the bumping and maneuvering jostled Sofia and me. I couldn't count all the food box corners that pressed down on me, poking and prodding my already tired and aching body. My heart pounded in my chest so loudly I felt certain everyone could hear it. I felt Sofia's tension through her taut muscles.

As the lift descended, I said, "Shawn, when we get to the warehouse, the others should distribute food and water like normal. I'll whisper directions to you so we can find our way to Conley and Barber."

"Okay, Nora."

"And don't forget that you'll have to be my eyes until it's time to spring our ambush," I added.

"Got it."

"Describe everything you see," I continued, "but only talk when none of the pirates can hear you."

Sofia's hand pushed through the boxes piled on top of us and gently covered my mouth. "Shawn's a smart guy, Nora, and he's lived among the pirates for years. I don't think he's going to risk ruining his best chance at rescue by doing anything stupid."

"No," Shawn said, "I will not."

"I'm sorry, Shawn. I'm just nervous."

"As are we," he said.

"And I'll bet my babbling is making it worse." I sighed. "I'll shut up, now."

Desperate for something else to occupy my mind, I called up an emotional map of the base. A few things had changed since the last time I checked it.

The bright red blob of the crew and children had divided in two. A smaller, far brighter red blob had separated from the main gathering. It didn't take a genius to figure out the smaller blob represented the forty women and ten men Rivera planned on giving to her celebrating pirates.

Crimson laced the bright red of the rest of the crew and children. Conley's spark pulsed with it. With a sudden flash of insight, I realized crimson represented anger. Unable to do anything to protect the unfortunate ones Marsh selected, my bodyguards must be seething by now.

A telepath could relay our entire plan to Conley. But I'm an empath, and that's not an option for me. At least not until Conley, Barber, and I can sit down and work out a code. But that's for the future. For now, I turned my attention to one last detail on the map.

The spark representing Rivera was much closer to the warehouse than the last time I'd checked. I considered how far she'd come since I first discovered she was on the move, and didn't like my calculations.

In a soft voice, I said, "Shawn, can you guys move faster? Rivera is closer to the warehouse than I thought she'd be, and we have to get there while she's still there with the guards and the prisoners."

In response, Shawn called, "We need to pick up the pace, guys."

A chorus of assents answered. Seconds later, our float pallet began moving faster. In a remarkably short time that seemed to take forever, I heard an airtight hatch grind open.

The hopeful pushing the first pallet in line said, "Food and water, as ordered."

"Bring it in," a bored voice replied.

A second voice chimed in, "Hey, you got any chocolate?"

"Um, no sir," the hopeful mumbled.

Curiosity tinged the bored voice as he asked, "What you want chocolate for?"

"It's for my girl when I get my turn with one," the second voice replied. "You know, give her a little romancing to get her in the mood?"

Both pirates laughed, and their casual disregard for other people chilled my blood. Then the line of float pallets began moving again. I held my breath when Shawn pushed our pallet past the two guards, but they were still laughing at the second pirate's so-called joke. Then I forcibly turned my mind back to the rescue.

The warehouse lift must have been larger than the one in the pantry, because the pallets didn't bump or jostle as the hopefuls guided them into place. With a lurch, the lift rose towards ground level.

I ran another emotional scan. Rivera's spark was next to the small, red blob of people she was giving to her crew. Conley's spark was fifteen meters away, on the near edge of the red and crimson blob. I relayed that to Shawn and offered a last, silent prayer for deliverance.

Then the lift jerked to a stop, and the doors opened onto the warehouse. Angry murmurs, wracking sobs, and impatient orders assaulted my ears as the hopefuls pushed the float pallets into the immense building.

Rivera's voice rose above the noise. "Just where do you think you're going with that, boy?"

"Food and water for the prisoners, ma'am," the hopeful said.

"*Captain*," Rivera snapped.

"Yes, Captain," he amended. "Ma'am."

"Did you order this, Marsh?" Rivera asked.

"I did, Captain," Marsh replied. "I figured it might settle the merchandise down a bit. Right now, a little food might distract them from the ones you're taking to the crew. Especially the kids. You know how whiny those brats get when they're hungry and thirsty."

Rivera remained silent for two long seconds, considering Marsh's words, no doubt. At long last, she said, "Yeah, all right."

Seconds later, Shawn pushed our float pallet off the lift and into the warehouse.

"Which way?" Shawn murmured.

"Straight ahead," I whispered.

"Who am I looking for?"

"A big guy. Two meters tall. Strong. Brown hair."

"Will he have another big guy next to him? Just as strong, with black hair?"

"Yes."

"Got him."

Ten seconds later, Shawn asked, "Food, sir?"

Conley's curt voice said, "No."

Afraid Conley might dismiss the food out of hand, I'd given Shawn a code phrase. He used it now.

"I have fresh strawberries, sir."

"I don't..." Conley paused. "Strawberries, you say?"

"Yes, sir."

Shawn's hand swept the boxes away from my face. My lips twitched into a nervous smile, and I pushed four blasters up through the food boxes covering Sofia and me.

"It's time to blow this joint, Conley."

Conley's and Barber's expressions barely shifted as they stared down at Sofia and me. Their eyes widened slightly, otherwise their faces might have been carved from stone. The two men had been with me for ten years, so I knew the eye-widening bit was their version of jaw-dropping astonishment.

Someday I may look back on this moment and laugh. God only knows I hope so. But not today. Not with thousands of lives depending on our actions in the next few minutes.

"What is your plan, Miss Connaught?" Conley asked.

With everything that was on the line, you'd think he could call me Nora. Just this once. Okay, I didn't really think he or Barber would ever approach their jobs with anything less than the formal detachment required to do it well. But I still hoped that just once they'd crack and show some emotion on the job.

"Take these four blasters, give two of them to officers you trust. The four of you position yourselves around the warehouse and get ready to shoot the pirate guards. I'll stay near Rivera and Marsh. The two best shots get things started by taking out the pirates watching the ten kids Rivera had Marsh pull from the crowd. That's the signal for the rest of us to blast the other pirates."

My bodyguards gave microscopic nods, but Barber added, "I dislike the idea of you putting yourself in danger, Miss Connaught, but I see no other choice."

"Agreed," Conley said. "Have you thought beyond putting down these pirates?"

"Yes, but Shawn can't keep this float pallet in one place for much longer," I said. "Meet at the big airlock after the shooting stops."

Without further comment, Conley and Barber picked up a box of food and two blasters each. The guns vanished into pants pockets designed to conceal weapons, and Shawn pushed the float pallet deeper into the milling crew and children.

Shawn waved several crew members to the pallet and hurriedly asked them to crowd around it. They did so, probably thinking he just wanted them to take food and hand it out. None of them controlled their expressions when they saw Sofia and me hiding in the container.

A middle-aged woman gasped, "Sofia?"

Sofia put a finger to her lips. "Shh."

The woman clapped a hand over her mouth, nodded, and blinked rapidly. The rest of the crew took Sofia's cue and remained silent.

"Get closer and bend over the container," Shawn whispered, "so Nora and Sofia can climb out without the pirates seeing them."

They did as Shawn asked and did a great job of blocking the pirates' view of the float pallet. But that also put them in our way. Instead of the graceful exit I'd pictured, I ended up wriggling head-first between a woman and a man.

My belt buckle caught on the container's lip. I had no leverage to lift my hips, so hissed, "A little help, sir?"

He glanced around nervously, then grabbed me by a back pants pocket and lifted. The belt buckle rose above the lip. I slithered over it and rolled into a kneeling position on the warehouse floor. Half-a-dozen young children watched me wide-eyed.

Afraid they might give me away, I followed Nora's example and held a finger to my lips. "That's the best hide-and-seek place ever! But I need to find a new hiding place."

One boy regarded me for a second, then whispered, "You're not 'sposed to move after you hide."

I flashed what I hoped was a friendly and reassuring smile. "Grown-ups play by different rules."

The boy considered that for a second and then nodded his acceptance of my qualification. The kids just watched as Sofia joined me. Behind us, the crew members gathered around the float pallet broke apart. With their movement masking ours, Sofia and I stood. I gave a little wave to the kids as we headed back towards Rivera and Marsh at the warehouse lift. Sofia stayed behind me, since Rivera knew what she looked like.

I glanced around the warehouse. Besides the two pirates watching the kids tied to the catwalk railing, seven more stood and surveyed the crew and children below them. They looked bored, to me, even the pair with the ten children. I didn't have time for more than that glance before Sofia and I neared the warehouse lift.

I'd never seen Rivera outside of emotionally laden memories, but I recognized her immediately. She had jet black hair pulled back in a severe bun, the pale complexion all spacers have, and I guess she was good looking in an authoritarian way. A tall man walked next to her as she inspected the forty women and ten men he'd selected as entertainment for her crew. Rivera appeared happy enough with Marsh's choices and turned back towards the lift.

"Let's get them moving," she said.

Two more pirates I hadn't noticed before began shoving the crying, cringing, terrified entertainment girls and guys towards the lift.

Sofia leaned close and whispered, "Can you take out all four of them?"

I shrugged. "I'll do my best."

Someone in the crowd caught Rivera's eye—not me, thank God—and she pointed. "Bring that one, too."

A girl off to my left whimpered as Marsh came her way. His path to the girl put him right between Rivera and me. At that same instant, two blaster shots echoed through the warehouse.

~

Children screamed.

Pirates shouted.

Marsh grabbed for his holstered gun.

Crew members around me shrank back from him.

I freed myself from the crowd with one step, raised my blaster, and fired.

My shot hit Marsh center mass. He jerked and collapsed to the floor. His partly drawn gun clattered to the floor next to him.

I looked past Marsh's crumpled body, searching for Rivera. I saw her pushing and shoving her way through the shocked crowd of fifty girls and boys chosen to entertain her crew.

This is why your blaster is set for stun, Nora.

With grim determination, I raised the gun and pointed it into the crowd. More shots sounded around the warehouse, and that was too much for the fifty people around Rivera. They panicked and ran for the imagined safety of their crewmates. My already dubious line of fire at Rivera vanished.

A blaster shot flashed to my left and burned into the floor.

I dodged left, towards the smoking hole. The pirate's hastily aimed second shot scorched the space I'd just vacated. I looked up at the catwalk, saw a pirate aiming for a third shot, and snapped off a quick shot at him. It missed, but he flinched from it. I took more careful aim, but a hail of blaster bolts splashed all around the pirate before I fired. One shot found its mark, and the pirate dropped.

I glanced around. Sofia was on one knee beside the unconscious Marsh and had his blaster in a good two-handed grip. A determined, unconscious smile played across her lips as she looked for another target.

Oh, Granddaddy, you're going to like this one!

"Thanks," I said.

"No problem," Sofia replied.

Her gaze stopped roving and her finger squeezed the blaster's trigger four times. A voice cried out from the catwalk as one of Sofia's shots found its mark.

As Sofia looked for another target, she said, "Go, Nora. Stop Rivera!"

Wishing I'd gotten a look at the lift and stairs down to the tunnels when Shawn smuggled us into the warehouse, I dashed after Rivera. The lift was far too slow for an escape, so I felt certain Rivera would take the stairs. But I'd already had one near-disastrous encounter with stairs recently, and Rivera had two pirates stationed at the bottom of the stairs. If she reached them, they could easily hold me at bay while Rivera escaped into the tunnels and summoned help.

Or was she already shouting for help over her handheld radio? I itched to turn on the radio I'd taken from the dead pirate. But as important as that was, stopping Rivera was my priority.

From behind me, Shawn suddenly shouted, "Look out!"

He tackled me as half-a-dozen blaster bolts sizzled all around us. Sofia must have spotted the shooter, because her blaster cracked five times and the shots stopped falling around us.

"Thanks, Shawn," I said. "It's safe to let me up now."

Shawn groaned, but didn't move.

I twisted under his weight. Agony etched his pale face.

"Shawn?" I wriggled to get out from under him. "*Shawn?*"

Sofia suddenly crouched down next to me. In a quavering voice, she said, "He's been shot, Nora."

"Is he... dead?"

"No, but he's hurt bad."

A strange silence descended on the warehouse as Sofia held Shawn while I slid free of him. My training made me glance around the warehouse and take stock of the situation.

Unconscious pirates lay on the catwalk or hung over its railing. Most of the crew and children crouched, making it easy to spot Conley, Barber, and Captain Riggs. They held blasters at the ready as their eyes swept the catwalk for additional targets.

"Clear!" Conley called.

"Clear," Barber said.

"Clear," Captain Riggs said. His gaze turned towards a small knot of people. "Doctor, how badly wounded is my first offer?"

An older man rose from the knot of people. "Lieutenant Blair is dead, sir."

Grief flickered in Captain Riggs' face as he nodded in acknowledgement. "Are there any other wounded?"

"Over here," I said. "The man who smuggled Sofia and me into the warehouse took a shot meant for me."

Other calls for a doctor rose from around the warehouse. The older doctor started our way, and several of the others gathered around the first officer stood and answered the other calls for help.

In a quiet voice, Sofia said, "Nora, go after Rivera. There's nothing you can do here."

I checked my emotional map of the area. To my complete lack of surprise, Rivera's spark was already a hundred meters away and receding quickly.

"It's too late. She's long gone," I said.

The doctor arrived and bent over Shawn. My bodyguards and Captain Riggs weren't far behind him.

Captain Riggs helped Sofia stand. "It gladdens my heart to see you alive and well, Miss Olson." He looked my way. "And you, also, Miss Connaught."

The doctor said, "I need to get this man to my surgery, Captain, or we'll lose him."

"We'll do our best," Riggs said, "but Rivera's software sabotage locked the *Pegasus's* controls. Unless we can break it—"

"I think Nora can get the code from Rivera, sir," Sofia said.

All eyes turned my way, and Conley asked, "Can you do that, Miss Connaught?"

"Maybe," I said. "If I can induce the right emotions in Rivera, it might make her recall a memory of entering the code."

Captain Riggs turned a thoughtful gaze on me. "I'm sorry to put so much responsibility on such young shoulders, Miss Connaught, but our fate is in your hands."

I looked at Captain Riggs' concerned expression and felt hysterical laughter welling up inside me. Not wanting to ruin the captain's solemn moment, I glanced at Sofia. She looked as if she was struggling to maintain a straight face, too. That tipped me over the edge, and I snorted a quick laugh. It was totally inappropriate—especially with Shawn lying wounded practically at my feet—but I couldn't help it. Sofia lost it right after I did.

Captain Riggs raised his left eyebrow. In a mild tone, he said, "I was unaware I said something amusing."

"I'm sorry, Captain," I gasped, fighting to bring my insane giggles under control.

"You didn't, sir," Sofia added. "Say something funny, I mean."

I nodded and pointed at Sofia. "What she said."

Then a fresh bout of hysterical laughter burst forth from both of us.

Captain Riggs shifted his gaze from me to Sofia. "Would you care to explain your laughter, Miss Olson?"

"You apologized for putting the lives of the crew and passengers on Nora's shoulders, sir."

"Yes, and I meant every word."

"We know you did, sir." With obvious effort, Sofia squelched her laughter and turned a serious expression to Captain Riggs. "But we've been carrying that weight ever since I took Nora's place so she could hide in the tunnels. Everything Nora and I have done since then has been for the ultimate safety of everyone onboard the *Pegasus*."

Captain Riggs' face turned thoughtful for a moment, then he said, "I hope you young ladies will accept my apologies for such a thoughtless comment."

My giggle fit ended as abruptly as it began, and the familiar, oppressive weight of expectations crashed down on me again. "Don't worry about it, Captain."

I turned to Conley and Barber. "While I'm busy digging the code to unlock the *Pegasus* out of Rivera's mind, you two need to sneak onboard and take our ship back from the pirates."

My bodyguards exchanged glances. I got the idea the looks hid an unspoken conversation. They came to a decision and nodded once at each other.

Conley turned back to me. "We'll need an atmosphere harness and as detailed a description of the situation on the *Pegasus* as possible."

I looked back and forth between Conley and Barber. "You're not going to argue and insist you must stay by my side?"

"You're more than capable of taking care of yourself, Miss Connaught," Conley said.

"And taking the *Pegasus* is the best way we can ensure your safety," Barber added.

Sofia immediately began unfastening her harness. "I can provide the description and the atmosphere harness for Conley and Barber. Nora, that means you're free to visit Rivera's cesspit of a mind."

All thoughts of laughter—hysterical or joyful—vanished from my mind. I stepped over to my bodyguards, reached an arm up and around each of their necks, and pulled them down to my level. I rested my head against theirs for a second, then kissed them each on the cheek.

I blinked back sudden tears, and said, "I love you guys."

My bodyguards put arms around me and squeezed gently.

"We love you, too, Miss Connaught," Conley said.

"Don't get yourselves killed taking back the ship," I said.

"Don't lose yourself inside Rivera's mind," Barber said.

As we broke our brief embrace, Sofia handed her atmosphere harness to Conley. She pointed across the warehouse at the airlock facing the *Pegasus*. "I'll tell you what we know while we walk."

As three of the people I cared the most for walked away, Captain Riggs asked, "Is there anything I can do to assist you, Miss Connaught?"

"I don't think so, sir."

I looked over at Shawn. The ship's doctor still hovered over him, doing what little he could without his surgery or instruments.

"Hang in there, Shawn," I whispered.

Turning back to Captain Riggs, I said, "I won't be able to respond to anything while I'm inside Rivera's mind. So don't worry if I just lie there, okay?"

The Captain nodded. "Is there anything I should do while you're... away?"

I shrugged. "Have someone stay by my side and keep others from tripping over me, I guess."

"I shall do that personally." He laid a grandfatherly hand on my shoulder. "Take care, Miss Connaught."

With a quick nod, I stretched out on the floor. "I'll be back with the codes as soon as possible, sir."

I closed my eyes and opened my mind to the emotions surging throughout the pirate base. The spark representing Rivera was right where I thought it would be. Her mind swirled with the bright red of fear, the crimson of anger, and the blue-green of hopeful desperation. Somehow, someway, I had to take those emotions and subtly manipulate them into an emotion evoked when Rivera entered the code for the software that locked the *Pegasus's* controls and weapons.

I dove into Rivera's mind.

PLAYING WITH EMOTIONS

The first time I entered Rivera's mind, I found a tranquil sea of joy and satisfaction. Joy, because she believed she'd finally avenged her brother's death. Satisfaction, because my supposed death was the instrument of her revenge.

This time, Rivera's mind was anything but tranquil. Emotional maelstroms raged inside her head, battling for supremacy.

A towering vortex of crimson anger swept through her emotional sea. It smashed the joy she took from her assumed revenge, shredded the satisfaction she felt when she blew up the lifepod she thought I was in, and scattered greed from her latest piratical score.

A tsunami of bright red fear slammed across her mind, crushing tiny pockets of lust and pride and hatred. Only anger withstood fear's relentless might.

A blue-green tempest of hopeful desperation whipped through emotions great and small. It battered cruelty and obsession and all other emotions except anger and fear. The tempest swirled around anger, lending its strength to the destructive vortex, and drove fear ahead of it, adding power to the tsunami's crushing might.

Rivera's anger engulfed me, and I spun helplessly in its grip. Then her fear crashed through the anger. It knocked me from the vortex, but threatened to drown me under the tsunami. I fought my way to the tsunami's crest, only to have the tempest blow me into the vortex again.

I felt the same as I had the first time my empathic ability manifested—overwhelmed and barely keeping myself together. How could I manipulate Rivera's emotions if I couldn't even protect myself from them? I had everyone from the *Pegasus* depending on me, and I was failing them.

God, I don't know what I'm doing. I'm terrified I'll let everyone down and doom us all.

A deep and desperate despair welled up inside me.

I can't do this, God. It's not fair to expect me to.

Resentment rose from despair.

I'm just an eighteen-year-old girl on her first trip away from home.

Self-pity washed over me.

I'm just plain old No-talent Nora.

Something bubbled up from beneath my self-pity and smacked me.

A fresh voice—Sofia's voice—said, *You are far more than that. You are Nora freaking Connaught, Badass Babe of the Cosmos. Stop feeling sorry for yourself and do what needs to be done!*

With a start, I noticed Rivera's emotions weren't tossing me around like a leaf caught in a tornado anymore. I floated inside an emotional bubble of my resentment. It rolled through the vortex, floated over the tsunami, and flat-out ignored the tempest.

I realized I no longer resented God for giving me this task. He obviously thought I could do the job, and who was I to doubt Him?

Wait, if I didn't resent God for my situation, how could a bubble of resentment protect me from the maelstrom raging inside Rivera's mind? You'd think an empath would know her feelings really well. But even with all the experience I've picked up with my empathic ability lately, I'm still new at this psychic stuff. I had to consciously examine my feelings to figure it out.

I resented the running and hiding I'd been forced to do over the previous two days. I resented experiencing those sick pirates' minds so I could sow the seeds of revolt in them. I resented everything the passengers and crew suffered during that time. I resented...

Rivera.

I resented the pirate captain as deeply as she hated my family. And my resentment was equal to her rage, her fear, and her desperation.

Okay, so I had a big job ahead of me. Big deal. Sofia and I already did the impossible. We faced the piratical storm without flinching. (Well, without *much* flinching, anyway.) We stared down insanity and psychopathic obsession. We faced the worst the uncaring universe has thrown at us. And...

We're still here.

We're still standing.

Yeah, I might be on my own inside Rivera's mind. But that just meant everything else about our escape was in Sofia's hands. And I know she's up to it.

Just like she knows I can do this.

I ended my self-reflection, turned my attention to Rivera's disaster area of a mind, and shouted, "Do you think you're angry now? Do you truly believe a revolt among your crew is your biggest fear? Ha!"

My voice barely rose above Rivera's emotional cacophony. But if I heard it, Rivera's mind could, too. That meant I could manipulate her emotions, and the first step was to stop her emotional conflict. That meant making one emotion dominant. Anger looked strongest, and I thought it would be the easiest one to mold. All I had to do was turn fear and desperation into anger. And I thought I knew how to do that.

"Feel shame!" I ordered. "Shame that you—a *Rivera*—were willing to waste fifty valuable captives because you could not control your own crew! What would your brother think of *that*, huh? Paco would be ashamed!"

Foaming crests of red so dark they bordered on black appeared on the tsunami of fear.

"Yeah, you shamed your brother. Shamed your father. Even shamed your pathetic mother. A Rivera *commands*, she doesn't *cower!*"

That last insult had an incredible effect. In a rush, the bright red tsunami of fear turned the red-black of shame.

Yes!

That made my next command incredibly simple.

"You feel shame, you horrible excuse for a Rivera? You should feel anger, instead. Anger at your crew. Anger at the *Pegasus*. Anger at everyone and everything that made you feel even a twinge of shame."

The vortex of Rivera's anger suddenly changed course and bore down on the shameful tsunami. They crashed together and in a blinding spray of emotions. The vortex of anger spun clear, and the red-black tsunami was gone.

With no prompting from me, the vortex swallowed the blue-green tempest, too.

If I'd had hands, I'd have rubbed them together in satisfaction. Now, to mold Rivera's anger into my triumph.

The crimson vortex of Rivera's anger roared through her mind. It destroyed lust, overwhelmed greed, and fed on fear. Her rampaging anger was a truly awesome spectacle.

Enough gawking, Nora. You've got a lot of work to do and time is not in your favor.

Right.

I gathered myself and shouted, "Yes, you *should* be angry! Just think over everything you've done for this crew! Things beyond their capacity to do *or* comprehend!"

Squishy memories shot out of the vortex as Rivera's mind embraced the buried emotions fueling her anger. They rained down around me, and I saw into the memories that brushed against me.

A woman in a business suit smiled at Rivera across a neat desk. "My examiners tell me your test scores and impressive range of practical knowledge more than make up for your lack of traditional education. You impressed them, and that is a rare thing. One even says you're destined for command."

Exultation exploded inside Rivera, but she simply said, "That's kind of them, ma'am."

The woman held her data pad up. "From everything I've read in your report, you more than earned it. The job is yours if you want it, Miss Riva."

"I want it, ma'am. More than anything,"

The woman stood and extended a hand across the desk. "Welcome to the Connaught Starlines."

That memory didn't surprise me. I mean, how else could Rivera the pirate turn into Lieutenant Riva of the *Pegasus*?

More memories grazed me, but one stood out from the rest.

Rivera walked the streets of an unknown city with half-a-dozen junior officers from the Pegasus.

"Twenty-four hours of shore leave, guys," one crowed. "What should we do first?"

An ensign who looked about twenty counted off on his fingers. "Pick up girls, ply them with food and alcohol, and charm their pants off. Literally."

"If your plan requires charm," a female ensign said, "you're screwed, Derek. And I don't mean that literally."

The others laughed as Rivera headed in another direction. "I'm sure you kids won't want a member of the senior staff spoiling your fun."

Rivera pasted on a false smile and waved off half-hearted protests. Five minutes later, she entered a hotel, made her way to a room on the fourth floor, and hit the buzzer on a door at the end of a hallway. It slid aside, and she entered.

A man waited within. "I got your message. What's the news?"

"The Pegasus *has a new course. The captain told us just before shore leave."*

"That's just great," the man growled. "Now we'll have to scrap the raid and—"

"No, we don't cancel it," Rivera said. "We adapt to it."

"Look, I know you want off that tub as soon as possible, but we don't have enough time to come up with a new plan."

"I already have one," Rivera countered.

The man waved off her comment. "It doesn't matter. Your mother is too cautious to—"

"She'll make an exception this time."

"What makes you so sure?"

"Because the new course takes us to Ark's Landing, where we'll pick up the oldest Connaught kid."

The man nodded. "You're right. She'll definitely make an exception for that."

I found a morbid fascination in the course Rivera followed to capture the *Pegasus,* and from her memories, I saw how isolated she felt. Hiding her vengeful nature behind the guise of a stern-but-fair officer. Maintaining an emotional distance from people she planned on selling into slavery, or worse. Knowing the pirate crew would believe her work on the *Pegasus* was little more than a cushy vacation from the drudgery and boredom of day-to-day life at a pirate base.

And that was about all of Rivera's self-pity that I could handle. I dodged around several more memories, then shouted, "You should be disgusted at how poorly the crew understands what you've done for them! Feel disgusted, they can't think beyond their latest desires. Feel disgusted that most of them are incapable of planning even a simple raid, much less something as complex as taking the *Pegasus.*"

I don't know if Rivera thinks that last bit is true. But I get the idea she's one of those people who believes she's smarter than everyone else and resents the idea that other people don't automatically shut up and do what she tells them to do. Then again, I got the same idea from half the pirate minds I entered when I kicked off my psychological warfare campaign.

And anger makes someone more likely to accept ideas they wouldn't normally believe. That's what Granddaddy taught me, anyway. Nothing I'd done and seen since the pirates took over the *Pegasus* made me think he was wrong, either. So I shouted more orders for disgust and watched the vortex for color changes.

I didn't catch the shift until it was well underway. That's because the color of disgust was gray, which blended into the crimson of anger so well I only spotted it when a big chunk of the vortex turned gray. When I knew what color to look for, I saw splotches of gray dotting the vortex. They grew quickly, and soon I watched a gray vortex with streaks of crimson.

That was good enough. I had Rivera's emotional state right where I wanted it, so I ignored the memories flying from the gray vortex and moved to the next part of my plan.

I shouted, "Those disgusting morons don't understand! They don't realize how successful this raid was. They don't realize it was an absolute triumph. And you should feel triumphant! You should feel like you did when you blasted Nora Connaught to atoms!"

This shift was easy to see, because it turns out that triumph is yellow. As soon as I issued the order for triumph, bright yellow streaks appeared in the gray vortex. They grew and spread, easily overriding disgust. As before, memories spun from the vortex. There were far fewer memories than anger and disgust produced, and that was good. Because I needed one memory in particular.

It wasn't hard to find. One triumphal memory glowed so brightly it could almost rival a star. Certain that was the memory I wanted, I willed myself to grab it.

Rivera stood near a crewman manning a weapons station.
"I wish I could kill you with my bare hands," she said.

My voice issued from the comm, calm and self-assured. "Well, you can't."

"No, but I can kill you."

"What? No! How?"

"The Pegasus is well armed, girl."

"But the weapons were sabotaged!"

"By me, you idiot!" Rivera turned to the man at the weapons' controls. "Have you targeted the lifepod?"

"Yes, ma'am," he said.

"Fire."

"No!" I liked the panic I put into my voice. "Please, don't!"

A broad, triumphant smile spread across Rivera's face, and she said, "Goodbye, Nora Connaught."

Rivera turned towards the captain's chair and—

Wait, that was it? That was the triumph? But she didn't enter the code to unlock the controls!

Then it hit me. She entered the code long before I launched the lifepod. She had to, otherwise the *Pegasus* would have just drifted on the same course forever. I associated the code with the lifepod's destruction because, in the memory I just watched, Rivera and I both mentioned her sabotage. But entering the code was something Rivera did to regain control of the ship, not something that made her feel triumphant.

Oh, God, I'd been so certain that triumph was the key to getting the code. But I'd been horribly, disastrously wrong. And unless I could discover the emotion Rivera felt when she entered the code, we were all doomed.

Stupid, stupid, *stupid*! How could I have been so stupid? So certain I knew all about Rivera's state of mind? What was I thinking?

You weren't, a voice inside my head said.

I thought I'd gotten rid of you, No-Talent Nora.

You wish, Nora. You'll never be rid of me, because you'll always be me.

Wrong. I have a talent and—

And what? You're going to be the hero and save the day? That's a little girl's fantasy, Nora, and you're not a little girl anymore. It's time to stop pretending you're a hero.

I think I've done pretty well so far.

Oh, you've had a few successes. But manipulating a woman as terrifying and smart as Rivera into revealing her secret code is beyond your ability. Sure, you made her remember her moment of triumph, but—

You're right. I *did* guide her from anger at her crew straight to her memory of blowing up the lifepod.

Like I was saying—

That means I *do* know Rivera's state of mind. Enough to make her remember what I wanted her to remember.

My point is—

If I can just figure out *when* Rivera entered the code, maybe I can guess her feelings. And if I can do that, maybe I can still get the code. Thanks, No-Talent Nora. You've been a big help.

The doubting voice inside my head, the one that's been plaguing me since my sister Nancy first got her psychic powers ten years ago, fell silent. Maybe she was gone for good this time. But I was glad she'd put in her latest appearance. Because arguing with her showed me that all was not lost.

The situation wasn't great, but it wasn't impossible, either. I turned my attention away from No-Talent Nora back to Rivera and figuring out when she entered the code that unlocked the *Pegasus's* controls.

She wouldn't have done it before the pirates had complete control of the ship. Let's see. The pirates stormed aboard shortly after I slipped into the *Pegasus's* maintenance tunnels, leaving Sofia to pretend she was me. I felt a shiver of dread as I remember how that switch nearly got her killed.

I pushed that thought out of my mind. Horrific as that experience was for Sofia, she was still alive. But she wouldn't stay that way unless I got that code.

Okay, the pirates boarded shortly after that. The crew

surrendered, and the pirates began herding crew and passengers into the dining hall. Was that when Rivera unlocked the controls? I mean, the pirates had control of the ship, right? And they couldn't do anything with the *Pegasus* as long as Rivera had them locked out. But...

With five thousand people onboard the *Pegasus* and only a couple of hundred pirates, wouldn't the pirates need everyone working on crowd control? At least until they had the passengers and crew inside the easily guarded dining hall? For a ship the size of the *Pegasus*, the bare minimum crew was around fifty people. And that just covered the bridge and engineering. There's no way the pirates could spare that many from their gang while they rounded up everyone.

Rounded up *almost* everyone, since they never found me.

No, the soon-to-be late pirate captain would have waited until her crew had everything under control before she worried about manning the bridge and engineering. After all, space is vast and filled with a whole lot of nothing. It's not like she had to worry about the *Pegasus* running into something. The original Captain Rivera wouldn't have turned her attention to other matters until she had complete control of the ship. Only then would she send her daughter—the current Captain Rivera—to unlock the controls.

So, what would Rivera—the daughter, not the mother—have felt while she did that? Satisfaction? Anticipation? Greed?

God in heaven, how could I manipulate her into feeling one of those emotions? Rather, the specific version of it she felt unlocking the ship's controls? They weren't really tied to anything specific I could use to make Rivera summon the memory of entering the code.

What else was going on at the same time?

Passengers were terrified, but they'd been terrified ever since Captain Riggs told them he thought pirates were waiting at the wormhole exit. Besides, Rivera was an experienced pirate. Passenger terror must be normal for her.

The *Pegasus's* crew was probably enraged. But that's another thing she must have seen lots of times in the past.

What else went on then?

And then it hit me.

Rivera's mother sent for me so she could terrify me, kill me, and claim revenge against my parents for their imagined crimes.

Where was her daughter during the confrontation that led to the mother's suicide? The younger Rivera wasn't in the dining hall because the two guards who brought Sofia to the dining hall argued over who should tell the first officer that her mother had killed herself.

But one of the earliest emotions I read after my ability manifested was the blazing hatred the younger Rivera felt for me. She would have wanted to see her mother's vengeance in person. But the *Pegasus's* traitorous officer wasn't in the dining hall.

Unlocking the controls was the only task that required her personal attention. And it was important enough that her mother made her go do that instead of staying to watch me die.

Since Rivera wasn't in the dining hall when her mother killed herself, I knew she'd followed her mother's orders. But she couldn't have been happy about it. No, I felt certain I knew what Rivera felt when her mother ordered her to the bridge.

Rage. Pure, white-hot rage.

I had no trouble evoking Rivera's anger. But how could I turn that anger into rage? By introducing the target of her rage? Yeah, that sounded right. Rivera aimed her rage at her mother. As an empath, I can order up emotions. Only, 'mother' isn't an emotion.

Or is it?

I associate all sorts of emotions with my mother. Love, concern, pride, and about a million other feelings. But no one ever lists all the deep emotions they feel for their mother. They just say they love their mother. And most people love their mothers—I sure do—but that was the one emotion I felt sure Rivera did *not* feel for hers.

How about hatred? Yeah, that sounded right for the Rivera mother-daughter relationship. Still, the younger Rivera hated way more people than just her mother. My whole family, for starters, and my father above the rest. So I couldn't just go straight for general hatred as her source of rage because Rivera's rage had to be directed at her mother. That was the necessary middle step to Rivera's feelings when she entered the code and unlocked the *Pegasus's* controls.

I needed another emotion to go with hatred, something that tied it all back to Rivera's mother. But what emotion?

Loathing? No, that was just another word for hatred.

Irritation? Normal kids get irritated at their parents, but it seemed too minor a feeling to show up on Rivera's emotional radar.

Disgust? Hm... That emotion came with revulsion and rejection built in, and they struck me as things Rivera felt for her mother. So, hatred first, and then disgust.

I raised my voice and ordered, "Feel hatred! Feel deep, implacable hatred!"

Unlike every other emotional shift I'd caused in Rivera's mind, this one was instantaneous. A yellow vortex spun before me one second, and the next second a deep purple one replaced it.

A part of my mind wondered how my empathic ability selected colors for emotions. I mean, I like purple. Why did it represent hatred?

That was speculation for the future, when everyone was safe. Now, I needed to twist the purple vortex into... whatever color would turn up for disgust.

"Now," I shouted, "feel disgust along with the hatred. Feel disgust! Feel hatred! Feel them both!"

The change in the vortex was subtle this time, and slower in appearing. I kept shouting my emotional commands until I finally spotted streaks of brown in with the purple. Did brown mean disgust? It must, right?

As with the anger I had summoned recently, the purple-brown vortex began spewing memories. They rained down around me, and when they brushed against me, they burned. But not with heat. They burned with arctic cold.

A fourteen-year-old Rivera held a blaster and concentrated on a target ten meters away. She pulled the trigger with quick, jerking motions that made the gun wobble in her hands. That threw off her aim, and her shots all missed the target.

The older Rivera knocked the gun aside and slapped her daughter hard across the face. "You missed. Again."

"Ow, Mom," teenage Rivera whined, "why did you hit me?"

"I didn't hit you, girl," her mother hissed, "a Connaught did. And that's mild compared to what will happen to you if you shoot at one of them and miss!"

Seriously? Did either Rivera truly believe I came from a family of monsters?

Another memory froze me.

A Rivera about my age wrapped her arms around a man's neck and looked into his eyes. He wore an incredibly attractive, very worrisome smirk. Rivera felt confusion, anticipation, and desire for some kind of human interaction that had nothing to do with the Connaught name.

Her breath quickened as his hands began unbuttoning her shirt. Then, a strange expression came over his face and his hands stopped moving.

Rivera's mother appeared behind the guy and pulled him away from Rivera. "I told the crew my daughter was off limits. That includes you, Porter."

Her mother pushed Porter against a wall. Then she raised a blaster and shot him.

I saw the last of the memories spew from the purple-brown vortex. I tried dodging them, but a final one crashed into me.

Rivera walked through a corridor in the Pegasus. *She glanced over her shoulder at two pirates struggling with an ungainly burden—her mother's shroud-wrapped corpse.*

She stopped before an airlock and opened the inner hatch. "Put her in there."

The pirates hurried to obey, dropped the body within, and almost ran out of the airlock. I got the idea the pirates were afraid Rivera would flush them into space with her mother. But the surviving Rivera waited until they were out before closing the inner hatch. Without ceremony, she opened the outer hatch, and the sudden decompression blew her mother's body into space.

As she watched the white-wrapped body tumble away, one pirate asked, "Ain't you gonna say something, ma'am?"

Rivera gave a slight nod and said, "Paco deserved someone better than you, mother."

Wow.

I no longer had to figure out how to tie rage and Rivera's mother together, at least. I just had to bring it to the surface.

"Keep feeling hatred and disgust," I said, "and feel rage along with them."

White mixed in with the purple and brown. Finally, a new color that made sense to me. White worked for hot or cold. And, along with the purple and brown, made for a really ugly vortex. Just right for Rivera's ugly collection of feelings. But it wasn't quite right. I'd just experienced a ton of Rivera's memories of her mother, and none of them had anything to do with entering the code to unlock the *Pegasus's* controls.

What was I missing? What other emotions would Rivera have felt when her mother ordered her away right before finally taking revenge on the Connaught family? I mean, the younger Rivera wanted vengeance as much as her mother. So...

"Feel vengeful!" I called. "Feel the vengeance that drove you from the time Paco died until your mother had a Connaught under her control!"

Silver streaks appeared in the ugly vortex. They spread and entwined with the other colors until a multi-hued storm raged before me. But I still felt as if it needed something else. Some other emotion that tied everything together and left the one memory I needed to see.

But what else had Rivera felt when her mother deprived her of a share of their vengeance? What—

Oh, yeah. It's right there in front of you, Nora. That has to be it.

I steeled myself and ordered up one last emotion.

I KILLED NORA CONNAUGHT

Before introducing the emotion I prayed would produce the memory I desperately needed, I reinforced the emotions already spinning in Rivera's ugly emotional vortex.

"Feel hatred and disgust!" I ordered. "Stay enraged and vengeful!"

The vortex twisted and turned and lost none of its intensity.

Okay, Nora, it's time to find out if you've read this right.

I'd have taken a deep breath if I had any sensation of breathing. Since I didn't, I ordered, "Feel deprivation! Feel deprived of the one thing you wanted more than anything else!"

I kept repeating the command for deprivation, bolstering the other emotions now and then, and watched for a change in the vortex. It took a long time before I saw something new, but green streaks eventually appeared in the vortex. Only, this green wasn't the bright shade of hope. It looked more like the putrid green of mold, rot, and decay. It was like the bright green light of hope curdled by the darkness of despair.

I finally had Rivera in the mental state I wanted. Now it was a matter of waiting until the vortex spat out the memory I needed to see. As if on cue, a single memory flew from the vortex. I immediately immersed myself in it.

Rivera walked past the pirates and pushed through the passengers being herded into the dining hall. A tremulous hand plucked at her sleeve.

"Lieutenant Riva?"

She turned and met the terrified gaze of a middle-aged woman. The woman had her arm wrapped protectively around a pretty preteen girl.

"Yes?" Rivera asked, her voice toneless.

"What will the pirates do to us?" the woman asked.

"We'll sell you as a drudge." Rivera's eyes darted to the girl. "Your daughter is quite attractive. She'll receive pleasure training before we sell her. Her life will be far more comfortable than yours, while her looks hold out."

Tears spilled from the woman's eyes, but she asked, "We?"

Rivera ignored the question and pushed on into the dining hall. Her mother, the pirate captain, stood apart from pirates and passengers, surveying their latest haul of human merchandise. The Pegasus's *crew glared at Rivera as she approached her mother.*

"We've rounded up the stragglers, Mother, and will have everyone in the dining hall soon."

"Excellent," the elder Rivera said. She raised a handheld radio and said, "Marsh? Release the bridge crew from merchandise collection."

The radio crackled, and Marsh's voice said, "Aye, Captain."

The captain turned to Rivera. "Go to the bridge and unlock the controls."

"Yes, Mother."

Rivera spun on her heel and headed for the dining hall exit. Her mother's radio crackled again.

"Sutton?" her mother said.

"Captain?" a man asked.

I recognized his voice. It was the man I dubbed Harsh Voice in the aftermath of the captain's suicide.

"Bring the Connaught girl to me."

"Aye, Captain."

A jolt ran through Rivera, and she turned back to her mother.

"What are you doing?" she demanded.

"I'm avenging your brother, girl." Rivera's mother glared at her. "Now, go about your business."

"But I want to be here!" Rivera felt shame at her whining tone, but continued, "I want—"

"You have your orders."

"But—"

Rivera's mother drew her blaster and pointed it at her daughter. "I said you have your orders."

Rage and hatred rose inside Rivera as she snapped, "As you command, Captain."

The trip to the bridge passed in a blur as Rivera created her own ugly vortex of emotions. She stormed onto the bridge, shoved past several members of the pirates' bridge crew, and dropped into a seat before a console. With a few swift taps on the screen, she opened a software application.

The words Enter Passcode *appeared on the screen. Rivera literally pounded on each key as she typed* noraconnaughtmustDIE *and hit* Enter.

I pulled myself free from the memory and found myself feeling disappointed with Rivera. I'd expected a passcode I would have to repeat to myself over and over, so it burned into my memory. Instead, she'd used a phrase so simple a child could remember it. Intellectually, I knew Rivera's passcode was no less secure against slicing software than a random string of characters and symbols. But she used a *guessable* passcode. Maybe not easily guessed, but I could imagine the snort of disgust Dad—the family computer expert—would make when I told him.

Which, I reminded myself, I could only do if I returned to my own mind. I slid from Rivera's mind and drew a deep breath.

"Are you back, Miss Connaught?" Captain Riggs' deep voice asked.

Something about my situation felt a little odd. Not wrong, just... different. I opened my eyes and found myself looking up at the blue haze of an atmosphere shield and, beyond it, the stars.

Captain Riggs held me in his arms as he strode through an atmosphere tunnel connecting the warehouse and the *Pegasus*. I glanced around and saw the bare-framed metal vehicles that formed the original tunnel lined up again. The hopefuls—Shawn's friends from the pirates' pantry—manned the vehicles. Sofia walked beside Captain Riggs, and the *Pegasus's* crew followed their captain back to the ship, shepherding their young charges.

"Miss Connaught?" Captain Riggs asked, again.

"Yes, sir, I am back," I said. "And I have the code, sir."

"I had no doubts on that score, Miss Connaught," the captain rumbled.

Sofia looked over her shoulder and shouted, "Nora has the code!"

A loud cheer rose from the crew and almost drowned out my next words.

"What about Conley and Barber?"

"Hale and hearty, Miss Connaught," Captain Riggs replied. "I believe retaking the *Pegasus* was quite therapeutic for them."

With trepidation, I asked, "And the wounded?"

"Your friend still lives, as do my wounded crew members."

I sighed with relief, then said, "Um, I can walk on my own, sir."

Captain Riggs swung me down to my feet with ease. "Very well, Miss Connaught."

It took me a moment to remember how to walk in the moon's low gravity, but at least I didn't go tumbling heels over head. Still, I breathed a sigh of relief when we entered the *Pegasus's* Earth-normal gravity field.

The crew scattered to their stations, and Captain Riggs led me directly to the bridge. Conley joined us along the way. He nodded respectfully to me, then turned to Sofia.

"A Mrs. Stanley asked to be remembered to you," he said.

Sofia grinned in response.

On the bridge, I slid into the seat Rivera used to enter the passcode, banged out the same keystrokes, and the words *Enter Passcode* appeared on the screen. With care, I entered noraconnaughtmustDIE and pressed *Enter*. I held my breath as the screen cleared.

Captain Riggs asked, "What is the status of my ship?"

"Navigation online."

"Sensors online."

"Helm online."

"Communications online."

"Weapons systems online."

Captain Riggs activated his comm. "Chief Engineer Lawson? Status report."

"Engine controls are online, sir. The pirates never completely shut down my engines. We'll have full power available in thirty seconds."

"Navigation, can you find the course the pirates followed after they took control of my ship?"

"Aye, sir. I'm calculating the reverse course now."

From the comm, Lawson said, "Full power available now, Captain."

"Helm," Captain Riggs said, "get us out of here."

The *Pegasus's* deck vibrated beneath my feet and the starliner lifted off. The bridge crew cheered, all except the woman at the sensor station.

"Captain," she said, "sensors show the pirate ship is powering up. They're coming after us, sir."

Work at the control stations slowed as the *Pegasus's* bridge crew exchanged nervous glances. Captain Riggs' gaze swept the room, then he rose to his feet.

Captain Riggs walked around his bridge and put a fatherly hand on the shoulder of each member of his crew. In his calm, steadying voice, he said, "From the moment ill fortune let the traitor Rivera slip through our fingers, we knew pursuit was inevitable. It comes sooner than I had hoped, but that changes nothing."

The captain completed his circuit, leaving a calmer crew in his wake. "*But* one thing has changed. The *Pegasus* is no longer crippled by the traitor's software. She can run. She can fight. And by God, so can we."

The trepidation in the crew's faces eased as they turned back to their stations. A few gave determined nods of agreement.

"Captain," the comm officer said, "Weapons Chief Roberts is on the comm."

"On speaker," Captain Riggs said.

The comm officer tapped on his control board, and then nodded to the captain.

"What's the state of our weapons systems, Chief?" Captain Riggs asked.

"Not good, Captain," Chief Roberts replied. "The pirates took most of our missiles and cannibalized half our blaster cannons for parts."

"How many missiles do we have left?"

"Five, sir."

Captain Riggs grew thoughtful. "Can you get a target lock on the pirate ship?"

"Not with the cannons, sir. They're line-of-sight weapons, and the pirates are beyond this cursed moon's short horizon. We *might* get a target lock with missiles, but we're too close to the pirate ship for the missile arming sequence to complete."

Sofia and I must have looked confused at that, because Conley said, "Without the arming sequence, a missile could go off close to the *Pegasus* and damage it." He glanced at me, his face expressionless as always. "Damage *her*, I mean."

I smiled at him. "After all this, you remembered what I said when Captain Riggs visited my cabin, before all this pirate stuff happened?"

"I always remember what you say, Miss Connaught," Conley said. "It's part of my job."

"Well, it will please Aunt Nancy when I tell her about it."

"And may the opportunity to tell her arise soon," Captain Riggs said.

"Excuse me, sir?" I asked.

"Your Aunt Nancy commands the Ark's Landing navy, doesn't she?"

"Yeah," I said. "Um, I mean yes, sir."

"While you were retrieving the passcode from the former Lieutenant Rivera, Miss Olson told me of the messenger drone you sent to Ark's Landing. I—"

"Pardon the interruption, Captain," the comm officer said, "but we have an incoming transmission. It's Rivera."

The captain's face hardened. "Put her on speaker."

The comm officer did as ordered, and Rivera's voice issued from the speakers.

"Blast you into a billion pieces. I repeat, surrender and return to base or we will blast you to atoms."

"We categorically refuse," Captain Riggs said.

Rivera was silent for a moment, then said, "Hello, Marcus. I believe you'll want to reconsider your response."

"I most emphatically do not, traitor."

"That's an interesting epithet, Marcus. I always worked for this band of buccaneers, so—"

Captain Riggs interrupted. "Gang of cutthroats is more accurate."

"That's just hurtful, Marcus." Rivera's voice took on an admonishing tone. "My men never cut a single throat."

"Play all the semantic games you wish, traitor," Captain Riggs said. "My rejection of your demand stands, and shall stand as long as I have breath in my body."

Rivera's tone hardened. "Which won't be very long once my ship is within firing range."

"You won't find the *Pegasus* defenseless this time. Unlike your first cowardly attack, we have full control of our ship this time."

"Yes..." Rivera said. "That raises an interesting question. How *did* you bypass my software sabotage?"

Sofia waved to catch the Captain's attention. He saw her, and said, "Comm officer, mute us."

After he did, Sofia said, "I apologize for interrupting you, sir."

Captain Riggs smiled at her. "If anyone in my crew has earned that right, Miss Olson, it is you. What do you wish to say?"

All eyes turned to Sofia, and I know she found the attention uncomfortable because her cheeks reddened. But she drew a breath and said, "I think you should tell that traitor exactly how we got the passcode. Better yet, let *Nora* tell her."

Captain Riggs' eyebrows rose in surprise, but he just asked, "Why?"

"Because Rivera is totally unhinged when it comes to the Connaught family, sir. When she finds out she didn't actually kill Nora..."

Sofia's voice trailed off, so I finished her thought. "She'll completely lose it!"

"And keep after us until we're *all* dead," someone said under their breath.

Captain Riggs heard it and replied, "Does anyone here doubt the traitor will pursue us to the borders of the Federation?"

Around the bridge, heads shook.

"Does anyone here doubt the *Pegasus's* crew and passengers will fight to the death defending our freedom, our lives, and our ship?"

Again, heads shook.

"Then we lose nothing by following Miss Olson's suggestion."

"But what do we gain, sir?" the helms woman asked.

"Miss Olson," Captain Riggs asked, "would you care to elaborate?"

The red in Sofia's cheeks deepened, but she said, "An unhinged opponent is far more likely to make mistakes than a coldly calculating one."

"Exactly," Captain Riggs said. He looked at me. "I cannot order you to do this, Miss Connaught, but—"

I looked at the comm officer. "Can you do visuals with that?"

"Of course," he sniffed.

I went to stand next to Captain Riggs and struck a casual pose. "Please put us on screen."

A holographic image of Rivera appeared before Captain Riggs and me. Rivera eyed me with disinterest and looked back at Captain Riggs.

He said, "I have nothing further to say to you, traitor. However, this young lady has something to tell you."

Confused, Rivera looked back at me.

I smiled and waved. "Hi! I'm Nora Connaught, the totally not dead object of your hatred."

Rivera's eyes bugged out and foam flecked her lips as she shouted, "*What?*"

I really couldn't have asked for a better reaction.

"You heard the young lady," Captain Riggs said. "You did *not* kill Nora Connaught. You could *not* hold my passengers and crew prisoner. You will *not* stop the *Pegasus* escaping your sad, remote pirate base."

Rivera's wild eyes darted back and forth between me and Captain Riggs for a few seconds. Then she did something unexpected. Rivera laughed, and it definitely wasn't a good-humored one.

"Oh Marcus," she cackled, "that was a good one. You almost had me believing that girl was Nora Connaught. I didn't know you had it in you to use a dead girl like that."

"I would never do something so vile." Captain Riggs sounded truly offended by the idea that he would stoop so low. "But I assure you, this *is* Nora Connaught."

Rivera's gaze returned to me. "She has a vague resemblance to the family, I'll grant you. But—"

"Do you remember the only words we ever exchanged?" I asked.

"Keep your puppet quiet, Marcus," Rivera said.

"You said *I wish I could kill you with my bare hands*."

Rivera's eyes snapped back to me.

I continued recounting our conversation. "Then I said, *Well, you can't*. To which you said, *No, but I can kill you*."

"Where did you hear that, girl?" Rivera growled.

"Then I said," I put my hands on my cheeks, mimicking the vid cliché expression of horror, "*What? No! How?*"

Rivera leaned closer to her vid pickup. "Which member of my crew talked in front of you? Tell me, and I'll see that you're sold to a benevolent master."

I adopted a rural Ark's Landing accent and said, "Gosh, Miss Pirate ma'am, that do be a fine offer you be makin' ta me. But my mama didn't raise no fools."

That sarcastic reply was the wrong approach. My tone of voice jolted Rivera out of replaying our brief conversation from before she launched a missile at the lifepod. She leaned back, smiled, and said, "You should have taken my offer, girl. With your looks and quick wits, you could have made a fine concubine for some rich rim world warlord."

In a monotone, I said, "Oh no. How foolish of me to turn down such an attractive offer."

This time, I got Rivera's goat. She leaned towards her vid pickup again. "Don't mock me, girl."

"Or what? You'll sell me to the lowest bidder?"

"I'll do worse than that. I'll give you to my crew as a present." She cocked her head. "I think I'll do that, anyway."

Rivera's crew let loose a disturbing bunch of obscene remarks, hoots, and hollers at her words.

From outside the range of the vid pickup, Sofia hissed, "You're going at this all wrong, Nora. Hit Rivera with something you found inside her mind."

Sofia's suggestion prompted a burst of inspiration. I locked gazes with Rivera and said, "Paco deserved someone better than you, mother."

Rivera's mouth opened and closed, but no words emerged.

I took advantage of her silence and hammered on her love for her brother. "But you were wrong. Paco got the mother he deserved. Got the sister he deserved. And when Dad shot him, Paco got the fate he deserved."

"I'll make your death slow and painful for that, girl," Rivera snarled.

Now I had to push her completely over the edge. "Do you know where I got all that, Rivera? From your *mind*. And let me tell you, it is one sick and twisted place! I mean, dreams about your mother blowing a hole in her head so Sofia and I could climb out? No wonder you're such a psycho."

"How——?"

"You're kidding, right? I'm the daughter of the most powerful psychic born in the last four hundred years."

"No, I killed Nora Connaught." Rivera wasn't talking to anyone except herself. "She's dead. This girl is just a ploy to distract me."

As darkly entertaining as my conversation with Rivera had been, we still hadn't quite convinced her of my true identity. If only she had seen me in person before the pirate attack, she would recognize me. I had Rivera at the tipping point, but I needed something irrefutable to push her over the edge.

No, not something. Some*one*.

I reached over, caught Sofia by the arm, pulled her into the vid pickup, and wrapped an arm over her shoulder. "You don't recognize me, Rivera? Fine. But you *know* Sofia. You *spoke* to her. And you *think* she was in the lifepod when you destroyed it. You can deny I'm Nora Connaught all you want, but you *know* this is Sofia Olson, and she's also totally not dead."

The version of Sofia who met me in my cabin when I boarded the *Pegasus* would have quailed under the glare Rivera turned on her. But this Sofia put an arm over my shoulders, smiled, and gave a cheery wave.

"Do you know what your big mistake was, Rivera?" Sofia

asked. "You went up against the Badass Babes of the Cosmos. *And you lost.*"

A sick, savage smile spread across Rivera's face. "Not yet, I haven't. And Nora?"

She apparently expected a response from me. In a bored tone, I asked, "What is it now, Rivera?"

"In your last moment of life—your *real* last moment—as my ship utterly destroys the *Pegasus*, remember that you die with the blood of five thousand people on your hands!"

Then Rivera cut her transmission.

I stared unblinking at the spot where Rivera's image had been. My gaze lost focus, but I couldn't make myself look elsewhere. Rivera's words played over and over in my mind.

Was she right?

If the pirates destroyed the *Pegasus,* would every death be my fault? I mean, everything I did from the moment the pirates intercepted the *Pegasus* led to this moment.

I let Sofia take my place when the pirates boarded while I hid from the pirates.

I promoted Rivera from first officer to pirate captain when I drove her mother to suicide.

I freed Sofia and tricked Rivera into believing she had killed us.

I sowed the seeds of rebellion in the pirates' minds.

I recruited Shawn and the other hopefuls to my cause.

I smuggled guns to Conley, Barber, Captain Riggs, and the late Lieutenant Blair, leaving them—

An elbow dug into my ribs, and Sofia said, "Stop it, Nora."

I blinked and turned to Sofia. "What?"

"Stop listening to that traitor, Rivera."

"I... can't. And she's sort of right, too."

Captain Riggs snorted. "She most certainly is *not*, Miss Connaught."

I offered the Captain a wan smile. "I don't doubt the crew will fight the pirates to the last man, but what about the passengers? They—"

"Captain," Sofia asked, "may I have permission to escort Nora from the bridge?"

"Do you wish to check on your friend in sickbay, Miss Olson?" Captain Riggs said. "I can comm the doctor myself and—"

"*Sir!*" Sofia interrupted.

Captain Riggs' eyebrows arched in surprise at being interrupted on his bridge, much less by a nineteen-year-old member of his crew. Instead of shrinking from her captain, Sofia glared him into submission.

"Ah, yes, Miss Olson. If you think that's best."

Sofia's glare faded, and she smiled at him. "I do, sir. Thank you."

"Shouldn't we stay on the bridge?" I asked. "The pirates will attack soon."

"No, they won't," Captain Riggs replied. He pointed to his command chair's sensor display. "The pirate ship isn't on our sensors yet, which means Rivera is taking a course around the moon instead of pursuing us directly."

"Why wouldn't she come right after us?" I furrowed my brow, then realized the answer. "If she did that, she'd be in range of the *Pegasus's* missiles and her ship's velocity would be so low it couldn't maneuver well enough to avoid the attack."

"It?" Conley asked. "Don't you mean *she?*"

I arched one eyebrow. "Ships like the *Pegasus* are ladies and deserving of respect. Pirate ships are not."

"So there's no reason for us to stay on the bridge right now," Sofia said. She grabbed my arm and started towards the corridor. "Come on."

I let her drag me from the Captain's side, and barely noticed when Conley automatically fell in behind us. Sofia had other ideas.

She held out her free hand in the universal sign for *stop*. "Not you, Conley. Just Nora and me."

Conley didn't stop. "I am Miss Connaught's bodyguard, Miss Olson. I must assure her safety."

Sofia kept her grip on my arm, but put her other hand on her hip in obvious exasperation. "Do you honestly believe anyone on board the *Pegasus* will harm Nora?"

"That is not the point, Miss—"

"Yes, it *is* the point," Sofia said. "Just... let me do this my way, Conley. Please, trust me to keep Nora safe?"

I can't imagine the mental conflict that raged inside Conley's head, because his face remained as expressionless as ever. But the battle went in Sofia's favor. Conley nodded once and stayed on the bridge while Sofia dragged me away.

Once we were out in the hallway, I said, "Wow, Sofia, you've turned into a holy terror!"

"Don't try changing the subject, Nora," Sofia said.

Honestly puzzled, I said, "I didn't know we *had* a subject."

"The subject is you and your attempt to shoulder all the responsibility for everything bad that might happen during this escape."

"Oh, that."

"Yes, *that*."

"But it *is* my responsibility, Sofia. I made all the decisions, formulated the plans, and—"

Sofia stopped and shoved me up against the bulkhead. Anger burned in her eyes. "*You* did that? By yourself? With no one by your side?"

I shook my head, unable to meet her gaze, and whispered, "Of course not. I didn't—"

"Shut up and listen to me, Nora!" Sofia snapped. "You are the single most frustrating person I've ever met. One minute you're confidently mouthing off to an insane pirate captain and the next you're letting that same pirate make you doubt yourself. You've been a walking, talking bundle of contradictions from the moment I met you. You can be an almost unstoppable force. Until the tiniest sliver of doubt enters your head. Then you stop yourself.

"For God's sake, Nora, look at everything you've done since you came aboard. You truly *are* the Badass Babe of the Cosmos. And everybody knows that except *you*. You're not No-Talent Nora. You never were. You just don't believe it. Not yet." Sofia began pulling me down the corridor again. "Now, come on."

I followed her. It's not like Sofia gave me any choice, right?

"You didn't drag me off the bridge just so you could shout at me in private?" I asked.

"No, but that was a side benefit."

"Then why—"

"You'll see when we get there."

Two minutes later, Sofia dragged me into the *Pegasus's* dining room. Even though Captain Riggs let the passengers return to their cabins if they wished, many of them remained here.

Sofia marched straight through groups of people, drawing startled glances and comments, as she muttered, "Where is she?"

Sofia's gaze locked on someone or something, and she changed course for whatever caught her attention. Ten seconds later, she pushed and shoved her way through a crowd of people packed around a table. She finally reached the front of the crowd and said, "I thought I'd find you at your favorite table, Mrs. Stanley."

My eyebrows rose as I got my first look at the woman Captain Riggs called *formidable*. She truly looked like someone's sweet grandmother. Even her eyes look sweet and loving. But steel supported the love.

Mrs. Stanley's face radiated pleasure as she rose from her chair. "Sofia, dear! It's so good to see you."

"I need your help, ma'am," Sofia said. She shoved me in front of her. "Rather, Nora needs your help."

Mrs. Stanley's gaze snapped to me. "My goodness, is this the infamous Nora Connaught?"

"Yes," Sofia said, "and—"

Gasps sounded from the people packed around the table.

"It's Nora and Sofia!"

"It's them!"

"Heroes!"

"Saved us!"

That last was too much. I raised my voice and said, "We saved no one! Sure, we got away from the pirates' base, but they're chasing us."

"We know, dear," Mrs. Stanley said.

"But did you know their captain hates me, and will kill you all if it means killing me, too?"

"No," Mrs. Stanley said, "but I'm not surprised. We all saw how the first pirate captain reacted when she thought she had you standing before her."

"But they're going to kill you," I said, "*because of me!*"

"You're wrong, Nora. They're going to *try* to kill us because they're pirates. But this time we have a fighting chance against them. And *that*, dear, is because of you." Mrs. Stanley reached out and patted Sofia's hand. "And Sofia, as well."

I blinked back sudden tears as the people around Mrs. Stanley chorused their agreement. Deep inside my mind, I felt something go *pop*. I knew No-Talent Nora was gone for good.

Mrs. Stanley, aided and abetted by Sofia, made me sit down and talk to a few dozen passengers. They weren't long conversations, but they were eye-opening and mostly went like this.

The passenger says, "I can't thank you enough for everything you have done for us, Miss Connaught!"

"Please, call me Nora," I say. "And Sofia deserves your thanks at least as much as I do."

The passenger gushes some more, this time including Sofia, and then Mrs. Stanley shoos them away so another passenger can gush at us. It was gratifying and exhausting. Strange as it sounds, there are only so many times you can hear people tell you how wonderful you are before it gets old and embarrassing. I could tell Sofia felt the same way, even though I had to remind at least half the people fawning over me they should thank her, too.

One passenger stood out, though. He was also the only person who addressed Sofia without prompting.

"Um, Miss Olson?" he said. "Please accept my apologies for doubting you. And for the bit about serving tea to the pirates. That was completely out of line."

I recognized his voice as belonging to the ringleader of the passenger revolt that had never happened.

Sofia offered her typical friendly smile and said, "There's no need to apologize, sir. You were under a lot of stress."

"That's very gracious of you to say, Miss Olson," he replied.

"Sofia is a very gracious young lady," Mrs. Stanley said. In tones of velvet covered steel, she added, "Even in the most trying of circumstances."

"That's an excellent point, ma'am," he said, nodding fervently. He looked back at Sofia. "Anyway, I just wanted to tell you how sorry I am for my earlier behavior, and to say thank you."

"You're most welcome," Sofia said, "but you should thank Nora, too."

He did, and then withdrew quickly.

Before the next person stepped up, Sofia leaned towards Mrs. Stanley and whispered, "What happened between you two when he returned and found me missing?"

"Oh, that," Mrs. Stanley said. "I told him you went ahead to ensure your secret exit remained undiscovered, and asked me to lead him to you. Then I led him to a remote corner of the dining hall and had two of my grandsons sit on him until Nora's bodyguards told us the *Pegasus* was making her escape."

I took Mrs. Stanley's hand and gave it a gentle squeeze. "You are a wonder, ma'am. How can we ever thank you?"

"Pish and tosh, Nora. It is I who owes thanks to you courageous girls."

Moments later, Sofia and Mrs. Stanley decided I'd suffered through enough thanks. The Grandmother of Steel plowed a path to the door and sent us on our way. She must have remained there and discouraged people from following us, because Sofia and I mostly had the *Pegasus's* corridors to ourselves.

We visited sickbay and checked on Shawn. The doctor from the warehouse met with us personally.

He telegraphed his news by greeting us with a broad smile. "We got your friend into surgery in time. He'll make a full recovery."

A weight I hadn't known burdened me lifted off my soul. "Thank you, sir. Is Shawn conscious? May we see him?"

The doctor shook his head. "He's sleeping right now, but I'll comm you the moment he awakens."

We thanked him again and headed back to the bridge, walking in silence for the first minute.

Then Sofia asked, "Do you still believe you'll have blood on your hands if we have to fight the pirates?"

"Yes."

"*What?*" Sofia said. "After all the thanks in the dining hall—"

"But it will be pirate blood. Because if those scum board our ship again, I'm going to be right there on the front line, kicking their asses."

Sofia grinned. "Spoken like a true Badass Babe."

Conley leapt to his feet when we entered the bridge and started towards us.

Sofia waved him back. "Relax, Mr. Conley. Nora is fine."

It didn't take an empath to read the tension felt by the bridge crew. Rather than interrupt one of them with questions, I asked Conley, "What's the situation?"

"The pirate ship used their moon's gravity in a slingshot maneuver. They came into view with considerably more velocity than we have."

"Can we reach the system's wormhole before the pirates get within firing range?"

"No, though, they will also be within range of our weapons. Such as they are."

"Can we hold our own until the *Pegasus* enters the wormhole?" I asked. "That will give Weapons Chief Roberts time to repair more blaster cannons, right?"

"In theory," Conley said, "but—"

"Sir," the officer manning the sensors called, "the wormhole is activating!"

"Did we miscalculate the wormhole's location?" Captain Riggs asked. "Might our salvation be closer to hand than we imagined?"

"No sir," Sensors said. "It's activating because another ship is coming through the wormhole."

Everyone on the bridge stared at the sensor officer until the comm officer spoke.

"Sir, Lieutenant Riva... I mean, the traitor is on the comm asking for you."

"Put her on video," Captain Riggs said. When the image of Rivera appeared before him, the Captain asked, "What do you want, traitor?"

Rivera pretended to pout. "Marcus, I'm hurt that you won't use my given name. You used to call me Isabel."

"That name masked a traitor. The next time it will pass my lips is when I testify against you in a court of law."

"Brave words, Marcus, but misguided. I've called to give you one last chance to surrender."

"Absolutely not," Captain Riggs thundered.

"Don't be so hasty, Marcus. May I assume your sensors have picked up activity from the wormhole?" Rivera offered a brightly disturbing smile. "And you realize a ship will exit the wormhole soon?"

"What of it?"

"I know the ship that will emerge. It's the *Wraith*, the flagship for our little band of buccaneers. And Marcus, the *Wraith* is almost twice the size of my ship." Rivera's smile widened. "Surrender before it arrives, and I'll let you all live. Well, all except the Connaught brat and her little friend. Refuse—"

"Which I most emphatically do!" Captain Riggs declared.

"*Don't interrupt me, Marcus!*" Rivera screamed.

"Mute her," the Captain said. As Rivera fell silent, Captain Riggs turned to his sensors officer. "Can you determine the size of the vessel coming through the wormhole?"

"I've been working on that, sir. All I can say for sure is it's a big ship." The woman at the sensor station turned a fearful face towards Captain Riggs and said, "It seems likely the traitor is telling the truth, sir."

The Captain stared at his sensors officer for a long moment, then settled back in his seat. "Weapons Chief, did you get that?"

"I did, sir," the chief responded over the comm.

"You have weapons free, Chief. Fire at will and as you see fit."

"Aye, sir," the Chief replied.

"Unmute the comms," Captain Riggs said.

Rivera's voice returned mid-rant. "Ever do that again, you pathetic old man!"

"Captain," the sensors officer called, "the ship just emerged from the wormhole!"

"Identify the ship as soon as possible and feed that information to Weapons Chief Rob—"

The comm officer interrupted, "Incoming transmission from the new vessel, sir! On speaker."

Rivera fell silent, no doubt waiting to hear whatever *Wraith's* captain demanded.

A woman's voice spoke over the comm. "This is Captain Nancy Martin commanding the Ark's Landing Ship *Defender*. *Pegasus*, do you read? Again, this is Captain Nancy Martin—"

"Captain Martin," Captain Riggs said, "yours is a voice long hoped for. The *Pegasus* is in dire need of assistance. Most of our weapons are offline and we have a heavily armed pirate ship on our tail."

"Roger that, *Pegasus*," Aunt Nancy said. "We are launching fighters now. They will escort you to the wormhole while the *Defender* deals with that pirate."

Rivera broke into the conversation, screeching, "*No!* You're supposed to be the *Wraith*!"

"Is that what you call the pirate ship we met?" Aunt Nancy asked, her tone conversational. "Do you know it launched an ambush on my lead escort ship as she exited a wormhole? I'll bet the *Wraith's* crew was surprised when the *Defender* popped out right behind them. I left that same escort ship combing the *Wraith's* debris on the off chance someone survived the explosion."

Rivera's holo image gritted her teeth and growled, "This is all the fault of that Connaught brat! Well, Miss Fancy Captain, you won't stop me before I can kill her!" Rivera's image turned around, and she shrieked, "Full speed ahead! Ram the *Pegasus*!"

We heard shouts of protest from Rivera's crew. The traitor's holo image raised a blaster and began firing at her own bridge crew. She stopped shooting, gave a triumphal glance at the comm, and then said, "Computer, patch the helm to my station."

Rivera turned her attention to the helm controls as thumping sounds came over the video. I guessed it was other members of Rivera's crew trying to break into the bridge and stop her from killing them all. From the expressions on the *Pegasus's* bridge crew's faces, I also guessed they wouldn't get through in time.

"Weapons Chief, did our missiles have any effect on the pirates?" Captain Riggs asked.

They must have launched those while Sofia was dragging me around the *Pegasus*.

"Two of five hit, doing minimal damage, sir."

Captain Riggs spoke into the comm. "*Defender*, can you launch your missiles in time to stop that ship?"

"Negative, *Pegasus*," Aunt Nancy replied. "The wormhole energy scrambled our sensors. By the time we can get a target lock on the pirates, you'll be inside our missile blast radius."

In the silence that followed, I checked my emotional map to see if my range extended as far as the pirates. To my surprise, it showed up as a bright red blob of fear with two dozen sparks for the minds I'd entered, including Rivera's.

"Captain, can Rivera tell her autopilot to ram us?" I asked.

"No, she'll have to pilot it manually. Why do you ask, Miss Connaught?"

"I might have a way we can stop her, sir."

"You can't stop me, little *Nora*!" Rivera adopted the mocking sing-song way of saying my name that her mother used just before killing herself. "Poor little *Nora* is going to die."

"Comm, block the traitor's transmission," Captain Riggs said. A second later, Rivera's image vanished. "Now, Miss Connaught, what is your idea?"

"Aunt Nancy, can you get Dad for me?"

In response, Dad's voice came over the comm. "I'm here, Nora. What do you need?"

"Can you use your empathic ability to pull the fear from everyone on board the *Pegasus*?"

Dad was silent for a few seconds. Then I suddenly felt lighter as he absorbed my fear. The faces of the bridge crew all brightened, as Dad absorbed their fear, too. I don't know how he does stuff like that, but my dad really *is* the most powerful psychic in the galaxy.

"Done," he said. "Now what?"

"Can you blast all that fear into Rivera's mind?" I asked.

"No. I can send it at the pirate ship, but I can't target someone's mind I've never touched unless I can see the person."

"Can you target me, Dad?"

"I've been reading you since before you were born, Nora. But I'm not blasting your mind with the combined fears of five thousand people. It could kill you."

"You won't be. I've been in Rivera's mind and can target her. I'll redirect your blast and send it to Rivera."

"But you don't have psychic abilities, Nora."

"I do now, Dad."

"When did this happen?"

"I'll tell you all about it after we take care of Rivera," I said.

"No, I won't do that to you," Dad said. "It's too dangerous."

"More dangerous than getting rammed by the pirate ship?" I asked.

Dad didn't respond to my question, so Aunt Nancy asked, "Captain Riggs, do you think Nora can do this?"

He looked at Sofia, who looked at me. I gave a single, decisive nod.

Sofia said, "Yes, she can."

From the comm, Aunt Nancy said, "Matt, I hate saying it, but I don't know another way to stop that ship."

I heard Dad draw a ragged breath, then say, "Tell me when you're ready, honey."

I closed my eyes and reached out for Rivera's mind. The connection was there, just waiting for me to open it. "Give me five seconds, Dad, then hit me with everything you've got."

Sofia wrapped her arms around me and whispered, "Don't die, Nora."

I opened my connection with Rivera and entered her mind. Dad poured the fears of five thousand people into my head. I did my best to channel it into Rivera's mind. Then my brain exploded and everything went black.

RED TIDE

Darkness as deep as that from the void of space engulfed me and dragged me, tumbling and flailing along with it. I fought its inexorable force. Struggled against its vast power. But I had as much chance of withstanding this dark force as I had damming a mighty river with my body.

Just as I got my bearings, the force and I slammed into a flimsy barrier. I barely had time to recognize it as the wall surrounding Rivera's mind before it shattered under the assault and the force poured into her head. Rivera's ugly vortex still roared through her mind. In the disturbing light inside Rivera's sickeningly familiar mind, I realized the force driving me wasn't the black found in space.

It was red. Bright, blinding red.

It was the fear of five thousand souls.

It was a red tide of terror.

And *nothing* could stand against it.

The tide swept over Rivera's once-mighty emotional vortex, and her maelstrom shattered. Memories spilled from the dying vortex, and the red tide broke them into splinters. A hail of memory shards sliced through me. The fragments of Rivera's life left sharp impressions.

Her fifth birthday party as her drunk father screamed at the children attending, "Sing like you mean it, you sniveling brats!"

Watching her first lover snore and drool as she idly considered killing him for failing to satisfy her.

Kicking open a bathroom stall and beating up a woman who wore the same dress as Rivera, and wore it better.

Sobbing as her brother's casket shot into space after his funeral.

Sitting in a courtroom and hearing the judge sentence her father to life in prison.

Desperate to shoot her mother in the back, but being too afraid to try.

Laughing with a fifteen-year-old Paco and his gang while he treated her to a milkshake.

The hail subsided as the red tide of fear swept on through Rivera's mind. Boring, uncherished memories of her day-to-day life on Rockville station shattered before the tide as it rushed into every nook and cranny in Rivera's mind. Soon, there was nothing left in Rivera's mind but stark terror, and *still* the tide poured into her head.

It was more than Rivera could bear.

It was more than *any* person could bear.

Rivera's mind burst. And the woman who hated my family and wanted to kill me was just... gone.

But the red tide still dragged me with it. After seeing its easy destruction of Rivera, I wanted nothing more to do with it. I fought to return to my own mind, to escape the red tide. But it was too powerful. In desperation, I searched for some place to send it, some place to hide from its strength—and raised my mental map. I spotted two dozen sparks nearby.

They were the pirate minds I'd entered to plant the seeds of rebellion. I jumped to the nearest one. But the red tide followed me, smashed through the pirate's meager mental barriers, and obliterated the mind beyond. Unwilling to watch the destruction of another mind, I jumped to the next spark. And the next. And I kept on jumping from mind to mind, praying I could somehow, some way escape the red tide and avoid the same fate it delivered to Rivera and her crew.

But still the terrible force of fear drove me ever onwards. It left a swath of mental devastation behind us. I thought I should feel guilty about that, but I'd seen inside the pirates' minds during their idle time. I'd seen their twisted dreams and diseased yearnings. Besides, I was worried about what the red tide would do to *my* mind when I ran out of pirate minds to jump to.

With only four sparks left on my mental map, a bright beam of golden light pierced the red tide. It enveloped me. Shielded me from the red tide. Showed me the way back to my own mind. And I rode it home.

Someone cradled me. "Please come back, Nora. *Please*."

I drew a deep breath, and said, "Yeah, sure."

"*Nora!*" Sofia shrieked in my ear. "Are you okay?"

I tried for a casual tone of voice, but heard the tremor in it as I said, "I was until you broke my eardrum."

Nearby, Captain Riggs said, "Your daughter has returned, Mr. and Mrs. Connaught."

I heard Dad ask, "How is she?"

"I'm fine, Dad," I called. "Was that your golden beam I rode home?"

"I don't know anything about golden beams, honey," he said, "but I gathered everyone's love for you and put that into your mind."

"Who's everyone?"

"Your mother, your sister and brother, your grandparents, and your new friend Sofia."

My mother asked, "Are you sure you're okay, Nora?"

"That depends," I said. "Is the pirate ship still going to ram us?"

Sofia's eyes widened. "It never changed course again, and flew past us twenty minutes ago."

"Oh..." I shrugged. "Then I'm fine, Mom."

"Don't worry, Mrs. Connaught," Captain Riggs said. "I'll have

Sofia and Mr. Conley take Nora to sickbay for a complete examination."

"There's no need for that," I said, climbing to my feet.

The bridge spun around me, and I would have fallen if Conley hadn't caught me. He scooped me into his arms and said, "Let's get you to the doctor, Miss Connaught."

I looked at my bodyguard. "Conley, are you... smiling?"

The smile vanished, replaced by Conley's usual stoic expression. "I have no idea what you're talking about, Miss Connaught."

Moments later, he and Sofia delivered me into the hands of the ship's doctor. By the time I escaped his scrutiny, my entire family was on hand to greet me.

Mom and Dad ran to wrap their arms around me. Then everyone else swarmed me with hugs and kisses and all the love and warmth you expect from your family. Your *normal*, loving family, anyway. Totally unlike the horrid parody of a family that Rivera sprang from. After a moment, I noticed Granddaddy— Mom's father, the one who trained me—standing off from the group hug. I pushed the late and unlamented Rivera family from my mind, worked my way over to him, and wrapped my arms around him.

"Thanks, Granddaddy."

"For what?" he asked, his tone one of gruff surprise.

"For teaching me to fight and shoot," I said. "For making me memorize the *Pegasus's* maintenance tunnel system. For telling me to wear an atmosphere harness under my clothes. I couldn't have done it without you."

"I just made sure you had the tools. You did all the work." Granddaddy's arms tightened around me. "I'm so proud of you I could just burst."

Suddenly, I found myself crying so hard I couldn't stop. Tears of relief and release, not sorrow, but they kept pouring from my eyes.

Granddaddy awkwardly patted me on the back. Then Mom

was there, and he passed me into her arms with obvious relief. After a moment, Mom pulled a now crying Sofia into our hug. We swayed and cried and purged days of pent-up emotions. I won't say we cried out everything that happened to us since my empathic ability suddenly kicked in, but we got a good start on it.

Finally, Sofia and I dried our eyes, and I dragged everyone off to check on Shawn. He was awake and—after years of having the pirates tell him to 'tough it out'—was overwhelmed by the way my family fussed over him and the serious wound he received saving my life.

Sofia and I kissed Shawn on the cheek, which made him grin. Then my family thanked him profusely.

Granddaddy even said, "You have a good head on your shoulders, boy. Have you ever considered a career in security?"

Hey, that's super high praise coming from Granddaddy!

While we were doing all that family stuff, Aunt Nancy was busy defeating the rest of the pirates. She did it all without firing a single shot. Not that she really planned it that way. I mean, the pirates on the ship just commed the *Defender* and surrendered. But only if Aunt Nancy promised she wouldn't use her mind-stealing weapon on them. She kept a straight face and accepted their terms. She laughed for five minutes after they cut their transmission, then sent a boarding party to the other ship to round up the pirates.

But that still left the pirate base. The base was enormous—it had close to fifty buildings—and not even Shawn and the hopefuls knew the whole layout. The marine commander was all in favor of staging an assault on the base, but Aunt Nancy took a different approach. She hailed the base and broadcast live vids of Rivera and the other mindless pirates. No one would let me see my victims, but from the whispering Sofia and I heard, those slack-jawed, empty eyed, drooling shells of people looked... disturbing. Aunt Nancy let the pirates get a long look at their former gang mates, then she threatened to turn her 'weapon' on the base if the remaining pirates didn't surrender. Like the pirates on the ship, the ones at the base couldn't surrender fast enough.

The thing is, I don't know how I should feel about that. Everyone on the *Pegasus* and in the Ark's Landing navy ships knows I'm the weapon Aunt Nancy threatened to turn on the pirates. And it's great that none of the Ark's Landing marines had to risk their lives in a firefight. But I don't *want* a terrifying reputation, you know?

The whole idea kept me tossing and turning when I should have been sleeping. In the middle of the ship's night, my parents knocked on my door.

"Nora?" Mom called. "Can your father and I come in and talk?"

I let them in. They settled at the foot of my bed and radiated parental love and concern.

Mom said, "Talk when you're ready, honey."

"What makes you think something's bothering me?" I asked.

"You do remember you're not the only psychic in the family, right?" Dad asked.

I nodded, leaned against the headboard, hugged my legs to my chest, and tried to figure out what to say. Finally, I blurted, "Am I a monster?"

"Absolutely not," Dad said, his voice filled with conviction.

"What gave you that idea?" Mom asked. From the look in her eyes, she already knew the answer, but was giving me an opening to voice my fears.

"I don't blame Aunt Nancy for using me as a threat to get the pirates to surrender, but..." I blinked rapidly and tears rolled down my cheeks. "Dad, I... destroyed something like twenty minds. Personalities, gone. Memories, crushed. Humanity, destroyed. How can I *not* be a monster?"

Dad scooted down the bed, kissed my forehead, and said, "You did what you had to do to save everyone on the *Pegasus*."

"And," Mom added, "the rest of those pirates. They'd have died, too, if you hadn't stopped Rivera."

"My brain understands that," I said. "But my heart doesn't."

Dad gently turned my head so he could look into my eyes. "I know, honey. Your heart says there had to be a better way, right?"

I nodded.

"But does your heart have anything to say about what would have happened if you *hadn't* destroyed those minds?"

I thought about that, then said, "Something... even more terrible?"

"Right," Dad said. "Five thousand people would have died if the pirate ship rammed the *Pegasus*. You stopped that. *You*, honey. You made one of the hardest decisions you'll ever make in your life, and that decision saved thousands."

"Are you saying my heart already knows I'm not a monster?"

"Yes. It's your brain that's confused, and it's trying to pass off the blame on your heart."

I considered his words for a minute, then said, "Thank you. But don't be surprised if my brain gets confused again and I need to talk some more."

"We're always here for you, honey," Mom said. "It's not like this is the first time we've dealt with something like this. Your father's brain still gets confused about shooting Paco Rivera. And I'll bet it's going to get worse after this latest Rivera confrontation sinks in."

I won't say I slept like a baby after they left, but at least I slept.

It took two days to secure the pirate base, but the marines found a real treasure trove down there. The older Rivera kept meticulous records. Ones Aunt Nancy says can be used to track down the crew and passengers of the *Perseus* and others the pirates sold.

A Federation Navy squadron showed up just as our Ark's Landing forces wrapped things up. Aunt Nancy didn't need their military help, but she gratefully accepted their offer of medical and psychological support.

Sofia and I spent most of that time in the suite originally assigned to me by Captain Riggs. We did incredibly decadent things like taking hot baths, wearing clean clothes, and eating good food. But when Captain Riggs invited us to dine at his table, Mom made us accept.

She and Dad insisted on escorting us to the dining hall. It still felt odd using the ship's corridors instead of the tunnels, and maybe that's why Sofia and I didn't notice we four walked through them alone. As we approached the dining hall entry, the doors opened wide and revealed a saluting Captain Riggs. Assuming this was for my parents—they own the *Pegasus*, after all—Sofia and I slowed.

Mom gave us gentle shoves in the back and said, "He's here for you, not us."

Captain Riggs linked arms with Sofia and me and escorted us inside. The lights came up, revealing a dining hall filled with what looked like every passenger and off-duty crewman on the *Pegasus*. At the sight of us, everyone surged to their feet and applauded.

My cheeks grew hot as I blushed. Sofia blushed, too, and we both stared about us in astonishment. Captain Riggs led us to his table and said, "I thank almighty God for bringing you young ladies onto my ship."

He raised his hands for silence, and proclaimed, "Passengers and crew of the *Pegasus*, I give you our saviors, the Badass Babes of the Cosmos!"

As the applause started again, I leaned towards Sofia and said, "Adventures are strange. First, they're terrifying. Then they're embarrassing!"

"I know," Sofia said. "Let's never have another one."

"You got that right, Sofia," I said. "One adventure is more than enough!"

Henry Vogel began his writing career in comic books way back in the 1980s, with the indie titles *Southern Knights* and *X-Thieves*. When the bottom dropped out of the black & white comic book market, Henry went into IT, where he worked for the next thirty-three years. Henry took up professional storytelling in 2006, and has performed all across his home state of North Carolina.

As a lifetime fan of science fiction, Henry always wanted to write science fiction novels. He began writing *Scout's Honor* in 2012, and released it to the world in 2014. He hasn't stopped writing since.

Henry makes his home in Raleigh, NC, and is hard at work on his next novel.

www.henryvogelwrites.com

ALSO BY HENRY VOGEL

Travis & Trouble

Trouble in Twi-Town

Trouble on Mars

The Fortune Chronicles

Fortune's Fool

The Scales of Sin & Sorrow

The Scout Series

Scout's Honor

Scout's Oath

Scout's Duty

Scout's Law

Scout's Training

Scout's First Mission

Hart for Adventure

The Princess Scout

Scout: The Lost Colony Adventures

Non-series books

The Lost Planet

Heart of Dorkness & Other Stories

The Connaught Family Chronicles

The Fugitive Heir

The Fugitive Pair

The Fugitive Snare

The Hostage in Hiding

The Captain Nancy Martin

The Counterfeit Captain

The Undercover Captain

The Recognition Series

The Recognition Run

The Recognition Rejection

The Recognition Revelation

Comic Books

Aristocratic Xraterrestrial Time-Traveling Thieves Complete Collection

Southern Knights Almost Complete Collection

Southern Knights Color Edition

Southern Knights: The Morrigan Wars

Southern Knights: Leaving Atlanta (prose novella)

Missing Beings

Illustrated Children's Book

I'm in Charge! and Other Stories